The Healer's Choice

by
Kathryn Hinds

The Healer's Choice

The Healer's Choice

Published by
Dark Oak Press
Kerlak Enterprises, Inc.
Memphis, TN
www.darkoakpress.com

ISBN 13: 978-1-941754-27-6
Trade Paperback
Library of Congress Control Number: 2015934740
First Printing: 2015

This book is printed on acid free paper.

Printed in the United States of America

Dedication:

For our mothers, in their memory:
Carolyn Lupton Fernquist
and
Jane Augusta Lindsay Hinds
with unending love.

Acknowledgements

From the initial idea to the final manuscript, this book was many years in the making. Along the way, it—and I—had the support of so many people that it would be nearly impossible to thank everyone by name. But you cheerleaders, advisers, and beta readers know who you are, and I want you to know, too, how very grateful I am to you all; this book wouldn't be here without you. Having said that, however, there are a few people whom I must thank individually, starting with my dad, Richard Fernquist, who not only bought me my own typewriter when I graduated from high school but made a point of telling the clerk in the store that I was going to be a writer. I am truly blessed to have had parents who always believed in me and made sure I got the education I needed to realize my dreams. I am equally fortunate to have a most wonderful husband, the caring, talented, and knowledgeable Arthur Hinds, who has supported me in every way possible: bringing me coffee and chocolate, answering my questions about swordplay and medical matters, reading and critiquing multiple drafts, bringing me more coffee and chocolate, setting the songs in this book to music, and so much more. (You can hear Taras's song from chapter 30, "The Mothers' Land," on Arthur's CD Dance in the Fire.) Our son, Owen, has also been a wonderful encourager and has been a model of patience and understanding when I've been in the throes of writing. In addition, I have to give a shout-out to Maria Boers Morris, the best writing buddy ever, who has never been afraid to ask the hard questions—which have always turned out to be the ones that put the book back on track. Finally, my deepest thanks to Allan Gilbreath and Kimberly Richardson for welcoming The Healer's Choice and me to the Dark Oak family. I love you all!

Table of Contents

Chapter One

The Kel Nira made a final check of the warriors cramped together in the wagon bed. Most were able to sit upright, at least so long as they propped themselves against their fellows. The last she came to was a man who had lost his right eye, and much of the flesh around it. She ran her fingers over his bandages. "How is the pain?"

"Bearable."

But only just; yet it was too soon to give him another draught of poppy syrup. She drew her hand across his forehead, saw it smooth and his remaining eye close, then lowered herself out of the wagon. "The two with concussion will need close watching," she told her apprentices. The girls acknowledged her instructions, and climbed up to finish settling the injured men.

Steadying herself against the cart's wicker side, the Kel Nira tried to rub the sting of sweat and exhaustion from her eyes. At the far end of the field rattled another wagon, this one carrying corpses to add to the pyres that veiled the late-afternoon sunlight with their smoke. The battlefield wavered a moment in her vision, the landscape spiked with arrow shafts and broken spears. Among the bodies that still littered the ground, the sole signs of life were the carrion crows, intent on their work.

The Kel Nira reached out with her mind, hoping to sense even a single flicker of life among the fallen. She touched only emptiness, save for a lingering restlessness of spirit. "O Mothers Beyond, give them good welcome," she prayed, and traced a sign of release in the air. A sighing wind brushed by, stirring the strands of hair that had loosened from her braids.

She could spare no further thought for the dead; there were living, suffering men who had a stronger claim on her attention. There always were—and no end to them in sight.

One of the field surgeons cleared his throat. "Lady, does the House of Healing have room for so many?"

Behind him, another cart bearing wounded men trundled westward to make its way past the vine-cloaked hills at the edge of the field; the

1

vineyards were untended now, the cottages nestled among the hillside terraces deserted, the people fled from the scene of battle.

The Kel Nira rolled the stiffness out of her shoulders as she considered. "The nearest House can take no more, but you cannot care for more men in camp, either." She gestured toward the warriors in the wagon. "These are not so badly injured as some of the others and can withstand more travel. We shall take them across the river to the Sanctuary; the House of Healing there will have places for them."

The surgeon frowned. "The Forstene prince has made camp on Summer Bluff . . . too close to the ford for my liking. I know you have a Guardian with you"—his glance flicked to the robust woman seated beside the wagon driver—"but still you'd better go northward and take the bridge. It'll be a longer way, but safer."

The Kel Nira nodded and relayed the information to the driver. As the cart lurched into motion, she and the field surgeon mounted their horses. Not altogether certain she wanted to hear the answer, she asked him, "Did we win this one?"

He cast a glance back at the corpse-strewn field. "We kept the Forsteners from advancing farther, Kel Nira . . . but I wouldn't exactly say we'd won."

The battle had been fought just south of the Lenasha Forest, and their route soon led them into the embrace of the ancient trees. The surgeon took his leave shortly afterward. As he headed toward one of the warbands' hidden woodland encampments, he called back, "Be careful, Kel Nira."

"Thank you, my friend. May you walk with the Watchers."

She settled into her saddle, welcoming the shade and the clean fragrance of early-summer leaves—a relief after the oppressiveness of the battlefield. The two apprentices were crooning a healing song in rhythm to the creaking of the wagon wheels. The Kel Nira almost smiled as she relaxed into the lulling tune, trusting herself to her horse's confident gait. It was a lengthy ride to the Sanctuary by way of the bridge; they would not arrive till long after moonrise. No harm in a little doze now. . . .

She dreamed. A pack of wolves ran down their prey in the forest, relentless and sure. But at the moment they prepared their final, killing rush, the hunted burst out of cover and turned on the hunters. Death came to the wolves in red confusion, and all were slain but one. He tried to drag his broken body from among his slaughtered packmates; his legs would not bear him. He lifted his muzzle from the dust and howled.

The Kel Nira snapped awake. She inadvertently jerked on the reins, but the little mare halted without protest.

"Lady, what's wrong?" called out her junior apprentice.

She answered the girl slowly, still sorting through the dream imagery for what it was that had really awakened her. "There is something . . . someone . . . off to the right, I think . . . badly hurt." Signaling to the wagon driver to stop, she dismounted, her medicine bag slung over her shoulder. "Treska, you will stay here and tend these men."

"Yes, my chief."

"Deela, you will assist me."

Before climbing out of the cart, the senior apprentice paused to whisper something to Treska and pat her on the shoulder. The gesture was not lost on the Kel Nira. Treska was looking wan—no surprise after all she had vomited today. It was her first time on field duty, and the Kel Nira wondered if it was too much, too soon. Probably so; she tended to forget just how young Treska was—a tall girl with little of childhood's softness left in her face, but she had, after all, only just started her bleeding cycle.

The Guardian had jumped down from her place beside the driver, ironwood staff in hand. "I'd better come with you, Kel Nira."

She shook her head. "Thank you, Fama, but I would rather you stay with the wounded. We will not have to go far, I think."

Following a deer trail, the Kel Nira led the way deeper into the forest. The weariness she had felt such a short while ago had been banished by the mindcall of someone in extremities of pain. When a swath of broken and trampled underbrush cut at an angle across the narrow path, she crouched to examine the soil, saw the impress of hoofprints, and knew she was nearing the source of that call.

Not many paces on, she and her apprentice entered a clearing. Deela coughed, and the Kel Nira wrinkled her nose. The stench of carnage, enclosed by the trees, was strong here.

Three men and a horse lay contorted on the ground, impaled by arrows; one man's hand still clung to his useless shield, the metal-clad oval pierced right through.

"My chief, these are Forsteners!" Deela whispered. "What if their people come looking for them?"

"I do not think they will come into the forest now, with the sun so far in the west." The Kel Nira scanned the clearing, looking for a fourth man—the one she knew must be here, holding to life, whose pain had summoned her. "There!"

He had been hidden from view partly by the bulk of the horse's body, partly by the bracken that edged the clearing. His right leg was dark with blood.

The Kel Nira knelt beside him. She brushed her hands over his head and down his back. "No head injury . . . no damage to the spine." She beckoned to Deela for assistance.

The apprentice hung back. She still looked fearful, and now there was something more. "After everything the Forsteners have done, how can we heal one of them? Who knows how many of our people this one has killed or maimed or raped—"

"Enough! A Healer knows nothing of a patient but the need for healing. We turn our backs on no one." That Deela, so far along in her training, would even consider leaving this man to suffer. And for what? Mere vengeance?

"But . . . he hasn't *asked* for healing."

"His pain has spoken for him. Do you not feel it? Or do you close your heart to all save those you believe to be deserving?"

The apprentice dropped her gaze to the leaf litter at her feet.

"We have no time for this, Deela. Do you wish to become a Sworn Healer or not?"

Deela's shoulders tensed. Then, without a word, she came to join the Kel Nira. They bent to their task and rolled the man over.

Deela made some remark about how much heavier the man's mail shirt was than the leather cuirasses their own fighters wore, but the Kel Nira was already engrossed in examining his chest and abdomen as she had his head and spine. "The internal organs are unharmed. It is only his leg we need worry about. Good." She unbuckled and pushed aside his sword belt, careful not to touch the weapon itself.

He stirred back to consciousness as Deela tossed the sword into the bracken. His dark eyes widened, taking in the Kel Nira's green tunic and sleeveless white overdress, stained with the blood of the other men she had tended this day. "Sharhay!" he gasped out.

"Yes, I am Sharhay. But I am a Healer; I will not harm you."

Confusion joined the fear in his eyes. She switched to his language and repeated slowly, "I will not harm. I am Healers' Order."

"A Holy Woman?" he whispered hoarsely.

She gave herself a moment to consider that. "In Sharhay, women of Orders are called Ma'Sharha. It mean 'Mothers of the People.'" Her tongue stumbled over the difficult *th* sound. "Now rest quiet. Leg is hurt."

Deela knelt beside the man and took out her knife. He tried to roll away from the blade, but the Kel Nira gripped his shoulders and held him down. "She needs uncover wound. I give my word we not harm. Believe me, and be still."

"Why"—he paused to moisten his lips—"why do you help me?"

It was a long time since she had had occasion to converse in Forstene. Again she hesitated, thinking how best to explain. "In Order, we have—" What was the word for *vows*? "We swear to give heal where need is. This is sacred word." She smiled a bit at the similarity between this conversation and the one she'd just had with Deela.

The Forstener appeared to relax slightly. The Kel Nira reached for the water flask Deela had brought along. "Water," she said, and took a swallow herself to reassure him, then lifted his head and helped him drink.

When he was done, she moistened a scrap of cloth and gently wiped his face. With the grime cleaned off, he was revealed to be a man of twenty-odd winters, who would probably be handsome enough under other circumstances. But while most Forsteners had a coppery or golden cast to their complexion, this one's face possessed a distinctly grayish tinge.

"Oh!" breathed Deela, who had removed his leg armor and cut away the cloth beneath. "Lady, this is not good."

She was right: the warrior's femur was fractured, a jagged end of bone protruding through an ugly wound on his inner thigh.

The Kel Nira eyed Deela critically. Though small and slim, the girl was strong—but not strong enough. "It appears we will need Fama's assistance after all. You can find your way?"

After a moment's consideration, Deela nodded and darted off toward where the cart waited.

The Kel Nira removed a vial from her medicine bag. "This is for pain," she told her patient. "Not good taste, but you want drink before I fix bone."

His eyes narrowed in suspicion, then he heaved a resigned sigh and dutifully swallowed the liquid she'd measured out.

"I must clean leg now. You may feel hurt."

Chanting under her breath, the Kel Nira removed every bit of dried blood, dirt, and debris from the wound. Her patient held his body stiff and did not flinch, even though the spirits with which she washed the injury must have stung.

"Will I . . . be able to walk again?"

"I do all I can. Then you keep leg bound, and rest for all next moon. You can do?"

"Yes, Mistress."

She gave him what she hoped was an encouraging smile. "You will walk."

He mumbled something unintelligible, his eyelids drooping. The poppy syrup was taking effect.

Deela returned with Fama, who looked none too happy. All she said, though, was, "Are you sure about this, Lady?"

"If by 'this,' you mean treating this wounded man, then yes."

"Treating this wounded *Forstener* is what I mean."

"I am still sure."

Fama started to shrug, then bowed instead. "It is my duty to serve you, Lady."

The Kel Nira ignored the fact that the Guardian's tone was nowhere near as acquiescent as her words. "It is well. Get two scabbards from the dead men so that we can use them for splints. Then I will need you to hold him and provide traction while I pull the leg into alignment and set the bone."

Fama glanced at the warrior, sizing him up. His shoulders were scarcely broader than hers, and he was not quite as tall as she was. She nodded. "Right, scabbards first."

While Fama collected the splints, Deela laid out bandages and salve, then threaded a needle with silk and set it in readiness in a jar of spirits. The Kel Nira once more examined the injury, with both eyes and mindsight. The break had just missed cutting the great artery that carried blood through the leg directly from the heart. She must be careful not to harm that artery as she brought the jagged bone ends back together, or her patient would almost certainly bleed to death.

Fama returned, wordlessly dropping two wood-and-leather scabbards beside the Forstener on her way to take her place at his head. He stirred as she lifted his torso so that she could link her arms under his shoulders and brace him against her chest. Deela spoke a few soothing words, laying her hand on his forehead, and he settled once more. His breath came deep and steady.

The Kel Nira poured a little water over her hands and said the words of purification. With a prayer to the Watchers, she reached her mind to her tree of power and felt the earth-strength flow through it and into her own limbs, like golden light showering over her from its leaves.

She placed her hands on either side of the fracture, breathed in the breath of the nearby trees, and pushed the protruding bone into position. She moved down to the man's feet, reached again to her tree, and braced herself. She grasped his ankle in both hands and tugged on the broken leg, hard.

The Forstener cried out. His body convulsed, then stilled.

Fama's unyielding grip on his torso provided all the resistance the Kel Nira could wish. Renewing her own efforts, she pulled with steady force to move the bone into alignment, broken end to broken end. The golden light flowed into her and through her hands, pulsing warmly, and she sent her mind into the bone. She envisioned the ragged halves of the fracture joining together, the torn fabric of the bone mending.

"Splints." The Kel Nira was sweating; she had not had time to recover from her labors on the battlefield, and it took all her strength now to keep the bone properly aligned.

Deela positioned the splints and bound them into place, leaving uncovered only the torn flesh where the bone had broken through.

The Kel Nira held her mind to the bone for several heartbeats more before releasing her grip on the man's ankle.

Now to the wound. Her hand hovered over it, and she let the radiant warmth of the healing power flow through her and into the mangled tissue, driving away the impurities that could turn wounds corrupt. Then, as she had done with the bone, she drew together the muscle and the skin. Deela handed her the needle and thread. Singing a final charm under her breath, the Kel Nira stitched the skin closed.

At last she sat back. Deela reached to check her pulse, but the Kel Nira shook her off. "I am fine. Dress the wound."

She let out a long, slow breath and regathered her awareness of the outer world, trying to fend off the lingering emptiness that always accompanied the receding of the healing energy. Dully, she noted that Fama had released the Forstener, gotten to her feet, and was now gathering up the dead warriors' swords.

"We are not a sword people," the Kel Nira admonished.

"Maybe we can't use these ourselves," Fama answered stonily, "but we can keep other Forsteners from using them." Almost too quietly to hear, she added, "We ought to get at least some good out of this fool's errand."

Then Deela was finished with her task, and the Kel Nira knelt again beside the injured warrior. She brushed her hands over his leg, heart, and head. He had slipped into a peaceful slumber; the color was returning to his cheeks. "All will be well with him. Deela, get the cloaks from the dead men to cover him, lest he take a chill during the night."

"We're leaving him here?"

The Kel Nira hesitated, for the first time registering the quality of the Forstener's garments, the wolf embroidered on his surcoat, the gold rings in his ears. His straight dark hair, escaping from the ribbon that bound it at the back of his neck, was long; his mustache and beard were precisely trimmed. All the marks of a Forstene nobleman.

"My chief?"

"We cannot do more for him than what we have done. His own people will come in search of him in the morning, in any case—of that I have no doubt." She stood up, yet remained a moment longer staring down at the Forstener.

A breeze rippled through the tree leaves, making them whisper. The Kel Nira shivered with a sudden knowledge: by healing this man, she had somehow woven a new and unbreakable strand into the web of her fate.

Chapter Two

The Kel Nira and her party crossed the bridge under the rising moon. Passing a quiet cluster of houses—not a light, not a sound from them, and the only movement a flight of bats leaving an attic—they headed across the meadow toward the forest on the other side. Drawing near to the trees, the Kel Nira heard the shivering cry of a screech owl; Fama answered with a nighthawk's *oh-poor-you*. There was a stirring in some shrubs at the forest's edge, and a rider emerged.

He waited for the wagon to pass beneath the branches of the first rank of trees. The moonlight paled his amber-red hair—the same color as the Kel Nira's own—but even the gentlest illumination could do nothing to soften the set of his shoulders or the rough contours of his profile.

She smiled as he guided his horse to fall in beside her. "Pieran, I had expected to see you in the Lenasha."

"Reshtas decided to double the number of warbands guarding the ways to the Sanctuary; he sent me across to command them two days ago. I should have been at the battle, though."

Always he is so ready to fight. His leather cuirass was supple with recent oiling, the metal studs gleaming. His back bristled with longbow and full quiver. His heavy, curved forester's knife hung in its scabbard from his belt, and he had two axes and a hammer fitted into loops on his saddle.

She shook her head. "I think Reshtas decided wisely; it seems safer that the Champion and his Second should not be at the same place."

"No offense, Kel Nira, but you're hardly one to be lecturing other people on matters of safety."

"I was not lecturing, Pieran." She looked more closely at him. "Is something bothering you?"

He shrugged and glanced away; then the words burst out of him. "You ought to stay in the Sanctuary, where you're safe. But instead you've been out with the army and slogging around the battlefield—"

"Lower your voice! You may be my brother, but you have no call to speak to me in that manner." She reined her horse to a slower walk, forcing him to match her.

"I was worried about you," he said softly—softly for him, at any rate.

"Pieran, you know that it is the rule of my Order. And if I were not head of the Order but an ordinary Healer, then you would complain"— she dropped the pitch of her voice to mimic his—"that it is not right for the Kel Nira to send you out where she will not go herself."

He gave a half snort that turned into a chuckle. "Yes, that's probably what I would say."

"Besides, it is hardly dangerous. Once a moon I take my turn in camp, just like every other Healer in Orders; I supervise the field surgeons and assist with anything that is beyond their skills." It seemed as though once a moon at least she had to explain this to Pieran, but she strove to keep her impatience in check. "If there should be a battle, I stay where I am until it is ended, and only then do I go out onto the field. *And* I have a Guardian with me the whole time." She ladled on a final dose of reassurance. "There is nothingto worry about."

The moonlight was bright enough now, even filtered through the branches, to illuminate his frown. "You know what that Listener foretold, what she heard from the trees."

"She gave us that foretelling a long time ago, Pieran."

"What difference does that make?"

"None, I suppose." The Kel Nira sighed. "Well, if you must insist on keeping yourself available for my salvation, you ought to be glad Reshtas has sent you closer to the Sanctuary."

It was his turn to sigh. "I wish I had been with you in the south last year, instead of over west at the ferry landings."

"It was a bad year," was all she could think of to answer.

They rode on in silence. The Kel Nira suspected Pieran's thoughts were borne along the same course as hers, remembering. Very early last spring—before the season had even taken hold—the Forsteners had split their forces, one branch attacking the market center on the bank of the Ghil River. The other branch waited until most of the Sharhay warbands were in the west, and then swept down on the Winter Sanctuary. They looted and burned it, and destroyed all the sacred forest surrounding it.

The Ma'Sharha had learned from that disaster; the Summer Sanctuary was far better protected than the Winter Sanctuary had been. And now Pieran and his warbands were added to the Sanctuary's guard.

But if the rest of Sharhaya were to fall, what good would the safety of the Sanctuary be then?

*****

From the wagon, Treska watched the Kel Nira's brother ride away to resume his post near the forest edge. "I always thought that when someone becomes a Chief, she has to give up her family," she mused.

"It's not a rule; it's just the way things usually work out," Deela said. "She only has to give up her name."

A name was a lot to give up—but at least it wasn't your whole family. "The other Chiefs don't spend time with their sisters and brothers, though."

"Their sisters and brothers are all back tending hearth and farm, not serving the Council like the Kel Nira's brother. She can't help seeing him pretty often."

"I wish we could see our families more. I've never even gotten to hold my new baby brother, and he must be eight moons old by now."

"At least you've *got* a baby brother."

One of the men moaned. Deela turned away to tend to him.

Treska bit her lip. She should have thought before she spoke. Deela's family lived only two days from the Winter Sanctuary, and Deela had not heard from them since the attack. She had stopped trying to get news of them now, even though the Kel Nira said there was still hope. Deela didn't think so. But she never cried about it.

A man plucked at Treska's sleeve, and asked for a drink of water. There wasn't much left of what they'd brought out to the battlefield, so Treska gave him a drink from her own flask. She wasn't sure her stomach was settled enough to keep water down yet anyway.

The wagon creaked on along the bumpy road. The main approach to the Sanctuary was from the south, and that route was wide and smooth and much more pleasant in every way. Well, except for the fact that the Forsteners were so near it now. But at least they were still on the other side of the river.

Treska yawned. She didn't see how the Kel Nira was managing to stay on her horse; she hardly seemed tired at all. *Will I ever be that strong?*

Deela, done with her patient, patted Treska's arm. "Go on and close your eyes; get a little rest if you can."

Using her medicine bag for a pillow, Treska curled up in her corner of the wagon and tried to follow Deela's advice. The night insects and the tree frogs were singing; the horses' hooves plodded rhythmically over beaten dirt and leaf mould. As exhausted as she was, she should have been lulled straight to sleep. But the men were so restless— muttering, groaning, snoring, shifting to get comfortable. And Treska could tell that even the ones who were still and quiet were not quiet in their minds. As her eyelids drooped, she felt their nightmares and memories rasp against her senses.

She adjusted her lumpy pillow, and tried again to sleep. But someone was staring at her. She could feel it. She opened her eyes to meet the gaze of a single eye; where its mate had been was only bloody bandage.

"I guess you seen some things today you wish you hadn't," he said, not unkindly.

"I wish none of us had."

"Aye, nothing pretty about war. I didn't want to go fight the Forsteners, you know. Not that I don't want them out of our land! But I'm no good at fighting—I'm not even a hunter. Not like that Pieran who was talking to the good lady awhile ago."

"I heard he speared three boar in a single day one time."

"I don't doubt it, not a bit. So let him and his kind do the fighting. Let them make a proper army, even, like those Forsteners have got, so's men like me can be left to trimming our vines and doing what we know."

Deela leaned over from the other side of the wagon. "Pay him no mind, Treska," she murmured. "It's the poppy syrup talking."

But Treska thought that, for now anyway, the conversation was a help to the man. "So you're a vinedresser?"

"I was; maybe I will be again now. Easier to grow grapes with one eye than to kill Forsteners."

"I don't doubt it. What's your name?"

"It's Wennas, miss, from Sweetspring. That's up in the west."

"Is it a beautiful place?"

"Oh it is, it is. It— What was that?" Wennas had started at a noise from among the trees.

"Just a nightbird, probably." It had sounded like a baby crying. "Don't worry; I'm sure everything's all right. Oh . . ."

Suddenly Wennas was sobbing, and nothing Treska could say would convince him that anything in the world was all right, or ever would be again.

*****

The Kel Nira had been dozing in her saddle but was awakened by a voice raised in question, perhaps alarm. The wagon slowed, and Fama spoke softly, reassuringly, to a man standing beside the road. The Kel Nira left her to it, scrubbed a sleeve across her face, and looked around to orient herself. Good: the night's journey was almost over. Just a little way farther through the wild forest, and they would come to the sacred wood that surrounded the Sanctuary.

Fama's conversation ended. The man bowed and retreated into the trees ahead. Peering after him, the Kel Nira saw that he was making for a cluster of tents and lean-tos. Moonlight silvered the rough shelters, but also deepened the shadows that clung to them.

As she drew closer, it became obvious the shabby camp extended far into the woods on both sides of the road. It being deep night, few people were about, although here and there a figure huddled beside a low fire. But the number of shelters . . . there had not been so many here the last time she took this route. She could not help thinking again of the Winter Sanctuary, and the refugees who had thought they were safe in the forest surrounding it. If only she could promise these people that they would not meet the same fate. . . .

She heard weeping. It came from a woman sitting on a fallen log, not far from the roadside. Rocking and keening, the woman clutched a bundle of ragged cloth to her chest. A breeze parted the tree leaves above her head, allowing moonlight to spear through and illuminate some of the tiny, limp form swaddled in the rags. The Kel Nira barely had to reach out her mind to know the infant had already returned to the Mothers.

The woman must have felt the Kel Nira's attention on her. She choked back her sobs, scrambled to her feet, and bowed as the Kel Nira passed. Clinging to her dead baby, she asked for nothing. It took every bit of the Kel Nira's discipline not to go to her. But she was responsible for these warriors. And she had news she must deliver. And the Kel Sharha would be needing her. Too much to do. *O Watchers, lend me strength.*

From the corner of her eye, the Kel Nira thought she saw Deela and Fama exchanging a look. Fama's opinion hardly mattered to her. The Guardians' Order cultivated fighting skills and a somewhat ruthless devotion to justice—compassion was not exactly one of their priorities. The Kel Nira wondered, though, if her decision to heal the Forstener was troubling Deela again.

13

It was not as though that one man had caused these peoples' sufferings; nor would their lot be different if she had refused him healing. And yet somehow, she still felt, that act had changed her own lot—and perhaps that of others with her. *I am a Healer; what else could I have done?*

She left off her brooding as her party passed into the sacred wood. The ranks of immense trees, growing in eleven rings to surround the Sanctuary, breathed out their green breath. The Kel Nira sat straighter and inhaled deeply.

They crossed the little bridge over the stream that curved around the western half of the Sanctuary, a certain cheerfulness in the drum of hooves on timber. A short way more to go on the loamy road, and then at last her horse set foot onto one of the cobbled lanes of the Sanctuary. Wooden buildings rose to either side. One of those structures, the horse knew, housed the stables, and it strained at the bridle.

The Kel Nira patted the animal's neck. "All right, Luma, pretty lady. Just carry me a little farther, then one of the kind grooms will take you to your manger." The horse nickered appreciatively, and the Kel Nira smiled.

She dismounted with pleasure when she came to the House of Healing, situated on the northwestern edge of the circular green at the center of the Sanctuary. The familiar sight of the House's painted gables and shutters, and the carved door and porch pillars of her adjacent residence, filled her with gratitude for the fate that allowed her to call this place her home. *May the Watchers preserve it.*

A small crowd of healers, apprentices, and servants had gathered to meet the wagon. The Kel Nira sent her own apprentices straight off to bed, while she oversaw the settling of the injured warriors in the House of Healing's lower ward. Most were soon asleep, though they had to make do with pallets hastily laid in the spaces between the ward's already occupied beds. By the wavering illumination of the lamps in their wall niches, she went from pallet to pallet and stopped by each man to run her fingertips over him, looking for any developing complications.

Her Second rose from a patient's bedside and came up to take her by the arm. "You need to get some rest, my Chief."

"Lillanna—," she began to protest, but gave in and allowed herself to be steered out the door and up the wide stairway. On the landing, however, she shrugged away from the younger woman. "I will just check the patients in this ward, and then—"

"You will do no such thing. Whenever the rest of us come late back from battle duty, you always send us straight to our beds. So 'take your own medicine, Healer'!"

"Very cheeky, quoting my own sayings back at me."

"I have learned from the best."

"Hmph." The Kel Nira crossed the landing to the door that led into her residence. "Just one thing more, then: when Yasma and her apprentices go out to the Lenasha tomorrow, they will have to take the west road and the bridge; the ford is no longer safe. On their way, I want them to visit the refugees in the forest. Their numbers have grown, and I am afraid there is sickness among them."

Lillanna was silent a few moments, pensive lines creasing her freckled face. "I had better send someone to wake Yasma; she'll want to get an earlier start now. Good night, my Chief. Healing dreams to you." She started down the stairs, but stopped to call back over her shoulder, "And don't you wait until I'm gone and then sneak across to the upper ward. Get some sleep!"

"Yes, Lillanna. Good night, Lillana." The last word ended in a yawn.

As soon as the Kel Nira was on the other side of the door, she stripped off her bloodstained overdress. One of the servants, a gangling but capable girl, came out of Treska and Deela's room just in time to take charge of the next layer of the Kel Nira's clothing.

"Will you bathe, Lady?"

She ought to; she needed to. But now that she was at her chamber door, she couldn't imagine remaining upright for the time it would take to have the jars of water poured over her. "In the morning, Arna." She stumbled in to her bed and lay down just as she was, smudge-faced, tangle-haired, in breastband and dusty linen trousers. Arna followed to pull off her low boots and drape a light coverlet of Ghildaran silk over her, then tiptoed out.

No nightmares tonight; I am too tired. She had never had a peaceful night's rest after returning from a battlefield, but perhaps the Mothers Beyond might yet take pity on her.

*****

The next morning found the Kel Nira entering the portico that fronted the Celebrants' guildhall. A slender, fair-haired young man leaned against one of the pillars, tuning his lute and oblivious to all else.

"Good day, Taras," the Kel Nira greeted him.

15

He looked up from the instrument, and his frown of concentration gave way to such a smile that she could not help returning it, in spite of the gravity of her visit.

"Kel Nira!" He finally remembered to bow. "You honor our hall."

She took his free hand and bowed over it. "Thank you, Taras. I need to speak with your Elder. Is she within?"

"She is; she's working with the new apprentices, teaching them the dances for the Summer Festival. We"—he searched her face—"we *will* be celebrating the festival, won't we?"

"Not on Summer Bluff, I fear, nor on the riverbank—unless the situation changes greatly. I suppose the Council will have to discuss how to mark the day, under the circumstances. . . ."

"But that is not your business with the Elder; come, let me take you to her."

Taras ushered her into the building. Behind a closed door on one side of the corridor, two flutes intertwined their melodies. The Kel Nira paused at an open doorway on the other side and looked into a spacious room, sparsely furnished but well carpeted. A man with a deep laugh sat in the center, surrounded by children, enthralling them with the tale of how Little Stripeback saved her gathering of seeds. He had reached the part where the resourceful chipmunk convinced a pair of marauding birds that her seed cache was in an abandoned ant hill—only of course the hill wasn't abandoned. The children burst into giggles as the storyteller mimed the encounter between the birds and the biting ants.

The Kel Nira smiled, and she and Taras moved on and out to the guildhall's courtyard. There, to the accompaniment of the Elder Celebrant's hand clapping, a group of girls and boys faced each other in two lines that moved together and apart, then broke into couples that circled around each other.

More children. All of the Orders and Greater Guilds had taken in some war orphans—her servant Arna was one—but she hadn't realized the Celebrants had adopted such a number of them. And it seemed they were all being brought up as apprentices. So many to carry on the songs and stories and dances—well, she supposed that bespoke a hopeful view of the future.

The Elder, a plump woman of middle years, caught sight of the Kel Nira and Taras. Waving the children to stillness, she came to greet her visitor.

"May I speak privately with you, Elder Rimenna?"

"Of course, Kel Nira. One moment." She turned back to her charges. "Children, here is Taras now to sing you the song that goes with the dance you've been learning. Pay attention; I will return shortly, and I want to hear good things of you!"

The two women walked back inside and into a small room crowded with musical instruments. The Kel Nira closed the door, shutting out all but a murmur of sound from without.

The Elder stood by a tall drum, tapping it in an idle rhythm.

"Rimenna, I . . ." The Kel Nira sighed, reached into the pocket of her overdress, and withdrew a silver medallion, a smooth oval of amber set in its center. She pressed it into Rimenna's hand.

The Elder turned it over, and over again. "This is Jedan's. His mother gave it to him, when he attained mastery."

"I know. He wanted you to have it now, in gratitude for all you taught him."

Rimenna closed her fingers around the medallion. "No . . ." Her eyes were full of appeal.

"Did you know he had gone to Reshtas in the Lenasha?"

"Yes. He wanted to make a song. To honor the warriors and increase their courage."

"He did that. I heard many men speak of it, and I know they fought the better for it."

Rimenna nodded slowly. "What happened to him, Kel Nira?"

"He rode out with one of the warbands. I do not know why he did it; I did not know he had gone, until we found him on the field afterward."

"What . . . happened?"

"He took a belly wound." She laid a hand on Rimenna's arm. "I came to him too late. He asked me to help him return to the Mothers, and I did; there was nothing else I could do for him."

Rimenna stared at the medallion. "He was my first student—the first I brought all the way from apprentice to master. He was like . . . like a son to me."

"I know."

"He would have been Elder after me. Everyone agreed; everyone loved him."

"I am so sorry, Rimenna."

"And his song . . . his last song. It's lost now, too."

"The men who heard it will remember it, I am sure. I will ask my patients—or you may come and speak with them yourself, if you like. Whenever you like."

"Thank you, Kel Nira." Rimenna stifled a sob. "I think I want to be alone now."

"Of course. I must attend upon the Kel Sharha in any case."

But she lingered in the doorway to the courtyard, where Taras was singing. The song was slower than usual, to accommodate the children's newness to the dance steps, and he took the unhurried tempo as an opportunity to add intricacy to his accompaniment. The Kel Nira watched his long fingers move over the lute strings as his silvery tenor conjured memories of past summers.

"A Mother for every kind of thing:
Beast and bird and vine and trees,
Winter snows and rain in spring,
Flowers, grain, the fruits of peace—
The Mothers danced all in their round
To stir the seeds within the ground,
And sang to make the rivers flow,
And sought their loves, that love might grow."

Taras had been watching the children, but as he finished the verse he lifted his gaze to the Kel Nira. She caught his smile before she turned to leave.

As she emerged from the portico of the guildhall, she paused on the steps to look out over the green. A pair of cats lay sunning themselves on the low stone dais at the Sanctuary's center. An apprentice from the Vintners' Guild was drawing water from one of the fountains built into the four rounded corners of the dais. A few sheep grazed placidly, ignorant that shearing was only days away.

"Peaceful, isn't it?" remarked a woman in green tunic and gray overdress approaching the bottom of the steps.

"Kel Mona, good day to you." The Kel Nira joined her fellow Chief on the green. "I was just thinking—"

"About Taras?"

The Kel Nira shook her head. "Nothing so pleasant."

"What a mild word to describe such a beautiful young man."

"And when did you become a connoisseur of male beauty?"

The older woman smiled. "I'm just repeating the general opinion. Still, even I can see that he's quite beautiful—for a man."

"A very *young* man. I am old enough to be his . . . aunt—a youthful aunt, but nonetheless. . . ."

"What does age matter? I see him looking at you as much as you look at him."

"Everyone looks at Taras—he's a Celebrant."

"You choose to miss my point, Kel Nira. Come now; he's young, he's beautiful, he's more than willing. And you surely deserve a little pleasure now and again."

"Not now. There is too much work—"

"That's exactly what I mean."

"Too much work," the Kel Nira repeated. "I could not, in good conscience, indulge myself in that manner."

"Not even on a festival night? After all, it's practically an obligation then. The Mothers and Watchers like no offering better."

The Kel Nira almost grinned; the Summer Festival was little more than a moon away. But then she remembered that this year there could be no procession to the riverbank, no archery contests in the meadow, no watching the sunset from the crest of Summer Bluff. And in the field below the Lenasha—as in so many other fields where the Forsteners had left their mark—there would be no wheat turning golden with the promise of harvest.

"Stop waggling your eyebrows at me, Kel Mona, and be serious." She turned her steps toward the Kel Sharha's residence.

The Kel Mona turned with her, and they walked wordlessly for several paces, until the tension in the silence eased. "You must still be dreadfully tired from the battlefield."

"I am." And she had slept ill, too—no respite from the nightmares after all. She did not know which were worse: the ones in which she was surrounded by the wounded, too many to heal, or those in which she was surrounded by enemies, too many to fight. And fight she did in those dreams—which was disturbing in itself.

"So what were you thinking when you came out of the Celebrants' Hall?"

"That we do not see the hand of the war here in the Sanctuary, but it touches us nonetheless."

"Ah." The Kel Mona's face became grave, and she fingered the end of one of her long, pale braids.

"The refugee problem is growing worse. Along the west road they are camped almost to the edge of the sacred forest now. And their condition is not good; I think many of them need care desperately."

"I don't doubt it. But what can be done?"

"I would like those who are able to make the journey to go farther north, where they will be safe so long as we can keep the Forsteners from getting past the Lenasha. But the others—I think we will have to make room for them within the Sanctuary somehow." She shook her head. "I do not know how we can accommodate so many."

"This is not your responsibility alone, Kel Nira."

"I know; I will bring the matter before the Council when we meet again."

They had reached the Kel Sharha's residence, adjacent to the House of the Listeners' Order, of which the Kel Sharha was also Chief. This northeastern edge of the Sanctuary green was oddly hushed, as if everything in the vicinity were holding its breath.

The Kel Mona cast a worried look toward the Kel Sharha's windows. She pitched her voice low. "How much longer do you think you can give her?"

"As long as she needs." The Kel Nira bowed to her friend, and went in.

Chapter Three

Corvalen and his army crossed the mountains from Forstene into Sharhaya at the time when fruit should have begun to swell toward ripeness. But when they came down through the foothills, they found the country's famed vineyards and orchards hacked, burnt, or plain untended.

No one challenged the army's progress except a handful of ragged children who scooped up stones a distance from the roadway and lobbed them toward the soldiers. The few rocks that reached their targets bounced harmlessly off the men's shields, and the urchins ran away, shouting taunts. Corvalen deemed them unworthy of his concern—until he and his bodyguard were past them. Then he heard their jeering change to cries of terror, swiftly drowned beneath the shouts of men.

Corvalen turned his horse and galloped back in time to see the children fleeing from three horsemen who had come up from behind a hillock. "Let them go!" Corvalen shouted, urging his horse in pursuit of the men.

Rossen, his aide, drew alongside as the riders wheeled to face him. "And who might you be?" one of them demanded.

It was Rossen who answered. "Is that how you address Corvalen of Brintora, the Lord Marshal of Forstene? Temper your words with respect!"

Corvalen's squire joined them then, bearing the red, black, and gold marshal's banner, with the royal crown surmounting the three ravens of the barony of Brintora.

The horsemen's eyes went from the banner to the ravens on Corvalen's surcoat, and their bravado slid away.

"Lord Corvalen," ventured one of the horsemen, "we was only—"

"In Vallar's name, what do you mean by riding down children?"

The man balked. One of his companions hastened to explain. "Prince Dursten's orders, my lord: no impudence to be tolerated from the Sharhay."

21

Corvalen's anger cooled enough for him to note the men's rough-cut hair and the prince's sword-and-stars badge sewn onto each of their jerkins. Their horses were not the long-legged steeds of the Forstene plains, but looked to be of the sturdy little Sharhay variety. These were levied soldiers on plundered mounts.

"I am come with new orders from the king. He desires the Sharhay in the parts of this country that are already subdued to be treated with the same tolerance he extends to all his subjects. His Majesty wants these people's loyalty, not their hatred. Is that understood?" He waited a moment for the riders' assent, then pointed to two of them. "You will continue your patrol with a view to keeping the peace. You"—he gestured to the third man—"will escort me to your commander."

*****

The three soldiers had come from an outpost that watched over the main approach to the mountain pass. Corvalen meant to stay only long enough to inform the commanding officer of the king's new orders. But the commander begged his company at dinner so insistently that Corvalen decided to remain behind with his bodyguard while the rest of his army completed the day's march; on horseback, it would be an easy enough matter to catch up with the column the next morning. Indeed, the gallop would be a pleasure.

The commander was a graying, coarse-faced man, and he kept a lean table. But though the meal was scanty, the wine was more than adequate. By the third slender course, the commander's tongue was well lubricated, and he spun a tangled tale for Corvalen and Rossen, who had also been invited to dine.

"A perverse people, these Sharhay; they never do things the way you'd expect. Most times they'd rather ambush you in the woods than meet you in an honest battle. Comes from being led by women, I suppose." He leaned toward Corvalen. "You know, none of us—not even the prince, may the Celestials favor him—has ever got so much as a glimpse of their queen."

"The Kel Sharha?"

"Aye, her. She hides in the woods with her High Council, and works her magics from there."

"I hardly think—"

"You're new in this country, my lord. But I was there, you know, at what they called their Winter Sanctuary. Strange place! These people have almost nothing you could think of as a city. Two capitals—one in

22

the north, one down here—and both of them in the right middle of a forest. And that's where their queen and all her council live. In the bleeding woods!"

"And so you have been to the Winter Sanctuary?" Corvalen prompted.

"Beginning of last season; I was there when we destroyed it! Put a torch to those cursed trees myself." He shivered, and edged his chair closer to the brazier that warmed the room—unnecessarily, Corvalen thought. It was summer, after all, and the cool of the night was still hours away.

"In every village we've seen some of those witch women," the commander rambled on. "Holy women, some call them. Unholy, say I! The Sanctuary was full of 'em. And, I'll tell you, more than a few tasted my steel!" He paused and blinked, as if having difficulty keeping to the conversational path he had meant to follow. "Unholy, aye. And indecent. D'you know they wear trousers, all of them? And their tunics slit up to here!" He pounded his thigh. "They stride about like men—especially those fighting women, with those ironwood staves of theirs. They don't fight properly, neither. Dead silent they are—it's uncanny. Nor do they fight fair; they'll kick you as soon as crack their sticks over your head, and you hardly see it coming. They killed some good men." He seized his goblet, bringing it to his lips with such haste that wine sloshed over the rim and dribbled into his beard.

Corvalen exchanged a look with his aide. With practiced nonchalance, Rossen moved the wine bottle out of the commander's reach.

"Amazing, isn't it? That Sanctuary was defended by *women*, and they nearly drove us back. Held us off long enough to let most of their people get away from there, anyhow." The commander brightened. "Left all their treasure behind, though! Look at this." He dug in his belt pouch and produced a ruffle-petaled flower of delicately engraved and enameled gold. "That'll make a pretty bauble to bestow on some fine lady, won't it?"

"Beautiful workmanship," Rossen commented.

"Oh yes. Great craftsmen, these Sharhay. This brazier here is their work, too. Prince Dursten himself gave it to me out of the spoils when he saw how I suffered from the cold. Of course, it's nothing compared to all the rare valuables he's got locked up in the storerooms at Southwood." The commander barked a laugh. "That's a joke, that is. His Highness ordered a fortress built on the hill across the river from the Winter Sanctuary. Only there's no sanctuary anymore, and all the trees that surrounded it we either burned or cut for timber to build the fortress. So it's called Southwood! Get it?"

"Prince Dursten is a man of rare humor." Corvalen half rose to take his leave.

The commander seized Corvalen's arm. "Only here's what's not so funny. We finally broke through to the center of the Sanctuary as the last of those women were getting out of there. I saw them retreating myself, and I saw this . . . unnatural gray mist rise up around them."

"Smoke from the burning, no doubt."

The commander looked as though this thought had never occurred to him. "Maybe . . . but somehow, I swear, the women called it to them, and wrapped it around themselves so we couldn't see them, so they could make their escape. And then there were voices in the mist—or smoke, or whatever it was. Awful voices, and it was all we could hear. It made some men shiver, with cold creeping into their flesh. Cold that's never gone away, and a man can never get warm again. I swear, those women have cursed us all." He cast a look of desperate longing at the brazier. "What happened to that wine bottle?"

Later, on their way to join the bodyguard in camp, Rossen asked Corvalen what he thought of the commander's story.

"The man is a superstitious fool—not to mention a drunkard. All the same, things are not right in this country. I am not certain. . . . Well. When we stop at Southwood, we shall hear what the commander there has to say."

*****

Corvalen had been informed that the fighting was now concentrated in the north, so he was not surprised that his army encountered no warriors as they made their way to Southwood. What they did see were the remains of roadside executions, and the faces of the living pinched with anger and want. For long stretches of the march the only people they saw were Forstene soldiers on patrol, while of the Sharhay the sole signs were ruined farmhouses, unplanted fields, more untended or burnt vineyards, and expanses of charred tree trunks reaching black talons to the sky. Veteran that he was, Corvalen could not feel sanguine in the presence of such despoilment.

And yet I did this, and worse, in Cheskara, he thought as they approached a burned-out village.

Rossen, riding beside him, was evidently thinking along similar lines. "This place looks like the Cheskari borderlands when we left them. I hate to think what King Delanar would say if he could see the state of his new province."

"He sent me to say it for him. And it's not his province yet."

"But it will be—though if the prince keeps up this level of destruction, we don't seem likely to get much good out of it."

"A worthless conquest, and one hard to hold," Corvalen agreed. "May Vallar grant that the Sharhay listen to reason."

"They'll not be able to do otherwise once they've seen the strength of your army, my lord."

"The kings of Forstene have always believed diplomacy is most effective when backed by spears." He smiled, thinking with satisfaction of the spearmen and swordsmen, knights and men-at-arms now under his command.

And yet . . . he hoped his army would not have to do battle in Sharhaya. Let the men be put to work building watchtowers and fortresses, bridges and roads. The country he was riding through was a wasteland now; it had once been a place of fabled beauty. He would rather not be the agent of further destruction here. But the king wanted Sharhaya, and Corvalen was pledged to do whatever it took to deliver it into his liege's hand.

The road—if the muddy, potholed track they were following could be called that—turned a bend, bringing into view a corridor of trees shading a river on their left. Gradually the willows, alders, and hazels gave way to clumps of rushes, where blackbirds sporting scarlet-epauletted wings whistled and foraged. The road curved closer to the river, and horses began to strain toward the water.

As Corvalen led his gelding to drink, a heron snaked its neck up out of the reeds in front of him, turning its head so that one unnerving yellow eye was full on him. Then the dusky-blue bird launched itself into the air, flapping away northward with languid strokes of its wings.

The reeds rustled and swayed in the heron's wake. Yet close to the riverbank a frosting of mist hung undisturbed over the water's surface. Toward the center, the current foamed around toothy rocks, and the sunlight sparked on water droplets flung into the air.

As sometimes happened, the first few lines of what might make a poem sprang full-formed to mind:

Heron flight,
Misted river
Washing rocks in sun—

Beside him, his squire spoke, and Corvalen lost the syllable count.
"The water makes patterns."

Corvalen followed the boy's pointing finger. Through the mist he,
too, could see the swirls and spirals. *Water churns in patterns—*

"Better not stare at them too long, Pellar," Rossen cautioned
teasingly. "The River Wife might lure you in, like Notar the Trader."
Fate-churning current.

"That's just a nursery tale," scoffed Pellar, but nevertheless took a
step back from the waterside. As soon as his horse's thirst was slaked,
he returned to the road.

"Rossen," Corvalen began, and shook his head. But he couldn't
help grinning as they made their own way from the riverbank. "Not so
long ago, you yourself were a young squire on your first campaign in a
foreign country."

"I remember all too well, my lord. I'll try to be a better friend to
Pellar."

"Then he will be a fortunate young man; there are few better
friends to be had." Corvalen smiled, clapped Rossen on the shoulder,
and swung back into his saddle.

He spent the next bit of the ride refining his poem. He did not
delude himself that he was truly a poet—certainly the high epic style
was well beyond him—but this latest fashion in court poetry seemed
well suited to the skills of a dilettante like himself. Yet it was more
difficult than one would think.

Another curve in the river, another curve in the road brought the
first sighting of Southwood, seated atop a hill in the middle distance.
Corvalen could make out a palisade, and behind it the stony bulk of a
single square tower. He ordered his trumpeters to sound the first signal
for their approach. Southwood's trumpets answered, and the army
picked up its pace, every man and horse eager for the end of the day's
march.

*****

Rossen let out his breath in a sigh of pleasure. Southwood had a proper
bathhouse, complete with sweat bath and cold pool. Truth to tell, the
"cold" water was actually tepid, but it was still a civilized pool, lined
with smooth stone benches just the right height so that one could relax
on them with the water soothingly up to one's neck.

"I thought I might find you here," came Corvalen's voice behind
him.

"And here you find me." Rossen stole a glimpse of his lord, fresh from the sweat bath, dark-honey hair clinging to his damp shoulders, then closed his eyes as Corvalen eased into the pool across from him. "How did your meeting with the commander go? More wild stories?"

"Mm."

Confronted with this minimal response, Rossen was forced to open his eyes in hope of learning something from Corvalen's expression. But the Lord Marshal chose this moment to splash his face with the tepid water. Rossen waited for him to settle down again before prompting, "Well?"

"The commander here is Fengal of Telthene. A solid man, I'd thought. But this fort seems rife with, as you say, wild stories: the weather turning stranger and stranger the longer the army's stayed; mysterious mists, and dry ground that suddenly goes boggy; odd-behaving animals, and voices in the wind. Not to mention all manner of curses and nightmares. Did every man here spend his nursery years listening to outlandish Sharhay stories? Fathers should take more care in selecting their children's nurses."

"My nurse used to tell me lovely stories about Sharhaya. There was one she called 'The Land of Vines and Trees.' It was about a brother and sister whose parents left them with some Holy Women while they went away to another country. The parents died, and the children found out about it from the trees, and—"

"Yes, I know it. 'The Talking Trees of Sharhaya' is what my daughter's nurse called that story, I think."

Rossen couldn't resist. "Fathers should take more care in selecting their children's nurses."

That brought Corvalen up short for a moment, then he broke into a grin and chuckled. "Quite. But at least Mellis's nurse didn't fill her full of all this nonsense about curses and such. Besides, Mellis knows the difference between romantic stories and real life."

In truth, Corvalen's eleven-year-old daughter was full of all kinds of story-derived romantic notions, but Rossen forbore to point this out.

Corvalen rubbed his knuckles against his beard, as he tended to do when mulling over something perplexing.

"What is it?"

"Fengal gave me quite a mix of information. Most usefully, he's provided an up-to-date description of the situation in the north and has offered a guide to show us the best route to the prince's encampment. On the other hand, he claims no one can find the Summer Sanctuary."

"It's the capital of the country!"

"As you say. But remember, it's in the middle of a forest. Rumor has it that after the Winter Sanctuary was destroyed, the Holy Women did . . . something"—he spread his hands in a gesture of exasperation—"to hide the forest paths. Since then, only Holy Women and their servants can find their way to the Summer Sanctuary. At any rate, this is the excuse, as Fengal tells it."

"Does he believe it?"

The door behind Rossen opened again, and Pellar came in bearing a length of linen toweling. "Pardon me for disturbing you, my lord."

"Quite all right; I'm not going to get any cleaner than I already am." Corvalen climbed out of the pool, shook away some of the water from his skin and hair, and accepted the linen from Pellar. As he toweled himself off, he remarked, "It ought to be nearly time to dine, and a good thing."

"I'm sorry, my lord, but it seems Sir Fengal never dines till after dark . . . till after he has saluted the first star."

"What are you not telling me, Pellar?"

"Sir Fengal has heard that you didn't bring a star reader with you on this campaign, so he offers you the service of his. Not for the whole campaign, of course"—the squire's voice careered from low to high and back as he hurried on—"because Sir Fengal says that he really couldn't do without his star reader for so long. But Sir Fengal is sure you would like to accompany him to the tower roof with the star reader tonight, and as the sun is setting now . . ." Pellar's words dwindled away before Corvalen's scowl.

"I do not travel with a star reader," muttered Corvalen, "because I do not need a star reader. Nor do I want one."

"I know, my lord," Pellar said.

Rossen decided to come to the boy's aid. "My lord, Fengal is clearly a devotee of the Celestials. We can't fault him for his faith in the star readers any more than we would fault ourselves for consulting with the acolytes of the Exalted Ones. Many people, in fact, revere both the Exalted Ones and the Celestials."

Pellar added, "During their lives, some of the Exalted Ones themselves honored the Celestials and consulted with star readers. Heldar the Unifier, for example—"

"Yes, yes, fine." Corvalen wrapped the towel around his waist and, flinging the long end up over his shoulder, grumbled, "Next time, just remind me of my duty to my host and have done with it. But no more theology, I beg you."

Pellar exchanged a grin with Rossen, then followed Corvalen out.

*****

From the tower rooftop, Corvalen surveyed the landscape around the fort. Even in the fading light he could make out a huge blackened circle of earth across the river. It could only be the former site of the Winter Sanctuary. He had thought there would be something of it remaining; he was unprepared for the oppressive emptiness Dursten's attack had left behind. The other men gathering for the evening devotion arrived with hearty voices, but he returned them only murmured greetings.

Fengal attempted to make light conversation with him. "I meant to ask you, earlier, about things at court. How are Princess Hannalis and little Prince Heldar? I was one of the sponsors at his naming, you know."

"Yes, that's right," Corvalen said, wondering, as he had on that naming day, if it really was wise or proper to name a child after one of the Exalted Ones. Then he realized Fengal was still waiting for an answer. "Her Highness graces the court as ever she did, though it is apparent her husband's long absence saddens her."

Fengal made sympathetic noises. "Still, young Heldar must be a great comfort to her."

Corvalen smiled in spite of himself. "Indeed. But something of a trial to his nurse, I fear. The lad runs everywhere and can hardly sit still through a meal."

"Prince Dursten will be glad to hear his boy is so full of life. He misses him very much, I believe."

"It's hard to leave a young child and go away on campaign." Corvalen thought of Mellis, and of how long it took her, each time he came home, to stop treating him like a stranger. "I have a packet for His Highness that should please him very much: Princess Hannalis has sent a new portrait medallion of their son."

"I should like to see that myself, if— Ah, but here's Reader Thannen arriving. Please excuse me, Lord Corvalen." Accepting Corvalen's nod of dismissal, Fengal moved off to confer with the star reader.

The sky dimmed by imperceptible stages, and the vista from the tower roof contracted. Corvalen was watching the thin strands of mist curling up from the river when the others sighted the first star. The star reader—Thannen—began the litany of greeting, with Fengal and his fellow devotees chorusing the responses. Then everyone stood in silence, staring upward as the stars appeared to blink into being one by one in the darkening sky. Corvalen abandoned himself to the beauty of the night, the burgeoning stars eclipsing the afterimage of the blighted land across the river.

"The Guide Star!" someone announced, and Corvalen's eyes, too, were drawn to it.

Thannen, his bass voice resonant, led them all in a hymn to the star that had guided the ancestors of the kings of Forstene to their destined realm:

> "Hail, O Star, thou guiding light
> Whom Stennar knew for sign of fate.
> Father of Kings, th'Exalted One
> Held thee ever in his sight
> While 'cross the seas with trials great
> He sailed through settings of the sun
> Many a long and weary night.
> His desire only thou couldst sate:
> To show where glory could be won."

Even while the echo of the last notes still hung in the air, most of the devotees deserted the tower roof, no doubt hastening to their dinners. But Fengal and the star reader lingered, so Corvalen was obliged to remain behind as well.

Still gazing at the sky, Thannen said, "May I ask, Lord Corvalen, what stars you were born under?"

"In Brintora, most people do not keep such close track of the stars. But," he added, for politeness' sake, "I believe I have heard it said that I was born under the Lion."

"Of course; it could be no other. You are a votary of the Exalted Vallar, I think?"

This was no example of astral insight—like most sworn devotees of Vallar, Corvalen made a practice of anointing himself with oil of cedar after bathing; anyone standing near him could hardly fail to notice the scent. He answered nonetheless with a gracious inclination of his head. "I am."

"'The worthy man does not lightly draw his sword,'" Thannen quoted meditatively.

"You know the Exalted One's sayings?"

"Some of them. I know many things, Lord Corvalen. And I therefore warn you that you may find it difficult to keep to the Precepts of Vallar in this country."

"The difficulty of a task only increases the honor of achieving it."

"Ah. Another saying of the Exalted Vallar?"

Corvalen smiled. "No, that one's mine."

The star reader's attention shifted back to the sky. "There is the Lion—there." He pointed, his hand a shadow in the thickening darkness.

Corvalen's eyes found the constellation easily enough; he was not quite so lacking in star knowledge as he pretended. But he could see nothing remarkable about the Lion crouching above the northern horizon—until a shooting star appeared from the depths of the night and traced its bright, ephemeral path through the heart of the celestial beast.

"A sign, Lord Corvalen," breathed Fengal.

"But what does it mean?" he asked, rather against his better judgment.

There was a long silence before Thannen answered. "I do not know, my lord."

Corvalen took a gold coin from his belt pouch and pressed it into the man's hand. "A donation for your temple." He didn't know if the man had a temple yet, or planned to build one, but truly he ought to. He was the first honest star reader Corvalen had ever met.

Chapter Four

While the rest of the army broke camp next morning, Corvalen and a few of his officers lingered over their breakfast tea, awaiting the appearance of the promised guide. As the other men talked quietly, Corvalen worked on a letter to his daughter, till Fengal called out a greeting to a man just entering the hall. The gathered officers fell silent as Fengal introduced the newcomer. "Lord Corvalen, this is Esban. Your guide."

The man was dressed in Forstene clothes, but he wore his beard full and his mousy hair loose, with only the front locks tied back from his pasty face.

Corvalen noticed one of his lieutenants, Rindal, exchanging a wary look with Rossen. No doubt the rest of his men would hold similar opinions of trusting themselves to a Sharhay guide.

Fengal could not help but sense their lack of enthusiasm. "I assure you, my lord, Esban is completely trustworthy, completely reliable. He's been of great service to us."

"Has he," Corvalen said.

"He's become quite fluent in Forstene; you'll have no trouble at all communicating with him. And if you happen to run into any Sharhay, it will be useful to have a translator along."

Corvalen looked more closely at the man, and guessed that he was not older than twenty. He had a pack on his back, sturdy boots on his feet; he appeared competent enough. Yet his eyes lacked candor, and his smile was lopsided as he smoothly saluted Corvalen in the Forstene manner.

"It will be my honor to be your guide, Lord Corvalen, and to return in your company to my royal master, His Highness Prince Dursten."

Ah, this was one of Dursten's protégés, then. Well, he would not find it so easy to make his way into Corvalen's good graces. But that did not mean he might not be useful.

He certainly proved to be a source of information. Since the beginning of the war, Corvalen had endeavored to learn as much as he could about this country—his friend Martos, a former Ghildaran ambassador to Sharhaya, had been particularly helpful—yet there remained many gaps in his knowledge. Even the things he'd already been told showed themselves in rather different colors when described by a native. But Esban could not, or would not, elucidate the matter of the route to the Summer Sanctuary when Corvalen questioned him about it soon after they rode out of Southwood.

"I am not from the north," Esban explained, a note of petulance in his voice. "I have never been to the Summer Sanctuary."

"Yet you must know where it is?"

"Oh, it's in the Parasha."

Corvalen recalled the rough-sketched map Fengal had shown him. "That's the forest on this side of the river, in the north?"

"Yes; this river is the Asha." Esban gestured toward the reed-edged watercourse on their left. "*Parasha* means 'east of the Asha,' you see. Up north there is also a great woodland west of the Asha—the Lenasha Forest. That is where most of the Sharhay army is."

"Why not in the Parasha, to protect the Sanctuary?" asked Rossen, riding in his usual place at Corvalen's side.

"There are some warbands on guard in the Parasha, but they have kept out of most fighting this season. The Champion—he has command over all warbands, you see—he is a crafty old badger. He lured Prince Dursten's army to the other side of the river, goaded them into battle just south of the Lenasha. The prince made camp on Summer Bluff, not far from there—a strong position. But it is too steep to ride his horsemen down the east or south sides of the bluff and cross over to the Parasha. If they go down the northern or western slope, the warbands come from the Lenasha to harry them."

So far Esban's account of the situation agreed with what Corvalen had learned from Fengal. Nevertheless, suspicion niggled at him. "If you knew that the Champion's forces were leading ours away from the location of the Sanctuary—"

"A natural question, my lord. But, you see, at that time I did not— what is your expression?—have the prince's ear."

"Ah. And how long ago was this?"

"A moon ago, perhaps a little more." Esban waved a negligent hand.

"And the Summer Sanctuary—why is it said that no one save the Holy Women and their servants can find it?"

"Because that is the truth! Prince Dursten has been able to get some scouting parties across the river; I went with two of them. I saw for myself: the paths in that forest are tangled. Once under the trees, you cannot tell your direction. You think you are walking deeper into the wood, but every path leads you out again—or straight to a warband on guard. We just got away in our skins last time."

Or you have been playing Dursten's men for fools.

As the morning waxed, their road climbed. Below them the landscape opened into ripening grain fields, interspersed with thriving orchard plots. From the crest of a hill they looked down onto a village that appeared to be completely intact. Within the square palisade that enclosed it, roofs of wood shingles or thatch rose over houses that showed no sign of having been pillaged or threatened with the torch. A few people were out on the common; it was too far off to see what they were doing. From somewhere in the village a dog barked; from elsewhere came the bleating of goats.

After everything Corvalen had observed so far in Sharhaya, the bucolic serenity of this place should have been reassuring. But its incongruence disturbed him.

"I thought the Sharhay didn't fortify their villages," remarked Rossen, as usual putting his finger on the matter.

Esban assumed a faintly superior air. "No, but it would serve them better if they did. It is your people who built that wall. Prince Dursten gave the village to some of his soldiers who can no longer fight, you see. His Highness is a man of the greatest generosity!"

"What of the Sharhay inhabitants?" Rossen asked.

"Most ran away when the Winter Sanctuary fell. Luckily for His Highness's men, a few of the women chose to remain." Esban winked at Rossen and smirked.

"'Chose'?" Corvalen echoed.

"Not all Sharhay are fools. Some of us know that the friendship of the strong is the best guarantee for survival."

Rationally, it was difficult to disagree with Esban's conclusion, yet Corvalen felt an instinctual urge to do so. Instead, he silently watched the village outskirts recede from view as he descended the hill. Over one of the fields a trio of hawks rode high, scouring the far-off ground for unwary rodents among the grain.

"Those fields and orchards looked well tended," Rossen was saying. "Have the veterans turned farmers?"

Esban shrugged. "Some. Mainly, they have Sharhay farmers to work for them."

"That doesn't bother you?"

"Most Sharhay men are farmers." There was a clear note of disdain in his voice. "What is the difference if they work for the village Mothers or for Forstene landlords?"

Corvalen decided to rejoin the conversation. "Sharhaya's farmers are also Sharhaya's warriors, I understand. If they all agreed with you, it seems unlikely there would still be fighting in the north. It appears to matter very much to them whether they farm for their Mothers or for us."

"As I said, not all Sharhay are fools—but a great many are."

*****

The next day offered a spectacle far different from the peaceful veterans' settlement. In the distance, to the north and northeast, great billows of smoke rose to the already clouded sky.

Corvalen frowned. "They're burning their crops. They know we're coming." He narrowed his eyes at Esban. "How would they know that?"

"How would they not? This is a large army—a magnificent army! Those loyal to the Ma'Sharha could easily have sent a runner north to give warning."

"So the Kel Sharha will know about us, too?"

"She would know even without a runner. The current Kel Sharha is the Kel Sula, the Chief of the Order of Listeners—what you might call Diviners. The trees will have told her."

"You believe in the talking trees, do you?"

Esban shifted in his saddle. "I am not a barbarian, my lord! But the Sula do have their ways of knowing that which seems unknowable. They call it 'listening to the trees'—though perhaps this is just a mysterious way of speaking, to make the people hold them in greater awe."

"That seems likely," Corvalen said. "But runners or trees or Diviners regardless, your people are acting mistakenly: burnt fields are not going to slow my army. We are well provisioned for the season; we have no need to forage for food or to make requisitions from the populace."

Rossen asked Esban, "What of Prince Dursten's supply lines?"

"They have proved . . . troublesome. That is why His Highness sent me to Southwood, to arrange with Sir Fengal—"

"The prince sent *you*? You are Sharhay."

"Exactly, Sir Rossen. No Sharhay seeing me on my ride south would have thought to interfere with me."

Corvalen half smiled. "Even riding a Forstene horse?"

"I rode a Sharhay horse *to* Southwood. *This* horse was given me by Sir Fengal so that you would not be delayed by the pace of my inferior animal. Of course, on this horse, and in this company, I can no longer disguise my allegiance to Forstene. But soon that will not matter—now that you are here, Lord Corvalen."

*****

In spite of the information he had gained since leaving Southwood, by the end of the day Corvalen found himself thoroughly irritated with Esban. The man's manner was both servile and smug, his motives were far from clear, and his whining voice was enough to grate on even a patient man. Yet none of this explained the degree of Corvalen's disdain for him.

Perhaps I have given too little attention to my devotions since I came here. Sharhaya is an unsettled land; I must not allow it to unsettle me.

As soon as camp was made, Corvalen retired into his tent and opened his small gilt-wood icon case. Silently, he contemplated the painted image of the Exalted Vallar, then drew a deep breath and began the ritual recitation of the Ten Greater Achievements. For good measure he followed this by chanting the names of the principal warriors who had served under the ancient hero. "O Exalted One," he closed, in the traditional formula, "I, Corvalen of Brintora, mindful of your deeds, pledge that my own will follow the same path of honor, that I may be worthy to be counted among your following." After a few moments, he shut the icon case, pressed it to his forehead, and returned it to its protective wrappings.

When he emerged from his tent, Rossen and Rindal hailed him, waving him to join them and a few others at one of the cookfires. As Corvalen settled himself, Pellar ladled out a bowl of stew and presented it to him together with the evening wine ration. When Esban insinuated himself into the circle of men a short while later, Corvalen felt magnificently able to ignore him.

Esban, however, made several tries at drawing Corvalen into conversation. At last he caught Corvalen's eye and blurted, "You don't like me, do you, my lord?"

Corvalen took a leisurely drink before answering. "I don't trust you."

"Why not? I have been a good helper to your people."

"And betrayed your own. A man who can turn traitor once will not hesitate to do so again if it suits his interest."

"My interest is to see the Ma'Sharha thrown down."

"Your Holy Women?" Rossen said. "But why?"

"You would not understand."

Corvalen signaled to Rossen to keep quiet. Esban would make certain that they heard his tale, but Corvalen had no intention of encouraging his sense of self-importance.

Esban poked at the fire with a stick. "I have the Healing Gift, you see," he said at last.

"The 'Healing Gift'?" Corvalen did not attempt to disguise his disbelief.

"Some men do," Esban said. "It is more often women that have the Gifts, this is true. But when a man does show himself gifted, what do you think happens to him?"

Although Rossen managed to contain his curiosity, Pellar did not. "What?"

"Well, if his Gift is healing, he can become a lay healer: a maker of remedies, a *servant*"—he loaded this word with bitterness—"in a House of Healing. Or a field surgeon, who goes out with the hunting parties and warbands. But lay healers are not taught to wield power. *That* is only for the Nira, the healers who take Orders. And the Orders are only for women. So a man in Orders—yes, there have been a few—is compelled to live as a woman."

Pellar's widened eyes reflected the firelight. "You mean . . . ?"

Esban laughed. "No. No, you see, a man in Orders has to wear the clothes and braids of a woman. And has to shave, of course." He paused, cupping his hands around his beard as if to protect it. "But I would have agreed to all of that," he murmured. "It would have been worth it, to control such power."

"What happened?"

"The Kel Nira—the Chief of the Healers—she said I did not have the . . . capacity."

Or the compassion, Corvalen thought, but said, "I suppose she was jealous of your potential, and did not wish to be shown up by a man."

Esban either ignored or completely missed the sarcasm in Corvalen's voice. "My lord, you understand the situation perfectly."

The Healer's Choice

*****

Rossen stretched, feeling much more relaxed since Esban had taken himself off to his bedroll. The conversation around the fire had turned away from serious matters as the men lightened their minds before sleep. In the camp around them, soldiers dowsed their cookfires and prepared to settle in for the night.

The sound of a signal horn cut through the trailing-off of the men's banter. Corvalen stood, cocking his head to listen as the signal was repeated.

"A messenger," Rossen said, also getting to his feet.

Corvalen nodded. "Approaching from the south."

"You don't think . . . the king?"

"He was well enough when we left; he's been gaining strength since the winter."

In spite of his words, Corvalen's brow furrowed.

They did not have to wait long for the messenger to be brought to Corvalen. In the firelit dusk, Rossen just made out the man's livery— not the royal colors, but the blue and white of the barony of Caldene.

Corvalen was already speaking as he returned the messenger's salute. "Do you come from my sister? Is something amiss with her?"

"The lady of Caldene thrives, my lord, although the news she received of me was not of the best."

"Speak to the point."

"Yes, my lord. I am just returning to Lord Torval after carrying a message for him to his mother."

"Torval? No one has given me news of him since I arrived in Sharhaya."

So far as Rossen knew, Corvalen had not *asked* anyone for news of Torval, or even mentioned his name before now. The young man was Corvalen's heir, but he had gone against his uncle's wishes when he joined Prince Dursten's forces. There had been hard feelings on both sides. Corvalen's, however, were clearly melting like last year's snow as he received the messenger's news.

"I'm sorry to be the one to tell you, my lord: your nephew has been injured."

"How? When?"

"Just over four weeks ago, in the Lenasha Forest. Sharhay archers shot his horse from under him. His leg was badly broken."

"Did he lose it?" Corvalen's voice was painfully steady.

"No sir, praise Vallar! When I left him, he had every expectation of getting back full use of the leg. A remarkable thing—" The messenger broke off, and seemed flustered when he spoke again. "But I am sure you will want to hear his experiences from his own lips, my lord."

"Indeed." Corvalen clapped him on the shoulder. "I thank you for your news, and hope to have more from you tomorrow. But you look like a man in need of a quiet meal and a night's rest. My squire will see to it."

Pellar led the messenger off in search of food, wine, and a place to spread his bedroll. The other men had discreetly left the fireside and gone to their tents, with the exception of Rindal.

Corvalen gracefully lowered himself back to the seat he had occupied before the messenger's arrival. He rubbed at his beard and stared into the embers; the rubies in his earrings seemed to reflect back their glow.

Rindal cleared his throat and moved to take his leave.

"No, Rindal, sit back down. I need to speak with you. You too, Rossen. I have decided to ride ahead to Prince Dursten's camp."

"Your anxiety for your heir is most natural, my lord," said Rindal.

"Most natural," Corvalen echoed. "Especially since that messenger was not telling all he knew."

Rossen nodded. "I had that impression as well."

"I don't like the things I have seen in this country. I don't like what this country seems to be doing to our people here. I need not only to reassure myself about Torval, but to get the king's new orders to Prince Dursten without further delay. Rossen, you and Pellar will ride north with me at first light. Torval's messenger can show us the quickest route to the prince's encampment."

"What of your bodyguard? You ought to take at least some of them," Rossen urged.

"Ten men; no more. I want to get there with as much speed as possible. Rindal, you will take command of the army. Keep to this side of the river; we need to be in position to march on the Parasha if necessary."

"Understood, my lord. And what about Esban?"

"Get as much information from him as you can, but use it with caution; he is not trustworthy. If he shows any sign of betraying us"— Corvalen's jaw hardened—"kill him."

Chapter Five

Treska paused at the window, looking out at a drizzly dawn. During the night's rain, another crop of lean-tos had mushroomed on the trampled green. Refugees filled the Sanctuary—word had come that a new Forstene army was marching up from the south, and people were fleeing ahead of it. Some of them were strong enough to keep going after just a rest in the Sanctuary, but a lot stayed. There wasn't room for any more in the houses, or even the stables, and so many were sick or hurt that the Guesthouse had to be turned into an annex to the House of Healing. Now the newcomers had to make do with whatever rough shelters they could pitch on the green. They looked miserable out there.

Across the hall, the Kel Nira's chamber door stood open; Treska heard something metallic hit the floor and the Kel Nira use a rude word.

"May I help you, Lady?"

"Please." She had her hair in three plaits and was just tying off the last one.

Treska bent to pick up the cords and ribbons that had spilled from their brass box; that was what had fallen. She could feel the Kel Nira watching her. "Arna is getting your rain cloak."

"Good." The Kel Nira finished braiding her three plaits into one; Treska selected a leather cord and secured them.

"More refugees came last night."

"Then you will have plenty to do. They will all need to be examined, and probably most will require some treatment or other. Yasma will instruct you."

"I'd rather go with you and Deela."

The Kel Nira laid a hand on Treska's shoulder. "It is too early for you to endure the rigors of field duty."

"I know I let you down last time"—it was still embarrassing to remember how sick and how little help she had been—"but I've been working on my control, and I really think—"

"No. It was wrong of me to subject you to field duty so soon. You are not ready."

41

"I *am* ready, my Chief."

"I said no. You have your work here, and I must get to mine."

Treska was too familiar with that tone of voice to argue further. But she *had* been working on her self-control, and she *knew* she could do a good job now. She would just have to prove it after the Kel Nira got back from the field.

If she got back.

The sudden worry propelled Treska to hurry out into the hall after the Kel Nira, who was already halfway down the stairs.

"Walk with the Watchers, my Chief!"

The Kel Nira turned at the foot of the stairs and held her palms out toward Treska. "The blessings of the Mothers on you, my child."

Deela, waiting by the front door, handed the Kel Nira her medicine bag, and Arna helped her on with her rain cloak.

"Take care of yourself, Treska!" Deela called. She tapped her forehead twice, the private signal they used to encourage each other when their teacher was hard on them, then waved as she followed after the Kel Nira.

Treska ran back to the window, and watched the two of them walk out onto the green. Deela turned to the right and headed for the path back to the stables, but the Kel Nira went the other direction. *I guess she has to see the Kel Sharha before she leaves.*

The thought made Treska uneasy. There were things going on in the Sanctuary that she didn't know about, but she knew they were going on all the same. And it wasn't just that everyone was worried about that new Forstene army.

Well, the Kel Nira always said work was the best remedy for troubled thoughts. And if Treska wanted to prove herself to her teacher, a good report from Yasma would be a fine start. Today she would do her best work ever in the House of Healing—and tomorrow she would do even better.

*****

An elderly servant met the Kel Nira at the door. "I'm glad you're here, Lady," she whispered as she led the way up the stairs to the Kel Sharha's room.

"A difficult night?"

"She was up twice with the pain. But she's finally getting a little sleep now."

"I will do my best not to awaken her."

Within the room, a single lamp burned on the bedside table, and the window shutters were latched. After the servant left, the Kel Nira took a moment to let her eyes adjust to the dimness before approaching the bed.

Ordinarily it was her policy to give Nihara only when another Healer could stand by to monitor the process and cut it short if necessary. But Lillanna had kept the night watch in the House of Healing; she would be needing her rest now. And the Council members had agreed that only they and their Seconds should know the true seriousness of the Kel Sharha's illness. She had more than sixty winters, and thin and frail as she'd grown, it was impossible for the folk of the Sanctuary not to realize her health was declining. But if it were generally known that she was only able to leave her bed at all because the Kel Nira and Lillanna were pouring Nihara into her every day, the effect on the people's morale would be devastating.

So the Kel Nira knelt alone beside the Kel Sharha, trusting the Watchers to make sure she closed the channels before the fire-river of Nihara washed away too much of her own vitality. She placed her hands on the Kel Sharha's forehead and chest, drew a breath, and whispered the chant: "I draw power up from the earth. I open to power that flows from the sky. I am a tree to connect the worlds. I am a river to channel the flow."

As she said the words, she felt herself hollow out, making way for the flood. She moved her hands down to press her palms against the Kel Sharha's lower abdomen, where the cancer had been growing these past three years. She continued chanting, losing track of the actual words, of time, of everything but the heat and rush of Nihara pouring through her and out her palms.

And then she felt the energy wash back into her, as if the flood had crashed against a levee. She lifted her hands and sat back, dazed, vaguely aware of pain sharp in her gut. Her pulse was drumming like a call to arms. She swallowed with effort, made herself breathe to a long, even count.

At last the pain subsided, her pulse quieted and slowed, and she was able to focus on the outer world again. The Kel Sharha stirred, looking scarcely less hollow-cheeked than she had before the treatment.

The Kel Nira ran her fingers over the older woman's belly, and frowned. *I am no longer holding back the illness's advance, only slowing it—and not by much.*

Skinny fingers brushed her hand away. "Don't trouble yourself over me, child," murmured the Kel Sharha.

The Kel Nira stepped back and bowed. "It is no trouble, First of Mothers."

"Your frown says otherwise."

The Kel Nira quickly pulled her face into a cheerful bedside smile.

The Kel Sharha, now fully awake, chuckled. "Help me sit up, if you would. I want to talk to you. And don't tell me I should be resting—I do more than enough of that." Once settled against her pillows, she paused to catch her breath. "So . . . you are once more heading off to the field."

"Yes, Kel Sharha."

"I understand that Guardian Fama is not enthusiastic about accompanying you again. The Chief Guardiansherself is . . . concerned."

"They still disapprove."

"True. They do not fully understand your Order's vows. But I, who do, am also concerned, though for different reasons." She paused again, but when she resumed, her voice was a shade stronger. "Since you returned to the Sanctuary last moon, I have been pondering your action. In itself, given your oaths, there was nothing extraordinary in your healing of that Forstener. And yet it has a portentous feel about it. . . . I am convinced now, Kel Nira, that you have brought yourself to the attention of great forces, far beyond our influence or even understanding."

"The Watchers know who I am."

"I am not speaking of the Watchers, child, nor even of the Mothers Beyond. We Listeners have found that there are other forces, little regarded outside our Order—and perhaps that is just as well. Once they enter the weaving, even we cannot decipher the pattern. You have shifted your fate, Finoora, and they will see that it keeps to its new course."

So this was what she had sensed when she heard the trees whispering in the Lenasha. But something else in the Kel Sharha's words struck her.

"You called me by my birth name. Why did you—" She fought down an irrational panic. "Why did you use my birth name? Am I no longer to be the Kel Nira? Is my fate so evil?"

"I'm sorry, child, I cannot tell you—though I can hardly imagine you not being Chief of your Order. But Finoora . . . it was your grandmother's name, too, of course. There *is* something of her in you."

"I have been told that I have her temper."

"Yes . . ."

The Kel Nira stared at her hands, feeling she might be on the verge of understanding something. "I think," she said slowly, "I dream of her sometimes. But I know nothing about her, except that she was a Guardian."

"Did your mother never speak of her?"

"It is not as though my grandmother raised her; they were virtual strangers to each other. And Grandmother died many years before I was born. When I was old enough to ask about her, I was proud to learn she had belonged to the Ma'Sharha."

"I suppose that made you hope the Ma'Sharha would choose you, too?"

The Kel Nira smiled a little and shook her head. "I do not remember anything but feeling proud of my grandmother."

"Now, that is interesting. Most girls with Ma'Sharha in their lineage either yearn to become Ma'Sharha themselves or hope ardently that the Orders will see no talent in them and leave them in peace. Such powerful emotions are not easily forgotten."

"I do not remember," the Kel Nira repeated.

And it was true. She could summon to her mind's eye vivid tableaux from her first ten years: she and Pieran and their parents, sometimes at home in Redcreek, sometimes at the summer marketplace near the ferry landings, most often in the merchants' quarter in Ghildarna's capital city, across the Ghil River. The emotions that had accompanied those scenes, however, were long lost to her. Her recollection of the two or three years after her tenth winter were even less certain. Why did the Kel Sharha wish to stir the cauldron of memory now?

"Kel Nira, my apologies. You have duties awaiting you, and much on your shoulders already. But your grandmother came into my mind for a reason—perhaps you should think on it. Somehow . . . she is part of the weaving. . . ." The Kel Sharha's voice faded on the last words, and she seemed to sink deeper into the pillows.

The Kel Nira took the older woman's hand and bowed over it. "Thank you for your wisdom, Kel Sula Kel Sharha. Sleep now, and you will awaken stronger."

She left the house as silently as she had entered and made her way back around the edge of the green. The drizzle was slacking, tapering off into syncopated clusters of droplets, and many of the refugees were now awake, preparing their meager breakfasts.

As she turned onto the path to the stables, she heard someone approaching from behind at a squelching run. The Chief of the Guardians slowed to a walk beside her.

"Good day, Kel Jemya. What brings you out in such a hurry this morning?"

"Concern. You're not looking well, Kel Nira. I think you must be spending yourself now, to keep the Kel Sharha alive. This is true, isn't it?"

The Kel Nira allowed her silence to answer for her.

"Why?"

"Because I am sworn to do what is necessary."

"Yes, you have your Order's devotion to life in full. It will be hard for you to do what is necessary when the time comes for her to return to the Mothers, won't it?"

"It will be hard for us all. But when she asks, I will do it."

"So sad . . . she was once a woman of such power. And now, what lies before her? What can she hope to accomplish if she continues this way?" The Kel Jemya lowered her voice. "Even you can't restore her to health—can you? Don't bother answering. If you could, you would have done it by now."

They walked some paces without talking, the Kel Jemya beating out an agitated rhythm on her thighs.

The Kel Nira tried to diffuse her companion's tension. "The Kel Sharha is still wise. Her mind remains clear and strong; that is something. A great deal, in fact."

"No, the fact is this: she is lingering too long."

"You must not speak so."

But the Kel Jemya pressed on in a fierce whisper. "Her weakness drains the land, drains us all. If she had crossed when she first knew the severity of her illness, the Winter Sanctuary would not have fallen—"

"We do not know that."

"—and the Forsteners would be gone from Sharhaya by now."

"We do not know that, either. Even the Listeners cannot be certain of such things."

"They can be certain of nothing while their Chief dies this slow death. They know, as well as the rest of us, that a change must come, and come soon."

The Kel Nira chilled her voice, lest it rise too high in anger. "Are you sure for whom you speak, Kel Jemya? 'The rest of us,' after all, are not next in line to be Kel Sharha."

The Guardian strode a step ahead, stopped, and turned to face the Kel Nira. "Would you accuse me of unwholesome ambition?"

"I accuse no one. But your impatience might be thought . . . unseemly."

"I am only impatient to drive out the invaders. And I think that can best be done if the land comes into the keeping of the Jemya. To have a Listener as Kel Sharha during wartime—where is the sense in that? *We* are the defenders of the Ma'Sharha, the protectors of the Sanctuaries." She cleared her throat and shook her head. "The Kel Sula Kel Sharha did not see or sense, or hear from the trees, that the Winter Sanctuary would be attacked—did she? Do you even need to ask yourself why not?"

They were in view of the stables now, but still too far away, the Kel Nira hoped, for the people awaiting her to hear any of this conversation.

"What is it you want from me, Kel Jemya?"

"Just that you think these things over. And when you come back, perhaps you will see a way to convince the Kel Sharha that it is time for her to pass on her office. She would listen to you, Kel Nira; you would know just what to say to make her see the necessity."

"I will not break my oath."

"Of course not. Just . . . consider what I have said. With that new Forstene army on the march, we may not have much time left to exercise our strength. Already Elder Rimenna and some others have been heard suggesting we sue for peace. It would be best for the Guardians to take things in hand sooner rather than later. You understand, don't you?"

"Yes, I understand. But you understand *me* now. If I return from the field and learn that you, or anyone else, has been trying to convince the Kel Sharha to ask me for her crossing—and I assure you, if this is the case, I *will* find out—I will see that you answer to the Watchers for it."

"Agreed. Oh, and one more thing." The Kel Jemya took a step closer. "I doubt you'll see battle this time, since the Forsteners on the bluff will most likely wait for their reinforcements, but if you do . . . well, there is the matter of your giving aid to the enemy."

The muscles in the Kel Nira's neck and shoulders had tightened; she made an effort to relax them before speaking. "Do you think you have something of which to accuse me?"

"Accuse you? Hunh. Everyone knows that the Kel Nira is above reproach. No Chief could be a truer exemplar to her Order."

What shade of bitterness was this—and why?

"No, I am only thinking that if battle comes while you're out there, and if your path crosses a wounded Forstener again—" The Kel Nira was about to interrupt, but the Kel Jemya forestalled her. "I *know* you have to heal him if you can. But then . . . I want him. I'm sending two Guardians with you this time, just in case—Fama and Kirtana. Fama has orders. She won't leave your side and, if possible, she and Kirtana will bring back a Forstene prisoner."

"We cannot bring an enemy into the Sanctuary! Once he sets foot here, all the paths will be open to his people again."

"The Summoners will rescramble the paths, reset the enchantment. Kel Nira, we *need* information. If the Listeners can't obtain it, we must have it somehow. It could make all the difference in our fight; it might even mean our victory over the invaders. You wouldn't stand in the way of that, would you?"

"No more than you would stand in my way." She looked pointedly past the Kel Jemya toward the stables.

The Kel Jemya chuckled and stepped aside. The Kel Nira walked the rest of the path with purposeful, unhurried steps, not glancing back.

But once she was on her horse, she sifted through her conversation with the Kel Jemya, till her thoughts turned on themselves like the cart wheels turning on their axles ahead of her. She hardly noticed as the plodding little procession of horses and wagons entered the sacred forest. Then a sudden gust, blowing raindrops from the tree leaves into her face, made her pay attention.

Her shoulders prickled. Among the trees moved shadows, one seeming clothed in smooth and shining bark that yet was not bark but something softer, difficult for the human eye to focus on. From her saddle the Kel Nira bowed to the Watcher of the Beeches. The figure rippled twiglike fingers at her, and moved from shadow to shadow through the wood, keeping just in the Kel Nira's peripheral vision. When she reached the unseen boundary between the sacred wood and the wild forest, the Watcher rippled its fingers at her again, then rose upward to vanish among the branches of one of the beeches in the last ring of trees. *Strength*, said the leaves.

And she did feel strengthened. At the same time . . .

The Kel Nira had the uneasy feeling that she'd received this gift of fortitude because she was going to need it.

*****

With every night the Kel Nira and Deela were away, Treska found it more difficult to sleep, so she was grateful Healer Lillanna had asked for her assistance on the night watch. There was more than usual to do tonight because several families of refugees had arrived a little after dark. Treska had been assigned to join her friend Graysa, Lillanna's junior apprentice, in assessing the newcomers for illnesses and injuries. They'd found no serious disease, and Treska was glad of that, but it seemed that every one of the refugees suffered from malnourishment or dehydration or heat exhaustion—sometimes all three.

As the midnight hours neared, all the worst cases were settled in the House of Healing or the Guesthouse. Now Treska and Graysa could tend to the smaller hurts, bandaging blistered feet, administering salve for sunburn, and the like. There was a breeze building, and Treska could feel the refugees relax under its cooling touch. For a moment it shifted, and brought a welcome scent from the Sanctuary bakehouse; soon these people in their tents and lean-tos and unsheltered bedrolls would at least be able to exchange their hunger for fresh-made bread.

Right now, though, many were still more thirsty than hungry, so Treska left Graysa with the pot of sunburn salve and went to fill a pitcher at one of the dais fountains. She made her way carefully, not wishing to disturb the refugees who had managed to settle into sleep. She had to trust to the moonlight since she didn't carry a lamp—her pitcher was a large one, and she would need both hands for it when it was full. The light was fitful, though, as clouds scudded across the moon. *We'll likely have rain tomorrow; I hope we can get all these people under cover before then.*

The moon was shrouded as she reached the dais, but she didn't need to see to fill the pitcher. When she was done, she set it on the fountain's wide rim and used the cup hanging from her belt to dip herself a drink while she waited for the moon to emerge and light her way back to Graysa.

There was a murmur of restless voices nearby. Earlier Treska had seen a couple of refugees spread their thin blankets out on the dais; she wasn't surprised that they found it difficult to sleep there. The stone was not only hard, but was itself restless, filled as it was with memories of all the centuries of rites that had been performed atop it.

Treska tried not to eavesdrop on the refugees—two men—but then she heard one of them mention the Ma'Sharha, and in no respectful tone.

His companion scolded him. "Cursed ungrateful you are! Haven't the Ma'Sharha given up everything to serve us? No husbands, no children, and all those years of hard training and all those rules they have to follow. Would you want to live like that?"

"If I had the power they have, maybe I would."

"And what would *you* do with power like that, anyhow?"

Treska didn't wait to hear the other man's answer; the moon was out again, and it would be terribly embarrassing to have them see that she'd overheard them. As quickly and stealthily as she could, she carried her pitcher back to the family she and Graysa had been tending.

As Treska poured water for the children to drink, she tried to shrug away what she'd heard. Those men had been walking for days to get here—no wonder if they were feeling disgruntled. But Treska had the sense that the complaining man had been voicing a long-held opinion. She'd never in her life heard anyone say such a thing—say anything at all ungrateful about the Ma'Sharha. But just because she hadn't heard them didn't mean the words weren't said. And people didn't always say what they thought, either. How many others might there be who thought like that man, and only pretended to honor and esteem the Ma'Sharha?

"Tres? Tres!" Graysa's voice sharpened. "Pay attention where you're pouring that water!"

"Sorry!" Treska set down the pitcher and used the hem of her overdress to dry the little girl whom she'd unwittingly dowsed—though the child didn't seem to mind either the wetting or the drying, and giggled the whole time.

When the rest of the family had their cups filled, Treska and Graysa moved on toward the next group.

"Are you all right?" Graysa asked.

"Yes. No. I'll tell you later."

"Tell me now."

"I can't. I—"

Treska sensed some kind of stirring at the edge of the green, near the House of Healing. No—next to the House: the path back to the stables. "There's a cart coming."

Graysa gave her a curious look. "How do you know?"

"The people in it are scared and sad and angry. Can't you tell?"

At that moment the cart emerged from the path; the moon went under a cloud again before Treska could make out its driver or occupants. The Kel Nira wasn't with them, though—that much she could ascertain. And that didn't feel right.

"Maybe we should go to the House of Healing to help," Treska said.

"Lillanna will just send us right back out here to finish our assignment; she's like that."

Treska nodded, steadied her hands on the pitcher, and she and Graysa carried on.

Treska was bandaging a child's blistered foot when Lillanna's senior apprentice, a buxom girl named Saffa, joined them a short while later. "Lillanna wants you, Treska. I'll finish here."

Saffa's face was set in grim lines, and Treska felt her mouth go dry. She licked her lips and wiped her hands on her overdress. She couldn't think what to do next.

"Go with her, Graysa," Saffa said, sounding almost gentle this time.

Treska was still crouching beside her patient. Graysa pulled her to her feet. "Come on, Tres."

Inside the House of Healing, a servant pointed them up the stairs. Graysa took Treska's hand and led her to one of the surgery rooms at the back of the upper ward.

They walked in on a woman in the brown overdress of the Guardians, pacing. Treska did not recognize her immediately, her look was so bleak. But perhaps that was only a trick of the lamplight.

"Jemaya Kirtana?"

The woman stopped and stared hard at her. "You're the Kel Nira's other apprentice."

Treska swallowed and nodded.

Kirtana was bruised and filthy. Strands of dark blond hair clung to her cheeks, stuck there by sweat and blood. She rubbed at her face to get her hair out of the way, and left a smudge of dirt on her forehead.

Lillanna joined them.

"The men?" Kirtana asked.

"All safe, all settled," Lillanna said.

"Good . . . good. Those were her last words: 'Get the men to safety.' Good."

Her last words?

Lillanna put an arm around Treska, and Graysa squeezed her hand.

"Sit down, Kirtana," Lillanna said in her kindest voice, "and tell us what happened. Graysa, pour her some water."

Kirtana accepted the cup with mumbled thanks. When she had drunk, she said, "Is mine the first news you'll have got from the field?"

"We had a message earlier that the Forsteners were trying to take the bridge."

Graysa stifled a gasp.

"They didn't, though," Kirtana said. "Pieran's got the best bowmen, and he's been training them to shoot in tight volleys. They shot down every man and horse that tried to come across, till the bridge was piled with their corpses. Some of the Forsteners tried to swim the river, but they didn't get far either."

Right now Treska didn't care about the bridge or the battle. Where were the Kel Nira and Deela?

"After the Forsteners retreated we came out of the Lenasha. There was awful fighting on that side of the river, when our warbands tried to stop the Forsteners from riding up along the riverbank to the bridge. We found a lot of dead men. And some not so dead.

"I didn't see everything. I was helping one of our men to the wagon. The Kel Nira and her apprentice were with a surgeon, looking for more of our wounded. Fama was sticking close to them. I heard her yell, and the girl screamed. When I turned around, they were surrounded by Forsteners—must have been lying out there, pretending to be dead or injured; I don't know. . . ." Kirtana rubbed at her face again, and took another gulp of water.

"I grabbed my staff and ran toward them. It was getting dark; it was hard to see everything that was happening, and it was all so fast. I fought with one of the Forsteners. The wagon driver was right beside me, but all he had was his knife; a Forstene spear got him. The surgeon went down, too. So did the girl."

Deela!

"She got back up. The surgeon didn't. Neither did Fama—she was keeping the Forsteners off, until one of them ran up behind her and put his sword through her." Kirtana stopped, and looked from Treska to Graysa. "Maybe I shouldn't have told you that. Sorry."

Lillanna spoke, her voice tight and careful. "Tell us about the Kel Nira."

"She shouted at me to get the men away. I didn't want to leave her, but she kept shouting it; it was a command. I ran back to the wagon. I was going to wait for her, but she shouted at me again—'get those men to safety!' So I had to. The last I saw, she and the girl were running toward the river."

"Deela," Treska said.

"What?"

"'The girl.' Her name is Deela."

"Yes. I remember now. I'm sorry." Kirtana closed her eyes. "I'm so sorry."

Gently, Lillanna disengaged herself from Treska and knelt beside Kirtana. "You did what you were charged to do, and you saved the lives of a dozen men. That was what the Kel Nira cared about most."

Is. That is *what the Kel Nira* cares *about!* Treska wanted to say it out loud, but her mouth had gone dry again, and she realized she was trembling. Graysa hugged her.

Lillanna stood up; she was shaking, too. "It will be morning soon. We'll need to send messages to Pieran and Reshtas; they . . . may be able to find out . . . what happened."

"Maybe," Graysa said, "maybe Deela and the Kel Nira are even with Pieran now. Maybe they got across the river, and they're spending the night in his camp, and after they've rested, he'll bring them home."

"That is a hopeful thought, indeed. Well, the Kel Nira has always maintained that hope is a powerful medicine—and the Mothers know, we could use a dose now."

Chapter Six

Corvalen and his small company had crossed the Asha at the first ford they came to. From that point there remained less than a two-day ride to the prince's encampment. They followed the riverbank, and the landscape unrolled around them all but unnoticed until the hills began to steepen. Then the road led away from the river and into gentler meadowland.

At last the high bluff came into view ahead of them, rough-edged and eroding on its southern face. The road curved to embrace the bluff, and as they drew alongside it, Corvalen saw the sheer vertical soften to a sloping rise; he imagined that if they had approached from the northwest, the bluff would have looked for all the world like an unsmoothed wrinkle in a vast green coverlet.

But no, that analogy was far too peaceable. He saw now that on this side, the bluff was spike-topped with wooden palings. Here and there along the palisade, the westering sun reddened the metal of helms and spearpoints.

The messenger, riding slightly ahead, raised his horn and blew his approach signal. As the answering horn sounded from the palisade, he fell back to ride beside Corvalen. He gestured northward, where trees clustered in thickening ranks. "The Lenasha Forest."

Corvalen saw that between their position and the forest edge, the meadow was disfigured by a number of low mounds. "Are those graves of our dead, or Sharhay?"

"Ours," the messenger answered. "The Sharhay burn their dead. In fact"—he squinted toward the northeast, beyond the bluff—"that looks like smoke from their funeral pyres."

As the company turned to the right and began to climb the slope toward the palisade's one gateway, more columns of smoke became visible, crows and vultures circling in the spaces between. A slight shift in the breeze brought with it the odor of burning flesh.

A gap-toothed soldier saluted them at the gate and let them through without ceremony. "I fear you'll find us a little out of order, my lord;

we had fierce fighting day before yesterday. We still don't have all the wounded well settled, and there's more dead to carry out, too."

The gatekeeper appeared ready to regale him with a full description of the battle, but Corvalen disengaged himself from further conversation. He would have to hear the details later; he had present matters to attend to.

He left Pellar and the bodyguard to take care of the horses and find tents or at least a place to lay their bedrolls, while a soldier escorted him and Rossen to the prince's pavilion. As they passed through the encampment, Corvalen resisted the urge to look for his nephew's banners. He must order his thoughts for the coming confrontation—and confrontation it would be, he had no doubt.

For as long as Corvalen could remember, Dursten, though great-minded in ways, had been sword-proud and glory-hungry. Even before receiving his knighthood, he had begun to concoct plans for conquering Forstene's neighbors. Immediately upon coming of age he had married; within a year he had fathered a son and ensured the succession. Barely a week after his son's naming he had formally petitioned the king for permission to levy troops and undertake the conquest of Sharhaya. Corvalen and some of the other barons had tried to dissuade the king from approving this course, but Delanar would not deny his son's desire. Perhaps, after all, Delanar harbored the same dreams of glory; there was reason enough. Moreover Sharhaya, although a small country, was a rich one. Or had been, before Dursten burned his way through half of it.

And that fact, combined with the limits on both King Delanar's patience and his purse, had brought Corvalen here to Prince Dursten's silken pavilion.

The man on guard outside saluted him and affably denied his request for admittance. "With respect, your lordship, His Highness is interrogating a prisoner and does not wish to be disturbed."

"Then he will have to be disappointed in his wishes; this is the king's business, and it will brook no delay." He strode past the guard and pushed through the door hanging.

He stopped just inside, so abruptly that Rossen trod on his heel. Rossen's murmured apology turned to a sharp hiss of breath as he evidently saw what had brought Corvalen up short.

The prisoner was a woman. She was lying on the ground, her chest heaving with long, ragged breaths. Two brawny soldiers stood over her, looking as if they were ready to kick her the moment she dared move.

Her torn and bloodied tunic was bunched around her hips, and bruises were beginning to discolor her thighs. The tunic was green.

Corvalen fleetingly wondered why the garment's hue should trouble him; then he remembered what he had learned during his preparations for this mission.

Rossen seemed to be struck by the realization at the same time. "Green is the color of the Holy Women," he whispered in a rush.

Corvalen stepped forward. Even as he did so, one of the soldiers squatted and made a grab at the woman. She tried to roll away, but the other drove a booted foot into her ribs, and she lay still.

"Well, if it isn't Lord Corvalen." Prince Dursten had stepped out from behind a tapestry screen, adjusting the wrinkled pleats of his short tunic. A conscious look flashed across his handsome face, then gave way to a grin of sorts as he waved his arm in a mock-grandiose gesture. "Welcome to Sharhaya!" He sauntered over to a table to fill a wine goblet, which he offered to Corvalen. When he refused it, Dursten shrugged, raised the goblet to his own lips, and took a leisurely drink.

"I was told that Your Highness was interrogating a prisoner," Corvalen said, his voice tight.

"Indeed!" The prince set down his goblet and combed his fingers through his hair, pulling the unruly waves into a club. "Only a short time ago, in fact, the interrogation had reached quite a delicate point. Your arrival was very well timed, I must say."

"Your Highness—"

The prince ignored him and spoke instead to the soldiers. "Pick her up; let us see what his lordship makes of our prize."

They hauled her to her feet, but she kept her eyes on the ground; her tangled red hair, escaping from its braids, obscured her face.

"Come on, let his lordship see," snarled one of the soldiers, grabbing her hair and yanking her head up.

"Not very pretty, these Sharhay women," remarked the prince. "Not that it matters much, of course, once one gets down to business."

The woman was so battered that it was hardly possible to tell whether she would have been pretty or not.

Almost despite himself, Corvalen moved toward her. He had expected to see shame in her eyes—but instead they glittered with an icy defiance. She met his gaze without flinching and, in spite of the soldier's grip on her hair, managed to lift her chin in an unmistakable gesture of pride.

Dursten stepped forward. "Insolent bitch! Hasn't learned her lesson yet—have to teach it to her again." He raised his hand to strike the woman.

Corvalen brought his arm up and blocked the blow.

The prince glared at him a moment, then backed off, chuckling. "You always were a stodgy old stick, Corvalen." He picked up his goblet again. "So what are you doing here anyway? My father wrote that he was sending you, but I confess I am still much surprised. Last I heard, you didn't care to dirty your sword with this little war."

"The king your father has much to say about your 'little war.' But we will speak of this after present matters are attended to. Rossen."

"My lord?"

"Take away the Holy Woman. Find a safe place for her and set Gar and Fidden to guard her. Make sure she has food and water, and anything else she needs for her comfort. No one's to see her without my permission."

Watching Rossen help the woman out of the pavilion, Corvalen managed to bridle his anger so that he could address the prince with decent courtesy. "If Your Highness would be so good as to dismiss these men," he said, "we may speak about the king's business."

"Of course," Dursten answered, with a graciousness that dissipated as soon as the soldiers had gone. "What do you mean by commandeering my prisoner away from me like that? How dare you undermine me in front of my men?"

"What are *you* thinking, capturing a woman? A Holy Woman, no less."

"Holy Woman?" Dursten snorted. "I'd like to know who decided to call them so. Makes it sound like they could belong to the Sisterhood of Marga—which they most certainly could not. These Sharhay 'holy women' are nothing but a pack of whores."

"So you may think, but to the Sharhay they are as holy as the Sisters are to us—and you not only capture and interrogate one but go on to torture and violate her!"

"Can you think of a better way to break a woman who thinks herself superior to any man? Besides, it is the conqueror's right."

"Not by the Precepts of Vallar."

"My dear Corvalen, the Precepts of Vallar are meant for civilized warfare, among men of nobility. It is nothing to do with savages and barbarians."

"The Sharhay are not savages."

"No? And yet they're hardly civilized. They don't even know how to build in stone—the most they can manage is a garden wall. I grant you they're fine enough woodworkers, but—"

"Your Highness, we were speaking of the Precepts of Vallar, which your father intended you to follow here."

"And did *you* follow them, Lord Corvalen, when you fought the Cheskari?"

Corvalen answered carefully. "It was always my intention to do so." And so he would have done, had circumstances not betrayed him.

Dursten walked over to a table spread with architectural sketches and scattered pieces of a model castle. He picked up a round tower and looked at it critically. "You know, I was watching the day you rode out for Cheskara. Torval, too—we were on the battlement overlooking the Great Yard. Torval annoyed me with all his chatter and fidgeting, he was so excited. I could think of nothing except how much I wanted to be going with you—or instead of you."

He set down the tower and placed a section of curtain wall next to it. "Of course, I was all of eleven years old. Our tutor was there, too—old Caunar the Star Reader—and he told me to stop yearning to ride against the Cheskari and instead to prepare myself for the deeds that lay in my future."

"Wise counsel."

"It was more than that. He'd read it in the stars. He said that when I came to manhood I would have the opportunity not only to restore but to surpass the glories of my ancestors. 'The greatness of the king's heir shall be known in every land this side of the sea'—that was his prophecy, the exact words." Dursten toyed with the placement of a barbican. "I wish Caunar had been fit enough to come on this campaign. The fellow I've got with me doesn't seem to see the same stars. . . ."

"Perhaps the stars have not so much influence in Sharhaya."

Dursten snorted. "These Sharhay certainly have no sense of the Celestial Order. They even have female fighters—and, if you can believe it, they count these viragos among their 'holy women.'"

"And is that what your prisoner was—a fighter? Did you capture her in battle?" Corvalen had affected a tone of interested curiosity. As far as he knew, however, the women warriors protected the nonfighting Holy Women and the Sanctuaries, but did not otherwise go into battle. And although this woman certainly appeared to have the spirit of a fighter, he would be willing to wager that she was something else altogether.

Dursten frowned. "There was a fighting woman with her—but we couldn't take her alive. It's well-nigh impossible to capture a Sharhay warrior, male or female; they always manage to get themselves killed before you can ask them more than a question or two. I tell you, these are the damnedest people—"

"And the woman you took prisoner?"

"Oh, she's some kind of a physician or herbwife or something." The prince shrugged.

"A noncombatant. A physician." *The warrior's quarrel is not with the weaponless,* said the Precepts of Vallar. "Just what did you expect to learn by interrogating this 'herbwife'?"

"The way to the Summer Sanctuary, for one thing. The secret of the Kel Sharha's power, for another. The strength of their remaining fighting force. Anything she might be persuaded to tell me."

There was no need—or point in it, Corvalen supposed—to voice his disapproval of Dursten's methods of persuasion. "So, what has she told you?"

"Not a damn thing. But what does it matter anyway? Soon Sharhaya will be firmly under our rule—"

"'Soon'? Three years ago, you assured the Council that you could conquer Sharhaya with ease, that the country was poorly defended, its warriors undertrained and badly armed."

"It's true, by Heldar! They have no warhorses, no cavalry to speak of. You get them hand to hand, and they fight with knives, not swords. And armor? They wear no more than hunting leathers, if that!"

"Yet the Sharhay continue to resist. This war has cost us the lives of many good warriors. . . ." He paused to push aside his worries for his nephew.

"The Sharhay have lost even more. And they are running out of resources; they can't hold out indefinitely." The prince glared at Corvalen. "It took you five years to pacify the Cheskari. Why should my father grow impatient in the third battle season here?"

Corvalen spoke carefully; Dursten's feelings on the subject of the Cheskari were apt to be volatile. "That war was different, Your Highness. My task was to destroy the raiders and their strongholds, to take control of the marches, and to secure the border—not to add Cheskara as a province. The country possesses little enough to make that worthwhile.Sharhaya, on the other hand, is a rich land, but much of its wealth has already been destroyed. Moreover, we have so far lost more men in fewer than three years here than we did in five seasons along the Cheskari border.And we will lose more." He let his voice drop. "These are a people who hold their freedom dear, and we are pushing them to desperation. I fear they will fight against us until there are none of them left able to so much as hurl a stone. They will take as many of our warriors to the grave with them as they can. They will drain our war treasury and ultimately leave us with a worthless conquest."

"For a man who has stayed comfortably in Forstene, you think you know a lot about these barbarians."

"I have taken care to inform myself. I have also read your dispatches to the king, and have drawn from them the same conclusion as he has done."

"Conclusion?"

"And decision: His Majesty desires you to make peace with the Sharhay."

"Peace? With *them*? But it is only a matter of time now until we crush the Sharhay utterly!"

"You are out of time, Prince Dursten. And the king does not want Sharhaya crushed; he wants it as a prosperous and trouble-free province. With every additional day of warfare, that becomes more difficult to achieve."

Corvalen removed a roll of parchment from his belt. The king's seal, stamped into red wax, adhered authoritatively to the ribbon that bound the scroll closed. Dursten received the parchment with ill grace. Looking him in the eyes, Corvalen emphasized the main point of the royal missive: "King Delanar orders you to cease hostilities with the Sharhay immediately and prepare to negotiate a treaty."

*****

A short while later, Corvalen strode through the encampment once more. The place stank of blood, manure, and unwashed men, but he welcomed the odors, together with the sounds of harness and steel, and men's voices raised whether in pain or jest—all this was real and honest. In his mind he saw again the ice-blue eyes of the woman prisoner. He inhaled more deeply: saddle leather. He would have to deal with her soon. But first he was going to see Torval.

A sentry pointed him toward the area where the men from Caldene had their tents. Like his barony, Torval's following was relatively small, especially as the young man had yet to make a name for himself. But when he inherited from Corvalen, he would be one of the most powerful lords in Forstene. Meanwhile, pray Vallar that Torval would make of himself such a man as could wield that power wisely.

The Caldene camp was neatly laid out, the following's tents in concentric squares around Torval's modest pavilion. A pair of camp followers, arms laden with laundry, bustled along the mucky aisles between tents, while another could be seen tending a pot over a small cookfire. The women were reasonably tidy and had no look of ill-use about them. How dreadfully cut and bruised that Sharhay woman had been; there had been burns on her arms, too. . . .

Corvalen shook his head and willed his mind clear of her. *Torval,* he thought. And his heart softened as he caught sight of his nephew, sitting on a camp stool outside his pavilion, his left leg stretched awkwardly before him.

"Uncle!" The young man's face split into a grin of open pleasure. He rose and limped a few steps forward to embrace Corvalen.

"Torval. It's good to see you." He heard the roughness in his voice and tried to smile. "Sit back down. I'm told you injured that leg quite badly; you must take care. Is it . . . is it healing well?"

"Very well, sir. Our surgeon thinks it nothing short of a miracle."

"Ah. Your messenger hinted that . . . well. Or at least I thought he did."

"Sir?"

"You must pardon my distraction." He seated himself on the ground beside Torval. "I've ridden hard these last two days, and . . . well," he said again. He had been on the verge of venting some of his frustration with the prince—which would have been completely inappropriate, as Torval was under Dursten's command. Moreover, as Dursten had just reminded him, the two young men had been friends since boyhood, when Torval had served as a royal page. *I must be tired. to nearly have forgotten that.* And he wondered just how close the two friends were now. Torval was the older by nearly a year, but Dursten had a dominating personality. . . .

Corvalen roused himself as a cup was pressed into his hand and the aroma of spiced tea displaced the other camp smells. He looked up to see one of the camp followers, a petite young woman, smiling at him.

"Thank you." He took a sip. "Almost like being back at court; this tastes very like the tea King Delanar favors."

The camp follower offered him sugar, which he waved away. "That it is, my lord. The messenger brought it back for Lord Torval today, and the sugar—gifts from His Majesty himself. He sent a letter, too."

Torval shrugged a shoulder, and added a lump of sugar to his own cup. "Just to wish me well on my recovery. He's always been very kind to me, ever since I served at court."

"His Majesty always takes care to notice your nephew," the camp follower assured Corvalen.

Torval colored slightly. "Um, this is Jennis, one of the laundresses. She's been taking care of me. My squire's not the best for changing bandages and that sort of thing."

"Then I must thank you again, Jennis. You have my deepest gratitude for looking after my nephew. I shall not forget it."

"Oh, sir." It was Jennis's turn to blush, then she bobbed a hasty curtsy and scampered back to her cookfire.

"I don't believe I've ever seen a camp follower blush," Corvalen remarked.

"She's not just . . . That is . . ." Torval frowned. "Jennis is a sweet girl. It's a shame she has to make her living this way."

"She has no father? No uncles nor brothers?"

"No guardian, no."

"Torval, she must have chosen this life. After all, she could have gone to serve the Sisterhood of Marga; the Sisters never turn away a guardianless woman."

"I suppose she might work in one of their charity hospitals. She likes taking care of people." He clucked his tongue. "If she'd been born Sharhay, she might have become a Healer."

"If she'd been born Sharhay, she'd be among the conquered instead of the conquerors, and that would hardly be a better lot for her." The whole of what his nephew had said suddenly registered with him. "Torval, what do you know of Sharhay Healers?"

"Ah, so that's what my messenger didn't tell you."

"He only said that your horse had been shot from under you and that you'd taken a serious injury to your leg when you fell."

"Broke the large bone in my thigh. The bone end was sticking right out through my skin and came close to cutting the artery."

Corvalen grimaced as Torval indicated the wound's site.

"It happened during the battle of the Lenasha Forest. Most of the fighting took place in the meadow, actually, but around midday I chased some Sharhay warriors into the forest itself. There were five others riding with me. We got to this clearing, and the Sharhay ambushed us there." He shook his head. "Great Vallar, I should have seen it coming! Archers. They dropped two of my men before we even knew what was happening; they died on the spot. Another took a mortal wound. Two got away; they met up with another detachment and came looking for the rest of us next morning. Somehow I didn't take any arrows, but my horse did, and fell on my leg. I blacked out when I hit the ground, and the Sharhay must have thought I was dead, because they left me there. . . ."

His voice dropped, the words coming slower. "When I came to, I was the only living creature in that clearing. I managed to crawl out from under my horse, but I passed out again before I could get to the shelter of the trees." He paused to take a swallow of tea.

"Next thing I saw was a Sharhay Holy Woman bending over me, and she was all covered in blood." He flashed a nervous grin. "I don't mind admitting to you that I was afraid of her. Who wouldn't be, after all the tales we've heard of those women? But she knew our language—was I surprised!—and told me that she belonged to the Healers' Order and that she was oathbound to do me no harm. Well, what did I have to lose anyway? I can't imagine I would have lasted the night out there alone. So I drank the medicine she gave me, and she and her assistant cleaned my wound, set my leg, bandaged me up, and even covered me with cloaks to keep me warm through the night."

"And then in the morning your men found you and brought you back."

"Yes, sir. When our surgeon examined me, he was frankly amazed; said that he didn't know how he ever would have dealt with such a dirty wound, and he almost certainly would have ended up taking the leg. You know as well as I the likelihood of surviving an amputation so far up." The young man shuddered, then smiled crookedly. "It's my claim to fame now: healed of an unhealable wound, and by the enemy at that. Dursten's taken to calling me Torval the Lucky."

Dursten. Corvalen hastily gulped down the last of his tea; it tasted like bile. "Torval, this Healer of yours—what did she look like?"

"Red hair, light skin. Mother's age, or maybe a little younger. I wasn't in a condition to take in much more—oh, but I do remember thinking that her eyes were a very odd color, such a pale blue. Why do you want to know?"

Yes, Corvalen had seen those eyes. He sighed. "I'm sorry to tell you this, Torval, but you have just described Prince Dursten's prisoner."

Chapter Seven

The Kel Nira lowered herself carefully to the pallet at the back of the little tent. She had meant to stay on her feet to await whatever the Forsteners next intended, but her very bones seemed to be failing her. Her breath was coming with some difficulty. Cracked ribs, she diagnosed automatically, and halfheartedly ran her fingers over the bruised skin. Her hand dropped into her lap. Her senses unfocused, she stared at the tent wall, the play of shadows on the canvas, and listened to the murmur of foreign voices and the scuff of guardsmen's boots outside.

Coherent thoughts began to piece themselves together. The Forstener who had taken her from the prince's pavilion had left immediately after escorting her here. Time had passed—she could not gauge how much—and no one else had come. She knew she was not safe, but perhaps they would leave her alone long enough for her to . . . to do what?

To kill myself.

But how? She had mercy drugs in her medicine bag. . . .

She pushed away the unbidden memory of the field around the bridge. There were too many men after that battle for whom she had not been able to do anything more than give them release. But their path to freedom could not be hers—her medicine bag was back on the battlefield, along with the bodies of those who had accompanied her. Deela. . . Another thought to push aside. This was no time for reliving the past; she must provide against the future.

She plucked at the rough sheet draping the pallet. It might do . . . except that the tent offered no convenient beam from which to hang a noose. No, the Forsteners had quite efficiently denied her any means of removing herself from among them.

Except my own will.

Few people, even among the Ma'Sharha, had such force of will. Did she? Strength enough to simply lie down and, through will alone, sever the bond between body and spirit? But if she had that much strength, then she had enough to withstand further torture. At the end of

65

which, she would no doubt die anyway. The question was, would death come before her will was broken, or after? That last bout of "interrogation" had been interrupted before the guards could take their turns with her, but she was sure they would not be put off for long. How many . . . assaults—her mind shied from the other words, and the knife of pain and outrage that accompanied them—would she suffer before she begged for an end and told the prince anything he wanted to know?

Next time, fight back. Fight hard enough, and they will kill you then and there.

Perhaps . . .

But she had been trained to nonviolence—so much so, that she had just stood and watched while others were cut down trying to defend her. She had not raised a hand to aid any of them, not even Deela, whom she had been teaching with such care for the past four years.

If I could not fight for them, how can I think of fighting for myself?

There was a sound of throat-clearing outside. She tensed as the tent flap was pulled aside. "Mistress?" came a voice she recognized. It was the young man who had brought her here. "I have water for you, so that you may wash and drink, and a bowl of porridge, if you are hungry. May I come in?"

A ridiculous question, considering that she was their prisoner. But the courtesy provoked an automatic response, and she heard herself answering, "Yes, come."

The man entered diffidently, accompanied by a lean-faced youth. They laid out bowl and spoon, jug and cup, pitcher and basin on the ground in front of the pallet, but ventured no closer. When they were done, the man said, "If you have need of anything further for your comfort, Mistress, you have but to ask. I am Rossen of Barasel, and I serve Corvalen of Brintora; this is Pellar, my lord's squire." He waited for her reply, but she could think of nothing appropriate or safe to say. After a moment he nodded to her and left, the squire following.

Corvalen of Brintora. That was a name she knew. People called him the Scourge of Cheskara, for the ferocity with which he had waged war against the last country to resist Forstene power. And now he was here.

It was an effort to keep her hand from shaking as she poured water into the cup. She drank slowly, lest she make herself sick in her eagerness to quench her thirst.

Corvalen of Brintora . . . He had driven from their lands many, many Cheskari—some bands of whom had then started to raid across the bit of Sharhaya that bordered Cheskara. When the trees had begun to speak to the Kel Sharha, near three years ago now, of invaders in the south, everyone had thought the threat came from the Cheskari. But the invasion had come from Forstene instead.

And now the Scourge is here.

She nearly dropped the cup as realization struck her. It was Corvalen of Brintora who had stopped the prince from harming her further, who had ordered her to be given shelter and food and water. What could be the meaning of this?

Cautiously, she took a spoonful of porridge. Oats, a bit of honey, some small chunks of dried fruit.

But she should not eat without washing first. Weakened as she was, she had to use both hands to lift the pitcher and pour water into the basin. The water was . . . warm!

The Scourge's people had put themselves to some trouble for her. Whatever their motivation, even if this was only seeming kindness, here nonetheless was an unexpected grace, and her heart unclosed itself a little.

Stretching her hand over the water, she called up the power of the Mothers to purify and renew, although she felt that her calling was as weak as an untutored child's. Still, she kept up the chant of purification as she washed, deliberately cleansing herself of the pollution she had endured. It was not an adequate washing by the standards of the Ma'Sharha, but under the circumstances she would make it do.

Once she was as clean as she could manage, she took a few more spoonfuls of porridge and drank a little more water. She had strength for nothing more. The trials of the past days finally claimed their toll, and she drooped onto the pallet. She had just enough thought left to reach her mind to her tree of power, then plummeted into sleep.

*****

The Kel Nira slept till after dark. On awakening she knew immediately that someone was in the tent with her. She sat up, forcing herself not to wince at the discomfort of the abrupt movement.

By the light of the candle lantern he held, she made out the knight Rossen standing just inside the doorway.

"His lordship wishes to speak with you, Mistress. Come with me, please."

So, the time of grace was ended.

She was unsteady when she got to her feet, and he stepped forward to offer his arm to lean on.

"I can walk alone." Her voice rasped weakly in her ears.

He regarded her a moment, then gestured for her to precede him out of the tent.

She steadied herself as she smoothed her torn and rumpled tunic as best she could, then walked out into the night. Her movements were slow and careful, but she made certain they betrayed no frailty, at least of spirit. She kept her eyes straight ahead, looking neither at the ground nor at the men on guard outside the tent. There was an unseasonable chill in the air, and dampness—rain would be falling soon—but she resisted the urge to wrap her arms around herself.

Rossen joined her and led her directly across the wide path to another tent, this one much larger, and well-lit within.

The tent's sole occupant was Corvalen of Brintora. He sat behind a table, making notes on a sheet of parchment. A plate with the remains of a meal lay disregarded at his elbow. Rossen silently directed her to stand in front of the table, then withdrew. She folded her hands at her waist and waited.

The Scourge did not look up until he was finished with his writing. When his attention turned full on her, she met the appraisal in his eyes with resolution in her own. In her mind, she prayed for strength against him.

At last he spoke. "I am Corvalen of Brintora, Lord Marshal of Forstene, appointed Royal Envoy to Sharhaya."

She moved not a muscle in response.

"I know that you can both understand and speak my language. It is no use pretending otherwise."

"I not pretend; I have nothing to say."

"You might at least tell me your name." He smiled slightly, as if to encourage her.

"Sharhay do not tell name to enemy." She braced herself, expecting that he would any moment rise from his chair and strike her.

"I see." He picked up a jug, filled two cups, and held one out. "Take it—you must be thirsty." When she hesitated, he added, "It's only water, from the spring."

Many times, in peaceful days, she had drunk the water from the spring that welled atop this bluff. Remembering the water's sweetness, and mindful that the bit of water she had drunk earlier was not enough to make up for two days of thirst, she at last accepted and took a sip.

"Very well," he resumed. "You need not tell me your name. I know who you are in any case."

Her heart jumped. If he knew that he had a Chief of the Ma'Sharha in his power . . .

"You belong to the Healers' Order, I am told. And as such, you are also one of your people's Holy Women." He paused, in apparent expectation of some reaction from her.

She did not oblige.

"Since you are a Holy Woman, you must know the way to the Summer Sanctuary. And since your Kel Sharha is also a Holy Woman, you may have the knowledge to break her power. Prince Dursten believes that you do."

"If I know, I not tell—not him, not you." To speak so strongly cost her. The night chill sank into her bones, and her legs felt as if they might fold at any moment.

He looked her up and down, and rubbed at his beard. "It is clear you have endured much already, yet you have divulged nothing. You keep the Kel Sharha's secrets well." He gentled his voice. "But are they worth your life?"

"I not fear death," she answered quietly. She would go to the Mothers, and she would rest. . . .

"Indeed. That is one of the problems with interrogation under torture. Too often it simply renders death the more welcome. But consider: no matter how stubborn a man—or woman—may be, the torturer can be yet more stubborn. It might be a very long, and very painful, time before death comes for you."

"I have considered."

He contemplated her silently, and she endeavored to bear it with steadfastness.

O Watchers, give me the strength of your trees.

But even trees could not keep their branches from shuddering when the wind blew. It might be summer, but she felt near as chilled as if she were standing in the middle of a river swollen with snowmelt. She managed to suppress the first wave of shivering, but not the next, though she gritted her teeth against it.

He saw her weakness, and now at last he was up and coming around the table, pulling off his cloak as he moved toward her.

The action triggered memory of a similar one; her mind filled with an image of the prince, whipping off his tunic belt. He'd flung its jewel-studded clasp across her face, then slapped it across her back until the repeated impact sent her to the ground. When she tried to get up, he had kicked her over onto her bleeding back. In the shock of that pain she had not realized what was coming next until the prince was already on top of her. She had felt able to do nothing except close her eyes against the sight of him.

No! She would not allow herself to be defiled again—never again! With the thought, her every long-trained restraint fled. In an instant she had darted to the table and reached for the Scourge's forgotten plate— and the knife that she had noticed resting amid the remains of the meal.

But as her fist closed on the knife handle, he was beside her. His hand came down upon hers. He wrenched her wrist, twisting until her fingers disengaged. She bit her lip to keep from crying out.

As soon as he had the knife he let go of her and strode to the tent flap to say something to the men outside.

Weakness overwhelmed her. She sank to her knees, shut her eyes, and waited in miserable resignation for what was to come.

It was not what she expected.

The Kel Nira sensed Lord Corvalen approach again. He was behind her. And then light folds of wool came gently to rest on her shoulders.

Lord Corvalen moved to stand in front of her. "Look at me, Healer."

She had to tilt her head back to do so. Looming above her, he was an imposing presence.

"I advise you not to try anything of that nature again. You are no wielder of weapons, and I would not like to have to treat you as one." He held the knife up before her, flipped it in his hand, then tossed it onto the table. The point struck into the wood with almost a musical note.

He dropped to a crouch to look her square on. "Listen to me, Mistress. You are in my charge now, but you must understand the situation: although I deliver the king's commands to Prince Dursten, I cannot myself command him. He has given me leave to deal with you according to my own methods for the time being—but should he lose patience, it is unlikely I will be able to save you from him again."

Shaking in earnest now, she managed nothing more than a nod in response.

He frowned and reached for her. She flinched away, but he caught her arm with one hand; the other settled briefly on her forehead. "You are feverish—you should be resting."

He stood abruptly, pulling her to her feet with him. The cloak slid from her shoulders. He picked it up, settled it around her once more, and fastened the clasp at her neck.

His fingers slid down to grip her arms. Steering her to the doorway of the tent, he said, "We will speak again tomorrow, Healer."

The Scourge handed her off to Rossen, who silently led her back to her own tent, and as silently departed.

The candle lantern he left behind showed that an additional blanket had been spread on her pallet. Laid out over it was a clean blue tunic—a man's, and in the Forstene style, but warm-looking.

Far off, thunder growled. A heartbeat later, rain began to patter against the oiled-canvas walls.

Her hands trembled as she changed her rags for the new tunic. She debated with herself briefly about rewrapping herself in Lord Corvalen's cloak; the cold lingering in her bones decided her.

Only as she lay gingerly down on the pallet did she think to examine her hand. What had she meant to do with that knife? She expected to find the flesh somehow burned or scarred where it had touched the weapon—but there was no mark at all, nothing but a subtle tingling in her fingertips.

That night her dreams were haunted by a bloody face, stark-eyed, mouth open in a silent scream. She could not tell whether the blood was hers or not.

Chapter Eight

Corvalen had the seasoned campaigner's trick of falling swiftly into deep sleep, with the awareness that a call to arms could interrupt his rest at any time. But he slept through his first night in the prince's camp, untroubled, till dawn. As soon as he awoke, the challenges of the day ahead commenced to march in review through his thoughts.

As he pushed himself up from his bedroll, his glance fell on his sword, laid, as always, within easy reach. He reached, and drew it from its scabbard, the hilt a comfort in his hand.

He traced an arc in front of him, cutting the air with a leisurely stroke from right to left, then another left to right, giving his muscles a chance to loosen. After a few repetitions of this, he brought the sword up and swept it down, pivoted a quarter-turn and did the same. Then he drew the sword across to the left and swung out with a wide cut to his right, letting momentum carry him around another quarter-turn.

Which brought him face to face with Pellar, who leapt away from the blade just in time.

"You're going to need faster reflexes than that, boy, if you decide to make a habit of sneaking into people's tents. Announce yourself next time."

"Forgive me, my lord; I thought you might still be sleeping."

"If I were sleeping, I wouldn't be wanting that tea and porridge you're carrying, would I?"

"No, my lord, but I know you like to make an early start—"

"Never mind, never mind." Corvalen sheathed his sword and relieved Pellar of the tea. The mug was only half full, a good portion of the beverage having sloshed onto the squire when he jumped out of harm's way. Luckily for Pellar, if not for Corvalen, the tea was barely warm.

Corvalen scratched at the stubble on his cheeks. "I need a shave." He sat down at the table and started in on his porridge.

"I'll find out if there's a barber in camp, my lord."

"Didn't we bring my razor and shaving glass?"

"I'm sorry, my lord—I left them in the baggage, back with the rest of the army."

"Ah. Well, they weren't essential, after all. See if Rossen has his along; I'll wager he does. If not, I can just borrow Torval's later. It's not as though I need to worry about the state of my beard in front of that Sharhay woman."

"So that will be your day's first task? Shall I fetch her here for you, my lord?"

Corvalen thought a moment, remembering how weak and ill she'd been last night. "No, I'll go across. Lay out my mail—I want to look as intimidating as possible."

But when he entered the prisoner's tent, helm under his arm, she merely lifted her eyebrows at him—a look that, if he was interpreting it correctly, bespoke disdain for his faulty sense of proportion in arming himself so thoroughly to confront someone so powerless.

Or was she? There was power in her will, that was clear. She sat cross-legged, straight as a spear shaft, on her pallet, neither shrinking back nor looking away as he stared down at her with what he knew was a formidable glare. And after that one small reaction to his appearance, her face settled into utter expressionlessness; she might almost have been a figure carved of birch wood. Almost, but for the cuts and vivid bruises that marred her pale skin.

Pellar brought in a camp chair; the tent was so small that when Corvalen sat down, his feet were only inches from the Holy Woman's. He passed his helm to Pellar and waved a hand to dismiss him.

After the squire had gone, Corvalen continued to regard the woman silently, and she him. *Let her be reasonable.* Finally he allowed his countenance to relax and said, in his most courteous manner, "I trust you slept well, Mistress, and are recovered from your fever?"

Her eyes narrowed slightly. "Your . . . concern is . . . without meaning."

Well, true enough, at least from her perspective. But he wouldn't have expected her to tell him so. *She believes she has nothing to lose.*

"Suppose I acquaint you with my greater concern, then. My king wants Sharhaya. I have sworn to deliver it to him. And it is not my way to be forsworn."

"Is not mine, too," she answered, her voice low and measured.

"You are sworn to heal—that I know. But what else?" When he received no response, he continued, "To serve your people, I'd guess. Do you think your silence serves them?"

"I not think. I know."

"Forgive me, Healer, but there you are wrong. Things will go easier for your people if you talk to me, tell me what I want to know. Help me, and I can help them."

There was a momentary light in her eyes. He had been right: she would not care about helping herself; her people, however, were another matter.

But she said, "No."

He waited for more; it was not forthcoming. He shifted his tactics.

"Mistress, I rode up through the south of Sharhaya. I saw how little is left. I saw the—where the Winter Sanctuary used to stand." He hardened his voice. "Would you want the same to happen to your Summer Sanctuary?"

Her chin lifted. "You cannot find."

"I don't need to. I have an army marching up the east bank of the Asha; they'll be opposite this bluff in a few days. If I don't know the way to the Summer Sanctuary by the time they arrive, my warriors will simply cut and burn their way through the Parasha Forest until they reach the Sanctuary. And then—"

"Our warriors will stop them."

"Will they? Most of your men are on this side of the river, if I'm not mistaken. And even if they can get across, what can they do, really? Because although you may call them warriors, we both know that they are just farmers and hunters, with hunters' weapons, hunters' training. And some of them, I warrant, with naught but scythes and mattocks, and no training at all. They have no hope of prevailing against an army such as mine."

"We have . . . prevailed before now."

Brave words—but he doubted she entirely believed them; not after almost three years of treating the wounded and watching so many die.

He rapped out his next questions.

"How many fighting men do you have left?"

She shook her head.

"Tell me how to get to the Sanctuary."

"No."

"Tell me how to break the Kel Sharha's power."

"I cannot."

Corvalen sighed. "Your fortitude is admirable," he said. "But it will do you no good."

"So I do *you* no good, I am content."

"Do not try my patience, Healer."

Almost without thinking, he reached forward and laid his palm at the base of her throat, letting his fingers curve around her neck. A muscle at the corner of her mouth twitched, and her pulse quickened beneath his hand. That was all.

He leaned in toward her. "I can do anything to you"—he dropped his voice and bent closer still—"anything I want." His breath stirred her hair as he pressed his fingers into her skin to give force to his threat.

She did not even blink.

Some obscure part of him had an urge to tighten his grip around her neck and see how long it would take to shake her composure. *Vallar help me.*

He dropped his hand and sat back. "I choose, however, to treat you with honor."

She drew a long breath and slowly uncurled her fingers in her lap.

"You might consider showing some gratitude for all I have spared you." Even to his own mind there was irony in the words; he was not surprised by the glare with which she favored him. He decided to try gentleness again. "Mistress, I would continue to spare you, but if you give me no return for my mercy, Prince Dursten . . ." He let his voice trail off and spread his hands, allowing her fears to finish the sentence for him.

In truth, she looked less fearful than exhausted. Enough to break?

"Give me something to tell the prince," he coaxed. "Please."

Her lips curled in a mockery of a smile. "Tell him he is damned."

*****

Rossen saw Corvalen leave the prisoner's tent and stalk across into his own. After a discreet delay, he followed. "My lord?" he called at the entrance, waiting till he heard a muffled invitation to go in.

Corvalen was at the washbasin, dashing water into his face. Pellar sat cross-legged nearby, working his way with a wire brush through a pile of greaves and gauntlets and vambraces that needed cleaning.

Rossen strolled over to the table, where Corvalen's mail shirt lay discarded in a heap. He set down the shaving kit he'd brought, picked up the hauberk, and laid it out neatly, running his fingers over the iron links. *Vallar protect my lord.*

Corvalen, water droplets still clinging to his beard, joined him at the table.

Rossen smiled sympathetically. "I take it your interrogation did not go as well as you'd hoped."

Corvalen sighed and dropped into his chair. "No. But perhaps I was a fool to think it could go differently. This woman is . . ." He shook his head. "She seems immovable."

"Why concern yourself with her, my lord?" Pellar asked.

Corvalen frowned and rubbed at his damp beard. "A good question. Earlier this morning, I would have answered it differently. Now . . . She is unlikely toever give me what Prince Dursten wants. But"—his voice took on a ruminatory tone—"she is no longer Dursten's prisoner; she is mine. So I must ask myself: What do *I* want from her? And what can I reasonably, and honorably, expect to get?"

Rossen tapped the pouch containing his razor and mirror. "Go on and have your shave; I know I always think more clearly when I'm well-groomed." He stroked his own just-shaven cheeks and newly trimmed beard. As he'd hoped, his exaggerated gesture made Corvalen laugh.

"You needn't look so fine here; this isn't court, you know."

Rossen shrugged. "Not the king's court, no. The court of Brintora, on the other hand, is wherever you are, my lord."

"Huh. Only in theory. But at least my mother and my seneschal have the barony well in charge. A good thing, too, since I seem to be forever away on the king's business."

It wasn't just that. After the end of the Cheskari War, Corvalen could have spent much more time in Brintora had he chosen. Since his wife's death, however, he seemed to prefer to be almost anywhere else.

Corvalen had taken the razor out of its pouch and was turning it over in his hand, but Rossen did not think that he was simply admiring the scrollwork designs etched into the silver handle.

"You appear . . . preoccupied, my lord. If you would allow me, I will be happy to shave you."

"What? No, no, that's kind, but quite beneath you, Rossen."

"I shaved you often enough when I was your squire."

"You're not a squire anymore, though, are you? In fact"—he pointed the razor at Rossen—"I gave you this very razor when you were made knight, did I not?"

"Indeed, my lord." As if Rossen would have forgotten that.

Pellar spoke up. "Well, since I'm squire now, *I'll* do the shaving."

Corvalen grinned. "I'm perfectly able to shave myself, thank you both. While I'm doing so, you can each run an errand for me. Pellar, you will go and take some porridge and water to the Holy Woman. Rossen, I want you to carry a message to Torval."

Had Corvalen's reconciliation with his nephew not lasted, then? Rossen ventured, "Wouldn't you rather speak with him yourself, my lord?"

"I would, but I haven't time now; the rest of this morning I'll be in conference with His Highness. I'd prefer to put my idea into action as soon as possible."

"My lord?"

Corvalen tossed the razor from one hand to the other. "Yes, I think I see the path to take. I came here to end this war and win Sharhaya for the king, and that I will do. But he does not want just the land and its wealth—he wants the people and their loyalty. If I can win over this woman"—he gestured in the direction of the prisoner's tent—"then I should be able to win the rest of the Holy Women. Perhaps even the Kel Sharha herself."

*****

Torval shifted on his stool and scooted it a little farther from his tent; Rossen could see him struggling not to express his surprise.

"We *are* talking about my uncle, aren't we?" Torval said. "Broad-shouldered fellow—deep voice, crooked nose, ruby earrings? Goes on a lot about honor?"

Rossen grinned at the description. "The same."

"How about that! He was gracious enough to Jennis yesterday, but I'd no idea— Oh, wait. I see. He's still angry with me, isn't he? He didn't want me to ride to this war, and now he's found another way to punish me."

"You have the wrong of it there, Lord Torval."

"Do I?"

"Your uncle has forgotten his anger in his joy at seeing you again. He merely wants the girl—"

"So that I won't have her."

"You do not know Lord Corvalen if you can believe him so petty."

"Why else would he want Jennis? It's not as though he has any interest in women."

"Hasn't he?"

"He's not remarried and looks to have no intention of doing so. My sister Ildanis often remarks in her letters that the ladies at court vie for his attention, yet he ignores them all. My other sister told me that Duke Beddar even offered Corvalen his youngest daughter—but he refused the match! Mother says it's been years since he looked at a woman."

78

Lady Ardalis did tend to exaggerate—and of course Corvalen was not likely to confide in her about his visits to the courtesan houses.

"She thinks he's made a vow to the Exalted Eldetal, the Hermit."

Rossen almost laughed aloud at the very idea. But really, if Corvalen's own relatives were gossiping about him, it would be well to know what they were saying, so he banished his smile and cultivated a casual air. "What do you think, Lord Torval, if I may ask?"

"Well, that or . . . I thought he might have decided he, you know, prefers the company of men. Either way would make it pretty odd for him to have taken a fancy to Jennis."

"Nor has he."

"So what does he want with her?"

"Perhaps I wasn't as clear as I might have been when I conveyed his request. Let me try again; I'll start nearer the beginning. Your uncle has taken the Sharhay Holy Woman into his custody."

Torval's face lost its habitual openness. "How is she?" he asked.

Rossen debated how much to reveal. "She's . . . taken some injuries. Lord Corvalen says you told him that your laundress is good at dealing with wounds. He also feels it would be well for the Holy Woman to have a female attendant. So if you can spare Jennis for a bit—"

"Of course; it's the least I can do. By all means!" Torval's expression had lightened somewhat. He pushed himself up off his stool, paused for a moment to stretch—he was one of the tallest men Rossen knew, nearly as tall as the king—and limped a few steps to the doorway of his tent.

He paused again. "Rossen . . ."

"Yes?"

"I . . . I said some unworthy things, and you were right—I ought to know my uncle better than that. Certainly he knew better than . . ." Torval shook his head and let out a little snort of rueful laughter. "He certainly knew what he was on about all those times he told me I needed to practice more listening and less talking."

"I've received the same lecture once or twice myself."

As Rossen had hoped, that expression of solidarity resolved the last of the tension between them.

"Well, I'll just get Jennis for you now. She's . . ." With a self-conscious grin, Torval jerked his head at the tent. "She's in there. I'll, um . . . go get her." He disappeared through the door hanging.

Rossen looked away and bit his lip to keep from chuckling aloud. So the girl had been right there the whole time; she must have heard every word they'd said. He wondered what she'd thought of it all.

Chapter Nine

Her last words to the Scourge echoed in the Kel Nira's mind: *Tell him he is damned.*

She had never said such a thing of anyone in her life. To wish—to pronounce—that someone die without the grace of the Mothers, that his between-life be full of torment instead of rest, that he never reunite with his loved ones in his next lives . . . She shuddered at the thought of such a fate, and at herself for wishing it on another.

And yet, if ever anyone had deserved damnation, surely Prince Dursten did.

Her brooding was interrupted by the entrance of Lord Corvalen's squire, bearing a cup and bowl. "My lord offers his apologies, Mistress, for not sending food to you earlier. He hopes you have not grown too hungry."

"How kind," she muttered.

The boy appeared to take her remark seriously, and responded with a definite note of pride in his voice. "Lord Corvalen is as well known for his kindness as for his courtesy and honor."

"He is known in Sharhaya for his"—what was the word?—"cruelty."

"Cruelty!" The squire seemed genuinely shocked. "Oh, no, Mistress, never Lord Corvalen. He's hard on his men, true—but always fair."

"And fair to enemies?"

"Yes, Mistress, he is."

"Not so we have heard."

"A man can be fearsome in battle and still be fair to his enemies."

"Can he?"

"Yes; and honorable and kind, too, Mistress—as you have good cause to know." He set down the cup and bowl then, and left her.

If her face and ribs hadn't hurt so much from the beating the prince's men had given her, she might have laughed at the notion of the Scourge of Cheskara being such a paragon of virtue.

Instead, she investigated the bowl: porridge again. But it was, she had to admit, rather good porridge, wanting nothing more than a splash of cream to make it very good indeed. She could stomach only a few spoonfuls, however, then a few sips of water. *I will have the rest later*, she told herself, and lay down, weariness overwhelming her once more.

She awoke with bright sunlight striking her eyes—it must have been about midday, and the tent flap was open for someone to enter. The Kel Nira squinted; it took a moment for her to discern that the person was a petite, slender young woman.

"Deela!" she gasped, and pushed herself upright.

Then her eyes focused, and she saw that it was not Deela—no, how could it be?—but a Forstene girl with wide brown eyes and dark hair peeking out from under a kerchief.

"My name is Jennis," the girl said. "Lord Corvalen asked me to attend you."

The Kel Nira's grief for Deela receded a bit in the face of this interesting development. Her first response was a rush of gratitude for a female presence. Then she realized that the girl—Jennis—had to be a spy for the Scourge.

But that did not mean she could not be helpful.

"Attend, how?"

"Well, first thing, I ought to take a look at your injuries. I'm not a physician like you, but I can apply poultices and bandages, at least. And then"—she frowned—"I'll get you something better to wear. A woman should not wear men's clothes."

"I wash first—clean wounds."

"Of course! I'll go and fetch water now." Without further ado, Jennis scampered off.

The Kel Nira was not certain she wanted this untrained girl treating her—but someone had to, or the burns on her arms and the torn flesh on her back would become corrupted. That could lead to a bad death—although not so bad, probably, as the other options that lay before her. Perhaps she ought to refuse the Forstene girl's help.

But when Jennis returned, the Kel Nira allowed her to clean, bandage, and reclothe her—and was grateful for it. Jennis brought her fresh water to drink, too, and a bowl of meaty soup.

The Kel Nira sipped at the broth a bit, ate most of the vegetables, but poked her spoon at the chunks of meat suspiciously.

"Don't you eat meat, Mistress?" asked Jennis.

"I not know what this is."

"It's rabbit. And don't worry, it's fresh—one of the lads snared it just this morning."

"But is it"—she didn't know the Forstene words for *buck* and *doe*—"man or woman rabbit?"

"It doesn't matter, does it?"

The Kel Nira set down the bowl and pushed it away. She felt she was being ungracious, but it couldn't be helped. "Ma'Sharha not eat woman animals. It . . . dishonor the Mothers."

"Oh!" Jennis looked dismayed. "I'm sorry, Mistress. I'll be sure to find out next time." She picked up the bowl to take it away.

"You eat. Rabbit gave life; should not be for nothing."

"Well . . . all right." After a couple bites, she asked, "Who are these Mothers? Are they great women of your country's past?"

The Kel Nira answered slowly, illustrating her words with gestures, especially where she was not sure she was getting the Forstene right. "They are *all* women of past, and all women of future—all who gave life, all who will give life. Now, they are Beyond, behind world eyes can see. They hold birth and death in their laps. To serve life, they lend powers to Ma'Sharha. . . ." She trailed off. It was difficult to explain in a foreign language, and perhaps she was not wise to tell a Forstener so much.

At the same time, she found that speaking of the Mothers had soothed her spirit, and she felt a little less wounded.

After this the Kel Nira slept a great deal; her body's need for rest was such that the nightmares scarcely disturbed her, leaving nothing more than vague uneasiness in their wake. She even had a dream that was not a nightmare, although only pieces lingered after she awoke: images of herself sitting by the Kel Sharha's bedside; seeing her brother, and Treska and Lillanna, and the Kel Mona; entering the chapel, where she was welcomed by Taja, the Second of the Listeners' Order. "We have not forgotten you," Taja whispered.

Still, the Kel Nira could sleep for only short intervals. It was hard to get comfortable on the thin pallet. Her burns ached and itched. Her ribs ached, and lanced pain through her if she rolled over onto her side. Lying on her back, no matter how well Jennis had bandaged the healing welts, was scarcely better. So she awoke frequently, then sat up and did her best to meditate until her eyelids weighed down with exhaustion again.

The Scourge came in from time to time. Oddly, he did nothing more than make polite inquiries after her health and chat with her about the weather and the various birds he had sighted since coming to

Sharhaya. He seemed particularly impressed by a heron he had seen during the course of his march up through the south. The Kel Nira refrained from telling him that her people regarded the heron as a bird of omen.

Jennis was there often. She saw that the Kel Nira ate and drank, and checked her bandages. When she learned that Ma'Sharha customarily bathed twice a day, she expressed some surprise, but then made sure to bring in wash water both morning and evening. She even combed and rebraided the Kel Nira's hair for her, telling a long story about some ancient prince's quest as she patiently worked out the tangles.

The Kel Nira listened and was grateful for all Jennis's care, but she avoided speaking to the girl as much as possible; she did not want to inadvertently say something that might be of use to her enemies.

The third afternoon following Lord Corvalen's arrival, the Kel Nira slept for a long, uninterrupted stretch—the most peaceful sleep she had yet had. She woke late in the day feeling stronger, and there were fewer aches when she moved. She heard Jennis just outside, bantering with the guards. One of them stifled a laugh, and then the girl came in, bearing cheese and flatbread.

As she ate, the Kel Nira thought about her situation. She wasn't sure why the Scourge and his people were taking such care of her. She found it hard to believe that it was simply for honor's sake, as the squire had insisted. Jennis had hinted there was some other reason, but had also treated the Kel Nira to some fulsome praise of Lord Corvalen's sense of honor (and nobility, and generosity, and so on). The girl had seemed quite sincere.

Very well, suppose the Scourge of Cheskara was in fact an honorable man. There were still a great many more in the camp who had no claim at all to his virtues—not least Prince Dursten. How long could, or would, Lord Corvalen protect her?

Until he gets what he wants from me.

As though her thoughts had summoned him, at that moment his voice floated in from outside. The tent flap lifted, and he ducked through. He paused, looking her over. She straightened her back and glared at him.

"You appear to be feeling better, Mistress."

"Yes."

"I imagine you must be rather tired of being confined to this tent, though. Do you think you are strong enough to walk outside a bit?"

She nodded slowly. What was he up to?

The Scourge turned to Jennis. "You need not accompany us; go and look in on Torval, if you like."

A smile lit the girl's face, and she was off.

Lord Corvalen stepped closer to the Kel Nira and offered his hand to help her up. She took it reluctantly, and dropped it as soon as she was steady on her feet. He led the way out of the tent.

She noticed immediately that the guards had gone.

Just as she began to weigh the possibilities, Lord Corvalen turned to face her. His hand clamped around her wrist, and he said in a low voice, "Do not try to escape. If you run away, there will be nothing that I can do for you. Do you understand?"

Over his shoulder she caught sight of the prince riding past on a great white stallion. "I understand."

"Good." He let go of her. "Come with me, then. I have something to show you."

They walked through the camp. He kept their pace slow, no doubt out of deference to her weakness. This would have been irritating, had she not been busy taking in the details around her: the arms, the horses, the condition of the men, the snatches of conversation—perhaps she would see or hear something that would help her people. But why was Lord Corvalen taking that chance? *Because, you fool, he knows that you will never leave this camp alive.*

She was recalled from her thoughts by his voice.

"I was just thinking, Mistress, how few of my questions you have been willing to answer. I understand, of course, but I'm hoping you might tell me one thing, just to satisfy my curiosity."

"If I do not wish to tell, I will say so."

He chuckled. "I'm sure you will. Well, then: I'd had the impression that not many Sharhay know the Forstene language, and I simply wondered, how did you come to learn it?"

She pondered a moment, but could think of no harm that could come of her answering. "My family are vineyard people, and my parents sold the wine. When I was child, we lived in Rezhenet." She paused, remembering the great city, the capital of Ghildarna. Even as shrouded as many of her memories were, she had never forgotten the fascination of the city's markets—the bright, rich colors of exotic goods; the scents of fruits and flowers, spices and savories; the sounds of music, braying pack mules, and conversation in half a dozen languages.

She resumed her story. "Then, merchants of Sharhaya and merchants of Forstene do much business together. Sometimes, in

Rezhenet, they friends. My parents have friend like this. He come very much to our house; his son, too. First we all speak Ghildaran language. But my brother and I like the way Forstene language sound—and we think, we can speak it to have secrets from parents. So we ask the boy to teach us. Then we speak it with him always."

She shrugged to indicate she had told all there was to tell, even though she could have added that in succeeding years she had practiced the language with others, in particular the Ghildaran envoy—a master of many tongues—whenever he came to Sharhaya. And there was no denying that, after these last few days of hearing constant Forstene, and nothing but, her facility with the language was increasing.

"So you have had Forstene friends before. You know, then, that we can be good and honorable men," Lord Corvalen was saying. "Did you ever hear from the merchant or his son after you returned to Sharhaya?"

"You know Great Fire of Rezhenet? It destroy the merchants' quarter. They died." She forestalled his next questions. "My parents, too. My brother and I . . . in Sharhaya then—time for begin our apprenticing." And that, she realized, was also when her memory began to fog.

She felt his eyes on her then and returned the gaze, challenging him.

He did not look away, but gestured at their surroundings. "Do you have questions about anything you see or hear?"

"You mock me?" she was surprised into asking.

"No, assuredly not. But this camp is not really what I wanted to show you. Can you walk just a bit farther?"

"I can." She was tired, but she certainly was not going to say so.

Although the Kel Nira was grateful to be out in the air and sunlight, her spirits grew heavier as they continued on. She could hardly believe that the Forsteners had taken over Summer Bluff. Not only that but, as far as she could tell, they had cut down all the trees—to build their palisade, she supposed, as well as fuel their fires. She mourned those lost trees, and remembered how sweet their shade had been to lie under with a lover during Summer Festival.

She stumbled; Lord Corvalen caught her in his arms before she could fall.

It should be Taras's arms around me!

She pushed the Scourge away, momentarily strengthened by anger. Yes, if she hadn't lost track of the days, *today* was Summer Festival. The irony of being a prisoner in this place of former joy, and on this day, was almost crushing. Now both she and the place were polluted, and she wondered if either would ever be restored to their native wholeness.

The Scourge had not reacted to her anger and did not try to rouse her from her silence as he led her through the camp perimeter to the very edge of the bluff. There was no palisade here; the Forsteners probably hadn't had enough trees left. *And they must think they are secure in this direction.* They were probably right. Most of this side of the bluff was dreadfully steep; even the pathway that the Summer Festival procession took was such a climb that many people preferred to half circle the bluff and go up the gentler slope on the northwest.

She let her gaze wander down the pathway, now much overgrown, to the wild cluster of boulders below (how the children loved to climb on them, uncaring for the state of their festival clothes and ribbons), and beyond to the hazel copse, where some of the older festival goers were wont to rest in the shade before climbing the bluff. They would have come across the river in little ferry boats, while younger and wilder folk splashed through the ford; she could almost hear their shouts and laughter, echoing from previous years.

Lord Corvalen touched her chin lightly to make her turn toward him. "Look," he said, and pointed away to the south.

She sank to the ground. What appeared to be a huge force of warriors was entering the valley. By this time tomorrow, they would fill the meadow between the river and the Parasha Forest, and there would be nothing to be seen from this vantage point but Forstene tents and fires, steel-armed men and long-legged horses, and banners the colors of night and blood.

Lord Corvalen sat down beside her. She wrinkled her nose at the smell of him, so close—old sweat, with a faint overlay of some woody scent that she couldn't place.

Pride was strong in his voice when he spoke. "In Forstene, Mistress, I hold in fief a great barony, wherein are raised the most noble and the most skilled of all fighting men. These warriors you see advancing have been under my command for many years, and I have given them the best of training and armed them with the finest steel. They are disciplined and versatile, able to fight as well in a forest or on a mountainside as on an open plain. And they will give no quarter to any who raise a weapon against them. These are the men with whom I won the Cheskari War."

She could feel him watching her for her reaction; she made sure not to give him one. She kept her eyes on his army, as she knew he expected, but her mind reached to the trees that shadowed the meadow

87

edge on the river's far side. Was Pieran, with his warbands, still there somewhere? Or had he fallen in the battle for the bridge? She did not even know.

Lord Corvalen was continuing. "Tomorrow, or the next day, I shall take you down to see my army up close. You'll see that I have not made empty boasts, that all is just as I have said. Then, if you are strong enough to ride, I shall give you a horse and an escort to the edge of the forest, and you will return to your people."

Did he intend to try to follow her to the Sanctuary? Little success would he meet! But she spoke cautiously. "You wish me to tell them about your army?"

"Yes."

"They already know, I assure you."

"You will tell your people, and you will go to the Kel Sharha. You will tell her that she must surrender to the overlordship of Forstene."

"I will not."

"You *shall* give her our treaty terms, and you shall give her this message: if she does not accept our terms, my army will destroy Sharhaya."

"Carry your own message! Why should I do it for you?"

His face was somber. "Mistress, I am offering you an opportunity to leave this camp alive. It is not likely you will receive another."

"Why care?"

"Let us just say that it is a matter of honor."

She almost believed him. But surely there was more to it—although she could hardly expect him to explain his motivations.

To her surprise, after a few heartbeats' silence he began to do just that. "About five weeks ago, you healed a Forstene warrior in the Lenasha Forest. It was a leg wound, a very serious one."

"I remember."

"No Forstene surgeon could have healed that wound—not as you did. The young man would have lost his leg, if not his life."

Her skin prickled. "And this young man?"

"He is my sister's son. My heir."

"Ah." She would have to think about that. "And how does he fare? His leg is well?"

Lord Corvalen smiled. "He has been asking to be allowed to visit you. Perhaps I will send him to you this evening; you may see for yourself how he fares."

The smile faded. "Mistress, I have made an oath that no one shall ever lay a hand on any woman in my charge—but I do not know how much longer I will be in a position to keep that oath. You have given me no information, and the prince grows impatient; I will not be able to hold you safe from him much longer." He sighed. "I have no wish to see my nephew's savior tortured to death—which is what will surely happen if you remain in this camp. Will you not save yourself, and carry the treaty terms to the Kel Sharha?"

She looked again at his approaching army, and remembered his threat to send it burning through the Parasha to the Sanctuary. He was ruthless; he would do it. But his people were right: he was trying, at least, to be fair.

She felt she would choke, but somehow she got out the next words. "Very well; I will take the message." Then she hesitated, as another realization came to her. "And . . . this is two times you have saved my life." She took his hand, as her people's custom was, and bowed her head over it. "I thank you, Lord Corvalen."

*****

The Holy Woman released his hand and turned away from him. Corvalen watched her profile as her gaze once more swept slowly over the valley. Today was the first time he had seen her in open daylight, and the first time he had noticed that there were some silver threads in her hair, and feathery lines around her eyes and mouth. With a start he realized they were laugh lines. It strained his imagination to picture this grave, proud woman laughing.

She said, "I have seen enough." He stood and stretched out his hand to her. She ignored the gesture, rising to her feet without assistance.

Corvalen cast one more look into the valley to take satisfaction in the orderly progress of his army. A mist was rising off the river, the sort of mist he had noticed hanging in many of the river valleys in this country. Sharhaya could be a damp and difficult place, he reflected, and felt a bit more sympathy for Dursten's failure to achieve a quick victory.

They walked away from the bluff and back through the camp in silence—until he saw Torval limping in their direction.

Corvalen smiled down at the Holy Woman. "It appears I will not be sending my nephew to you this evening after all; here he comes now."

She smiled a little in return, but she looked very fatigued.

"Uncle! Well met!" Torval grasped Corvalen's shoulder, and Corvalen returned the gesture. Then Torval turned to the Holy Woman.

"Mistress—" He broke off as he took in the bruises. Consternation plain on his face, he looked to Corvalen for guidance.

Corvalen decided it was best to adhere to the common courtesies. "Mistress, I realize you have already met this young man, but please allow me to formally introduce to you Lord Torval of Caldene, the son of my sister, Lady Ardalis of Brintora and Caldene. And allow me to thank you on her behalf, as well as my own, for your care of him when he was wounded." Remembering how she had thanked him earlier, he reached for her hand and bowed his head over it.

He looked up in time to see her eyebrows lift in surprise, and he almost grinned; getting a reaction from her was an achievement.

But the next thing he saw sobered him. Scuttling toward them was Esban.

*****

The sound of hurrying footsteps on the well-beaten path scarcely warned the Kel Nira in time that someone was behind her.

A hard hand grabbed her arm, pulling to turn her about. The fingers dug into one of her burns, making her gasp aloud.

Before she could register who her assailant was, Lord Corvalen stepped forward and struck out with a blow to the man's jaw that made him stagger backward. Released, she stumbled a little herself; Lord Corvalen reached out a steadying arm.

As her heartbeat slowed to its normal thrum, she saw that the man who had grabbed her was one of her own people.

And Lord Corvalen obviously knew him. "Esban. I thought I had left you with my army."

The man's voice was nasal and drawling. "The army moves slowly, my lord, and I was eager to rejoin my prince. I rode ahead, you see, and I am on my way to him now."

Esban . . . Esban . . . The name was familiar, as was the face, and the voice. . . .

He was still speaking; his Forstene pronunciation was almost flawless, even those difficult *th*'s. "But permit me to say, that was not a very friendly greeting for a loyal servant, my lord."

"I promised the Healer that no one would lay a hand on her while she is in my charge. I do not care to have my word gainsaid."

"I beg your pardon—I did not know." He sketched a bow to the Kel Nira. "And my apologies to you, Lady; I was only overwhelmed by my eagerness to see if you were indeed who I thought you were."

Suddenly, the Kel Nira remembered this Esban—and the bitterness with which he had received her refusal to admit him to apprenticeship in her Order. Seven years ago that had been, but she could see that he had hated her ever since.

Esban turned to Lord Corvalen and grinned. "Congratulations, my lord. You have a prize here that I think you do not know the value of— but allow me to tell you. And then you may congratulate *me*, for it was my idea."

There was no mistaking the disdain in Lord Corvalen's voice. "Congratulate you? For what?"

"Well, you see, after I heard of Lord Torval's healing—and how good it is to see you up and about, Lord Torval—"

Torval grimaced.

"—I suggested to His Highness . . . that is, I told him how he might catch himself a Healer, a Holy Woman. Ah yes, I got his ear *then*. It was my idea, you see, to have your so-great Forstene warriors lie down and wait among the wounded. I knew it would work, but I never expected you would catch the Kel Nira herself!"

Lord Corvalen and his nephew both stared. Torval looked stricken.

Esban apparently took their silence as a sign that they had not completely understood him. "That's right, my lord—your prisoner is the Kel Nira: the Chief of the Healers' Order, a High Councillor of Sharhaya."

"Is this true?" Lord Corvalen asked her quietly.

She lifted her chin, but said nothing.

Chapter Ten

The confines of her tent allowed the Kel Nira little room to pace, but she trod back and forth nonetheless. She did not know what would happen if she stopped, if she sat or lay down on her pallet.

She ought to sit; she ought to meditate, to think things through.

They knew who she was.

She had seen immediately that there was no point in trying to convince Lord Corvalen that Esban was mistaken. She had no skill in dissembling; all she could do was refuse to speak.

And escape had been so close. Tomorrow, or the next day, she would have been on her way back to the Sanctuary—carrying the Scourge's message, true, but still. . . .

It had been hard enough to agree to convey the treaty terms. What would they want her to do now, now that they knew who she was? Or what would they do *to* her?

Lord Corvalen's deep voice, outside, brought her to a standstill. She turned to face the tent door, and he entered, everything about him solemn and deliberate.

"I have just come from Prince Dursten; Esban has acquainted him with your identity."

"Then . . . our agreement?"

"Is no longer in my power to keep."

There was an edge in his voice, and she remembered what he had told Esban: "I do not care to have my word gainsaid." For a moment, she actually felt some sympathy for him.

"Tomorrow His Highness will send a herald to your people." He spoke now with a careful absence of emotion. "He will tell them that we hold you hostage, and that they must surrender."

"They will not."

He took a step closer to her. "Then Prince Dursten will kill you, and strip your body and hang it to rot on the palisade. And he will make certain that your people see it."

He watched as that sank in.

The Kel Nira fought to maintain her control. She knew what the prince was capable of, and she could see what would befall if he did as he threatened. The sacrilege would enrage her people, and their fury would make them precipitate, reckless. They would not plan; they would not wait. They would hurl themselves against the Forstene armies—and be crushed.

Clearly, Lord Corvalen knew this, too, but there was no triumph in his look. When he spoke again, his voice was soft. "You can still prevent this, Lady."

"How?"

"Send a message with the herald, telling your people that surrender is their only hope. Surely your words will convince them."

"What terms—," she whispered. She steadied herself. "What are the terms for . . . for this?"

"His Highness demands an unconditional surrender."

She narrowed her eyes. "When you talked of a treaty, before, it was not this way."

"The situation has changed. *Kel Nira.*"

If a look could knife a man, the one she gave him then would have done so.

But he ignored it, and gentled his voice still more. "Lady, you are a Healer; you serve life. Do you not think that too many of your people have died already? But no more need die, now. Think how many lives it is in your power to save."

He was trying to manipulate her. He was frighteningly close to succeeding.

He had spoken her own buried thoughts.

"Think about it, Kel Nira. You have the night; I will return to hear your answer tomorrow morning, before the herald departs." He hesitated, then gave her a grave nod and left.

She dropped to her pallet. *O Mothers, O Watchers, what shall I do?* She lay down, certain that the morning would find her still worrying at the question. But the day's exertions claimed their toll and, eventually, she slid into an uneasy sleep.

*****

The evening she was captured had been a living nightmare; the Kel Nira's dream compressed the horror into vignettes that dwelt excruciatingly on details and jumbled events out of order in a way that made them all the more vivid and terrible.

94

Walking the twilit battlefield with the surgeon . . . dead and wounded men tumbled together in a heap. Hands reaching out from among the corpses—Forsteners, alive and hale, reaching for her.

Deela, thrown to the ground, screaming, then fighting for breath with a soldier's hands closed around her neck. Fama's staff cracking his head. Deela screaming.

Running toward one of the wagons, shouting at Kirtana to protect the wounded men; Kirtana leaping to the driver's seat and taking the reins herself, the driver lying dead.

The field surgeon falling, clutching a wound in his side. "Leave him!"—a harsh Forstene voice. "His Highness wants the women."

More running. The river ahead, reflecting the rising moonlight.

Fama laying about her with her ironwood staff. Bloodied Forsteners lunging at her, then one rushing up behind and driving his sword through her body. "Run!"—her last word.

The river. Deela diving into the current, the Kel Nira wading in behind. A spear, then a crossbow bolt skimming the water. A second spear. Deela struck, the Kel Nira screaming her name. Blood, strangely colored in the moon-limned twilight, gilding the river's surface.

From above and behind, a hand seizing the Kel Nira's tunic and hauling her from the water.

She gasped awake, and the nightmare river gave way to the realization that she was being pulled from her pallet—by Prince Dursten. She let loose with a cry of rage and protest, but she could not struggle free from his grip.

*****

Corvalen had awakened early and restless. A good bout of sword practice was what he needed, and he'd gone to the open area around the spring to run through his forms as the Celestials hid their shining faces behind the gray veil of the new day. He was working up a healthy sweat, and the eastern sky was just showing a tinge of red, when alarms sounded in the western part of the camp. Only then did he hear men shouting and notice the smell and haze of smoke creeping over the ridge. He swore, and set off at a run.

Pellar came sprinting to meet him. "My lord, the camp is under attack! Longbowmen"—the boy paused to get his breath—"shooting fire arrows from down on the meadow. Some of the arrows have hit the palisade, and some have gotten over and set tents alight—"

"Rouse as many men as you can to fight the fire. Now!"

The air was thickening around them as the squire hurried away to follow his orders. But most of the smoke seemed to be rolling in from the opposite direction of the attack. Smoke . . . or mist?

Corvalen lengthened his stride, and almost collided with another runner.

"Lord Corvalen!" the man-at-arms got out. "There's a small force of Sharhay burst through on the east!"

To battle, then. Even as he thought this, Rossen came hurrying from the direction of their tents.

"My horse!" Corvalen ordered.

"Yes sir!" Rossen turned and ran for the camp paddock. Corvalen followed at a brisk walk, continuing to question the man-at-arms, who had fallen in beside him.

"How many?"

"Half a hundred riders, perhaps more."

"Where did they break through?"

"At the low edge of the bluff. Their archers took out the sentries there in a matter of seconds."

"Damn!"

The camp had turned into a chaos of running, swearing men. Mist—Corvalen was sure now that it was indeed mist, a veritable fog, mixing with the smoke—swirled thickly among the tents, increasing the confusion. A woman's cry rose above the shouts and pounding footsteps. The Kel Nira! Corvalen swore again, and ran toward her tent.

Dursten had the Holy Woman; he was pulling her into the pathway, where his horse stamped impatiently. The guards stood by, at a loss—humble men, they could hardly be expected to act against the heir to the throne.

Corvalen felt no such hindrance. "Dursten! What are you doing?" he bellowed.

"There's a rescue party come after this whore. Right into my camp—the impudence! Well, if they want her back so badly, I'll give her to them—in pieces, if they don't call off this attack."

The Kel Nira appeared to be in shock. No sound escaped her lips, and her widened eyes seemed fixed unseeingly on the prince's horse. Corvalen's remonstrations were lost in the tumult surrounding them.

Corvalen lunged forward, but at the same time Dursten grabbed a handful of the woman's hair, yanking hard, and used his other hand to swing himself into his saddle. He hauled her up in front of him, snapped the reins, and dug his heels into the horse's flanks.

At that moment the Kel Nira seemed to find her voice. A single, unintelligible sound escaped her lips. The stallion bucked, then reared. The woman's hands were tightly wound in the horse's mane, but Dursten was startled into losing his grip. He tumbled off, landing with an ignominious thud.

The horse's front hooves slammed back to earth, the Kel Nira cried out again, and the mist closed around her and the stallion as they bolted forward.

*****

The fog was becoming impenetrable. Rossen, riding Corvalen's horse from the paddock at a gallop, heard the approaching hoofbeats barely in time to avoid colliding with Prince Dursten's white stallion. It took him a moment to realize that the rider, however, was not the prince but the Kel Nira.

What would Corvalen want me to do? There was no time to debate with himself; Rossen turned his mount to follow after the Holy Woman.

It was an uncanny ride. Rossen knew that he was close behind the Kel Nira, but he could scarcely see her through the clinging mist. At the same time, the horses' hoofbeats resonated with eerie loudness.

He was only vaguely aware of anything going on outside their hazy, echoing world. Shouts reached him, but the words were incomprehensible. There was an occasional clash of metal on metal, and twice a flash of steel pierced the edge of the mist.

Rossen prayed he wouldn't be felled by his own people. And that wasn't his only worry. He and his quarry were being joined by other riders, on all sides. Hearing them calling to one another, he realized that he had been caught up in the midst of the Sharhay rescue party.

If only he had a clear field of vision, he probably could maneuver himself out from among them. But both times he tried to get away, he narrowly missed crashing into another rider. He began to think that his pursuit of the Kel Nira might be an exercise in foolhardiness.

The horse troop swept toward the eastern perimeter of the Forstene camp. The mist was beginning to thin now, and Rossen could make out their location. They were not at the lower edge, where the Sharhay must first have broken through. They had chosen a more unexpected escape route, higher up the bluff.

The horses were in for a steep downhill run. All right, perhaps, for the scrabbly little Sharhay mounts—but for Corvalen's charger?

Rossen braced himself as they approached the perimeter. He and the woman were at the center of the horse troop, so he caught only glimpses of a few Forstene soldiers—some scattering, one falling as a thrown ax embedded itself in his skull.

Behind him, Rossen heard a man scream, and a moment later a riderless horse plunged past.

The Sharhay reached the edge of the bluff, and time seemed suspended as rider after rider leapt over.

Rossen urged his mount to kick free of the earth, and for a moment he felt borne up on the air. Then there was a plunge, and a jolt as hooves connected again with solid ground. They were a good way down the bluff and on a steep incline, but the horse kept its footing, praise Vallar.

The riders turned up the valley, away from Corvalen's advancing army, then slowed to ford the river. One more burst of speed took them across the meadow, up a rise, and into the Parasha Forest.

Among the trees, there was no concealing fog. Rossen, surrounded by half a hundred warriors who regarded his people as their mortal enemies, had to admit that he felt distinctly nervous.

*****

The Kel Nira was breathing hard by the time they reached the clearing; her slowly healing body had not been ready for such a ride. She slumped in her saddle, scarcely aware of the men dismounting and their chatter rising around her. Then she saw, standing at her stirrup, the most welcome sight in the world.

"Pieran!"

He reached up, and she slid down into his arms.

She could not tolerate his tight embrace for long. Gently, she disengaged herself, and reached up to touch his face. It was wet with tears. "So, you've finally fulfilled that prophecy." Her voice was a little unsteady, but she smiled.

Pieran tried to do the same. "Wouldn't want the Watchers after me, would we? Anyhow, I didn't do it alone. Plenty of volunteers for the warband, and the Kel Mona raised the mist—she and the others'll be along shortly; they're up by the old yew—and . . ."

He seemed to really look at her for the first time; he touched a gingerly finger to one of the cuts on her face. "I'm sorry we took so long," he whispered. "I'm so sorry."

"No, no, you were very timely," the Kel Nira began, but was distracted by footsteps pattering toward her.

"My Chief!" Treska called out. Lillanna followed close behind, and barely managed to restrain Treska from throwing herself at the Kel Nira.

"My Chief," Lillanna greeted her, and bowed. She could not entirely maintain her sedate manner, however, and a smile spread her face. "Mothers and Watchers, we thought we'd never see you again!"

"Never mind me now. We should treat any injuries the warriors have taken."

Lillanna was eyeing her with some concern. "I will see to you, my Chief, and Treska shall take a look at the men." She turned to the apprentice. "Go on; anything you can't tend to yourself, you call me over."

Treska bowed and went to do as she'd been told.

"Now then . . ." Lillanna stepped closer to examine the Kel Nira's facial injuries. Pieran moved a discreet distance away.

"Why did you bring Treska instead of one of your own apprentices?" the Kel Nira asked quietly.

"It was dreadfully important to her."

"And I am happier to see her than you know. But she is so young; I would not have her near to any danger. For that matter, I would wish that none of you had risked yourselves for me in this fashion. We do not need more deaths—and certainly not on my account."

Lillanna paused in her examination. "Once Taja knew you were alive, and where you were, can you think that we could bear to leave you imprisoned and suffering?" Her voice had trembled on those words, but she brought herself under control again. "As for Treska and myself, at least, you have no cause for concern; we simply waited here till Pieran and the others brought you back—along with another friend of yours." With a smile, she nodded toward the near edge of the clearing.

There stood Luma, loosely tethered to a sapling. *You got away, pretty lady!* The mare whickered and nodded.

Before the Kel Nira could reach to pat her horse's neck, Treska screamed.

The first scream was wordless, but the second was "Forstener!"

*****

Rossen had dismounted with the others, staying at the outskirts of the group and hoping to remain lost among the weary riders until he could edge away into the trees or think of something better to do. He had neither gotten far nor thought of anything, however, and now a girl in green tunic and white overdress was approaching him. She halted, her eyes widening as she took in his hauberk (the sole piece of armor he'd had time to don) and the huge gelding at his side. She screamed.

It took only moments for the Sharhay men to close in around him, knives drawn, arrows nocked. He judged it best not to try for his own weapon and raised his hands in surrender. A red-haired man stepped forward to seize him by the arm, while another relieved him of his sword.

As little as Rossen knew of the Sharhay language, there was no mistaking the intent of the men's mutters and shouts. Then came a different voice, a familiar one; the mob settled a bit and made way for the Kel Nira, attended by another Holy Woman.

Seeing Rossen, the Kel Nira clucked her tongue and shook her head. She said something to the crowd that made them fall silent. Slowly, men resheathed their knives; a few of the archers, however, remained with their arrows trained on Rossen.

"*Na Kel!*" exclaimed the girl who had started the outcry. That meant, Rossen thought, "my Chief," but he was unable to follow the rest of what she said as she scurried to the Kel Nira's side. The Kel Nira put an arm around her and spoke in reassuring tones. Then she turned her attention back to Rossen.

"I have tell them," she said to him in Forstene, "you not do this"— she touched a hand to her bruised face—"and I said you are one who act with honor. No harm comes to you in my care."

Rossen dared a small bow. "Thank you, Mistress."

"Hm."

She nodded to the red-haired warrior, who still held Rossen in his grip. "Pieran," she addressed him, and called him to her with a few more words. Shooting Rossen a warning look over his shoulder, he moved off to confer with the Kel Nira and the other Holy Woman.

Rossen sank to the grass to catch his breath and to show he was no threat. The Sharhay around him stood warily, exchanging few words with one another. Farther away, the Kel Nira and Pieran spoke in low, hurried tones that rose once or twice in intensity.

It did not take them long to decide Rossen's fate. Pieran marched straight up to him, scowling. Rossen scrambled to his feet.

"The Kel Nira will speak you," Pieran said, in uncomfortable-sounding Forstene. He led Rossen across the clearing to a tumble of boulders, where the Holy Woman had seated herself on one of the smaller rocks.

She looked exhausted. "Rossen, your lord had plan to give me terms of peace, to take to the Kel Sharha. I am sorry he not yet tell me those terms . . . for we wish to know them. I not say we accept—but we wish to know." She paused, and the other Holy Woman laid a light hand on her shoulder. "Tell your lord: come to the ford of the Asha on the morning after three nights, and Council will hear him."

"But," put in Pieran, "if you fight before then, we will not hear."

The Kel Nira nodded. "We will hear your lord only if your people not attack."

"And what if you attack us?" Rossen ventured.

"So you leave us in peace, we will not. Now you go, and return safe to show our good faith." At her nod, four mounted warriors came forward, one of them leading Corvalen's horse. "These men ride with you to the river. You have honor and mercy in your spirit, Rossen; fare well."

Before he could answer, his escort led him away.

Chapter Eleven

Treska had brought fresh clothes for the Kel Nira and offered to help her change. She demurred and, ignoring curious looks from Lillanna and the others, went behind the boulders to shed her worn Forstene garment in private. It was an awkward business stepping into her trousers, and she bit her lip as the process of easing into her tunic strained her ribs and pulled at the adhesions on her back. But the fine-woven linen settled over her, cool and smooth—soothing.

Her worst injuries now covered, she left the shelter of the boulders and allowed Treska to help her with her overdress. She was just knotting the belt when the Kel Mona rode into the clearing, accompanied by two others of her Order, a Listener, and an escort of three Guardians.

The faces of the Summoners were nearly as gray as their woolen overdresses, as though their skin had been glazed by the mists. The Kel Mona herself looked like a creature of mist—insubstantial, almost wavering in the Kel Nira's vision.

The Kel Nira shook her head and sat back down, heavily, on her rock. *My dear friend, how much have you spent yourself for me?* It was not a question she could ask aloud. And if she did, the Kel Mona would only answer, "You would spend as much of yourself for me"—which was simply the truth.

As the Summoners dismounted, Lillanna and Treska hurried to them with water flasks, made them drink, then pressed them to eat hard seedcake and dried venison. Color and solidity began to return to them. Light shifted in the clearing, and the tree leaves whispered.

"The current is fast; we must make haste to the Sanctuary," said the Listener.

It was Lillanna who answered her. "The Kel Nira is not strong enough for a hard ride, and the Summoners must rest."

At last the Kel Mona's gray gaze met the Kel Nira's, and held for a heartbeat. Then the Kel Mona said, her voice gravelly from long chanting, "It does not matter if we come behind, but the Kel Nira must not delay. Healer Lillanna, surely you can lend her the strength she needs?"

The Kel Nira stood, protesting, "I am perfectly fit."

"You don't look it."

"The Kel Mona is right, my Chief." Lillanna stepped closer and placed one hand on the Kel Nira's forehead, laying her other hand over her chest.

"If you think you are going to give me Nihara, young woman, you ought to think again," said the Kel Nira, with less force than she would have wished.

"If our places were reversed, my Chief, you would do the same." Lillanna removed her hands and folded them in supplication. "Lady, please. The Kel Sharha has been calling for you these past three days. You cannot go to her without your strength."

"You are a fine enough healer for even the First of Mothers, Lillanna—she did not have to go to such lengths and risk so many lives to summon me to her bedside!"

"Lady, there is one duty that only the Chief of Healers may perform for the Kel Sharha."

The Kel Nira felt a stillness descend. "She is asking to cross?"

"I believe she will ask, once you are there. She has refused Nihara from me; she said there was no more good in it for her, and no more good in her for Sharhaya. So, my Chief, do you truly believe you can ride to the Sanctuary in this state and then be ready to do your duty?"

The Kel Nira sighed and closed her eyes. "Very well."

Lillanna drew a long breath and placed her hands once more. The Kel Nira also breathed deeply, willing her mind to blankness and her whole being to receptivity. "I draw power up from the earth," Lillana murmured. "I open to power that flows from the sky. I am a tree to connect the worlds. I am a river to channel the flow." Warmth from Lillanna's hands began to soak into the Kel Nira. The heat thawed her last reserves, and without further thought she opened to the vitality that Lillanna was offering. She became conscious only of a pulsing radiance that gradually enveloped her. After a suspension of time, the light faded, leaving behind a comforting warmth.

"Kel Nira." The Kel Mona's voice was like a splash of cold water.

For a moment longer the Kel Nira savored the splendid absence of pain, the return of strength, and the energy that vibrated through her with every breath. Opening her eyes, she swiftly reoriented herself. Lillanna stood over her, pale and swaying, her eyes shadowed. The Kel Nira reached for the younger woman's wrist and nodded in satisfaction as she felt the steadiness of her pulse. "Well done, Healer. And thank you."

Lillanna smiled and nodded.

"I hope you have more seedcake and venison. You and I must both have a bit to eat, and then we must ride."

*****

Rossen's escort reined in at the ford, but kept watch as he crossed. He breathed easier after they turned back to the forest.

As he neared the bluff, he saw plainly the trampled path that the Sharhay had ridden up to break into the camp. He considered making use of it himself, rather than riding around to the other side to enter through the palisade gate. But he'd already risked his lord's horse once; better to take it up the gentler slope.

Then he realized there might still be Sharhay warriors in the meadow below the palisade, and he was, to his shame, without his sword. Up the path, then; there was no help for it.

Corvalen's horse, a confident creature, made the climb as placidly as if it were ambling through its home pasture. As it neared the top, a sentry hailed, and Rossen called back to ask about the state of the fighting.

"All over, sir—the barbarians ran away to their woods just as soon as they got what they came for." He waited till Rossen reached him to continue, "Guess their courage ran out, or maybe they don't know to press an advantage when they have one."

"Well, they *are* barbarians, after all," Rossen remarked, causing the sentry to snigger in agreement. "Would you know where the Lord Marshal is?"

The sentry was still grinning. "Just follow the sound of the shouting, sir, and you'll find him alright."

Rossen frowned. Off the battlefield, he had seldom known Corvalen to shout.

As Rossen rode toward the paddock, he could not but notice a feeling of unease abroad in the camp. Well, no wonder—the enemy had just carried off a rather spectacular feat, apparently with magic to aid them. What else might these Sharhay be capable of now?

There was confusion, too. Knights threw sharp words at squires and grooms, who ran about with armloads of armor and horse trappings. A minor lordling was haranguing his men-at-arms into marching formation. Another group of soldiers lolled about, armed for a battle that, to read their faces, they didn't think would come to pass. Rossen saw their commander dismount his horse and pull off his helm in obvious, impatient disgust.

The nearer Rossen got to the prince's portion of the encampment, the readier for battle the men looked—at least, they were fully armed and armored, mounted or standing at their horses' bridles. Yet uncertainty showed plain on some faces, guardedly on others.

But the countenance of the man who ran up to greet Rossen was suffused with relief. It took Rossen a moment to recognize him: Gar, of course, one of Corvalen's bodyguard.

"There you are, sir! Are you all right?"

"A bit dazed is all; it will soon pass." Just a natural reaction to the waning of the excitement of his chase after the Kel Nira and his near-capture by the Sharhay. And, he realized, he had never had any breakfast that morning. Food would have to wait a little longer, however. "Where is Lord Corvalen, Gar? Is *he* all right?"

"Oh, never fear for his lordship; not a scratch on him from this day's doings. You'll find him in the prince's pavilion, sir—and it will be a relief to him to see you, I'm sure."

Rossen let Gar take over with Corvalen's horse and headed to the pavilion on foot. He passed among the tents of Dursten's bodyguard, who stood about oddly silent. The reason soon became obvious: every ear was attuned to the voices coming from the pavilion. The men closest kept their backs to it, ostentatiously pretending not to be listening.

But no one could fail to hear the prince's bark: "You forget yourself, Lord Corvalen. I have already said that we will retaliate for this outrage and attack this very afternoon, and *I* am in command here!"

"We are *both* of us under the *king's* command," came Corvalen's reply—not shouting, precisely, but in a forceful voice that certainly carried.

The sentry on duty caught sight of Rossen, cleared his throat, and greeted him loudly. "Sir Rossen, what news?"

The voices in the pavilion fell silent, and a moment later Corvalen was rushing out and seizing both Rossen's shoulders. "By Vallar, I am happy to see you, Rossen—I wondered if I would ever lay eyes on you again!"

Reciprocating the shoulder clasp, Rossen managed to suppress the chortle that welled up in response to Corvalen's obvious pleasure in seeing him safely returned. "I have been given a message for you, my lord."

Corvalen cocked his head ever so slightly toward the pavilion; when Rossen nodded, he took his arm and said, "You had better come in, then."

Dursten had mastered himself, and greeted Rossen with suave courtesy, offering him a seat, wine, and cold fowl—all gratefully accepted.

There was a speculative look in Corvalen's eyes as he watched Rossen chew and swallow the first few mouthfuls. Dursten stood by with folded arms, his fingers tappingarrhythmically. Finally he said, "And so, Sir Rossen, you attempted to apprehend our runaway hostage—and horse thief now, too, I might add. Very quick thinking; a brave initiative." He tilted his head, his look expectant. "But . . . ?" So Rossen left off eating and drinking to recount his adventure.

Dursten's fingers tapped faster and faster as the tale was spun. At the end he burst out, "The impudence! She thinks she can summon *us* to treat with their barbaric council? She says they will *deign* to listen to our terms? She practically *orders* us not to attack them? The insolence!" He paced across the front of the pavilion, his voice rising in volume. "Serve them right if we met them at the ford with crossbows— rid ourselves of the whole damned council and the whole damned problem at once! What a lot of trouble—"

"Your Highness!" Corvalen spoke as sharply as Rossen had ever heard him. But as Dursten stopped pacing and turned toward him, Corvalen metamorphosed into the perfect courtier—almost. "Your Highness," he said, with only a hint of a growl. "Take some wine; you are agitated—"

"Agitated? Of course I'm agitated! This slut who presumes to give us orders, issue us invitations, set the time and place for us . . ." He blew out a puff of air, and for a moment it seemed that his storm of temper had exhausted itself. But at least one more flare remained. "To think that we had one of their chiefs in our hands, and she slipped through our fingers!" He glared at Corvalen.

Corvalen's jaw tightened. "She should not have been 'in our hands' in the first place, Highness. When her people learn how she has been treated here, they will hardly be sanguine about accepting our treaty terms."

"Good; I hope they reject the treaty! Then, Lord Corvalen, you will have to mobilize that army of yours and help me thoroughly conquer these accursed Sharhay."

"That is not the king's wish."

"No? Then why did he command you to bring your following here? Just to threaten the Sharhay—a mere show of our superiority?" Dursten laughed. "You are naive, Lord Marshal, if you think that my father would go to the expense and trouble of putting such an army in the field if he does not intend it to be used. He believes in diplomacy no more than I do. What's more, I don't think you do, either. Not really. You've been a warrior all your life. Warriors don't talk, don't negotiate; we fight. Or has something happened to take the fight out of you, Lord Corvalen?"

Corvalen answered softly. "Many things have happened to me, Highness, but I assure you, there is fight enough in me for any needful battle. I believe it is time for peace here—but if the Sharhay still want war, they shall have it."

There was little more to say after that, and Rossen and Corvalen soon left the prince.

They went to Corvalen's tent, Corvalen insisting on giving him a proper meal—Rossen had never finished his cold fowl in the prince's pavilion. Pellar waited on them, plainly eager to hear about Rossen's recent exploits, so Rossen obliged by telling them over again.

Corvalen sat quietly through this narrative, often looking past Rossen to the open tent door; he was not listening, not wholeheartedly. Of course, he had already heard it. But when Corvalen frowned for the third time, it occurred to Rossen that, glad as Corvalen had been to see him, he had said nothing in praise of his actions. Did he think Rossen had been foolhardy? Did he feel Rossen had disobeyed his orders? But perhaps he simply felt that he had been deprived of a chance at action. Rossen knew how irritable inactivity could make Corvalen, especially if his battle fury was awakened and then found no outlet.

Rossen swallowed the mouthful he'd been chewing and, catching Pellar's avid expression, told the last part of his tale. The squire's eyes shone with admiration. "How brave you were, sir!"

"What else should we expect from our Rossen, my boy?" Corvalen smiled absently, his gaze straying away again. Rossen thought, *I may have been brave, but I failed him all the same.*

At last Corvalen looked straight at Rossen, now with a genuine smile. "Forgive me, my friend; I have been most abstracted. My mind is still full of my argument with the prince, and . . . Well. Our situation is changed yet again. But though our hostage may have escaped us, your riding after her has yielded a good result. If you had not been there, she would not have proposed our meeting at the ford; I cannot thank you enough for bringing back that news. It accords well with the king's wishes. And"—his expression turned rueful—"I am glad she gave us three days; I only hope that will be enough time to persuade the prince to a more amenable frame of mind."

"The meeting time is good for another reason," Rossen observed. "Your army will be well in position and fully battle-ready; the Sharhay will see what they have to face if they refuse the treaty."

"Yes, my army will be in position. That, I think, is what chafes Prince Dursten so."

"My lord?"

"He wanted this victory for himself. That's why he made that push to take the bridge, and why he tortured that poor woman for information. He wanted to storm across to the Sanctuary and have Sharhaya won before ever I got here. You should have seen him right after the Kel Nira escaped—actually, no, be glad you didn't. I've seen His Highness in some rages before, but this crowned them all." He shook his head and lapsed into silence once more.

Rossen could not tell just what Corvalen was thinking, but his face was lined in an expression of perplexity mingled with something that looked very near misery. Rossen felt his own spirits sagging in response.

Corvalen shook his head again, and stood up. "Well, whatever happens, Dursten can have his 'glory'—I want none of it. He is right about one thing, however: I am a warrior, and I am made for fighting. It is my duty to subdue or destroy the enemies of Forstene, and if I must, I will kill every last man of Sharhaya. But I tell you, Rossen, I shall never in my life be able to forget that these people were not our enemies until we *made* them so."

*****

The afternoon was well-advanced when the Kel Nira and her party rode into the Sanctuary. They were greeted with subdued cheers from people gathered on porches and balconies, and by the refugees encamped on the green; relief and anxiety mingled in the faces turned toward her. She tried to smile back with reassurance—her face hurt much less than it had—but faltered when she saw Taras. She had to look away, his expression of concern was so avid, and so searing was the sudden memory of what she had planned and what had come to pass instead. *This is no time for personal considerations*, she chided herself.

At the dais, Yasma's junior apprentice stepped forward, offering a beaten-copper bowl freshly filled with water from one of the fountains, for this was a formal homecoming. The Kel Nira dismounted and washed her face and hands, murmuring the words of purification. She thanked the girl, then, with Lillanna and Treska following, made her way among the tents and lean-tos to the Kel Sharha's house, the refugees bowing as she passed among them.

Inside, Taja was descending the stairs. Weariness and concern were written in the lines of her plump, pretty face, but her expression lightened as the Kel Nira stepped forward to meet her. "Thank the Watchers, you are safe!"

The Kel Nira returned Taja's bow, then took her hand and bowed again. "I thank the Watchers, and I also thank you, Listener; I dreamed of you, and I know it was a sent dream. It gave me comfort when comfort was most precious to me."

"I only wish . . ." Taja trailed off, then shrugged. "You had better go up. But," she added, soft and sympathetic, "if you want to talk with me at any time, I am at your service." She bowed again, and walked away toward the Kel Sharha's kitchen.

"It was kindly meant," Lillanna said beside the Kel Nira.

She realized that she was frowning after Taja, and a sharp answer was almost on her lips. She stilled herself, rolled her shoulders back, and composed her expression as she mounted the stairs.

The shutters were open in the Kel Sharha's room, but the daylight was feeble against the clinging shadows around the bed. The Kel Sharha lay propped against her pillows, and moaned in her sleep.

Yasma was conversing quietly with her senior apprentice by one of the windows. As she turned to greet her Chief, her welcoming smile faded; she covered her obvious dismay with a deeper than usual bow.

I must look really dreadful. The Kel Nira wished people would stop reacting this way, and her reply to Yasma's stammered greeting came out terse and impatient. She had to steady herself, again, to listen to Yasma's report on the Kel Sharha's condition. *I have my duty to perform; I cannot permit myself to become disturbed by the words and deeds of others.*

At last, having dismissed Yasma and her apprentice, she was able to turn to the Kel Sharha's bedside and make her own examination. It did not take long. There was no help for the Kel Sharha now; all the skill and power of the Sworn Healers could do no more than alleviate her pain—and she might linger with that for a moon or more. Would she indeed ask to cross, to return to the Mothers?

As the Kel Nira knelt beside the bed to await the Kel Sharha's waking, her thoughts turned upon themselves. No woman in memory had ever headed the Council for as long as this Kel Sharha; she had been First of Mothers for most of the Kel Nira's life. Her crossing would be a grave disruption to the people in the best of times—and this was not the best of times at all. Yet cross she would, and before the season changed, one way or another. But what way was best?

The Kel Sharha stirred, as though the Kel Nira's thoughts had waked her, and answered the silent question aloud: "I am ready now, Kel Nira." Her voice was a creaky whisper. "I should have asked long before this; I should have asked when I stopped hearing the trees. But I am an old fool, alas, and my weakness has nearly doomed our people." She paused; a tear slid from the corner of one eye. Then she seemed to collect herself, even smiled a little. "There is a tree outside the window here—do you see?"

The Kel Nira glanced toward the window nearest the bed; it looked out onto a courtyard garden, and just outside the window a graceful branch reached up, the leaves rippling in a light breeze.

"A beech tree," said the Kel Sharha. "Your tree, Finoora." Her voice had dropped so low that the Kel Nira had to lean very close to hear.

The Kel Sharha gazed off into a vision that only she could see. After several heartbeats, she turned her eyes to the Kel Nira. "Do you know that I was the Listener who divined your tree for you? You would not remember, of course, having been just a babe in arms; but perhaps your mother told you?"

"She did; it became quite a point of pride with her, after you became the Kel Sharha."

The old woman chuckled—or it would have been a chuckle, had she been stronger. "I imagine so. But did you ever know why the beech is your tree, not the willow or the elder or some other?"

The Kel Nira shook her head.

"Because it perseveres . . . it perseveres. Those leaves outside my window will turn brown in the autumn, but they will not fall. They will cling to the branch until the new leaves are ready to unfurl. Only then will they let go. That is your nature, too, Finoora. And mine—the beech is my tree also. But now that you are here, I will let go; I can rest with the Mothers, knowing that you will bring the springtide strength back to our people."

An odd feeling twisted around the Kel Nira's heart. "Lady, I am not—"

"You are!" The old voice was suddenly firm. "You are more than you think you are, Kel Nira."

A shutter banged as the breeze outside kicked up. Lillanna and Treska, who had been hovering all this time by the far wall, ready should their Chief need them, each hurried to a window to make fast the shutters.

"Send them out," whispered the Kel Sharha.

As soon as the door closed behind them, the Kel Nira said, "Please do not set riddles for me, Kel Sharha—not now." *Not when this may be our last conversation in this life.*

"I do not know that you are ready to hear. Yet you are readier than ever you were before." Her head cocked in speculation. Then her hand darted from beneath the covers, unexpectedly strong as it seized the Kel Nira's chin. "Tell me about your dreams," she commanded.

The Kel Nira recoiled. "No!" Then, flustered by her own vehemence, she said, "Forgive me, Lady. You must not tax your strength over me."

"I intend to cross tonight, Finoora. I have no more need of strength—but you do."

"I was weak; I know." The Kel Nira felt herself tremble with the admission, but she did not look away.

"What nonsense!" The Kel Sharha made a strange sound; after a moment the Kel Nira interpreted it as a laugh. "You, weak? My dear child, your only great weakness is that you so fear being weak!" She paused; her breath caught, and she grimaced.

The Kel Nira laid her hands over the Kel Sharha's belly, willing Nihara to flow through her and numb the pain. She was a poor channel in her present state, but the spasm subsided even so.

She sat back on her heels, breathing hard for several heartbeats, then reached for the bottle of poppy syrup that Yasma had left on the bedside table.

The Kel Sharha caught her hand. "No. Time is short, and I wish to be clearheaded. You are going to have to go and prepare for the ritual very soon, so you must listen to me now. I do not know what has been done to you, though I can guess much of it. The details do not matter to me. What matters is that a door is opening in you, one that we believed was locked for good and all. . . . Why do you dream of your grandmother?"

"I . . . I don't know."

"Do you see her in your dreams—or in your dreams, do you see through her eyes?"

"I . . . oh!" The Kel Nira felt as though she had been slapped. She shook her head as a memory resurfaced: her mother, scolding her yet again for losing her temper. *You have your grandmother's own spirit,* her mother had exclaimed, in an exasperation that had reached its limit. And . . . in truth?

The Kel Sharha was nodding as though she, too, had watched the scene replayed.

"First of Mothers, why is this important now?"

"Because I see, Kel Nira, that you have survived a terrible ordeal—yet kept your honor throughout it. I know your strength, and it is great. But for all that lies before you, you will need even more. You are going to have to accept who you are—*all* of it—and who you were. You are going to have to let that door open."

Chapter Twelve

The chapel hummed with chanting as the Kel Mona, her Second, and their apprentices readied for the coming rite. The Kel Nira and Lillanna passed quietly among them, Lillanna carrying the tray of wood and copper ritual vessels to its place beside the small chapel hearth. The Kel Nira added her mortar and pestle to the arrangement.

In front of the closed north door of the chapel, the Kel Sharha's usual place, cushions had been piled and laid out to make a low couch; one of the apprentices draped it with a fine-woven white cloth. Another apprentice began to lay a new fire in the hearth; the Kel Nira and Lillanna moved away to give her more room to work.

They stood silently as the Kel Mona closed and ritually sealed first the chapel's western door, then the eastern. The Kel Nira watched her friend attentively. The Kel Mona, some years her senior, was no longer a robust woman. She had already done a major working today, one she must have begun well before sunrise, and this would be an arduous night. *May the Mothers lend her strength.* The prayer reminded the Kel Nira again of the Kel Sharha's final words to her. They had been more than commonly premonitory. . . .

Lillanna touched her elbow and whispered, "You are wanted, my Chief." She made a little jerk of her chin toward the chapel's southern door. The Kel Jemya stood there, looking at her expectantly.

With an inward sigh, the Kel Nira went to join her fellow Chief, and together they stepped out into the moonless night and walked a little way off from the chapel. The circular, vine-covered building, on the northern edge of the Sanctuary, was overshadowed by towering trees at the back. At the front, the chapel looked out on a wide path, paved in white stone, that led by a serpentine course from the green. The two women stared up the path, in the general direction of the Kel Sharha's house.

"I wanted to speak with you before the procession arrives," the Kel Jemya said.

"I do not think this is a good time. We need to prepare our minds and spirits for the rite."

115

"This is part of my preparation." She turned to face the Kel Nira straight on. "The last time we spoke, I said things that . . . that perhaps I should not have."

"I believe you spoke only out of your anxiety for Sharhaya."

"Just so. But . . . you were right that my impatience was unseemly. And now . . ."

Now you feel guilty about it. The Kel Nira quelled her impatience and folded her hands at her waist. Back among the trees, an owl moaned a deep *hu-hoo*.

"So I wanted to assure you, before the rite, that I did *not* try to convince the Kel Sharha to ask for her crossing—nor, to my knowledge, did anyone else."

"I know, Kel Jemya." The Kel Nira heard a note of weariness in her voice; to her dismay, her companion heard it, too, and peered closely at her.

"Are you all right?"

What do you think? Of course I am not all right! But aloud she said, "I am well enough to do what is required."

There was a silence, disturbed only by a breeze that ruffled the women's hair. It stirred the flames of the torches at either side of the path, and the light glinted in the Kel Jemya's eyes. Slowly, as though feeling her way, she said, "You will remember, Kel Nira, that the Guardians are sworn not only to protect but also to exact justice."

"And you will remember that I have no taste for that kind of justice, Kel Jemya."

"Have you not? We remember differently, then. When I first knew you . . ."

"Yes?"

The Kel Jemya frowned, then a bit of a smile curved her lips. "You were a very angry girl. Who would have thought you'd grow up to be such a peace-loving Healer?"

"This is hardly the time to talk about my childhood. Now, please—I must return to the chapel and still my mind. The duty before me is the gravest I shall ever perform."

The Kel Jemya seemed about to speak again, but was stilled by the sound of drumbeats, joined a moment later by mournful flutes; the Celebrants had gathered on the green.

"They are ready for you, Kel Jemya. You must lead your Order in the procession."

"Yes . . . duty." She paused a moment longer in reflection, then drew herself up to her full height, looking suddenly very martial and

116

very, very sure of herself. "Duty," she repeated. "I to mine, and you to yours." She bowed, received the Kel Nira's answering bow, and strode off up the path.

The Kel Nira stared after her, her mind straying. "Justice," she whispered, and then wondered just what the Kel Jemya had been remembering. It was so hard to concentrate tonight, yet vital that she do so. . . .

A step behind her, and a light hand on her shoulder; she started, and turned to see Lillanna.

Silently, Lillanna drew breath and laid her hands over the Kel Nira's forehead and chest, and in grateful silence the Kel Nira received her Second's offering—not a great flood this time, but like standing under a gentle waterfall, just long enough for refreshment.

*****

The drums kept up a steady heartbeat outside as the Councillors and their Seconds took their places in the chapel. Last of all the Kel Sharha entered, carried in a chair litter by two warriors. Champion Reshtas stepped forward and tenderly lifted her out, then supported her on her last walk around the chapel. He settled her on the couch, kissed her brow, and took up his position beside her.

The warriors made a quiet exit with the empty litter. The Kel Mona shut and sealed the door behind them as her Second threw a handful of herbs into the hearthfire, making it blaze with green-hearted flames. The smoke spiraled up to the smokehole, but the air thickened nonetheless, so that the oil lamps shone but feebly.

More chanting, and the Kel Nira joined in with the others, her voice pitched lower than usual, roughened already both by emotion and the smoke. It was a wordless chant, and the participants in the ritual all sang what notes came to them naturally, so it was discordant at first. Gradually the tones blended into a harmony that somehow, in its perfect lack of plan, reminded the Kel Nira of the wild forest. She forgot the heat and closeness of the chapel: the Watchers were near, and her heart welcomed them.

The chant ended by mutual, unspoken consent, and Elder Falessan presented the Kel Mona with a chalice. She drank, then carried the wine to each of them, lastly to the Kel Sharha, Reshtas helping her to drink. The fire hissed and flared as the Kel Mona poured the remaining wine into it. She nodded to the Kel Nira; it was time.

The Kel Nira picked up her mortar and pestle. The herbs within were well ground already, but she must offer the mortar to the Kel Sharha for the last, symbolic grinding. She knelt by the couch; she had to take a long breath before her voice would come. At last she managed to push out the ritual words, beginning with the Kel Sharha's full threefold title, and said so that all could hear, "Kel Sula Kel Ma'Sharha Kel Sharha, you have asked me to help you cross this night. Tell me now, in the presence of Chiefs and Elders, Champion and Lawspeaker, if you still choose this time to return to the Mothers."

"I do, Kel Nira."

Silently, the Kel Nira held out the mortar and placed the pestle into the Kel Sharha's hand. The old woman pounded the herbs once, twice, thrice.

"So be it," murmured the Councillors.

The Kel Nira bowed to the Kel Sharha, and carried the mortar and pestle back to their place beside the hearth to set about mixing the herbs with wine and poppy syrup. While she was at her task, the others, one by one, approached the couch and made their farewells.

"Is it ready, Kel Nira?" the Kel Mona asked in her ceremonial voice.

"It is ready." Cradling the cypress-wood cup in both hands, she knelt again beside the Kel Sharha. "First of Mothers, First of the People, you know who I am; the Mothers know; the Watchers know. I stand at the gates of life and death; I see the entering and the leaving, and by the grace of the Mothers I sometimes wield the power of both. I offer you this cup in love, that the gates may open gently for you."

A universal in-drawn breath as the Kel Sharha received the cup and slowly drank. The drums pulsed outside; the fire cracked and hissed.

The Kel Nira took back the empty cup. "Rest well, my Chief," she whispered. It was all she could manage. She got up, bowed, but before she could resume her place, the Kel Sharha caught her hand and squeezed it.

"Beech tree . . . perseveres. Remember."

The Kel Nira nodded, her throat thick. She watched the next part of the ritual dazedly: the Kel Mona's invocatory gestures as she intoned, "From Sula to Jemya, the keeping of the Motherland passes"; the Kel Jemya kneeling beside the Kel Sharha; the Kel Sharha cupping her hands around the Kel Jemya's head.

"Open, and receive," said the Kel Sharha, and her hands shone beneath the dimming oil lamps.

The Kel Nira gasped; she was not the only one. The Mayahara, the power that every Kel Sharha embodied, flowed visibly from the Kel Sharha to the Kel Jemya. It looked like flame; it looked like a river at flood; it looked like a rainbow; it sounded like wind in the treetops and tasted of rain on the wind, and smelled like damp dark earth.

It was done. The Kel Jemya got to her feet unsteadily, staring down at the Kel Sharha in wonder. She bowed, and bowed again, then stepped back as the Kel Mona came to the Kel Sharha's side.

The gate was opening; the Kel Nira felt it, felt the beckoning of the Mothers Beyond and the Kel Sharha's yearning toward them.

The Kel Mona took the dying woman's hands in both her own and said to her, "Kel Sharha, you have given your life to the People, first among us and First of Mothers. In gratitude we give back to you the name you relinquished for our sake. Go, Serelha, to she who called you by this name at your birth. Be reborn to her now in the realm of the Mothers, to take your rest there until this world calls you again. Serelha, we will speak well of you."

A sigh, and Serelha crossed Beyond.

The Kel Nira laid the cypress-wood cup in the fire, and knelt staring into the flames until Lillanna pulled her to her feet and led her from the chapel.

*****

The Council, along with the refugees and all the Sanctuary folk, sat out on the green for the rest of the night. Serelha's pyre had been built on the dais, the fountains covered with stone slabs to keep them pure, and the gathering remained solemn as the body burned. Toward morning, though, people began to reminisce and tell their favorite stories about Serelha; Taras and some of the other Celebrants sang, and the Vintners kept all supplied with wine, drunk unwatered on this occasion.

The Kel Nira took little to drink. All the same, in spite of her best intentions, she caught herself dozing several times throughout the proceedings. And when the fire on the dais died down, she began to shiver, though others remarked on how warm the night was. Treska brought her a shawl, Pieran put his arms around her, and she nodded off yet again.

At last the sun rose, and the Kel Jemya could be publicly acclaimed as the new Kel Sharha. She made some kind of a rousing speech, the Celebrants struck up some kind of an inspiring tune, and, after cheering with all the rest, the Kel Nira said, "I am going home to bed now; come, Treska."

Lillanna followed behind them, unsteady from her wine and leaning on Pieran's arm. The Kel Nira was only vaguely aware of her brother and her Second conversing until Lillanna's voice took on an obstinate tone. The Kel Nira turned in time to hear her say, "Well, that's my opinion: I *do* think it's a pity the keeping of the Motherland didn't pass to the Nira next instead of the Jemya. You *must* agree that your sister would be a much better Kel Sharha than the Kel Jemya."

"Mothers and Watchers forbid," murmured the Kel Nira, and gave Lillanna a look that spoke quite loudly enough to silence her on the subject.

It was with immense relief and gratitude that she finally climbed the stairs to her chamber. Arna met her to help her undress, but the Kel Nira sent her below for a basin of hot water and worked her own way out of the heavily embroidered ceremonial overdress and tunic while she waited for Treska to come up from the workroom. Then she lay facedown on the bed, and fell asleep without a pause—though not for long. She heard her door shut, and opened her eyes.

Treska stood over her, plainly distressed.

"You see why I sent you for bandages and ointment. As soon as Arna brings the water, I need you to wash my back, then dress the injuries."

"She just brought it," Treska stammered out. She hesitated. "Should I use it to purify my hands first?"

"Use the pitcher and basin on my washstand. There is a bottle of spirits there, too; pour a little into your wash water, and the rest into mine."

Having done as she was told, Treska set about dabbing at the Kel Nira's back with a soft piece of linen. The spirits stung, but the Kel Nira knew they concentrated the water's power against impurities; she breathed more deeply and focused on the sensation.

"Perhaps," Treska said, "perhaps . . . maybe you should have Lillanna or Yasma look at these welts, my Chief."

"Are they corrupted?" She did not sense that they were; but then, she was hardly at her best.

"I don't *think* so. But I think a full Healer would do much better for you."

This might be true, but Yasma was something of a gossip, and Lillanna, as Second in the Order, would feel honor-bound to report her Chief's state to the rest of the Council.

"No. I trust only you to see this—and to keep silent about it."

"What about Arna?"

"She saw yesterday, when I bathed before the rite of crossing, and I told her the same: this is not to be spoken of."

"But why? Men do not keep their battle injuries secret, nor do Guardians hide their wounds."

"Warriors and Guardians are expected to take injuries; Healers are not. You tell me, Treska: looking at my back, how do you feel about the Forsteners?"

"I *hate* them. More than ever!"

"Exactly. I will not have the people incited to further hatred and violence, and certainly not on my account." If they knew—especially if they knew the whole of it—the result would be every bit as dreadful as if Prince Dursten had carried out his threat to kill her and hang her naked body from his palisade. To abuse, to defile one of the Ma'Sharha—a Chief, moreover . . . There would never be peace so long as Dursten lived.

And even not knowing the whole of it, the Kel Jemya Kel Sharha had already spoken of justice. Would she even consider listening to Lord Corvalen's offer of peace?

*****

Treska rubbed the ointment over the Kel Nira's raw skin, trying not to imagine how those wounds had been made. And she knew that the injuries went much deeper than the torn flesh. The Kel Nira might be impassive on the outside, but everything inside her screamed pain. Treska knew she was not supposed to hear that screaming, but it had been getting louder and louder. She did not want to think about anything that could have been bad enough to cause that. How could the Forsteners be so cruel? And to the Kel Nira, who was so compassionate that she had even healed one of them! It was all so wrong, it made Treska feel sick to her stomach.

She helped the Kel Nira sit up so that she could wrap the bandages around her, and the Kel Nira tried to make a joke about her new fashion in undergarments. Treska only smiled weakly in response. She turned away to lift a nightrobe off its hook, but she could feel her teacher's attention focusing on her.

As the nightrobe's soft folds settled around the Kel Nira, the screaming inside faded to a whisper. The look she gave Treska almost spoke her concern aloud. It made Treska realize that her own fears and worries were clamoring for attention.

She had been afraid to think about them, but now she had to know. "May I ask you something, my Chief?"

"Of course."

Treska fixed her gaze on the bedside rug, with its delicate design of birds perched in interlaced flowering branches. "It's about Deela. Did they . . . do anything to her?"

"They only killed her, child, and it was quickly over. You need not worry for her; she is well with the Mothers."

"I won't worry, then, but . . . oh, my Chief, I miss her so." The tears started before Treska could even try to hold them back. "I miss her so much."

"Come, Treska." The Kel Nira wrapped an arm around her and pulled her close.

Treska sobbed against her shoulder, while the Kel Nira stroked her hair and made small comforting sounds. It reminded her of how her mother had used to soothe her when she was a little girl and suffered some little hurt. The hurts were so much bigger now. . . .

At length Treska pulled away, sat up straight, and scrubbed at her eyes. "I'm sorry, Lady." She sniffled. "I know I should be more like you and bear it calmly. I'm sorry."

The Kel Nira gave her the smile she used with patients who needed reassuring. "I may not have the luxury of indulging my emotions, Treska, but you are young—it is a luxury you can still afford from time to time, especially in such a case."

"Thank you, my Chief. I . . . I should let you sleep now. You have a Council meeting this twilight, and you'll want your rest beforehand."

"You should also sleep, Treska; you have been awake all night, too."

Treska wished the Kel Nira would let her stay here, curled up on the beautiful rug beside her bed. That was what Treska's mother would have done. But the Kel Nira was not her mother, and Treska could not bring herself to ask for such a favor. Especially not when the Kel Nira had such sorrows of her own. With slow steps, she went to her room, lay down, and stared at Deela's empty bed until the tears came again and she cried herself to sleep.

*****

The Healer's Choice

The Kel Nira slept till the middle of the afternoon. After a good wash (being careful of her bandages) she'd pulled on trousers and tunic, and gone down to her garden to enjoy the sunshine and a light meal. Now she sat in her basket chair among her herbs and flowers, sipping watered wine, tossing crumbs to the pair of doves that had alighted on the other side of the lily pond.

With a trill, the birds took flight, alarmed by heavy footsteps, and Pieran came out of the house and into the garden.

"You're not at work!" Pieran's surprise was genuine; he knew her well.

The Kel Nira smiled. "I went to the House, but Lillanna chased me off. She says I must rest."

"She's right. I could wish, for your sake, that Council was not meeting so soon."

"Ah, that reminds me." She pulled a folded sheet of parchment-cloth from her pocket. "This letter awaited me when I returned. It is from Martos, and Arna said he'd sent one for the Council as well. Will you read this to me, please?" While she could converse fluently in Ghildaran, she was no great reader, especially of foreign languages—the letters seemed to scramble themselves before her eyes. Pieran, on the other hand, might have no ear for an accent, but he could read almost anything put before him.

He accepted the letter and read aloud:

Most revered Kel Nira, greeting from Martos, Viscount of the Fifth District, counselor in diplomacy to His Majesty, Zhorzos of Ghildarna, the Serene.
I have written of these matters to the High Council of Sharhaya as a whole, but I write to you also and privately, in token and honor of our long friendship.

"You'd think that, in token and honor of your long friendship, he wouldn't write so pompously," Pieran remarked. "And he might have considered writing in Sharhay for your sake."

The Kel Nira shrugged. "He is a diplomat, and diplomats all use Ghildaran."

Pieran rolled his eyes, and continued:

His Majesty has considered your Council's renewed petition for aid against the Forstene incursion into your Blessed Country. I regret to inform you that, after due deliberation, His Majesty still concludes that it is not in the interest of our Most Serene Realm to intervene in this conflict.

Pieran swore. "Zhorzos is a—"

"An impious and an ungrateful man." The Kel Nira shook her head. "We expected no different from him—we only hoped for more."

"He wouldn't even be on that throne if the Ma'Sharha hadn't *intervened* in the Ghildaran civil war to help his family."

"Zhorzos is evidently not a man of long memory—that war was in our grandmother's time, after all." The Kel Nira frowned; her words brought back to mind the Kel Sharha's—Serelha's—unsettling counsel. *Serelha must have known my grandmother; I wish I had asked her to tell me more.* A useless regret, of course.

She looked up to see Pieran regarding her with an expression of respectful and only slightly curious patience; he was used to her dropping into silent thoughtfulness. She smiled, and motioned to him to resume reading.

There: that is the official version, for which I am most sorry. Indeed, I can scarcely express my regret that all of my efforts—and I have worked at this problem from the most unlikely angles, I assure you—have come to naught. I know what you will say, and justly. I myself can say little more, for I have but small expectation that my letters will actually achieve their destination, as things stand.

But in the hope that this does reach you, allow me only to say further that, in any circumstance whatsoever, you and your worthy brother—and whoever else might attend on you—may expect every welcome and hospitality in the Mansion of the Fifth District. My good lady wife bids me add that she would rejoice to see you again, and that she meanwhile prays every day to the Golden Mothers for you—as do we all.

Your servant, and most respectful devoted friend,
Martos

Pieran stared at the letter for several heartbeats before refolding it. As he handed it back, he said, "Perhaps you should accept his invitation, Kel Nira. I fear for you, if the Forsteners prevail."

"I fear for us all. But I will not leave Sharhaya. Would you?"

"No, but my duty is to stay and fight—to the last, if need be."

"And mine is to heal—even beyond the last. Nor would it be honorable in me to leave; I am Chief, and must set the example for my Order. You know this."

Pieran fell silent, chewing on his lower lip. She could tell that, in spite of what she'd said, he was working himself up to argue her into fleeing, so she forestalled him. "Listen, Pieran. We spent so much of our childhood in Ghildarna that when we first came back, we did not feel at home in our own country—I could not even speak our language properly! But now our roots are in the land. This is where we belong, where all our love is. Even if it were not my duty to stay, I would not leave Sharhaya. I could not."

"Not even to save your life?"

"It would be worthless to me, anywhere but here."

Chapter Thirteen

Twilight, and the Councillors gathered once more in the chapel. The hearth held only a token fire, and all four doors stood open to let in any breeze that might happen to stir in the balmy evening. Still, much of the previous night's heaviness clung about the Councillors as they stood by their cushions, their Seconds behind them, awaiting the new Kel Sharha.

The Kel Nira had brought with her a folding fan, and she opened it now. The other Chiefs had unlaced the sleeves from their tunics, but she had felt the need to cover the burns and bruises on her arms— probably a foolish indulgence, since the cuts and bruises on her face, though healing well, remained eminently visible. Now in the heat of the chapel, she regretted her long sleeves extremely, not to mention the added weight of the embroidery and assorted bits of official regalia. But everyone else had their ceremonial robes on, too, and before long others were bringing out their own fans.

The Kel Sharha arrived at last, and circled the chapel to exchange bows with each Councillor in turn. Once she took her place, the Kel Mona stepped forward to invite the Watchers to bear witness to the Council's actions, that the Councillors might be ever mindful of their duty to the Mothers, the People, and the Land.

"So be it," everyone responded, and looked expectantly to the Kel Sharha.

The Kel Jemya Kel Sharha was nothing if not expeditious; she moved forward into the evening's business without pause. "The Listeners are without a Chief," she said, in the ritual formula. "Who will fill that place?"

The other Councillors seated themselves, leaving only Taja standing.

"First of Mothers, I will fill that place," said Taja, and took a trembling step toward the Kel Sharha.

The Kel Nira watched the ceremony, but in her mind she heard again the words of her own investiture, as clearly as if eight years had not passed—the voice of the old Kel Sharha strong and vital, her own voice quavering under the weight of the burden she was accepting:

"Healer, by what name are you called?"

"Finoora is the name with which my mother greeted me."

"That name binds you to the life of attachment and personal desires. No woman may be a Chief of the Ma'Sharha who is so bound. Will you renounce that life and lay aside the name that symbolizes it? For the Mothers of the People call you to their service."

"I am a nameless one, and offer my life to serve the People."

"I am a nameless one, and offer my life to serve the People," Taja whispered—but no longer Taja, now: Kel Sula.

"On behalf of the People, I accept your offering," intoned the Kel Sharha. "And know that as a Chief of the Ma'Sharha, you may one day be called to stand in the place I now fill." She took the Kel Sula's face between her hands. "Here I set the channel for the Mayahara, that you may open and receive when your time comes."

The Kel Sula's eyelids fluttered; her eyes rolled back. The Kel Nira well remembered this part of her own initiation as Chief: the chain of rapid sensations from sudden heat to deep chill to black senselessness, then the scent of earth and the sound of running water, and her head feeling pinpricked all over.

The Kel Sharha dropped her hands; the Kel Sula's eyes closed, and she sagged with a long exhale.

All was still for several heartbeats as the two women regathered themselves. The Kel Mona offered a chalice to the Kel Sharha, then to the Kel Sula, pronouncing, "Whatever comes, the Mayahara finds its channel, always flowing, from Chief to Chief. The rite is done."

The others responded, "So be it," and each drank from the chalice in turn to seal the ceremony.

Next came the matter of the Champion. People sat straighter or leaned forward; no one knew what to expect from the new Kel Sharha on this. It was entirely possible that she would dismiss Reshtas and ask for the nomination of a new Champion. But what a time to contemplate such a change.

The Kel Sharha motioned Reshtas to stand, giving him a hard stare. At length she said, "Many a year has passed since the hunt councils proposed you as Champion, Reshtas, and many a year you have served the People since you were accepted by the Kel Sharha who last stood here. You have shared in the Mayahara through her, and are therefore bound to the service of Sharhaya."

Reshtas held himself expressionless, but his shoulders slumped, and he looked all of his fifty-odd winters. The Kel Nira knew it was beyond difficult for him to see another in Serelha's place—he had been devoted to her from first to last, and now to have this loss added to all his other burdens . . .

The Kel Jemya Kel Sharha's look softened; her next words were delivered in almost gentle tones. "You have served well, Reshtas, and are deserving of rest from your labors. I can release you from your bond—but I would rather not. Sharhaya is in too much danger, and a trusted, proven Champion . . . That is to say, we need you, Reshtas, and I hope you will continue your service."

"I will, First of Mothers. My life belongs to the Mothers, to the People, and to the Land."

"So be it," came the unified response, and the chalice circled among the Councillors again.

"The High Council is complete," said the Kel Sharha, "and it is well. We have much to plan tonight, for tomorrow we must attack the Forsteners, before that new army can settle in." As she seated herself, some of the Councillors exchanged looks or whispers with their neighbors.

The Kel Nira shifted on her cushion, aware of Pieran's gaze on her. Slowly, deliberately, she folded her fan and lay it beside her.

"Now, what I have in mind is this," began the Kel Sharha.

The Kel Nira cleared her throat. "I beg your pardon, First of Mothers, but I have information—"

"We are all eager to know what you learned in the Forstene camp, Kel Nira, and will hear you in due time."

"I ask the Council to hear me now, please. I have a . . ." She swallowed. "I have a message from . . . from Corvalen of Brintora."

That got everyone's attention, and no one troubled to keep their reaction to a whisper.

Reshtas's voice carried over all the others. "The Scourge of Cheskara is *here*?"

"He is the commander of the new army."

"We'd heard rumor of this—but our scouts have had that army under observation, and none have been able to confirm the Scourge's presence."

"He rode ahead; he was in the camp on Summer Bluff when I was there."

"You saw him?"

"And spoke with him. As I said, he gave me a message for the Council."

"Very well," said the Kel Sharha. "Let us hear it, then."

The Kel Nira hesitated. She could not bring herself to tell them Lord Corvalen's original message—to surrender to the overlordship of Forstene or be destroyed. No, for a variety of reasons, she could not deliver such a blunt ultimatum. "He has brought terms of peace," she said slowly. "He will tell them to us at the ford, the morning after tomorrow."

"Indeed? And what if we will not hear his terms?"

"He says his army will burn its way through the forest to the Sanctuary."

Almost everyone in the chapel had been at the Winter Sanctuary when it was attacked, and some—including herself and the Kel Jemya Kel Sharha—had barely managed to escape. Lord Corvalen's threat bore serious consideration, and silence hung over the meeting for many heartbeats.

"Well," said the Kel Sharha, "all the more reason to strike when he's not expecting it, and disable his army before he can attempt anything of the kind."

Reshtas's brows drew down. "That army will not be easy to disable—maybe impossible."

"Some people did not think it would be possible to rescue the Kel Nira from the Forstene camp—but it was done."

Pieran nodded; as a Second, however, he was in Councilonly to observe and assist and could not speak unless invited to do so.

The Kel Mona joined the discussion. "I thank the Mothers and Watchers that we succeeded in bringing back the Kel Nira. And yet, we hardly disabled the army on the bluff. With the mists, with Pieran's horse troop, and with the surprise and the distraction of the archers' attack at the other side of their camp, we were able to achieve what we intended. But I don't know that we could have done more."

There was no point in letting this go on. The Kel Nira drew a deep breath, ignoring the ache in her ribs. "I gave my word," she said.

The Kel Sharha stared at her. "You what?"

"I gave my word that we would hear Lord Corvalen's proposals."

"By what authority?" Reshtas shouted, and at the same time the Kel Sharha said, "How could you—what gave you the right—?"

Something in the Kel Sharha's manner broke the Kel Nira's restraint; she was on her feet before she realized. "*This* gave me the right!" She gestured to her scarred face, to her black eye. "And these!"

She pushed up her sleeves, showing the bruises and the bandaged burns; she pulled off her bracelets and held out her wrists, where the raw marks of ropes were still to be seen.

She was trembling, but she cared nothing now for the other Councillors' looks and exclamations of pity, outrage, dismay. "I know what it is to suffer at the Forsteners' hands—and I have not suffered the worst. When is the last time any of you visited the House of Healing? If you saw every day what I do—bodies crushed by the hooves of the Forstene warhorses, limbs hacked through, eyes gouged out—"

As she paused to draw breath, Reshtas said, his voice quieter now but still forceful, "I have seen as much as you, Kel Nira, and I like it no more than you do. But this is the cost of defending ourselves. The warriors know what sacrifices they may be called to make."

"I am not speaking only of warriors. I am speaking of children, infants, women with child, old women and men. Ask those refugees out there what they have seen and suffered!"

The Lawspeaker cleared his throat and ran a hand through his shining gray hair as he got to his feet. "Kel Nira, I grant you—I think we all grant you—that your recent experience endows you with even more than your usual authority. And no one can fail to appreciate the difficult position you must have found yourself in. I, for one, do not wonder that you consented to hear terms of peace, especially when faced so closely with the might of Forstene."

"Thank you, Tigannas. And indeed, all I gave my word to was that we would *listen* to Lord Corvalen's proposals."

"That seems only reasonable," put in Elder Rimenna. She looked to Reshtas and the Kel Sharha. "Where is the harm in hearing what he has to say?"

"The harm is in the time and opportunity we will lose," the Kel Sharha said. "And besides, what possible peace settlement can the Forsteners offer us that will be acceptable? You of all people, Kel Nira, by those very injuries that you display—those Forsteners beat and tortured you; they killed your apprentice—how can you even consider making peace with them?"

"They hurt me, yes; they killed Deela." These words were hard to get out, and her voice came quietly now. "I do not want them to hurt anyone else, to kill anyone else's dear ones. I want our people to live."

"Without freedom?" Reshtas asked.

"Freedom with despair," said the new Kel Sula unexpectedly, "or survival with hope?"

Into the silence that followed, the Kel Nira said, "The Scourge's army is ready to crush us utterly, and even if any of us survive, what hope of freedom—or anything else—are we likely to have then? A treaty, even if its terms are harsh, will let us hope, so long as it lets us live."

The Kel Sharha folded her arms. "Say, then, that we do give ear to these treaty terms. Do you really believe the Scourge of Cheskara can be trusted?"

"He is a ruthless man, and I believe him when he says that he will destroy Sharhaya if we refuse to treat with him. I also believe he is an honorable man, and that he will abide by any terms he gives us."

"And you can say this, even after the treatment you received at his hands?"

"It was not he that did this, but common soldiers, of the prince's army." This was mostly true; until the last, the prince had not laid hands on her himself, but had only given the orders—and smiled as they were carried out.

Memory assaulted her: she was alone in that miserable tent again, bound to a stout pole at the center. But the soldiers had gone out—to refresh themselves, no doubt, having worked up a thirst flogging and insulting her. She must have passed out, or perhaps she'd actually fallen asleep, in spite of all. She came to consciousness screaming, with hot iron burning into her skin. The next thing she knew, she'd been dragged to the prince's pavilion. She'd said no word, made no sound in response to her interrogators before now, and he was delighted—delighted!—that they'd finally gotten something out of her. How had they done it? They demonstrated: knife blade heated in candle flame, then pressed into her arm. Dursten laughed as they did it yet again, and she bit her lip until the blood streamed to keep from crying out.

O Mothers, O Watchers! She forced herself away from the recollection, smoothing her sleeves over her arms, ashamed that she had made a show of her injuries. What had she been thinking?

The debate carried on around her. "We are finally learning how to fight them!" "Finally, but too late. There are too many of them now." "They don't know the forests; we do." "The trees will be bare in a few months, even if they're not burned; what protection will they give us then?" "Surely with the new powers the Summoners have found—" "We don't know the full extent or costs of those powers yet."

The Kel Nira's back was to the west door, and a breeze—a strong one—was finally sighing through it. She could hear the tree leaves. . . . She looked across the hearth to the Kel Sula, who was also silent, listening—not to the discussion, judging by the tilt of her head and abstraction in her eyes, but to the trees.

Gradually the others were drawn in by the Kel Sula's stillness. Ingas, the Elder of the Artisans' Guild, leaned toward her, asking in his breathy voice, "What do the trees say, Kel Sula?"

"They say that to fight tomorrow is to fight the current. But there is no meeting the enemy without cost, whether to do battle or to treat with him."

"Which course has the greater cost, then?" asked the Kel Sharha.

The Kel Sula shook her head. "The Watchers do not know. There are other forces at work. . . ."

The Kel Nira clenched her fists to suppress a shiver. She could hear Serelha again, on that long-ago-seeming day when she'd left for her last field duty: *"There are other forces. . . . You have shifted your fate, Finoora, and they will see that it keeps to its new course."*

But hers was not the only fate that had shifted. What had she brought upon her people?

*****

Corvalen inspected his army with immense satisfaction. The encampment was as neat as he could wish, the men cheerful and busy, the horses full of vim. "Well done, Rindal; you've led the army up in fine form."

"Thank you, my lord. The camp is situated to your liking, then?"

Corvalen nodded. The tents, in their orderly grids, marched far down the valley in the south and stopped just out of bow range of the forest in the east, where the last pickets were now going up. The northern perimeter of the camp was roughly half a mile below the ford, which left plenty of room at the upper end of the valley for exercising the horses, drilling the men, and, perhaps, mustering for battle. On the west the river, now dappled pink and gold under the sunset, offered all the fresh water an army could desire.

He strolled up the riverbank, calling out greetings to the men, happy to be among his own soldiers again. Every now and then he and Rindal exchanged observations about the terrain or the weather, speculating on the likelihood of rain during the night. Then Rindal said, "Is it true, my lord, that we will really see the Kel Sharha tomorrow? It's been a great topic of curiosity among the men."

"The Kel Nira told Rossen that she would bring the Council, and I presume that includes the Kel Sharha."

"Their whole council? These barbarians are very trusting folk, aren't they?"

"I did my best to convince the Kel Nira that she could trust in my honor; it is a quality they, too, value. They will come here in peace, and we will receive them in peace."

Rindal looked faintly disappointed. "Then we won't draw up for battle?"

"On the contrary, we will be fully battle ready, cavalry to the fore." He swept his arm to indicate the open area below the ford. "Let the men look as intimidating as they can; I want these Sharhay to be in no doubt about the advisability of accepting our treaty."

"And if they don't accept it, my lord? Then we fight?"

"Yes; then we fight."

Corvalen thought about this later as he returned to his pavilion in the center of the camp. When he had answered Rindal, he had felt his spirits rise at the prospect of action. Eager anticipation—that was what he had felt. Here he had the best army in the Five Lands and, by Vallar, he wanted to take it into battle. All the preparation—the training, the provisioning, the long march—all of it, right down to the mending of harness and polishing of armor—it had but one end: to mount horse, draw sword, and kill as many of the king's enemies as he could, leading his men after him to do the same. That was what they were made for; that was their purpose.

King Delanar knew this as well as anyone. Was Dursten right, then—did the king in fact want Corvalen to crush the Sharhay? The treaty certainly contained a number of harsh provisions, any one of which might be enough to make the Sharhay reject it. Delanar had given Corvalen and the prince some room to negotiate, but there was much on which he was immovable. He was, perhaps, pessimistic about their success—the Sharhay were notoriously stubborn.

Or perhaps Delanar did not care at all, one way or the other, so long as the war ended and Sharhaya bowed to the overlordship of Forstene.

Corvalen sat down at his camp table and sighed. "'The worthy man does not lightly draw his sword,'" he murmured, reaching for his icon case. He contemplated the image of Vallar until it grew too dark to make out more than the faint glint of the gold leaf. Putting away the icon at last, he remembered another of Vallar's sayings: "A man never feels so much alive as he does on the edge of death."

He lit a candle lantern, then began to sort through the rolls of parchment on the table. His hand came to rest on a small scroll of particularly fine vellum. He smiled as he opened it. He never tired of looking at this, though he knew its words by heart. It was a copy of the ancient "Blessing on the Man Who Fares in Lands Abroad,"written out in elegant calligraphy—Mellis's laboriously made gift to him when he departed on this campaign. He sighed again. Mellis would be a woman before another summer or two passed, no doubt with many suitors eager for her blessings. He must treasure his daughter's girlish devotion while he could.

A hesitant voice disturbed his reverie. "My lord?"

"Rossen, come in; sit down."

"I bring wine—which is well, I think. You are not cheerful, my lord."

"Oh, just thinking."

"Plotting strategy?"

Corvalen smiled. "In a sense—though not for battle. I was thinking that I will soon need to choose a husband for Mellis."

Rossen chuckled. "Far be it from me to contradict you, my lord, but I think perhaps you *are* facing a battle there. Mellis has been a long time with Lady Ardalis, after all, and, I think, has begun to take after her."

"I have observed that they are both of them very decided in their opinions."

"And your sister's feelings on marriage are particularly decided."

Corvalen rubbed at his beard, remembering all the trouble over his nieces' betrothals. "Why Ardalis is so adamant on the matter, I cannot fathom. Our father chose her a good husband, and their marriage was a happy one."

"Yet even I have heard her declare—loudly, and more than once—that no young girl should be married to an old man, as she was."

"He was in fact a man of only middle years—although still much older than she, of course. But what of that? If she had had her own choice from among her suitors, and had chosen a man of her own age, who can say if she would have been happier? Time could well have taken her from desire to disappointment, but instead took her from duty to love. Well, friendship, at any rate."

"True as that may be, I think you'll still have a hard job convincing either your sister or your daughter that an arranged marriage can ever be preferred to a love match."

Corvalen was starting to feel decidedly cross. "Then I must presume that they have both of them spent far too much time listening to the minstrels; perhaps I should ban the fellows altogether."

"Come, my lord; you cannot mean that. And you must admit that your Brintoran minstrels at least know how to compose a decent song. Only listen to this thing that was making the rounds in Barasel the last time I was there." Rossen struck a pose and sang, his expressive voice doing full justice to the lugubrious melody:

"Her knight clung to the garden gate,
Brought low by a frowning fate.
'Why, oh, why could you not wait?
Our love was pledged so long!'

She could not speak, but only moan,
'Too many years I spent alone.
My life was harder than a stone—
You left me for too long!'

Too long he watched her where she stood,
Till he lost all hope for good.
'I'll have no more of drink or food;
Farewell, my love, so long!'"

"Rossen, that is truly *awful*. 'My life was harder than a stone'? Dreadful; by Vallar, dreadful!" He laughed heartily, sharing Rossen's merriment.

At the same time, he was thinking, *What an excellent, good-humored young man he is.* And he remembered that when Rossen had first joined his service, Mellis had puppy-dogged after him around the castle for days, announcing to anyone who would listen that she intended to marry him when she grew up. *I wonder. . . .*

From outside came the sound of more singing: the hymn to the Guide Star.

Hail, O Star, thou guiding light
Whom Stennar knew for sign of fate. . . .

As the hymn ended, Rindal's strong baritone began a ballad about Vallar's Fifth Deed, the holding back of the sea. Still smiling, Corvalen rolled up Mellis's parchment and put it carefully away. Then he and Rossen went out to join in the choruses.

Chapter Fourteen

As Corvalen's horse splashed into the ford, a heron that had been fishing in the shallows on the other side stretched out its neck, spread its wings, and took to the air. Corvalen admired its flight till his attention was drawn by movement across the river: Dursten and a band of retainers were coming around the base of the bluff. Corvalen glanced over his shoulder to exchange a nod of satisfaction with Rossen, for Dursten's escort, like his own, were all spearmen and swordsmen. He had not forgotten the prince's ill-considered words about bringing a party of crossbowmen to the ford, and he was relieved that Dursten had evidently been in a more sober frame of mind when selecting the men to accompany him for this parley.

Indeed, the prince's mood as Corvalen joined him below the bluff was quietly genial. After exchanging salutes and greetings of the day, they sat their horses side by side, looking toward the river and the forest in an easy and even companionable silence.

The sun had just broken over the treetops; the early-morning light turned the grassy riverbanks golden green and vivid. Corvalen wondered if he could find words adequate to describe the colors, the clarity of the morning air, the sense of expectation . . . but no, it would take a better poet than he to do it all justice.

A light breeze, blowing from the south, carried the pleasant sounds of men and horses as the ranks of Corvalen's cavalry, commanded by Rindal, took their places a short distance from the ford.

"A fresh army, well drawn up—a fine sight on a summer's morning," Dursten said, with perhaps a note of wistfulness in his voice. "I'm afraid my men will not look so handsome when they take the field."

Corvalen thought of saying, *If all goes well today, they will not have to take the field*, but instead replied, "They have had near three years of hard campaigning, Your Highness. That does tend to wear on men, horses, and arms."

"Still, their spears shine bright enough." Dursten twisted in his saddle to look up at the top of the bluff, and Corvalen followed his gaze. The climbing sun burnished a solid line of spearheads up there, and as Corvalen watched, another line of spearmen fell in behind the first, and then another.

"Very fine," he said. The ford was well out of spear range, of course, but the ranks of soldiers atop the bluff would make a daunting spectacle for the Sharhay.

Dursten was fidgeting with a chain around his neck; after a bit, he pulled it off and regarded the medallion depending from it. "Did I ever thank you for bringing me this?"

Corvalen saw that it was the new portrait medallion of young Prince Heldar. "I was but the messenger; it is your good wife who deserves the thanks."

"Yes, I must write to her. . . ." Dursten contemplated the bronze profile of his son for some time, during which his mind seemed to travel a winding path, for when he looked up again he said, "Heldar the Unifier was twenty-two years old when he conquered Brintora. No offense intended, Corvalen."

"None taken. I am, after all, only Brintoran by blood on my mother's side."

"Well, you're still more fortunate in your maternal line than I."

Corvalen knew that if the prince were permitted to follow this thought along its usual course, he would soon launch into a diatribe on the subject of female treachery—not a promising prelude for the coming meeting. Grasping for something that would deflect him, he said, "We both of us have reason to look back on the Brintoran campaign with pride, Your Highness."

"Oh yes." Dursten's frown cleared. "Your great-grandfather was something in my great-grandfather's army, wasn't he?"

"He was the Exalted Heldar's Lord Marshal, in fact, and made Baron of Brintora for his service in that war."

"They must often have sat their horses together, as we do now. How odd history is," the prince mused. He looked down at the medallion again. "In five days I shall be twenty-two, you know. So if this goes well, I shall still make my first conquest younger than the Unifier made his. And the kingdom I pass on to my son will be greater than that inherited by any previous king of Forstene. That'll be something fine, won't it, Corvalen?"

"It is a noble ambition, Your Highness." When the prince was in this mood, it was hard not to feel something like friendship for him. But Corvalen had seen enough of his other moods to know this one would not last.

Yet it was Corvalen whose good nature faltered first. As Dursten was tucking his medallion and its chain under his gambeson, Esban and two other riders rounded the base of the bluff. "What is he doing here?" Corvalen asked.

"In case we need a translator, of course." Dursten raised his voice to hail Esban. "Well, good morning there! Finally slept it off, did you? How's your head?" He laughed.

Esban laughed, too, but looked none too happy to be out under the bright morning sun.

The sun climbed higher and the day grew hotter as they waited for the Sharhay to appear. Corvalen had insisted that Esban wait in the back rank until he was needed, but his voice carried forward, whining about the heat. Corvalen, sweating in gambeson and mail, glanced back reprovingly; Esban wasn't wearing so much as a jerkin over his light tunic.

"Some people will always complain," murmured Rossen, on Corvalen's right. "In truth, though, it *is* hot. I don't know how those fellows back there with him can bear to keep their cloaks on."

"Some men would rather be uncomfortable than unfashionable, I suppose," Corvalen replied, absently noting the men's deep-dyed, scallop-edged cloaks.

Rossen grinned. "If those fellows are suffering for fashion, they're suffering in vain—alas, to be both uncomfortable *and* unfashionable!"

Corvalen gave his aide half a smile, but he was becoming ever more aware of Dursten's burgeoning impatience. If only the Sharhay had arrived earlier, when the prince had been relaxed and affable. The longer he had to wait, the more irritable he was going to get, and the less smoothly this meeting was likely to go. With such reflections preying on him, Corvalen found himself growing impatient, too. It was with a sense of relief that he discerned movement at the edge of the forest.

"At last," said the prince. "I thought they would keep us waiting here all day."

"The morning is hardly gone, Your Highness," Corvalen replied. "And we do not know how far they had to ride."

"Oh, well, I suppose we should get ready to meet them." Dursten pulled up his coif and beckoned to his squire for his helm, an impressive thing with constellations worked in gilded bronze on the crest, cheekguards, and nasal. Corvalen preferred plain iron, and no massive cheekguards to interfere with his peripheral vision. They urged their horses forward, and halted at the river's edge.

As the Sharhay drew nearer, the sight of the Holy Women, most of them bare-armed and all of them riding astride, occasioned some muttered commentary from the Forstene soldiers. "Silence in the ranks!" Corvalen called back, although he was morally certain that the rude remarks he'd heard had come from Dursten's men, not his.

The Sharhay councillors were accompanied by an honor guard, women in green tunics and brown overdresses, to all appearances armed—if one could call it that—with no more than wooden staves. Three rode in front, three in back, and two on each side of the councillors. And Sharhaya's High Council itself: four women in the green robes of the Ma'Sharha, each in a different-colored overdress; another woman, rather stout, with an hourglass-shaped drum slung from a shoulder strap—she and the two men who rode either side of her must be the heads of the Greater Guilds, Corvalen thought; a slight, soberly dressed man with gray hair, probably the official they called their Lawspeaker; and a powerfully built man in leather armor, who could be none other than the Champion of Sharhaya.

Many of the women, and the two Guildsmen, were wearing broad-brimmed straw hats against the sun—hats unfortunately similar to those most often seen in Forstene on the heads of farm laborers.

"Can a nation really be governed by such as these?" said Dursten sotto voce, and the aide to his left answered, "It is a barbarian nation, Highness; what more natural than a barbarian government?" Dursten sniggered.

"Your Highness," Corvalen murmured, but let it go at that. He was trying to make out the Kel Nira's expression, but she was still too far away. Her posture as she rode was straight and proud, but not easy. There was tension in the set of her shoulders—and indeed, an air of apprehension seemed to hang about the entire Sharhay party. He could hardly blame them.

Movement at the forest edge caught his eye again: men with longbows, stepping out from the shelter of the trees. Near two hundred, Corvalen estimated. But as they formed ranks, he saw that in fact only one in four actually carried a bow. And they were too far from the ford to be much of a threat in any case. Still, they made a good showing. Corvalen did not blame the Sharhay for that, either.

"Esban!" Dursten called, and when he came forward asked, "Which is the Kel Sharha?"

Corvalen, in spite of himself, looked over, and saw Esban peer, frown, and shake his head. "She is not here; she is an old woman, a Listener."

"What does that signify?"

"She would be wearing black over her green. But, you see, the *kel*—pardon, I mean the chief—in black is much younger."

Dursten glowered. "Shall we stand for this insult? Here am I, Heir of the Blood of Stennar, kept waiting in the sun, and this barbarian queen will not bestir herself from her woods?"

Corvalen tried to conciliate him. "Being old, Your Highness, perhaps she was not strong enough to make the ride."

"Now that's a thought," said Dursten. "Old, weak, sick—ready to fall!"

"No," said Esban, with sudden decisiveness. "She has died, it must be, and the Kel Jemya has succeeded her. She has the brown dress over her green, and the cloak she wears—always the Kel Sharha wears a garment of that color, you see."

The woman Esban indicated was riding next to the Kel Nira, and now Corvalen saw that she had a russet cloak thrown back from her shoulders. She was tall and muscular, and had such an air of strength and authority that Corvalen was surprised he had not recognized her for the Kel Sharha without being told.

The honor guard and most of the Councillors drew up a little way from the river. The Kel Sharha and the Champion continued forward. As they reached the river's edge, Corvalen urged his horse into the ford to meet them, and beside him the prince did the same.

The first words of the formal greeting were on Corvalen's lips, when he heard a sound behind him. In that moment he could not put a name to it. The next moment brought the thud of a crossbow bolt embedding in flesh.

With a strangled cry, Sharhaya's Champion fell from his horse, the bolt protruding from his eye. He was dead when he hit the ground.

Corvalen shouted—what, he could never remember afterward. But it was too late. Another bolt was already flying. It struck the Kel Sharha, and she, too, fell.

*****

Shocked silence from some of the Councillors, screams from most—but the Kel Nira had only one thought. She leapt from her saddle and dashed forward, ignoring the cries that followed her. A spear hurtled past. She threw herself to the ground and crawled the last few feet to the Kel Sharha's side.

The Kel Jemya Kel Sharha's face was distorted in a grotesque expression. She gasped for air, blood flowing from the corner of her mouth. It was like the face the Kel Nira had seen in her nightmares for so many years. She shook off the horror, and reached her mind to pour out Nihara. But the moment she placed her hands, she knew that the First of Mothers was beyond healing.

"Healer," the Kel Sharha said in a voice that the Kel Nira could just hear if she bent close. "It seems . . . the land must pass . . . from my keeping." With effort, she raised her hands and cupped them around the Kel Nira's head. "Open, and receive," she commanded.

There was no resisting. The Kel Nira hollowed herself as if she were preparing to channel Nihara, and spun out of time. The Kel Jemya Kel Sharha's hands on her were cold, yet burned. The Kel Nira could feel her fellow Chief's pulses, and each straining beat pumped out power, energy—the Mother-strength of the land, that which the Kel Sharha embodied. The Kel Nira had watched this process from the outside, only days before, but living it, receiving the Mayahara, was like nothing she could have imagined. Its power was far, far beyond that of Nihara, even at its strongest. The Mayahara was the imperative of the land, of the people who belonged to it, and of the long centuries of their belonging. She was part of that belonging—and now, embracing the power that thundered into her, she was its summation.

Just as she thought she was utterly filled with the power of the Kel Sharha, the First of the People and the First of Mothers, she felt some other force insinuating itself into acquiescing corners of her being, an energy that vibrated as a faint harmonic, holding echoes of something familiar but unremembered. She thought she heard the Kel Jemya Kel Sharha's voice: *Receive this, too; it is your birthright, though it was taken from you.*

Then came a moment when her whole being completed its long inward breath. She exhaled, and plummeted back into moving time.

She found herself staring into the glazed dead eyes of the Kel Sharha. But beyond this still point where death had settled, there was a storm of running, shouting, fighting. Her sense of disorientation dissolved with the realization that her people were under attack.

She stood. "Kel Mona!" All she could think was that her friend should raise the mists, conceal the remaining Councillors from their enemies. "Kel Mona!" She looked about, and finally saw the Kel Mona struggling toward her, a crossbow bolt in her arm.

The Kel Nira ran to her and caught her as she stumbled. She eased her to the ground and began to pull her clothing away from the wound.

The Kel Mona pushed her away. "You must not trouble yourself with me now, Kel Sharha."

For a moment she lost her sense of time and place again, and it seemed she could hear generations of Lawspeakers chanting: *From the Mona to the Sula, from the Sula to the Jemya, from the Jemya to the Nira—so the passing is ordained for the keeping of the Motherland. . . .*

"From Jemya to Nira, the keeping of the Motherland passes," said the Kel Mona.

"Oh, dear Mothers," the Kel Nira whispered. Only now did her mind fully comprehend what had passed between her and the Kel Jemya Kel Sharha.

The Kel Mona grimaced. "Go on! My wound is not mortal, but we will all die here unless you do something soon!"

It was true. Standing up again, the Kel Nira tried to school herself to her new role. Swiftly but fervently, she called on the Mothers and Watchers to give her aid.

She took in the situation. Most of the honor guard were in the ford, matching their ironwood staves against Forstene swords. The other Guardians were trying to herd the rest of the Councillors back toward the forest. Beyond them, the archers had just been given the order to attack; Pieran was at their head as they ran forward to take position.

The Forsteners across the river jostled at one another, some pushing their way to the ford and others seeming to hold them back. Lord Corvalen was in their midst, shouting; what he was trying to accomplish, she could not tell. The prince had pulled back from the fray, and called to a band of spearmen scrambling down the bluff.

All this she saw in a moment's sweeping glance. And then she turned to the Forstene army on her side of the river, Lord Corvalen's army. So far they were holding their position, though the horses stamped, and every man had drawn his sword. This cavalry was all that Lord Corvalen had said it was—and she saw that the commander had his eye on Pieran and his warbands.

A cry from the ford: one of the Guardians was down, and four more Forsteners were charging into the river; the remaining Guardians were outnumbered now two to one.

A battle horn sounded from the head of the cavalry. Instinctively, the Kel Nira knew that a second blast would be the signal to charge. The lines of knights were poised to run down not only the warbands but the retreating Councillors, too. She must act now.

What could she do? Her powers of healing were utterly useless in this situation. She was forbidden to touch weapons—and there were none to hand in any case. But . . . there was that other small, anomalous talent of hers. She picked out a likely horse and reached her mind to it. It would not be charmed, so she tickled and taunted till it began to prance and buck. The second horse was easier, the third was even eager to do her bidding. Before many moments had passed, she had more than a dozen horses dancing with agitation, a few throwing their riders.

It was enough confusion to keep the knights from advancing for a bit. Now to make the most of the time she had borrowed.

She called her own horse to her, leapt astride, touched her heels to the creature's flanks, and rode for the Sharhay line. She raised one hand and shouted, "Hold!"—over and over, her only hope being that if the archers withdrew, the knights would not charge. At last she heard Pieran take up her cry and saw him lift his hand in a signal to halt the advance. Silently, she thanked her brother for trusting her.

She turned her mount to see the cavalry commander riding before the front line of knights in similar fashion, calling them to order; thank the Watchers, they were sheathing their swords.

But still the Guardians were struggling in the ford, though their opponents were fewer. Without thought, she rode for the river, shrieking like the high winter wind. As her horse splashed into the churning, bloodied water, she did something she had never known she could do—nor did she know just how she did it—but she focused her scream and made of the sound a lash, and with a sweep of her arm she wielded it to part the ironwood staves and the iron swords. The air reverberated; the river rose up between the Guardians and the Forsteners, and as it settled, she was between them herself, her horse rearing away from the sword blades.

A spear came down in the water next to her, but at the same moment Lord Corvalen bellowed a command. The Forsteners hesitated, and Lord Corvalen shouted again. They withdrew to the riverbank, and scabbarded their blades. At another word from Lord Corvalen, the spearmen laid their weapons down in the grass.

The Kel Nira Kel Sharha allowed herself a sigh of relief, and then another as she saw a field surgeon and his assistants hurrying from Pieran's lines to tend to the Kel Mona and the other wounded Sharhay. She bowed her head as the men retrieved the bodies of the Champion and the former Kel Sharha. For many heartbeats, stillness reigned.

The silence was broken by Prince Dursten's voice. "Councillors and warriors of Sharhaya, your leaders are dead! In the name of King Delanar of Forstene, I command you to surrender."

The Kel Sharha's head snapped up. She felt an anger welling in her such as she had seldom felt before. She faced the prince straight on and, the newly wakened power making theForstene words comewith ease, called out in her strongest voice: "Sharhaya is not leaderless, for I am First among the People now. What is the name of your king to us? We will never surrender our freedom to men without honor—rather will we make you beg *us* for terms of peace!"

She threw a final icy glare at the Forsteners, then made to rejoin her council.

Lord Corvalen called after her, and she heard his horse splashing into the ford. "Lady, please, do not ride away yet!"

She turned back, sitting up even straighter in her saddle. "Why should I not? Our Council came here in good faith to hear terms of peace, but you have brought treachery. Your honor is a lie!"

"No, Lady—I swear it! Look: even now, those who killed your leaders are in the custody of my men."

She followed his gesture and saw that it appeared to be so. "Kel Sula!" she called over her shoulder. To Lord Corvalen she said, "We will see for ourselves if these are the men responsible. Bring them to us."

Lord Corvalen beckoned to his men, who hauled the prisoners forward. They struggled briefly, but paled and went still under the Kel Sharha's gaze.

Dursten rode nearer, trailed by Esban. "What are you doing, Corvalen? Are you seriously going to allow this?"

"Your Highness, these men were seen wielding crossbows; they had them ready-loaded, concealed beneath their cloaks. If the Sharhay wish to satisfy themselves even beyond the evidence of our own witnesses, I can see no reason to object."

The Kel Sula had ridden into the ford. She looked at the two men, in their absurd cloaks, but her pupils were already dilating. Her voice seemed to come from a distance as she spoke the ritual words: "You stand in the river, the place of truth, the place of judgment. The waters wash away all concealment, but if crime you have committed, even they shall not cleanse you of your guilt."

The Forsteners gaped back at her, uncomprehending. She leaned down from her saddle and seized the nearest man by the chin, stared into his eyes. Her face hardened, and she released him. The other man's guards shoved him forward, and she repeated the process.

"These are the killers," she pronounced, and let go of the second man in distaste. "I have seen their guilt; it paints their souls."

The Kel Sharha translated the Sharhay words for Lord Corvalen's benefit.

"Let her look at my soul, too," he said. "Let her prove to you that my honor is no lie."

He seemed in earnest.

She beckoned the Kel Sula, who reached for Lord Corvalen without question.

"Innocent," the Kel Sula said almost immediately, though she gave him a long look before releasing him. "He had nothing to do with this; he was as shocked as we were. His soul is painted with sorrow for this day's deeds, and anger."

"I thank you, Kel Sula. You may return to the others."

The Kel Sharha turned her regard on Lord Corvalen. It was difficult not to respect his willingness to be examined by the Kel Sula. "She says you do not lie," the Kel Sharha told him, "and you came here in honor."

"Do you believe her?"

He was ruthless; he was manipulative. But he was honest. "Yes. I believe her."

"Then may I take it that you are satisfied with these men's guilt?"

"They are guilty, but I will not be satisfied until I see justice." She leveled her gaze at Lord Corvalen.

Moving with deliberation, he pulled his sword from its scabbard and held it out, hilt toward her, offering it. "The wrong was done to you and your people, Kel Sharha; the right of justice is yours."

She stared at the sword. She estimated its weight, its balance; her hand lifted, her fingers already curving to grasp the hilt.

She caught herself, and settled the willful hand back on her reins. Looking Lord Corvalen in the eye again, she said, "I am no wielder of weapons."

"So I recollect," he answered quietly.

She motioned to him to put away his blade. "The Sharhay are not a sword people. It is the place of the Guardians to carry out justice, and they will do it in their own manner."

Already four Guardians were coming forward. Lord Corvalen moved aside, signaling to his men, and they handed the assassins off to the women.

One man cried out, "Your Highness! Prince Dursten! Please!"

Dursten urged his horse to the edge of the riverbank. "Have you taken leave of your senses, Corvalen? You can't mean to hand soldiers of Forstene over to—"

"I have been appointed royal envoy to Sharhaya, Your Highness, to act on the king's behalf in all matters pertaining to the treaty. His Majesty has no place in his soldiery for truce breakers, men who act on their own command without regard for their sovereign's wishes. They have destroyed their king's desired peace, so yes, I do mean to hand them over to Sharhay justice. I will have the Sharhay know that our king is not to be made mock of by such as these, or by anyone!"

Dursten was silent for several heartbeats.

"Oh, please, Your Highness!" cried the man. "We only did what we did to help you, to help you win your war! We're loyal servants, we are, and we thought it would please you, we thought it was what you wanted—"

"Silence!" Dursten's voice was terrible. "Loyal, do you say? Were you following orders? Did I give you a command? *Did I?*"

The man was sobbing now, too overwrought to answer. But his companion said, "No, Your Highness. It was our own idea. Our own mistake."

"Then go pay for it like men."

The Kel Sharha followed the Guardians and their prisoners up the riverbank. At a decent distance from the water, the men were made to kneel and bow their heads. A Guardian stood over each; the Kel Sharha could sense the air about the women vibrating, as though a drumhead had been struck and was about to be struck again.

Even as she thought this, Elder Rimenna began to drum the death rhythm, and the Lawspeaker rode up beside the Kel Sharha.

"Now, Tigannas."

"Do you not wish to say anything first, Kel Sharha?"

Her hands gripped the reins tighter, but she shook her head. "Have it done."

Tigannas cleared his throat and raised his sonorous voice. "Where there has been dishonor, justice must follow. Those who have brought death shall be given to death; this is the law. If the condemned have any beings whom they honor, let them pray to them now that they be not damned—for they who have shown no mercy shall receive none from the People." He paused, then addressed the two Guardians at either side of the assassins. "Have it done."

The Guardians raised their ironwood staves. Elder Rimenna's drumbeat quickened. With a final slap of the drum, the staves cut down through the air, then came another percussive sound as each staff struck the base of a man's skull.

It was the first time the Kel Sharha had watched men die and felt no wish to save their lives.

Chapter Fifteen

The Kel Nira—no, Corvalen corrected himself, she was Kel Sharha now—had declared she was satisfied by the execution of the assassins, but it was obvious that many of her companions were far from content. The Sharhay council had withdrawn some way toward the forest, and he could make out none of their words; clearly, however, they were debating whether or not to stay and hear the treaty terms.

As so often happened, Rossen spoke Corvalen's own thought. "Amazing that any of them would even consider the treaty now. I'd think that such treachery as was done here today would put an end to the least idea of making peace."

"So it still may. But the Kel Nira, I believe, is too opposed to needless bloodshed—and too stubborn—to be swayed by the ill-considered actions of two low soldiers."

Corvalen, Rossen, and Pellar were sitting on the riverbank, somewhat apart from the rest of their party, while Dursten and his escort had sought the shade of a hazel grove nearby. Enjoying the opportunity to relax a little, with no one by but his squire and his dearest friend, Corvalen did not bother to disguise the fact that he was watching the Kel Nira as she stood and addressed her council. He admired the way she calmed her people's justly inflamed tempers, with harsh words and soft words in turn. He wished he could hear just what she said, but the breeze carried only her tone of voice across the river. There was something, too, he thought, in the very nature of her presence—both calming and commanding.

Damn—he liked the woman! And now she was the Kel Sharha. . . .

Rossen had been making some remark, agreeing about her stubbornness. He continued, "But if I may say so, my lord, I believe your own conduct, your honor, has much to do with it, too. You stopped our men from crossing the ford; you signaled Rindal not to charge. You handed over the assassins, and you promised to discipline the soldiers who attacked without command. She cannot fail to take all of this into account."

"Perhaps."

"My lord?" Pellar said. "I'm not sure I understand why . . . well, why you did those things. If you hadn't . . ."

"If I hadn't," Corvalen answered, "the council would have been destroyed and the war won—like that." He snapped his fingers.

"And then the king would have had Sharhaya, as you have sworn."

"The councillors would all be dead or captured, and most of those men who came out of the Parasha. But the rest of the Sharhay force is in the Lenasha. What do you think they would have done, and all the other people of Sharhaya, if we had massacred their High Council? How long would the war *stay* won?"

"But surely without leaders, it would be an easy matter for us to defeat the rest—"

"Nothing in this country is an easy matter, boy. And would they indeed be without leaders? Look how the Kel Nira stepped into place as Kel Sharha."

Rossen commented, "They seem to have a most orderly succession."

"And even if none of this were the case, Pellar, what sort of victory would that have been, if I had taken advantage of treachery? Then indeed my honor would be a lie."

"But your duty to the king . . ."

"I swore I would deliver him Sharhaya—not my soul."

The squire opened his mouth, evidently thought better of what he'd been about to say, and shut it again.

"This evening, Pellar, I suggest you spend some time studying the sayings of the Exalted Vallar. You can recite the first twenty to me during breakfast tomorrow. Now go and tell His Royal Highness that the Sharhay Council has finished its deliberations; it looks like the Kel Sharha is coming to speak with us."

Corvalen picked up his helm and stood, shaking his head as Pellar hurried off. Still, he could not blame the boy for his questions. There had been a moment, indeed, when Corvalen had nearly yielded to a sharp temptation to take advantage of the treachery. It was Vallar's hand on his shoulder, he thought, that alone had kept him from drawing his sword and spurring his horse into the river to join battle.

The Kel Sharha and her guard reached the ford before the prince had left the shade of the hazels. But if Dursten thought to keep her waiting in her turn, he thought wrong; she addressed Corvalen without delay or preamble, in a tone of voice that admitted no interruption or discussion.

"We have many wounded who cannot travel back to the Sanctuary with comfort, so we will camp by the forest. You will leave us in peace, and so will we you; tonight we hold our funeral rites. Tomorrow in the afternoon you will come to me, and we will discuss the conditions by which the council hears your treaty."

"Thank you, Lady. In the meantime, by your leave, I would attend the funeral rites, to do honor to your predecessor and your Champion—if it would be acceptable."

"It would not. And Lord Corvalen, if there is treachery again—"

"There will not be."

"May every word of yours be cursed if there is." She held her gaze—cold, severe—on him a moment longer, then turned her horse and galloped back to her council.

Corvalen did not believe in curses—but if there were indeed people with the power to effect such things, surely the woman he stared after now was one of them.

He turned to see Dursten approaching on horseback, looking none too happy. "Where does she think she's going?"

"To prepare for a funeral—two funerals."

"Well, call her back!"

"To what purpose, Your Highness? What would you say to her? Will you express your sorrow for the losses she has just suffered? Will you apologize for the contemptible deed done by men wearing your badge?" *A deed you would have praised and rewarded if you could decently have managed it.*

"Don't you take that judgmental tone with me, Corvalen. It's not my fault they chose a poor way to curry favor."

"Isn't it? You said—"

"I know what I said! But I was drunk; I was . . . all right, I was careless. But any sensible man would have recognized it as idle speech and discounted it. Those two were fools."

Yet you chose them to serve in your bodyguard.

Dursten had the grace to look uncomfortable. "What did she say, then?"

"I am to meet with her tomorrow, to hear their conditions—"

"*Their* conditions? For what? Surely they don't think *we're* going to surrender."

"They still want to hear our treaty terms. If we meet their conditions."

Kathryn Hinds

Dursten snorted. "Conditions!" he said again. "Fine. But no more delays after that. Five days till my birthday, and Sharhaya is going to be mine before then. One way or another."

*****

The Kel Nira Kel Sharha sat apart, according to custom, as the pyres blazed, the flames reaching up into the night, the black smoke joining with the darkness and blotting the starlight. Two pyres: the Kel Sharha and her Champion at once, both dead by violence. Such a thing had never been, in all the memory of Sharhaya. *What has brought us to these evil days?*

Word had been sent to the Sanctuary, and there had just been time for some of the Sanctuary folk to reach the meadow between the river and the forest before dark. Still, it was a sadly small gathering that bid farewell to the fallen leaders and now kept vigil. Lillanna and Treska had come, but no one else could be spared from the House of Healing, nor could more than a few Guardians leave their posts. Taras and two other Celebrants had joined Rimenna; their flutes and drums played counterpoint to the sputtering percussion of the flames, the only sounds in an island of silence.

The Kel Sharha forced her gaze to stay on the pyres. Taras's beauty was no temptation to her tonight, but she was uncomfortably aware of other lights punctuating the darkness beyond the encircling guard of Pieran's warbands: the campfires of Lord Corvalen's army and, across the river, the watchfires burning atop the bluff.

She could not see the Kel Jemya—no, Edda, now that she had been given back her name—within the flames, but she could hear her voice, speaking of justice. What was it she had answered Edda? *You will remember that I have no taste for that kind of justice.*

And yet she had demanded exactly that kind of justice from Lord Corvalen, and she had even taken a savage satisfaction in it—as Edda would surely have done. It was her due, after all.

We remember differently. . . . You were a very angry girl, Edda had said.

And now I find that I am a very angry woman, the Kel Sharha reflected—and again wondered just what it was that Edda had been remembering.

Edda was someone that she had always known, or so it seemed. They were—had been—almost the same age, and their families were from neighboring villages. There had been a feeling of wary friendship

152

between them, and of something mutually understood but always unspoken—a shared past, and a rivalry of sorts, occasionally shading near to hostility.

Edda's dying words echoed in her mind: *Receive this, too; it is your birthright, though it was taken from you.*

What had that meant? What birthright, and how taken? What had Edda known about her that she did not know herself?

Whatever it was, Serelha also knew it, came the thought, and pieces of that last conversation came back to her: *You are more than you think you are, Kel Nira. . . . A door is opening in you, one that we believed was locked for good and all. . . .*

She should not be thinking of this now, not here beside her predecessor's pyre. The flesh was burnt nearly all to ash; soon she would have to raise the first cup of wine, and pour the first libation. Then there would be the stories and the songs, until the sunrise brought her formal acclamation as Kel Sharha. She would have to make a speech; what would, what could, she say? She would have to take up her new duties . . . and one of the first would be to meet with Lord Corvalen.

At last the Kel Sharha allowed herself to look toward the enemy campfires. He was there somewhere, thinking, planning—what? She had thought she could rely on his honor, but now, again, she questioned that judgment. He was a man not only ruthless, but full of guile.

During the Council's deliberations that afternoon, the Kel Sula had revealed a disturbing thing: when she examined Lord Corvalen in the ford, she received the strong impression that he had understood her every word—understood Sharhay very well, in fact.

The Kel Sharha did not know whether she was angrier at Lord Corvalen for deliberately concealing his knowledge—he had never given even the slightest hint or sign of it—or at herself for having had no suspicion. But there was no doubt that she was angry indeed about having been deceived.

So, we shall see what he has to say for himself tomorrow. Everything depended, now, on whether or not she could trust the word of this enemy.

*****

"There, Kel Mona; you will do well." The Kel Sharha stroked her fingers once more over the newly rebandaged wound and smiled her habitual bedside smile.

153

The other Sharhay injured at the ford, tended by Lillanna and Treska, shared a long tent, hastily brought from the warbands' camp. For the Kel Mona, though—her uneasiness at confinement in small spaces being well known—some of Pieran's men had built this airy bower at the forest's edge. The Kel Sharha rather wished the men had made a bower for her, too. It was much cooler and pleasanter here under the interwoven branches than within the walls of her tent— Pieran's tent, in fact, brought for her with such efficient generosity that she had felt compelled to cheerfully accept its loan.

"And you . . . you will do well, too, you know," said the Kel Mona.

The Kel Nira Kel Sharha's smile turned rueful. "What will the people think? Only days ago we sent out messengers with news of the death of one Kel Sharha and the acclamation of the next, and now they ride out again, carrying the same tidings—no, worse, for we have lost our Champion, too. How will the people maintain their spirit; how will they keep faith?"

"How will they not, with you as Kel Sharha?"

She ducked her head. "I did not want this. I was not prepared for it."

"Nonsense! You may not have wanted it, but you were prepared for it the day you became a Chief of the Ma'Sharha. Each of us knows this duty may one day come to us; why did you think you would escape it?"

"I just . . . I did not think it would come so soon, or in such circumstances."

"You have received the Mayahara. You have felt it; you have used it."

Yes, that first rushing inflow of the Mayahara had been undeniable in its force. Perhaps Edda had helped, too, giving her life's last energy to swell the flood. But after the ford, the Mayahara had subsided. It flowed now in the Kel Sharha like a quiet stream, and she was not altogether sure what to do with it.

The Kel Mona laid a hand on the Kel Sharha's cheek. "You know you can do this."

"Do what?"

"Whatever you have to."

The Kel Sharha remained silent, letting her thoughts turn while her gaze drifted to the meadow beyond the bower. She found herself squinting against the sun, past its zenith and beginning its slow slide into the west. Afternoon. "Lord Corvalen will arrive soon," she murmured.

154

She stood, gathering the russet cloak around her. Sized for Edda, it was too long, and it was stained with Edda's blood. But it would have to do for now—and it would not hurt for Lord Corvalen to see those bloodstains, to be reminded of his people's perfidy.

"Be careful of that arm," she told the Kel Mona as she left the bower.

"Be careful of that man," the Kel Mona called after her.

Indeed.

Leaving her tent door open, she went in and settled herself on a cushion to wait. She performed three deep breathings, and reached her mind to her tree for strength. *Beech tree perseveres.*

"Your pardon, First of Mothers." Guardian Kirtana stepped in hesitantly, and bowed as the Kel Sharha rose to her feet.

"Kirtana! I have hardly seen you since . . ." Again came the sudden collage of memory, images from that terrible night. "I have wanted to tell you how sorry I am for Fama's death."

"And I for Deela's, Lady."

The more recent deaths were too much, too palpable to be spoken of. After a moment the Kel Sharha reached through the silence and took Kirtana's hand, bowing over it. "I have also wished to thank you for getting those men to safety. Every one of them survived, because of you."

"In that, at least, I did not fail you."

"In nothing did you fail me, Kirtana. Nor shall you. If I understand aright, you will be the new Kel Jemya's Second?"

"That is her intention, if it please you."

Please me? Kel Sharha or no, who am I to say what the Guardians do in their Order? She covered her confusion with a smile and a nod, and said something vague, then, "So, I think you are here to stand guard while I meet with Lord Corvalen?"

"Yes, and to tell you that he has come out from his army, alone, and willingly given up his sword to your brother. He only awaits your summons."

"Bring him, then." She stood straighter, arranged the drape of the bloodstained cloak, and folded her hands at her waist.

Beech tree perseveres.

Kirtana returned. "First of Mothers, will you receive Corvalen of Brintora, envoy of the king of Forstene?" she intoned.

"I will."

Kirtana bowed, and as she went to take up her post outside, Lord Corvalen entered. He did not bow; nor did the Kel Sharha take his hand as she thanked him for meeting with her.

"I have come here placing my trust in you, Kel Sharha; I have left behind companions and armor, and brought no other weapon but my sword—which, as your men will tell you, I gave up without hesitation as soon as it was asked of me—so that there might be good faith between us."

"Good faith . . . yes." She nodded him toward a cushion, though she remained standing.

As he sat down, she said in Sharhay, "Why did you not tell me that you understand our language?"

His look of surprise lasted only a heartbeat. "You never asked me," he answered in awkwardly accented Sharhay. Then he switched back to Forstene. "Your pardon, Lady—I comprehend your tongue better than I am able to speak it. I'm sure that you can understand why I would not volunteer such information. But I tell you truly that if you had asked me, I would have admitted to it readily enough."

Her skepticism must have shown plainly on her face, for he continued, "I would even have told you how I learned Sharhay. From a Ghildaran envoy, as a matter of fact—Martos of the Fifth District. Do you know him?"

Martos had helped Lord Corvalen? She pushed down her consternation; she could not let this revelation distract her. She answered cautiously, "He is an old friend."

"He is an old friend of mine as well, and a canny man. I could not but agree with him that it would be far easier to negotiate a treaty with you if I understood your language."

Negotiate! Inwardly she seized on the word, but she kept her face and voice stern. "I, too, agree with our friend—but I do not agree it was 'canny' to hold secret your knowledge of Sharhay language." She took a step toward the tent door, consciously emanating an air of dismissal. "There will be plain dealing between us, Lord Corvalen, or none at all."

He did not leave. She stared down at him, but still he kept to his seat. She folded her hands again and waited; she would simply stand here and meditate, for the rest of the day if necessary. To give way to him in this contest of wills was unthinkable—will was virtually all her people had in their favor now.

"Very well," he said at last, and stood to face her. "Plain dealing. Both of us want this war over. That will be done, one way or another.

Both of us want to walk away from this with honor. That will be harder—especially for you."

"*I* will walk withhonor, Lord Corvalen," she said softly. "I am Chief of a free people, who fight only to hold our freedom. *You* are with those who try to take what is ours. Where is the honor there?"

When he answered, his voice was as cold as if she had slapped him. "The honor is in being a true and loyal servant of the king to whom my allegiance is sworn. But unless I misjudge, you will feel your honor stained indeed when you are required to swear that same allegiance to that same king. And that, my lady, is one term of the treaty that is not negotiable."

It took her some moments to comprehend all he had said. "How"— she moistened her lips and swallowed—"how . . . to offer this . . . allegiance?"

His voice was still brittle. "You are to go to Forstene, to be displayed in Prince Dursten's triumphal march through the streets of Forstene City. That is our custom, when we are victorious. The same would befall your Champion, if he still lived. He would then be executed, having borne arms against us. You, however, will be given the opportunity to become a loyal subject of King Delanar."

"And then?"

"That will be for the king to decide."

She drew a steadying breath. "We should . . . we should not continue this conversation. This matter, it is for the whole Council."

"You are willing, then, to hear our terms?"

It took her a moment to remember the conditions the Council had settled on, and she found it maddeningly difficult to keep her voice from quavering. "So you come with no weapons but your swords, and stand in one rank only so that no man can hide what he does, we will hear."

"When?"

"Tomorrow. After the mist is off the meadow."

"Tomorrow morning. Good. And Kel Sharha . . ."

"Yes?"

"Tell your warriors to lay aside their weapons tonight—for my men will have theirs at the ready to answer any provocation. If our forces meet, it will be the worse for Sharhaya."

Her patience snapped. "Enough, Lord Corvalen; your point is made! Leave me!"

With a slight bow, he did so.

She turned her back to the tent door. Her heart drummed loud in her ears; she hugged her chest and clenched her fists to stop from shaking.

"Lady?"

Mastering herself and dropping her arms, she turned to see Kirtana, looking troubled, but also puzzled. Good—the Guardian, who knew no Forstene, clearly had understood no more of the conversation in the tent than what was suggested by the raised voices.

"Lady, are you well?"

"I must go to the trees," the Kel Sharha answered with sudden decision. "I will be back by dark, to initiate the new head of your Order. Bring my horse, if you would be so good."

*****

Her thoughts spun as she cantered into the forest. "'Rather will we make you beg *us* for terms of peace,'" she muttered.

The proud words she had flung at the prince the day before were utterly empty. She had gotten a good look at Lord Corvalen's army, and saw how it compared with her own. *His* words were no empty boast or idle threat; it did not take a Listener to predict what would happen if those forces met. And at heart, the Kel Sharha had known this from the moment she had first seen the Scourge's army marching into the valley. She had realized then, as little as she had liked to admit it to herself, that her people's only hope for survival was to make peace, at virtually any cost. But it had never occurred to her that she would have to pay such a high personal price.

"Yet if by doing so I can save Sharhaya, the price is well paid," she whispered.

Tree leaves rustled all around, seeming to speak with Serelha's voice: *You will bring the springtide strength back to our people.*

The Kel Sharha reined her horse and willed herself to stillness, listening. Had those words emerged from her memory, or had she truly heard the trees speaking—and might they speak to her again? Perhaps this was another gift that came with the Mayahara?

It had always been rare for her to hear tree voices. Certainly she received information from trees and other plants—healing knowledge—but that came in the form of intuition, a wordless understanding. Yet though she might not hear messages that translated into words, as the Listeners did, she felt the full force of the greenery around her. There was healing here for the soul as well as for the body.

158

The Watchers were abroad.

She dismounted, and let Luma amble along behind her as she waded through a fern brake.

On the edges of her vision, the forest was full of movement: figures made of light and shadow, staying close to the trees so that it was impossible to tell their hair from vines or leaves, their skin from bark. They spoke to one another in a humming, rustling whisper. But if the Kel Sharha turned to look at one straight on, she saw only brush and tree trunks, heard only birdsong, the breeze moving through leaves, branches creaking against one another.

The Watchers could hound cowards and those forsworn to their deaths, driving them to some black forest pool or pit of sinking sand. But that was not their business with the Kel Sharha. She sensed curiosity—they must see her, examine her, know who it was that now embodied the Mayahara.

She stood still to let them gather close about her, and closed her eyes that they might move more freely.

Twiglike fingers brushed her cheeks, stroked her hair. Bark—rough, smooth, knotty—pressed upon her bare arms. She was breathed upon, with the sensation of soft new leaves wafted about her face and shoulders. Vines and lithe willow branches seemed to drape around her.

An odd feeling grew upon her—odd because so relaxed, so without fear or worry or discomfort of any kind, a singular lassitude. A blessing, and she sank gratefully into it.

She awoke to find herself lying on a mossy bank under the arching branches of a grand matriarch of a tree. A beech, of course; as her muddled vision focused, she saw the Watcher of the Beeches pass through the smooth gray bark and into the heart of the tree. Then, to her surprise, she began to sob.

Most Sharhay cried openly and freely, when the occasion warranted. But Ma'Sharha were trained to dampen their feelings, lest unrestrained emotion interfere with their work. The Kel Sharha truly could not remember the last time she had cried. Now years' worth of weeping poured forth all at once. There was so much to mourn: so many friends who had died in the war, patients she had been unable to save, the Winter Sanctuary looted and burned, villages razed, at least a dozen Houses of Healing destroyed.

She felt her country's tragedy as keenly as her personal griefs, and the prince's violation of her seemed only a reflection of the rape he had visited on all Sharhaya. The catalog of the invasion's toll went on, and it was all for naught. All their fighting, all their struggle had gained them nothing. Any concessions that she might win from Lord Corvalen would not change the fact that Sharhaya was conquered.

She had never wanted to be Kel Sharha. She should not have been; both her predecessors should have lived longer. She was furious at her own inability to save either woman. So here was the punishment for her impotence: now she was Kel Sharha in her turn, and she was the one who would surrender her country's freedom, disgrace her lot thereafter.

Yet what else was there to do? The only alternative was to keep fighting, when any hope of prevailing against the Forstene armies was little better than an idle dream. If it were still only the prince's army to contend with, things might be different—but with Lord Corvalen's ten thousand poised at the edge of the Parasha. . . Oh, she knew there were many among the people who would prefer death to losing their freedom—but what kind of freedom was it to bow to annihilation? For that was surely what the Sharhay faced if they fought on; they were too weak now, too worn down.

She had said it before, and she believed it still: it was better to live, and to hope. Things might not always be so bleak; there could come an opportunity, somehow, for her people to reassert their sovereignty. But that could only happen if they survived, and it was her responsibility to make sure they did. She was the Kel Sharha. She stood for the Mothers of the Past and the Mothers to Come, and for all those who watched over the Growing World. They would give her the strength for whatever happened.

The tears had ceased to flow, leaving her feeling tired but cleansed. She got to her feet and faced the tree.

"O Grandmother Beech," she whispered, "you have watched many generations of the Growing World, you have fed and sheltered people and animals both, and now you have given rest and nourishment to my spirit. I humbly thank you, Great Lady of the Forest. As you are rooted in this soil, so may I, wherever my path leads, ever know the strength of this my Motherland. And as you give of your own being to replenish this soil and nurture those with whom you share it, so do I offer my life for this land and this people whom I love and serve, and to whom I am sworn. May the Mothers and the Watchers guide my steps, even when I must walk among foreign trees. It is I, Finoora, who beseech you, who am known among the people as Chief of Healers and First of the Mothers of the People; may I be ever worthy of the names."

She bowed to the tree and lingered awhile longer beneath its shade. A breeze kissed her cheeks and again stirred the leaves overhead. From the whisper of the leaves, a voice spoke in her mind: *Fear not for tomorrow. Brave words will save many. The strength of the land is in you—but you must have its patience, too.*

Chapter Sixteen

The next morning found Rossen once again at Corvalen's side on the west bank of the river, squinting into the sunrise. To Corvalen's left the prince, in full battle array, sat tall in his saddle. Beside Dursten was hisherald, and next to him stood Esban, waiting to be called on to translate. A string of retainers and bodyguards lined the riverbank to both left and right, but every man—even Dursten—carried no weapon but his sword, and that in plain sight.

The Sharhay did not keep them waiting this time; they had left their camp even as the Forstene party was taking up its position. They rode through the clearing mist at a sober pace, as people meeting their fate only reluctantly.

At the center of the Sharhay group was, of course, the Kel Sharha, wearing her predecessor's bloodstained russet cloak. No Champion accompanied her, but to her left were the other three chiefs of the Holy Women, and to her right the Lawspeaker and the elders of the Greater Guilds. Rossen remembered that he had heard Martos of Ghildarna telling Corvalen, during their many long talks last winter, that the Greater Guilds were artisans, vintners, and . . . something Martos called Celebrants, who were evidently singers and storytellers and the like. Odd, that—to represent minstrels on their High Council. The Sharhay were strange folk, undoubtedly.

The councillors reached the riverbank; there was a pause, the silence of a held breath. Somewhere down the Forstene line a horse stamped, the sound abnormally loud. Across the ford, the leader of the warrior women shifted in her saddle and adjusted her grip on her staff. Back among the trees, two crows called to each other. And all this time the Kel Sharha stared down into the river, where the current swirled and spiraled. At last she raised her gaze; for a moment her eyes were as troubled as the water, but as she glanced across at Corvalen, her expression went remote, and stayed that way.

She lifted a hand from her reins with a small gesture to the Lawspeaker. He began, delivering a formal greeting to Corvalen and

161

the prince in slow, careful Forstene. Corvalen returned the greeting in equally labored Sharhay.

It was Dursten's turn to gesture—but his arm moved in a great, dramatic sweep. It was answered by trumpeters atop the bluff behind him, brazening out a fanfare. *He has planned this moment since the day he set forth on campaign.*

His movements grand as could be, the prince dismounted and drew his sword. He raised it high, holding the blade poised aloft for the morning sun to gild it, then plunged it into the earth.

Two of the Sharhay elders flinched, but the rest of the council kept their countenance.

"Chiefs and Elders of Sharhaya," Dursten shouted across the water, "we claim these lands for the crown of Forstene, by right of conquest. Yet King Delanar is mighty in mercy as he is in arms, ever prepared to show clemency to the vanquished. If you would sue for peace and the king's mercy, hear now the terms of our treaty."

Esban translated the prince's words, which the councillors received stonily. The warrior woman, however, once more shifted her grip on her weapon. At last the Kel Sharha called across in Forstene, "We will hear."

Prince Dursten retrieved his sword, remounted his horse, and signaled to the herald. The man cleared his throat and unrolled a parchment. In ringing tones, with pauses every half sentence for Esban's translations, he read out, "Article One: Immediately upon the signing of this treaty, all Sharhay warriors will disarm and turn over their weapons and horses to the armies of Forstene. They will likewise surrender all Forstene arms, equipment, and mounts taken in spoil."

Rossen had read the proposed treaty, and had heard and even taken some part in numerous discussions of it, so he gave only half an ear to the herald and Esban as they set forth the conditions of peace—the viceroy who would govern Sharhaya, the garrisons that would be established, the curfews, the limits on travel and assembly. . . .

The Kel Sharha, he saw, would not look at Prince Dursten, and only once did she flick her glance over Esban—a scornful, dismissive glance that took some of the gloating triumph out of his voice as he translated the conditions under which the High Council would be permitted to meet. Her gaze then returned to Corvalen, and Rossen turned his head enough to see that Corvalen was giving as good as he got. It was almost funny: the two of them, each easy on horseback but spear-shaft straight, locked in a staring contest across the ford. Yet Rossen found himself suppressing a frown.

"Article Five," sang out the herald. "The office of Champion is hereby abolished forevermore. Anyone attempting to fulfill this office will be outlawed immediately and will be put to death as soon as apprehended."

Far behind the Sharhay councillors, Pieran and his men stood on alert. Rossen wondered how that last condition would go over with them; it was, however, one of the terms that was absolutely not open to negotiation.

"Article Seven: The people of Sharhaya shall be subject to the laws of Forstene, without exception." The Lawspeaker shook his head at this—a small movement, but perceptible. The whole party's tension became even more tangible as Esban translated the terms regarding indemnity, annual tribute, and work service. Rossen braced himself for what was coming next; out of the corner of his eye, he saw Corvalen sit even straighter, if that was possible.

"Article Nine: The Kel Sharha is required to participate in Prince Dursten's triumph and to personally render homage to the crown of Forstene. Immediately upon the signing of this treaty she shall be taken into the custody of the king's envoy."

The elders had been growing restive as the articles were read and translated. Now there was a positive outcry, and even the disciplined faces of the Holy Women showed consternation. The Kel Sharha alone remained impassive, and raised her hand for quiet. When she had it, she asked, her voice frigid, "Are those all your terms?"

"There is one more article," Dursten answered, nodding and smiling with mock graciousness. He gestured for the herald to continue.

"Article Ten: Five hundred Sharhay, to be chosen by Prince Dursten or his officers, will be sent to Forstene as hostages for the peaceable behavior of their fellow countrymen. To further ensure the keeping of the peace, the remaining fighting men of Sharhaya will be assembled, every tenth man to have his weapon hand cut off. So it was done in the time of Heldar the Unifier—"

The rest of the words were drowned out as the Sharhay council erupted in outrage. This time even the Kel Sharha reacted. Her voice rose above all the others: "If this is your king's 'clemency,' we will have none of it—the treaty is not acceptable! Do you want Sharhaya? Then you will buy it with your blood!" Her words hung in the air as all stilled around her—though Rossen saw that the woman warrior had urged her horse forward, in position to move quickly between the Kel Sharha and harm.

The Kel Sharha was glaring at Corvalen in pure fury, clearly holding him responsible for the proposed decimation of her warriors. She continued in a voice like iron, the Forstene words coming to her easily now. "Does your king want a province burned and soaked in blood? Or does he want one that can send him the wine and precious things he covets? If he wants Sharhaya peaceful and productive, the treaty you have proposed will not give it to him. I tell you now, we will never accept any terms that include your tenth article."

"The tenth article—," began the prince.

"Is barbaric! And unnecessary, if we accept your ninth article. Your king will have me in his power—and I alone am a more than sufficient guarantee for the peace of Sharhaya."

The prince sat silent, apparently thinking over her words.

Rossen almost felt sorry for the Kel Sharha; she had been well and truly manipulated—as Corvalen had said she would be. It was true that decimation had been carried out in the Exalted Heldar's time, but only after some of the new-won provinces had risen in rebellion. King Delanar and Corvalen both knew full well that maiming one-tenth of Sharhaya's able-bodied men was not the way ensure peace here. The article was in the treaty only so that the Sharhay council could negotiate it away—and then, feeling that by doing so they had achieved a great thing for their people, they would be the less inclined to demand much in the way of further concessions.

They would also, Rossen reflected, be all the more hardened in their opinion that Forsteners were inhumane monsters. Rossen sometimes wondered if they might be right.

Dursten spoke again. "There is no 'if' about the ninth article. Accept that—and some of the rest may be open to discussion."

*****

The encampment was still roiling from the day's events; the burr of discussion and argument was such that the Kel Sharha could barely hear the nightbird songs, though she strained to listen. Sitting on a cushion beside her in her tent, Pieran continued reading, his jaw clenched.

She passed a hand over her eyes. So tired. The gamble she had taken in initially refusing the treaty, in the heat of her anger, had left her shaken. She was going to have to do something about Prince Dursten's power to inspire her with overwhelming rage. But this time, at least, the rage had worked in her favor. The tree voice had been right, and her brave words had indeed saved many hundreds of her people from imprisonment or maiming.

"It's intolerable!" Pieran muttered, throwing down the parchment, a draft copy of the new treaty.

The Kel Sharha retrieved it, and thoughtfully laid it beside her copy of the original treaty. "It is far better than what we were first offered."

Pieran stabbed a finger at the first treaty's last article. "*That* is monstrous."

"Indeed. And not only is that article struck off, but we have been able to get some of the other articles modified. We will be able to keep to our own laws of marriage and inheritance, as you have seen, and an exception has been made to the curfew for Healers attending patients."

"But surrendering all our weapons. . . . Don't they understand that these are *tools*?" He patted the hilt of his forester's knife, for the moment still safe in its scabbard at his side. "How are we supposed to tend the forests without our knives and axes? How are we supposed to hunt without our bows and arrows?"

"They will give 'license,' they say, to hunters and foresters who meet their conditions." She scanned the new treaty, trying to sort through the scrambling words and letters. "Does it not say so?"

Pieran took the parchment back from her. "Yes, here it is"—he pointed—"but all the same—"

"And does this treaty say everything else that I told you it should?" She could remember all that had been decided in the Council's negotiations with Lord Corvalen, but the Forsteners trusted to parchment, not memory, and she wanted to be certain that their written words were the same as the ones she remembered.

Pieran nodded slowly. "But—"

"Good. Then Tigannas can write out fair copies in Sharhay; it would be well for you to help him with the translation."

"This all seems so hasty," Pieran grumbled. "I mean, only one day for negotiation! Can't you ask for more time to consider the treaty's ramifications?"

The Kel Nira frowned, no happier with the situation than her brother was. "The Forsteners were adamant that we come to an agreement by this nightfall."

"And if not?"

"Then tomorrow Lord Corvalen would lead his army into the Parasha. Your archers are good, Pieran, but not good enough, and not numerous enough, to bring down ten thousand Forstene warriors."

"But this treaty—"

The Kel Sharha faced him sternly. "Do you question the Council's wisdom, Pieran? Believe me, we know how little we have won from the Forsteners. But that little is far more than we might have hoped for."

"Lady, you know I have faith in you and the rest of the Council to decide what's best for our people. And you have not done so little; after all, no man's going to lose his work hand. It's these Forsteners—they'll likely twist this treaty to mean whatever they wish it to, or ignore it altogether to gain what they want. And . . . they're taking you away! Lillanna can act for you in your Order, but no one can act for the Kel Sharha." His eyes shone with tears. "Will you ever come back?"

Her throat tightened. Looking down, she bit her lip and blinked furiously. When she thought she could be sure of her voice, she whispered, "I do not know." She swallowed, and reached for Pieran's hands. They were rough and hard-knuckled and not altogether clean.

The two of them had sat like this once before, hand in hand, facing an uncertain future—only then, they had faced it together. For a moment her mind was distracted by the effort to remember more about the day they'd learned of their parents' deaths, and the days that had followed. But the prospect of her own uncertain future loomed too near. The certainties of that future were bad enough: held captive by Lord Corvalen, paraded and humiliated by the prince. . . .

"Finoora—"

She started at Pieran's use of her personal name.

"Finoora, what if you did not go to Forstene? What if we could get you to the Ghil River and across? Martos has offered you refuge; you would be safe with him."

She allowed the idea to linger between them for several heartbeats before answering. "To do that would break the treaty."

"But if you go tonight, before the treaty is signed—"

"Pieran, think! What would be the consequences for the rest of the Council, for the rest of Sharhaya?"

"I'll wager that any of us would gladly suffer any consequences rather than to know you humiliated in the prince's triumph and—and—and who knows what else in Forstene. You are the Kel Sharha, damn it!"

"You are right: I am the Kel Sharha, and it is my responsibility to care for this land and its people. If I do not go to Forstene—as I have already given my word to do—then it matters not whether I live or die in any case. The Forstene armies will lay this country waste, and there will be no Sharhaya for me to return to, ever. I will be damned indeed if I so betray my trust."

Pieran's head drooped. "I'm sorry I suggested it; I shouldn't have. But I didn't realize you had already given your word . . . and I wasn't thinking clearly." He smiled sadly. "Or rather, I was thinking only about my little sister, worrying for her future, and forgetting for the moment that she has grown to be a wise and mighty woman, the First of Mothers."

"Oh, Pieran . . ."

His hands had tightened on hers. "Only a few days ago you told me that your life would be worthless to you anywhere but in Sharhaya."

"Well . . . it appears that I was wrong. I sometimes am, you know." She gave him a sad smile of her own and said, so low that he leaned closer to hear, "I do not feel either wise or mighty. I do not want to go among the Forsteners. Pieran . . . I am afraid, so afraid. . . ." She squeezed her eyes shut, and felt his arms wrap around her.

"I'll come with you," he whispered fiercely.

For a moment she let herself imagine it. Then she remembered what Lord Corvalen had told her. "No. You bore arms against them; they would kill you during their triumph. I could not bear it." She sighed. "You should go back to Redcreek, help Aunt Hoba with the vineyard, watch your children grow up."

"They're Silna's children, not mine," he said flatly; he and Silna had parted with little friendship remaining between them.

"Better Silna to contend with than the Forstene viceroy." She pulled back to look him full on. "I want you out of his reach, Pieran. I would bear my own troubles more easily knowing you to be safe."

"I'll"—he cleared his throat—"I'll do my best, then."

They sat together in silence for a while. The Kel Sharha tried to savor his nearness, pushing away the knowledge that these were almost certainly the last moments she would ever have with her brother.

At length Pieran cleared his throat again. "So . . . when exactly is this treaty to be signed?"

The time for being just sister and brother was past; the weight of her office settled on her again. "The day after tomorrow, before the sun nears its height. That will give you and Tigannas time to make our copies of the treaty. And you will need to prepare your warriors."

"Those in the Lenasha, too?"

"Yes; the field between the Lenasha and Summer Bluff is where the surrender will take place, after the treaty signing."

"Lady . . . what if"—a sly light had come into Pieran's eyes—"what if all our warriors cannot be found? Some might slip off to their homes, taking their weapons with them. . . ."

The Kel Sharha put some sternness into her voice. "I am accountable for our people, Pieran. I expect the warbands to make a creditable surrender the day after tomorrow, and I expect there to be no trouble afterward. We will not in any way antagonize the Forsteners. Do I make myself clear?"

"Lady, they will have you hostage." He paused, in a palpable effort to master the bitterness and sorrow that had crept into his last words. "None of our people would act in such a way as to risk harm to the Kel Sharha."

"Yet the provocation will be great. Years may pass, Pieran"—she held up a hand to forestall another outburst—"and I may not . . . remain in a position to act as guarantor."

"They might kill you," he said tonelessly.

"So they might. But it does not matter—that is what I am trying to tell you, Pieran. This is not about me; it is about our people. They are wounded in body and spirit, and the only battle they should wage now is to regain their health, their strength. That in itself is a long, hard fight; they cannot waste themselves on any other. So I ask you again, do I make myself clear?"

"Yes, Kel Sharha." He heaved a great sigh. "I will prepare the men, and will myself set them a sterling example of peaceful fortitude. You can trust me, Lady."

"I know." She brushed her lips across his cheek. "Hold fast for me, Pieran. We must endure."

After Pieran walked out into the quieting night, she almost ran after him. But she did not want to make a habit of weeping.

Chapter Seventeen

Dursten swatted at a cloud of gnats; Corvalen resisted the urge to do likewise. One more reason he would be glad to get this done with.

The treaty pavilion was a spacious affair of silk striped in royal gold and purple, its sides open to admit any breeze that might come off the river to lighten the heaviness of the day. Unfortunately, the only movement in the thick, damp air was that of gnats and midges, and the heat was more oppressive than Corvalen had known it since coming to Sharhaya. Thunder had rumbled in the distance throughout the morning, but as yet there had been no rain.

As royal envoy, bearing the king's signet, Corvalen sat at the head of the table. On his right, Dursten continued to fidget; on his left, the Kel Sharha sat apparently composed—but Corvalen could tell, by the set of her shoulders, that her hands were clenched tight under the table.

Beside her, the Lawspeaker at last finished looking over all the copies of the treaty, put the parchment sheets into a neat stack, and pushed them across to Dursten's scribe.

The Kel Sharha turned to Corvalen. "The treaties are in order. We thank you for your patience. We—"

Dursten cleared his throat and stood. Behind him, the purple and gold standards borne by the front rank of his escort hung limp.

Corvalen resigned himself to listening to another speech. Dursten had arrived at the treaty table announced by his trumpeters and acclaimed by his herald, then had spoken at length on the destiny of Forstene. Now, however, he abandoned speechmaking in favor of recitation from one of the old epics:

"Then that hero, harsh of voice
From command amid the battle's crash,
Took measure of the foreign men:
Their strength waned, as waxed his own.
He offered mercy, the magnanimous ruler—
Not only friend, but father would he be,
To guide the base and barbarous. . . ."

Dursten droned on, reciting the surrender of the Brintoran tetrarchs to the Exalted Heldar—"the Unifier." Corvalen tried not to take it personally, recalling that he himself had reminded Dursten that he was only half Brintoran, and moreover descended from the commander who had been at Heldar's right hand in the conquest of Brintora. *But today Dursten sits at my right hand*, he reflected, and remembered how the prince had flushed at seeing the royal signet on Corvalen's finger. Clearly, this day was not exactly as Dursten had envisioned it when he first set out for Sharhaya.

Corvalen glanced over his shoulder at the men of his escort. Some of them *were* pure Brintoran—had even grown up speaking the old Brintoran tongue. If anyone felt resentment at the prince's recital, however, he kept it to himself; the men all stood at rigid, perfect attention—just as Corvalen expected them to. They were impervious even to the gnats.

Dursten's tone grew more ponderous; he was drawing to a close:

"So Heldar took this land to hold,
His first enrichment of the realm—
A worthy scion of great Stennar,
Exalted first of Forstene kings."

The recitation was heartily approved by Dursten's escort, who banged swords against shields until he raised a hand to silence them.

Dursten looked around him, and said, "As many of you know, tomorrow is my birthday"—another burst of shield banging—"but today I receive all the gift I could want. I do not claim it for myself alone, however. I have won Sharhaya for the glory and honor of all the Blood of Stennar, for all Forstene. This rich new province is my gift indeed—my gift to His Majesty my father, and, even more, to my son and to his sons after him."

Corvalen's men joined the cheers for King Delanar and Prince Heldar. As the shield banging died away, Dursten sat down to the stack of treaties.

The scribe presented him with an inkpot and a plumy quill pen, and Dursten—with a flourish, of course—signed his name at the bottom of the first sheet of parchment. He had left hardly any room for the Kel Sharha's signature.

Corvalen took the treaty from Dursten and passed it to the Kel Sharha. The scribe had opened a second inkpot and given her a plain quill, which she held awkwardly. It occurred to Corvalen to wonder if she even knew how to write.

As subtly as he could, he pointed out where she should sign. She just stared at the parchment. Dursten smirked.

The only sound now was the hum of insects. Then Corvalen became aware of another hum, lower and more melodious. It was one of the councillors standing behind the Kel Sharha—the chief in the gray overdress, he thought. Someone else picked up the hum, then someone else, till they had all joined in a soft, many-toned resonance. Dursten scowled, but it was just a sound—no words, nothing that could really be objected to, any more than the buzzing of a passing honeybee or the song of a thrush in the hazel copse.

The Lawspeaker touched the Kel Sharha's shoulder. She nodded, blinked hard, and drew in her breath. She dipped the quill into the inkpot. She hesitated; a drop of ink fell onto Dursten's signature.

She signed—slowly, carefully, the quill pinched between her long fingers.

Corvalen took the parchment from her. She had written her full title: *Kel Nira Kel Ma'Sharha Kel Sharha*, in small Ghildaran-style letters but quite clear.

The scribe's assistant dripped purple-red wax onto the bottom of the treaty, and Corvalen pressed the royal seal into it. It seemed to him that he should say something, but he felt strangely bereft of words. His actions would have to be sufficient; besides, the less attention he called to his role here, the more equable Prince Dursten was likely to be.

The first copy done, the signing of the others proceeded efficiently and with no sound but for the humming and the scratch of the pens. By the end, the hums drifted into silence as more and more of the councillors struggled to hold back tears. The Kel Sharha's face as she signed the last copy of the treaty was blank, any emotion she felt completely shuttered from view.

Corvalen pressed the seal into the wax, and now his charge from the king obligated him to speak. He rose from his seat and pitched his voice to fill the pavilion and roll out over the river. "In the name of His Most Solemn Majesty Delanar, Sovereign of Forstene, Heir to the Exalted Stennar, the Merciful and Just, Perfect in Majesty, Beloved of the Celestials: I proclaim Sharhaya a province of Forstene, under Forstene sovereignty, subject to the lordship of Forstene, in the royal possession of Forstene's king, by this accord signed here today. I proclaim it in King Delanar's name, and it is done."

"It is done!" roared the soldiers, and beat their shields.

"It is done," Dursten echoed. He had stood, too, for the proclamation, and now he clasped Corvalen's shoulders and laughed. "Done, and well done!" He raised a hand in signal to Esban, who stepped forward bearing a tray with a wine jar and three goblets.

"Let us drink to the treaty," Dursten said as Esban poured the wine and handed him the first goblet. Esban passed the next to Corvalen, then offered the third to the Kel Sharha.

Her reserve wavered. "You have forgot yourself, Esban," she said in Sharhay, her voice so low and steady that she must be exerting great control.

Beside the Kel Sharha, the Lawspeaker had gone rigid, his lips pressed together. Corvalen saw that the faces of some of the other councillors, too, showed dismay, perhaps even suppressed outrage, as though Esban had just done something exceedingly offensive. The effrontery of this traitor offering wine to the woman he had betrayed was an ample insult on its own, of course, but Corvalen sensed something more subtle going on as well.

Dursten affected not to notice. "Come, Kel Sharha," he said with his most charming smile, "we cannot drink our toast until you take your glass."

She did not return the smile—and Corvalen would not have liked to be the recipient of the look she gave the prince. It was gone in a heartbeat, though, and she answered with a careful absence of expression. "It is not done in Sharhaya to drink unmixed wine but for such rites as births and weddings and deaths."

Dursten took the goblet from Esban and waved him away. "But this great occasion is all those things, Kel Sharha: the birth of a new and glorious era for Forstene, the death of Sharhay independence—and, truly, the wedding of Sharhaya to Forstene. Won't you drink to your bridegroom?" He leaned across the table and thrust the goblet at her. "Come, you must. I insist."

For just a moment she looked as though she might be ill. Corvalen felt his own innards twist as a flash of memory showed him the Kel Sharha as he had first seen her, raped and beaten, lying at Dursten's feet. He was certain that Dursten saw her that way too—and meant for her to know it.

Before Corvalen could formulate a tactful way to keep the prince from attempting to humiliate her further, the Kel Sharha stood and took the goblet.

She did not look away from Dursten; she did not raise her voice. "This is a forced marriage; to such I can never drink. But I will drink to

the death of your war and the rebirth of peace between our peoples."
She raised the goblet, then drank, though shallowly.

"To the peace," Corvalen said, and drank off his glass.

"To Sharhaya, Forstene's newest province," the prince declaimed,
his patent displeasure at the Kel Sharha's response to his taunts erased
by the equally obvious satisfaction of having the last word.

Except he didn't have it. As he downed his wine with exaggerated
relish, the Kel Sharha deliberately overturned her goblet, letting the
ruddy liquid run out upon the ground. "Better wine spilled than blood,"
she murmured in Sharhay to the Lawspeaker.

Dursten appeared not to hear. He motioned Esban for a refill, but as
he prepared to offer another toast, the Kel Sharha looked to Corvalen.
"Now what happens?"

"We shall ride to the other side of the bluff to receive your army's
surrender. Our herald will read out the treaty, and your Lawspeaker will
read the Sharhay translation, so that all of your warriors will
understand. After that, your men will come forward one band at a time
to give up their weapons to His Highness's army. The men will be
instructed to return to their homes, traveling in groups of six or fewer,
in accordance with the treaty's limit on the number of Sharhay who
may assemble together. You understand, the treaty is now in effect."

The Kel Sharha folded her hands at her waist. She answered him in
her own language. "In compliance with the treaty, then, I surrender
myself into the custody of the king's envoy."

A sob choked in the throat of one of the councillors; with startling
incongruence, the thrush in the hazel copse began a new song.

Corvalen looked down into the Kel Sharha's face, pale under the
last shadows of bruising and the still-red scars on her left cheek. "I
accept your surrender, Lady, and promise to hold you in honorable
custody. Your movements will be as little restricted as possible while
you remain in Sharhaya, but you will be under guard at all times
henceforward." He beckoned to Fidden and Gar, two of the steadiest
men in his bodyguard, who came to stand behind the Kel Sharha.

Dursten put down the goblet he had drained while Corvalen spoke,
and slapped the stack of signed treaties. "Let's to horse then; a fine
show awaits us! What a victory we'll celebrate tonight!"

*****

The Kel Sharha watched the mound of surrendered weapons grow, a
wall of axes, knives, bows, and arrows separating her from her people.

Pieran had brought the warbands out of the Lenasha in good order and assembled them across the field from Dursten's army. And she sat her horse here, at the head of the Forstene cavalry, sharing an awning with Lord Corvalen and Prince Dursten, and a guard on either side of her—on show before her own people.

She watched it all as from a distance. She saw the men lay down their weapons, tools of their livelihoods for the most part; some also threw down Forstene swords and bits of armor they had gleaned. They left their horses, too—those who had them, for her people had no tradition of fighting on horseback. Unlike the Forsteners.

She saw the Councillors grouped around Pieran and the other war leaders, all solemn-faced, but steady. A few Celebrants had joined Rimenna, including Taras; from time to time the Kel Sharha noticed the sun in his hair and heard his flute soar high above the others, or, when he switched instruments, heard his drum beat deeper. But she could not let him mean anything to her now.

She scarcely noticed the heat, yet odd things caught her attention: near the edge of the Lenasha, a lone vulture struggling to maintain its glide in the torpid air; at the far end of the field, the hillside village still deserted; closer at hand, Lord Corvalen removing his helm and pushing back his mail coif, his hair slick with sweat. His horse, and Dursten's, stamped frequently, pawing the ground in frustration at being made to stand in a single spot for so long. Luma stood patient and placid, merely swishing her tail to fend off the flies, and from time to time the Kel Sharha stroked the mare's mane or patted her neck to reinforce the charm.

The first warriors to surrender their weapons had tried to approach the Kel Sharha, calling out for her blessing. But the Forstene soldiers had barred their way with brandished spears, had thrust them back roughly, had cuffed a few about the ears, so that she had looked across to Pieran with a shake of her head—enough to tell him to warn the men off trying to come near. Yet they all looked to her after they laid their weapons down, as though they wanted something, expected something of her. What more had she to give?

Still, she held out her hands in blessing and smiled a smile meant to reassure and encourage as each group of men came forward. But her mind stayed distant. And as the mound of weapons grew and the warriors of Sharhaya walked off with bowed heads and slumped shoulders, she asked herself, *Did I truly choose this, or did I simply allow it to happen?*

She knew that a great many of those men wanted to keep fighting, did not want to surrender—yet they did it, because they trusted in the Kel Sharha, the woman touched by the Mothers as no one else was. *Just because I received the Mayahara, does that mean my decisions as Kel Sharha are always correct?* For she *had* made the choice to accept the treaty. Rimenna and Tigannas had supported her and helped convince the rest of the Council, but the impetus and the ultimate responsibility were hers. She prayed to the Watchers that she had not done wrong.

The last to surrender his weapons was Pieran. Now she paid attention, and she was grateful that he made no show of his reluctance or of his disdain for the Forsteners. She also noticed that his additions to the mound of weapons amounted to only one knife, one ax, one bow, and half a dozen arrows; if he had hidden the rest of his personal armament somewhere, she hoped he'd have the sense to leave it there.

Like most of the others, he bowed deeply to her, hands over heart and belly. When he straightened, she could see that tears were starting; she was not surprised by the abruptness with which he turned and strode away into the forest.

Finally, as the sun sank behind the hills, it was over. Carts rattled onto the field to be loaded with the surrendered weapons; grooms moved to take charge of the Sharhay horses. The last groups of warriors—former warriors—were disappearing, six by six, into the distance and the approaching twilight.

The Councillors, after some obvious uncertainty, stepped forward one by one to bow to the Kel Sharha, then turned to make their way to the river and across. At the last moment, before their path took them out of sight, the Kel Jemya, the Kel Mona, and the Kel Sula turned back to gesture protection and blessing upon her; she reached out and traced the same signs in answer.

Suddenly the prince let out a whoop, spurred his horse, and galloped up the field and back. He drew his sword—its blade gleamed red in the sunset—and rode four times around the mound of weapons, still roaring and hooting. The Sharhay horses nearest him shied; there was a great deal of nervous whickering, and one animal kicked out as a Forstene groom reached for its harness.

Luma laid her ears flat and shifted uneasily. The Kel Sharha patted her neck again, and to the other horses she thought, the images strong in her mind, *Run now, if you can, while you can—into the forest, through the forest—to the meadows beyond the trees—fresh grass and freedom!* She was answered by a confusion of animals jostling one another, grooms exclaiming and shouting as horses eluded them. Then there was a surge, and perhaps a score of horses managed to break away and reach the trees; a couple of men started after them but were called back to help control the remaining animals.

As the Kel Sharha allowed herself a bit of a satisfied smile, she realized that Lord Corvalen was looking at her. She made herself aloof again, keeping a watch on her captor out of the corner of her eye.

Prince Dursten cantered back toward them. "Damnedest thing about those horses!" he exclaimed as he approached, but he sounded cheerful. "By the Unifier, it's good to move about again!" He flourished his sword in the air once more and resheathed it, with a grin and a contented sigh.

Lord Corvalen looked suddenly very tired. "Your Highness, will you require my assistance any further this evening?"

"What? Oh, no, not at all." Dursten's eyes lit up, and he leered. "Of course, you have your prisoner to attend to. Well, go along—we can do quite well without you tonight. Ha!" He spurred his horse again and took off down the line of soldiers, exuberantly shouting out to the troops, who answered him back as boisterously.

Lord Corvalen turned to the Kel Sharha. "Come, Lady. There is a pavilion for you in my camp; I will escort you there and have food and drink brought for you."

She hesitated, looking after the prince.

"Do not mind His Highness's . . . pleasantries. I said I would hold you in honorable custody, and so I will; you have nothing to fear from me."

"But my Council—will they be safe tonight?" She locked eyes with Lord Corvalen. "Will any of my people be safe?"

Lord Corvalen observed the scene for a moment. "I doubt that anyone will harass your council or go chasing after your warriors. . . . But once I've seen you safely to your tent, I will order guards for your councillors' camp—just to be certain."

She took his hand and bowed over it. "I am grateful, Lord Corvalen."

*****

The nightmares stabbed at her sleep over and over. They were a jumble of images—some from memory, some from fear, some from the abyss—and growing more horrific: the bloody face, the mound of weapons, trees rooting themselves in the corpses of her Councillors, children with hacked-off limbs begging at the door of the House of Healing. Toward dawn she dreamed she was watching her own violation, and she could not make a move or a sound to help her dream-self, nor could she so much as close her eyes or look away, but she must watch every moment of it.

She woke in a cold sweat, with a surging of nausea. One of the guards was peeking in through the doorway, looking worried; she must have cried out in her sleep.

"I am ill," she blurted, and pushed past him out of the tent, into the predawn gloom.

There was a latrine trench a short way off, provided with a loose-woven screen of green willow branches for nominal privacy. She plunged behind the screen and retched. She vomited again and again, till she brought up only bile.

When she returned to the pavilion, she found wash water awaiting her. Though still shaky, she cleaned herself with care, and thought. So much had happened to her recently that she had lost track of her cycle—which had been irregular the last year in any case. How many days was it now since she last bled? And—Mothers and Watchers forbid—had she been fertile when the prince raped her? Her stomach roiled anew, and she clamped down against the nausea, willing it away.

Ridiculous. Everyone knew how difficult it was for Ma'Sharha to conceive—it was said that so much of their life force flowed into the use of their powers, little was left to water the growing of a new life. Moreover, she had long set her will against conception, and taken her monthly herbs besides. But she was not sure that "everyone" was right, and herbs could vary in their potency, and her battered will had been exerted elsewhere. . . .

She ought to be able to sense whether she was pregnant or not. She ran her hands over her belly and opened her awareness, but she could get no clarity. Her churning emotions were in the way. This would not do; she must think clearly.

She had her medicine bag with her, as always. But abortifacients were not among the herbs she carried on an ordinary basis. If she could only get back to her house in the Sanctuary—all the herbs she needed were there, in their neatly corked jars on her workroom shelves.

And if she could get back to the Sanctuary, she might contrive to speak privately with the Kel Jemya and ask her to curse Prince Dursten. It was the least that he deserved. It was too bad he was out of the Guardians' physical reach. They would castrate him, and cut off his nose, too, so that any beholding him would know that he had committed the sacrilege of violating one of the Ma'Sharha. Death was too great a mercy for such a man.

Then suddenly the Kel Sharha found the clarity she had sought. It was not, after all, pregnancy that had made her sick. It was hatred, hatred poisoning her spirit. And for this she had no ready antidote.

Chapter Eighteen

It began to rain midmorning. The Kel Sharha lay on her cot, listening to the drops pattering onto the canvas overhead. She made the words she was thinking follow the rhythm of the rain: *Strength of the land; its patience, too. . . .* Eventually she drifted into sleep.

The rain had stopped by the time she awoke. She pulled on her boots and the russet cloak, and went outside.

Two guards were seated on mats under an awning in front of the tent, playing at dice. They jumped up when they saw her. "Feeling better, M'Lady?" the older of the pair asked. "The night watch said you was very ill this morning."

"Perhaps I was too long in the sun yesterday," she answered. "I am better now; thank you."

"Good then. Now, I'm called Gar"—he thumped a hand against his broad chest—"and this here is Fidden."

"Fidden it is. We been in Lord Corvalen's following through Cheskara and since, me and Gar, and there's no finer lord a man could serve. So he sets us to look after you, by Vallar, that's what we'll do, and you can consider yourself well guarded—and there ain't no harm we'll let come to you neither, because that's his lordship's order. Which we wouldn't need that order anyways, 'course, you being a lady and all."

The Kel Sharha smiled and nodded; Fidden spoke a variety of Forstene she had not encountered before, and with an unfamiliar accent, but she thought she understood most of this speech.

Gar apparently didn't care much for his companion's loquaciousness and shot him a look before saying to the Kel Sharha, "So . . . is there something we can do for you?"

"I would like to walk. Is it permitted?"

"As long as we come with you. Where to, then?"

"Along the river." The rain had washed the air of its heaviness, and the gnats were negligible today.

"Right-o. You lead, and we'll just follow on behind."

179

When they reached the ford, the Kel Sharha stood for a long time looking toward the forest. The Councillors had returned to the Sanctuary; their tents were gone, but the Kel Mona's bower still stood. Not far from where the encampment had been, a number of Forsteners were moving busily about.

"What do they do?"

"Surveying, Lady," answered Gar. "There's a watchtower going to be built there, and barracks, and them surveyors are figuring the layout."

"I see." It was a sensible location, allowing the soldiers to control the ford. But it pained her to think of this place transformed into a military base. She turned her back on the surveyors and headed on downstream. As she walked along the riverbank, another question occurred to her. "Who will be in the garrisons? Lord Corvalen's men?"

Fidden answered this time. "Word is, the prince is having a right castle built up on that bluff there—his own men'll garrison that, most like."

"I don't know," said Gar. "Prince Dursten's men've been in the field a long while and mostly want to get back home, I'd say. I think the guvner'll be bringing his own troops to man the castle."

"The . . . governor?" asked the Kel Sharha, not sure she'd understood the word.

"Right. The viceroy, you know."

"Lord Corvalen is not viceroy?" It had not occurred to her that he wouldn't be—but now she realized that she'd never had any basis for that assumption.

"Oh no, he's what you might call a sort of a regent for the guvner, till he gets here," Gar explained.

"I see." Forsteners certainly had a confusing way of arranging things.

She walked on in silence. Fidden and Gar seemed unobjectionable in themselves, but it was difficult to feel complaisant about their presence. She tried to think of them in the same way that she had the Guardians who had accompanied her on so many occasions—but there was no comparison. And as she thought of the Guardians, here by the river, she couldn't help remembering Fama's death. And Deela's.

The river was no comfort.

The Kel Sharha had decided she might as well turn back when she noticed some plants growing along a rivulet that fed into the larger stream. She knelt, pinched off a leaf, and was about to pop it into her mouth when Fidden grabbed her hand to stop her.

"Here now, here now, what's that? What greenery are you eating there?" he demanded.

She pointed the herb out to him. "I do not know its name in Forstene language. We call it *dan-ajlas*."

"Huh, like *den-eljas* in Brintoran. *Bog mint* is its Forstene name. But there's another plant grows almost just like it, and that one's poisonous as can be. However"—he crushed a leaf and inhaled its fragrance—"this ain't it. Aye, bog mint alright."

"I am not much of a healer if I do not know such plants."

"Oh, I never thought you'd mix them herbs up—I know you know better. I was just feared you might be about to, well . . . make off with yourself."

"Dolt!" whispered Gar, with a swift elbow to Fidden's ribs.

The Kel Sharha stood with her arms folded and eyebrows raised, staring at them. Then she plucked another leaf and slowly, deliberately chewed it up. Finally she addressed the two guards. "I was ill this morning, and my mouth tasted like"—she did not know the Forstene word for *midden*, so she just made a face. "Now it tastes like mint, much nicer. The other plant—not nice at all. And I do not want to 'make off with myself.' I know my duty; I will not try escape—of any sort."

She turned back toward Lord Corvalen's camp. After a few steps she beckoned to Fidden. "Tell me, how you learn those herbs?"

"Oh . . . that." Fidden dragged a hand through his short brown hair, leaving it sticking out at odd angles. "My gran showed me them two plants, and some others. She's like you with the plants, she is—'cept of course she's just a village cunningwoman, not a great lady like yourself, Lady. Begging your pardon."

"Another day perhaps you tell me more of your gran. Now I am ready—" She was going to say, "to return to my tent," but she realized she was not.

At the same time, her spirit felt more and more oppressed out here. She remembered this river valley as a place of fishing parties and festivities, grain fields and grazing, summer camps for the fieldworkers and herders, music in the bowers at night. . . . Now it was an armed camp, populated by foreigners save for herself.

She knew that what she was feeling was only the smallest foretaste of what awaited her in the months to come, and suddenly wished that she could, after all, escape. Just to get on her horse's back and gallop into the forest, if only for a little while . . .

"Where is my horse?"

The soldiers exchanged looks.

"I am not going to ride away." And she wasn't, in spite of that moment of fantasy. "I want to see my horse and know she is well."

"Oh, if that's all . . . She'll be in the paddocks with the rest of 'em, I reckon. And them grooms look after all the horses proper, I can tell you—but I don't blame you wanting to see for yourself. It'll be this way, then."

The tents in Lord Corvalen's camp were set up in orderly blocks, separated by a gridwork of muddy paths. Fidden led the Kel Sharha along the wide lane that had been left open between the tents and the paddocks, which were located at intervals along the river to give the horses easy access to water. She was grateful she did not have to pass among too many of the soldiers to get here, although all the tents along this path opened to face the paddocks, so that the horses were always under watchful eyes. Now many of those eyes followed after the Kel Sharha. She ignored the stares.

"Here we are, M'Lady," said Fidden with a flourish. "Third paddock. That be your little mare right there, if I'm not mistaken."

She called to the horse, who was already trotting toward the fence, "Luma, pretty lady!"

Luma whickered, nuzzling her velvety nose into the Kel Sharha's hair. The woman wrapped her arms around the horse's neck, whispering, "How are you, my girl? Are they treating you well?" She combed her fingers through Luma's mane, pleased to encounter few tangles.

The mare nudged at the Kel Sharha's hand. "I'm sorry, dear friend. I know you would like a treat, but I have nothing for you."

Luma whinnied and tossed her head. Hoofbeats approached, and the Kel Sharha turned to see Lord Corvalen riding up to the paddock. He swung from the saddle, patted his horse's neck in a friendly manner, and handed the reins to a groom who had hurried forward.

On his approach, Fidden and Gar had moved closer to the Kel Sharha and assumed their most erect and guardlike posture. Corvalen smiled at them. "At ease, men. I need no show to know that you're discharging your duty to a fault. I'll stand a turn at guard myself now— go and take some refreshment."

When they had gone, Lord Corvalen gave the Kel Sharha a courteous nod and said, "I was told that you had been unwell early this morning. May I take it you are feeling better now?"

"I am."

"And your guards"—he gestured in the direction where they had gone off—"I hope they suit. They're only common men-at-arms, but I have found them to be as brave and trustworthy as any knight—and a good deal kinder than many. But if a more noble guard would better suit your dignity—"

"No. They are fine; I like them well. And you need not trouble over my 'dignity,' you know."

"I promised to hold you in honorable custody, Lady. I do not intend to be forsworn."

"Of course not." She was spared further awkwardness by Luma's nickering plea for more attention. The Kel Sharha turned back to the horse and stroked her nose. Once again Luma nuzzled her hand in search of a treat.

"Perhaps she would like this," said Corvalen. He reached into his belt pouch and pulled out a small white lump that sparkled in the afternoon sunlight.

"What is it?"

"Sugar. It comes from over the sea. It makes things taste sweet, like honey."

"Oh . . . In Rezhenet, sometimes on a holiday we had little cakes with sugar on the top. But I never saw it like that before. And horses like it?"

"Mine does. All horses like apples and other sweet things, do they not?"

She accepted the sugar from him, and, unable to resist, touched the tip of her tongue to it. The taste was as she remembered from the Rezhenet holiday cakes—which had been a rather extravagant treat; she could scarcely imagine the wealth of a man who thought nothing of carrying sugar lumps in his belt pouch and handing them out to horses.

When she offered the sugar to Luma, it was received without hesitation. The horse whickered appreciatively—or hopefully. Lord Corvalen produced another lump, which was consumed as quickly as the first.

The Kel Sharha patted Luma's neck. "No more, dear. You must not presume on Lord Corvalen's generosity."

"She may have another tomorrow, when we ride to the Sanctuary."

Had she heard him rightly? She must have, for he was smiling when she turned to face him. "You will let me go to my home? And do my work in the House of Healing?"

"It will be the end of summer before we return to Forstene. I see no reason to make you live in a tent until then."

"I thank you, Lord Corvalen."

His smile faded before she could take his hand; he reassumed his official air. "In any case, the king has charged me with holding your capital until the viceroy's arrival. Prince Dursten is sending out detachments to secure the country, and he too wishes to establish a presence in the Sanctuary." A hint of tension had entered his voice, but it dissipated with his next words. "Torval has volunteered to undertake this office, so he and his following will accompany us. You understand, we will be quartering soldiers in your Sanctuary."

Forstene soldiers in the Sanctuary! But what else could she expect? Sharhaya was their province now, and they would go wherever they pleased.

Only later did the irony strike her: Lord Corvalen had finally gotten her to agree to show him the way to the Sanctuary.

*****

They left camp before the morning was far advanced. Corvalen placed the Kel Sharha between himself and Torval, her guards and Rossen just behind with the squires, at the head of the long column of men-at-arms who would occupy the Sanctuary. He was surprised when she turned to him, a questioning look on her face, as they set out.

"Lord Corvalen, you said yesterday you wait for the viceroy. Are you viceroy until he comes?"

"No, Lady. Sharhaya is not a barony, but a royal province, and I am not of the blood of Stennar."

"This means . . . ?"

"The Exalted Stennar was the ancestor of our kings. His sons shared the rule of Forstene, and neither the country nor its provinces may be entrusted to any but men of the royal house."

She seemed to puzzle that over before asking, "What if none of these men are fit to rule?"

"The viceroy of Sharhaya is very fit, I assure you."

"You know him well?"

"I was his squire; he made me a knight."

Torval laughed. "That was long ago, of course, Lady. I, too, served the duke as squire—but much more recently."

"The duke?"

Corvalen explained. "The king has chosen as viceroy his cousin Duke Beddar, whose lands in fact border Sharhaya. That being the case, it may be as little as four or five weeks until his arrival. He has had ample time to make his preparations, and only awaits my messenger with the news that the treaty has been signed."

"What sort of man is he?"

Corvalen thought how best to sum up his old mentor. "An excellent swordsman; a capable commander; an honest and efficient administrator—"

"He's got a pretty daughter, too," Torval put in.

Corvalen ignored this. "The duke has managed his lands exceedingly well, and long served King Delanar as chancellor. He passed that responsibility on to his eldest son a few years past; I imagine—"

"Is he honorable?" the Kel Sharha asked.

Corvalen regarded her a moment before replying, "I have always found him so; he is a lawful man and loves order. But he will not tolerate any threat to his authority. He can be . . . uncompromising."

"What does this mean?"

"His justice is rarely tempered with mercy. And he is like to be harsh at first, till he is sure of your people. If they continue peaceably under him, however, they should find him a good lord."

She nodded in acknowledgment of his answer, but her air now was distracted. Her gaze wandered away from him and to the trees; the column was entering the Parasha.

Corvalen had seen where the Sharhay councillors left and then returned to the forest, so he knew there would be a path of some kind here, or several paths, leading to the Sanctuary. But he had not expected the road that opened before them. It was unpaved, of course, but it was wide, level, and well defined. He was struck again by the superstitious folly—or colossal ineptitude—of those who had insisted that the way to the Summer Sanctuary could not be found.

Then he looked farther ahead, and saw that the road faded away into undergrowth and bracken, and past that point the trees crowded together; there was no discernible route among them.

Frowning, he reined his horse. As the column behind him halted, he heard Rossen let out a long, low whistle.

Corvalen turned to the Kel Sharha. She was wearing her shuttered look again. "Lady?"

"I will have to open the path; the protection is still on it."

"So . . . no one can travel to the Sanctuary without a Holy Woman?" He hardly liked to admit that this was a possibility.

"Once I open the path, it will remain open; I destroy the protection by leading a stranger to the Sanctuary." She glared at him, as though she expected him to gloat.

A saying of Vallar's was in his mind, however—*Unseemly and unwise, to remind the vanquished of their humiliations*—and he said, as gently as he could, "I'm sorry, Lady, but it must be so. Ride ahead; we will be close behind."

She seemed to gather her resolve, then urged her horse forward.

Corvalen was about to follow when there came a great rush of wind through the treetops. A silence just as startling settled in the wake of this.

Out of the corner of his eye, he thought he saw movement among the trees, but when he turned, there was not so much as a squirrel.

Fidden muttered something in Brintoran.

"Yeah, woodwights for sure," Gar whispered back.

And then, from some distance off to the left, came another sound.

The Kel Sharha looked back at Corvalen, her eyes full of accusation. "What is that? That sound like axes?"

"It is my men cutting trees—timber, for the building of the watchtower and barracks."

The wind was picking up again, and the more slender trees along the roadside swayed; higher up, branches creaked against one another.

The Kel Sharha cocked her head as though listening. Then she swore in Sharhay, and with no more warning than that took off up the forest road at a gallop.

"Hoy!" yelled Fidden and Gar after her. "Not again!" Rossen exclaimed. All three would have pursued her, but Corvalen held up his hand.

"Wait here," he commanded, and spurred his horse. *This is between her and me.*

He had almost caught up when she veered off the road. Cantering through underbrush and over fallen branches, weaving among the trees, her surefooted Sharhay-bred horse was able to outdistance his charger. Though forced to slow, he managed to keep her in sight, only momentarily losing her to view when a clump of trees now and then came between them.

What in Vallar's name is she playing at? On reflection, Corvalen found it hard to believe she meant to try to escape, but he could not fathom what her intention was.

She leapt off her horse, almost before the animal had come to a halt, in front of one of the largest beech trees he had ever seen. Only then did he catch sight of the pair of soldiers approaching, each shouldering an ax.

Corvalen reached the mossy bank beneath the tree a few moments after the soldiers. The Kel Sharha, her back pressed against the beech, was staring them down. They looked round at Corvalen in mute appeal.

"Lady, come away—," Corvalen began.

"They shall not cut this tree!"

"They shall, if I order it," he answered calmly.

Her eyes narrowed as she transferred her gaze from the soldiers to Corvalen. She looked to be on the verge of giving him a serious tongue lashing; then her face changed, softened. "Lord Corvalen, I know I am in no position to ask a favor of you. . . ."

Nor, he thought, could she easily stomach the idea of asking; further words seemed unwilling to come forth.

But she had shown the good sense not to challenge him in front of his men; he decided to help her along. He dismounted, and walked toward her. "Is there something special about this tree, then?"

With him standing as he was now, she had to tilt her head back to look at him. "Do you know of the Watchers? They stand between this world—the Growing World, we say—and the other, where the Mothers Beyond are. The Watchers make a . . . a bridge between us and the Mothers, and they . . ."

"Watch over you?" he supplied, trying not to sound facetious; apparently he succeeded, because the Kel Sharha continued in all sincerity.

"Over all the Growing World—they watch, yes." She nodded. "And they love . . . things that are like themselves, that connect worlds. They attach themselves to trees especially."

"This one, for example?"

"This is a Watcher tree. Such old and great trees often are, for they have seen so many seasons, so many lives. All people honor them."

Corvalen had never seen her this open and earnest. "Then we will do so, too."

He turned to the soldiers, whose faces plainly showed their skepticism about these Watchers—but it didn't matter what they, or he, believed. "The province will be more governable if we make some effort to keep to Sharhay customs, even those we don't understand. So you'll leave off cutting trees until I've had time to learn how we can get our timber without giving offense. Find the other details and tell them the same, then report back to your commander."

One of the men looked as though he would have liked to question the order, but he made his salute and ambled away with his companion with every show of obedience. These soldiers belonged to the royal troops under Corvalen's command; it occurred to him that perhaps some of his Brintorans might be more suited to the task of timber cutting, more sensitive to Sharhay feelings. *Too sensitive, some of them.* It was another thing to consider, at any rate.

"Thank you, Lord Corvalen." The Kel Sharha reached for his hand. "I am grateful," she said as she bowed.

"Then perhaps you will oblige me by not riding off in that precipitate manner again."

"If I waited to explain to you, the men would have been here already with their axes."

"You could not know that."

"Could I not?"

She had never let go of his hand; now, with surprising strength, she pulled him closer to the tree and made him press his palm against the bark, her hand on top of his. "Close your eyes."

Corvalen would never have obeyed anything like a command from this woman and was about to pull away from her—then suddenly he was overwhelmed by the feeling that some other presence was near, and that *it* wanted him to close his eyes. A thought came to him: *Vallar once sought the Wights of the Wood*—an old, old story, not even in the canon of the Exalted One's deeds. But it was the first story of Vallar he'd ever heard, when he was but a small boy. He closed his eyes.

"Now you will understand," the Kel Sharha whispered; she had switched to her own language. In a low, wooden-flute voice, she sang,

"Roots deep, branches high,
Bridge between the earth and sky . . ."

Under his hand, the bark warmed and yielded slightly, like skin. He almost jerked away, but the Kel Sharha pressed harder on his hand; he could feel her pulse.

No . . . it was the pulse of the tree—or of something within the tree, something with neither sap nor blood in its veins, something with a green breath. It emerged from the tree with a sigh, and he felt the breath stir his hair. More beings, of the same kind, seemed to be gathering around him. Things tugged at his hair and earrings, poked at his ribs, pulled at the hem of his surcoat. Thorns scratched at his free hand; it itched for his sword.

He gritted his teeth. Surely he was only imagining it all. The Kel Sharha had made him close his eyes so that he would be more suggestible; if he opened them, he would see right away that there was nothing there but a manipulative woman. Still . . . *Vallar had to blindfold himself when he went into the Wood, so that the Wights would come to him.* And he had come out of the Wood with the honor-name Oakheart.

Corvalen's muscles ached with tension; he relaxed his breathing and dropped his resistance. The ground under his feet seemed to heave, as though deep roots shifted beneath him. A breeze hummed through the leaves all about, a many-toned humming that resonated through the beech tree before him.

It was alive; it almost seemed to have a soul.

A long silence. Breathing—his, and the Kel Sharha's.

He opened his eyes, and he was staring at smooth, gray bark—an ordinary tree.

The Kel Sharha lifted her hand off of his.

Corvalen turned to her. "What did you do to me, woman? Why?"

"The Watchers desired it—for their own reasons, which I do not know."

"It was not real; somehow you made me imagine—"

"I did nothing but lead you here, as I was led. I am the Kel Sharha; the Watchers know me," she said. "And now they know you, too."

Whether this was a good thing or bad, Corvalen could not tell.

Chapter Nineteen

Rossen's first thought, after the surprise of the Kel Sharha's bolting away, was that she had led them into an ambush. He ordered Corvalen's men into battle readiness, and Torval ordered his followers likewise. Then they waited.

They waited till arms grew tired of keeping shields raised high, ready to block a torrent of longbow arrows that still did not come. Rossen would not let the men relax—if Sharhay insurgents were lurking among the trees, they would be waiting for just such a lapse in vigilance.

"We should send out scouts," murmured Torval.

Rossen shook his head. "It would be sending them to their deaths, if the Sharhay are out there."

Torval dropped his voice even lower. "What about my uncle? *He* is out there."

"I'm well aware of that! But he commanded us to remain here. We would have heard something if he were in trouble."

They both fell silent to listen—as they had been listening for a long while, straining to catch any telltale sound. There was nothing to hear but some birds twittering to one another.

Torval shifted in his saddle. "I'm going to look for him."

"No. I'll go. Your leg's hardly well enough—" Rossen broke off. He'd not ceased to scan the forest, and now at last he saw movement. He tensed.

Then every man's shield arm relaxed, and there was a collective exhale, as Corvalen and the Kel Sharha were sighted among the trees. She was leading the way, keeping her horse to a slow trot. She looked thoughtful and faintly unhappy, though her air was far more collected than seemed right for a prisoner who'd just been apprehended in the act of escape.

Corvalen's expression was deeply pensive, his carriage wary. His surcoat was skewed and snagged as though it had been caught in a bramble thicket, and locks of hair had come loose from the ribbon at his nape and hung about his face. Rossen could not stop himself from darting another quick look at the Kel Sharha: her braids were as tidy as could be, her garments no more disarranged than anyone's were when riding. But Rossen felt sure that something had happened between them—something not entirely to the liking of either.

Corvalen rejoined the column, his face now studiously blank. He cast a glance over the men, said, "Let's be on our way, then," and that was that.

As the Kel Sharha took her place ahead of them, so that she could do whatever it was she had to do to clear the way to the Sanctuary, Rossen settled into position beside Corvalen and Torval. They set off at a walk.

The road opened to them as they advanced—a phenomenon all the stranger for its lack of overt drama. One moment Rossen might see nothing but a dense thicket ahead, the next he could discern a possible path through it, and the next he was in that very place, on a road as wide and level as that which they'd been riding all along. The effect was disorienting at first, almost as though they were standing still with the forest shifting around them.

Rossen would have expected the horses to be nervous, but perhaps they were reassured by the confident gait of the Kel Sharha's mare. Before long the men relaxed into the quiet talk, jokes, and bursts of song with which soldiers were wont to alleviate the tedium of a march.

Corvalen, however, was little inclined for conversation. Not so Torval, who chatted amiably away; after a while Rossen found his prattle a welcome distraction from Corvalen's self-contained silence.

Although Torval had been absent from court for close on three years, his mother and sisters were enthusiastic letter writers and kept him well informed. And, as a former royal page, Torval enjoyed the acquaintance and correspondence of many prominent courtiers; even the king, it seemed, wrote to him now and then. Torval consequently had a great fund of anecdotes and gossip, some of which Rossen had not heard before.

Torval had tried several times to draw out his uncle, but was unsuccessful until he began describing a new show-swordsman who had enthralled the court. "Mother says the ladies all dote on him, and the chancellor says that on a rainy afternoon you can't stroll the galleries without having your way blocked by some group of boys practicing this Odasen's moves."

"I hope," Corvalen said, "those boys have no thought of riding to war when they're grown. Such moves will get a man killed in battle."

"That's why it's called *show*-sword, Uncle," Torval answered with a teasing smile. "And admit it, you enjoy the performances as much as anyone. Or at least admit that they make a nice change from listening to ballads and epics and poetry recitals."

Corvalen gave a fleeting smile to acknowledge the point, adding, "It's good to have balance in one's enjoyments, as in everything else."

Torval chuckled. "Odasen would no doubt agree—although he would probably define 'balancing one's enjoyments' differently. There's a young man or two who's practiced more than one kind of swordplay with him; but that doesn't stop him from paying frequent visits to the house of Neldis the courtesan, too."

Rossen wondered what Corvalen, another frequent (though discreet) visitor to Neldis's house, thought of this news.

But Corvalen only said, "I trust you didn't have *that* gossip from your mother or sisters, Torval."

Torval assured him that he had not and segued into another anecdote, but Rossen saw that he had lost his uncle's attention again; Corvalen's gaze was fixed forward, as though he was pretending not to be looking at the Kel Sharha.

*****

When they stopped to rest the horses and have something to eat, Corvalen left the Kel Sharha under Rossen and Torval's watch and took Pellar aside to hear his recitation of the third twenty of the Sayings of Vallar. The squire faltered only once; Corvalen corrected him without impatience, then together they chanted the names of the Exalted One's principal warriors. This was solid ground, on which a man knew himself for himself.

There might indeed be Watchers or woodwights in this forest, but they were nothing to shake a man of honor. Nor was some fey woman who claimed to hear voices among the trees.

Fed, tidied, and refreshed in spirit, Corvalen remounted with a good will for the task ahead. He attended to his duties as both commander and comrade, pulling away from the column to survey it from time to time, riding back to check on the rearguard, and making desultory conversation with the men and with Rossen and Torval.

At the same time, he found he remained acutely aware of the forest around him; on more than one occasion he caught his attention drifting from his companions to focus on some particular tree. At one point, as he was scrutinizing the shadows, a large red-crowned woodpecker flew overhead, its cry a raucous laugh. Inwardly Corvalen laughed, too, at the notion of himself becoming superstitious.

They rode deeper into the afternoon. Then all other feelings dropped away in the face of honest awe as the forest changed its character. Now on each side of the road grew a line of majestic trees, their branches meeting overhead to form verdant arches. From many boughs hung small silver, bronze, and copper bells, beautifully wrought, that rang sweetly in the stir of movement created by the riders. The sound was like the song of birds before dawn, yet some of the bells rang in a lower register, suggesting women's voices heard from far off. No man spoke.

Emerging from the leafy passageway, Corvalen saw the forest change again. The trees looked to be mainly birch, beech, oak, and maple as in the wild forest, but here they grew in so regular a pattern that they could only have been planted that way—and that must have been done generations ago, for these trees towered even more massively than those the company had just passed under. In addition to more bells, strings of colored beads—glass, amber, stone, and painted clay—garlanded many of the branches.

The Kel Sharha halted, and Corvalen went forward to join her. She had gone very still. Too late, he realized that he was in all likelihood interrupting a prayer; he certainly would have wanted to pray, were he in her place. He waited beside her in silence, till she stirred again.

"Are these . . . Watcher trees?" he asked quietly.

She nodded. "But not only the Watchers; we bring the ashes of our beloved dead here."

No wonder she had been praying. Corvalen was still trying to think of some suitable remark when she spoke again.

"This is sacred forest: eleven rings of trees to circle the Sanctuary. You must not cut or burn these trees, nor kill any animal within this place. It is sacred. You understand?"

"Yes."

"And you will make all the soldiers to understand?"

There was an edge of urgency in her voice, and he remembered the charred, empty circle of land he had seen in the south. It came to him that she must have been there, in the Winter Sanctuary, when it was attacked.

"The war is over, Kel Sharha. There is no reason for my people to harm your sacred places."

"There never was, Lord Corvalen."

194

For a moment he had a glimpse of sorrow deep as a mountain lake, then ice coated the water's surface.

The Kel Sharha kneed her horse into motion again. Corvalen followed, pulling up his coif and donning his helm, mindful of the impression he wanted to make when he entered the Sanctuary. He glanced back and was satisfied to see Torval and the others doing likewise.

From nearby, some forest hawk cried; it was answered almost immediately by another farther ahead. Then there was silence, but for hoofbeats and harness and the bells among the branches.

Nagged by the feeling that he and his men were being watched, Corvalen occupied his mind with counting the rings of trees as he passed them. After the eleventh ring there was a bit of loamy clearing, and then, stepping onto a cobbled street, they entered the Sanctuary itself.

Never had Corvalen seen such a place. Martos of Ghildarna had told him of it, but he'd had difficulty forming a picture in his mind to match the description. Here was a small town, completely surrounded by forest. The houses were arranged in neat concentric circles, with lanes paved in colored stone running between the rings of buildings. All the houses were wooden, stave-built, most of them two-storied. They looked immaculately kept, many brightly painted, many with doors and porch pillars elaborately carved. Flowers and herbs spilled from window boxes and baskets; fruits and vegetables rioted in gardens. Here and there Corvalen saw a croft of wheat, or a cluster of fruit or nut trees. Among the plants, he sometimes glimpsed a well, often protected, shrinelike, by a wood-shingled rooflet, its supports carved and painted to look like flowering vines.

Just as Corvalen was thinking that this place seemed completely untouched by the war, the Kel Sharha led the way out onto the circular common at the center of the Sanctuary. Ringing this area were more well-made wooden buildings. But the green itself was blanketed with tents and lean-tos, around which hovered shabby, careworn people, staring at the advancing soldiers. Corvalen was aware of even harder stares from people gathered on porches and balconies; he was sure that there were more hostile eyes on the other side of every window facing the common.

The Sanctuary fairly vibrated with loathing, fear, uncertainty, and sorrow. It was a dispiriting mix—but one that would soon yield to an authoritative hand.

The Kel Sharha had paused—looking about her home with what bittersweet thoughts Corvalen could only imagine. Now as she moved forward again, some of the refugees sent up a cry and rushed toward her. She slowed her horse as hands reached to touch her gown, her boots. She nodded to one side and another, graciously, but her own hands stayed tight on her horse's reins.

Eventually the refugees fell back to let Corvalen and his vanguard pass. They had to ride single file, and carefully, to make their way along the narrow clear space between the crude shelters.

This would not do. Martos had told him that when the High Council was in residence, the Sanctuary was occupied by roughly two hundred people. These refugees looked to double that number. *They'll have to go.* Even though Corvalen planned to have a large percentage of his men camp in the forest, keeping the Sanctuary surrounded, there was no room for both soldiers and refugees here.

As for the peoples' obvious adulation of the Kel Sharha . . . it was problematic in its way, but it did tend to confirm her value as a hostage.

At the center of the common the remainder of the High Council had gathered atop a shoulder-high stone platform, with shallow steps at each side and a fountain at each rounded corner. The Kel Sharha dismounted before the nearest fountain on the left, where a young Holy Woman greeted her, offering a copper bowl she had just filled with clear water. The Kel Sharha bowed, then ceremoniously washed her face and hands.

Corvalen swung down from his saddle and approached, curious to see if the bowl would be offered to him as well. The young woman cast an anxious glance at the Kel Sharha, and Corvalen saw her consider, then nod. She gave him a look as if to say, "Remember, and do not betray this welcome."

He answered with a slight bow that he hoped conveyed appropriate gravity and consciousness of her indulgence, then gladly splashed away some of his travel grime.

As he finished, he realized that he had nearly allowed the Kel Sharha to take control of this situation. Ignoring her therefore, he motioned to Torval and Rossen to dismount and wash.

Meanwhile he eyed the councillors, taking their measure. He could not expect any of the chiefs of the Holy Women to be very accommodating. As for the elders of the Greater Guilds: however honored they were by the Sharhay, they were mere artisans and minstrels. But that silvery-haired fellow, Tigannas the Lawspeaker . .

.he might be someone that Corvalen, and later the viceroy, could work with.

When Rossen had finished washing, Corvalen allowed himself to glance toward the Kel Sharha again. He expected to be met with a frown, or a challenging glare. He got cold dignity, as she turned away from him and mounted the steps to the top of the dais to receive the greetings of her council. He followed.

He would take the lead from her soon enough.

Chapter Twenty

The Kel Sharha had made her escape to the House of Healing as quickly as possible after completing the formalities of her return, of introducing Lords Corvalen and Torval and adjuring the Sanctuary folk to cooperate with their authority. It still pained her to have uttered those words. But they were necessary; this was the lot she had chosen for her people.

Peace—I chose peace for them! And survival; it was the right choice.

She forced herself to concentrate on her patient. His symptoms worried her, especially as they were shared by a number of others in the ward.

A familiar footfall made her look up.

Taras stood before her, cradling his lute in his arms. "Kel Sharha." He bowed.

He was so beautiful.

"You should not be here, Taras."

"I thought you might like me to play for your patients."

Ordinarily, she would have welcomed him to do so; he had such a way with his music, almost as if he could channel healing power through it. "Not today; I do not want you to *become* one of my patients. I fear we have an epidemic brewing here."

Epidemics were always a danger in wartime, when so many were in such close quarters and conditions made it difficult to maintain the proper state of cleanliness; she had heard that more people died from disease during the Ghildaran Civil War than were killed in the fighting.

"You'll stop it, though, just as you've stopped every other epidemic that has threatened us."

"My Order has done well enough till now, yes." This had been a point of no little pride, in fact, and she did not relish the irony of disease scything through the people now that the treaty was signed. "We might yet halt this fever's spread, but still it will take many lives before it is done." *And I do not want yours to be one of them.* "You should go, Taras."

199

Her patient had been lying restlessly, eyes open but unfocused, occasionally muttering odd words. Now he thrashed his blanket off, and the Kel Sharha could see the rash covering his chest. She placed her hands to quiet him; his flesh burned, and it was slack and doughy.

Taras plucked one of his lute strings, then another, and let them vibrate in gentle harmony. "If you command me to leave, Kel Sharha, I will. But *you* are here, and isn't your life at risk?" He touched a third string; it echoed the same sweet, quiet note as his voice.

"The longer we work with the healing power, the stronger it is in us; I think I have little to fear. Our apprentices, however . . . they are still vulnerable." She looked up the ward, to where Lillanna's junior apprentice lay in the grip of the fever; Treska sat by her, lifting her head to help her drink a glass of salted honeywater, sip by sip.

Taras followed her gaze. "Is that young Graysa?"

"Yes."

"Don't you fear for your Treska, then?"

"I do. But if she is to take Orders, she must . . ." She lost her thought as her eye was caught by movement in the doorway at the end of the ward.

"Kel Sharha?"

She resummoned her composure. "I can no more discourage Treska from nursing her friend than I can dissuade you from bringing your music into this House." She tried to smile. "Play if you will, till I get back."

"Back?"

"There is a matter to which I must attend. Excuse me."

She looked again to the doorway, where Lord Corvalen leaned against the jamb in an attitude of apparent leisure. Yet even from across the length of the room, she could see that his eyes were keen, observing everything.

She did not hurry up the ward. She paused to speak a word of encouragement to Treska, and again to confer with Lillanna, who was just leaving a refugee boy's bedside.

The Kel Sharha kept her voice low. "As soon as you can spare anyone, send an apprentice out to the green to examine the rest of the refugees. I am sure that those who have been brought to us are not the only ones who are ill."

Lillanna frowned. "We have no room for more, either here or in the Guesthouse, my chief."

"The warriors nearly recovered from their wounds can be moved to the House of the Guardians. If that does not free enough beds . . ." She puffed out her breath in exasperation. She had been about to suggest the guildhalls, but the Celebrants' Hall was already full of orphans, and disease certainly could not be admitted to the Vintners' Hall. That left only the Artisans' Hall, where she doubted there would be much room for beds or pallets among the craftworkings.

"There's a field surgeon serving in the Guesthouse," Lillanna offered. "He could set up a tent hospital below, in the House garden."

"Good. Send for him and have it done. I will speak to the Kel Jemya about her Order's assistance." She should speak with the other Chiefs, too; if the Kel Sula could find the source of this contagion, the Kel Mona could perform the proper rites. . . .

First, however, she had to send Lord Corvalen on his way.

As she approached, he straightened and began to greet her, but she gestured him to silence. "Let us speak elsewhere. Your presence disturbs the people here."

On a stand beside the doorway rested a bowl containing an herbal infusion mixed with watered spirits. She washed her hands and murmured the words of purification, their rhythm counterpointing the music of Taras's lute. She glanced back, to see that he had settled himself beside poor Graysa and that many of the patients already appeared to be resting easier. Then she joined Lord Corvalen in the corridor.

He gave her a curious look. "I did not expect to find you still working as a Healer now that you are Kel Sharha."

"Every Healer is needed. Sickness has spread among the refugees—there are too many for the Sanctuary."

"I agree. They cannot stay here. In fact, I came to talk to you about sending them on their way."

"Have you heard me, Lord Corvalen? They have sickness!"

"Not all of them, surely. Kel Sharha, I am not a hard-hearted man—I would not deny your care to the sick and injured. But those who are strong enough to travel must leave this place."

"To go where?" She heard herself bite out the words, and instantly regretted the show of temper.

"Back to their homes," he said. "The war is over, after all."

"And what of those who have homes no more?"

He shrugged. "They will make new homes."

"Where? How, with no living and nothing but what they carry?"

"They will make their way as best they can. How is not my concern, so long as every able-bodied one of them is gone by high-sun tomorrow."

"Not your concern? But you—"

"My concern at present is the quartering of my men and the elimination of potential sources of disorder—and that means clearing out those refugees." His voice had hardened; the Kel Sharha knew he would not give way before her.

And why should he? Why would he? He had his duty to his king, and that surely did not include accommodating her.

And yet . . . he had humored her wishes before—when they did not stand between him and his duty. This very morning, he had agreed to halt the timbering until he could find a better way to do it. If she could convince him that showing compassion to the refugees would serve his own purpose . . .

"Lord Corvalen," she said, and chose her next words with care. "You do not want disorder. I understand. But these people . . . they are already poor and without power; many feel they have nothing to live for. If you send them away by force, you will have more order in the Sanctuary, true—but not in the rest of Sharhaya. These people will leave with anger in their hearts. Many will find something to live for then: hatred of Forstene. Anger and hatred—they can give power to the powerless, and it is a power that spreads like flame in a dry season. How easy to govern will be a land where such fires burn?"

"Not easy," he acknowledged, but he studied her warily.

*****

Corvalen was being manipulated, and he knew it. At the same time, he knew there was truth in what the Kel Sharha said. And he had to admit that she did seem to understand his desire to establish order. She was an astute woman, too; he gave her credit for endeavoring to convince him that it was all part of his duty to do what she wanted. Well, two could ride that horse.

"Not easy," he repeated. "But even so, the fact remains that there are more refugees here than the Sanctuary can support. You said it yourself. And if sickness is spreading among them, isn't it best to get as many of the unstricken as possible away from here, before they also fall ill?"

The Kel Sharha crooked him a half smile. "So, our object is the same—or near enough. But there are still the questions: Where shall they go, and how live?" She folded her hands at her waist and looked at him expectantly.

Can't the woman ever stop setting me problems to solve? This day alone there had been that business with the trees. . . .

Corvalen caught at an idea. "It may be that I can give a living to some of these people . . . if they would accept it."

The Kel Sharha's eyes narrowed. "Work for Forsteners? Doing what?"

"Helping with the timbering, so that we have no more problems like that of this morning. If they could show my men which trees are acceptable to cut"—a thought occurred to him. "Or can only Ma'Sharha recognize Watcher trees?"

"Most Sharhay know these trees well, and they know the proper way to receive the forest's gifts."

Did she mean there was some kind of rite or prayer that had to be done before cutting a tree? A form of apology perhaps; these people seemed to believe that trees were alive, almost as alive as people. Fast on that thought came a moment's vivid sensory recollection of her hand on his, and his on the beech, and the breath and movement of the forest, the sense of being in the company of living spirits. . . .

He turned abruptly, gesturing to her to accompany him down the stairs. "Let us see what we have to work with," he said as he walked out onto the porch of the House of Healing.

The evening gathered in, but the light was still far from failing. He looked over the green and contemplated the refugees. Some of those nearest stared back. He glanced aside, expecting to see the Kel Sharha standing next to him. But no, she had halted in the shadows of the doorway. He strode back to her.

"There do not look to be very many able-bodied men among your refugees."

"But what you want is not men's work—anyone can do it."

"Kel Sharha, if women without men mix with my soldiers, the soldiers are likely to expect them to . . . do more than forestry."

She did not seem to understand him.

"My army quick-marched to Sharhaya." He tried to explain in a way he hoped would not offend her sensibilities. "I did not allow any women to accompany or follow us."

"What about Jennis?"

"She came to Sharhaya with Torval and his following. Women often travel with a Forstene army. They do the soldiers' laundry and provide . . . other comforts."

She frowned, then frowned more deeply and drew herself up with full dignity. "No woman of Sharhaya would provide such 'comforts' to

Forsteners. Our women do not"—she struggled to find the Forstene words; not finding them, she switched to Sharhay—"do not make merchandise of their bodies, and our men would be ashamed to purchase the gifts of love!"

Corvalen felt the scorn in her words, the clear disdain she must feel for men like him. But what did she know of men like him, of the knife edge they honed between honor and dishonor? The mores of Forstene were not those of Sharhaya. Nor, for that matter, were those of Sharhaya all that she thought them to be; for a moment he was tempted to tell her about the Sharhay women who "comforted" Dursten's veterans in the village near Southwood.

He pressed down the unworthy thought and strove for a reasonable tone of voice. "In that case, it would be best if my army employed only your men, at least until we become better accustomed to the ways of your country."

Really, though, it was the Sharhay who were going to have to accustom themselves to the ways of Forstene—and the Kel Sharha's expression told him she understood this all too well.

*****

Treska swallowed, trying hard to calm her stomach. She took a deep breath, but that just made it worse—the Guesthouse reeked of vinegar and pungent herbs from the daily purifications the Kel Sharha had ordered, here and in the House of Healing.

But no amount of washing floors, walls, and furniture had been enough to save Graysa.

Treska felt tears stinging her eyes, even as the nausea surged again.

The Kel Sharha had refused to let her stay the night beside Graysa's pyre, out in the wild-forest clearing where the bodies of the epidemic victims were burned. The House of Healing, the Guesthouse, and the tent hospital were all full, and there were patients to see from first light on. "I cannot do without your assistance," the Kel Sharha had told her.

So here they were on the second floor of the Guesthouse, come at the request of one of the lay healers to deal with an old refugee woman's gangrenous foot. And as if gangrene was not already disgusting enough, now the foot had to be amputated.

Treska finished purifying the Kel Sharha's surgical knife with wine spirits and laid it on a tray next to the woman's bed, ready. She could feel the woman's fear, her anticipation of the pain not entirely damped by a strong dose of poppy syrup. Treska tried not to look at her foot and fought the urge to gag, but was not quite successful.

The Kel Sharha gave her a sharp look. "Go outside; the lay healer can assist me with the rest of this procedure."

Treska knew she should refuse, should declare her determination to stay and help, but she bolted.

Out on the balcony, she gripped the railing and took great gulps of the morning air. *Why did I ever want to be a Healer?* But of course, what she wanted had nothing to do with it—the village Listener had seen the gift in her, and so she was sent to the Order for training, as must be. And really, she did want to use her gift, and help her people, and she did like the idea of being a Healer. The reality of healing was just so much bloodier and uglier and smellier than she'd expected. . . .

Below her the green was empty except for some Forstene soldiers marching around. No more tents and lean-tos, no more refugees; they had been gone since yesterday. Most were on their way back to the remains of their homes or looking for someplace new to settle, but the Kel Sharha said that some were going to work for Lord Corvalen's army. She said he was giving them food and shelter in return for their help in the forest. Imagine working for the Scourge of Cheskara! Now that she had seen him, he didn't seem quite as scary as in the stories, but he was scary enough all the same.

And he was going to take the Kel Sharha away to Forstene. *First I lost Deela, and then Graysa. Soon I won't have anyone. I hate Forsteners!*

A soldier passed under the balcony, and Treska almost wished that her nausea would come back so that she could accidentally-on-purpose throw up on him. Instead she found herself crying again.

"There now, child." The Kel Sharha had come out onto the balcony without Treska hearing her. She put an arm around Treska and drew her close.

The Kel Sharha smelled like vinegar and sweat and blood. Treska's stomach churned again, and she pulled away.

Through her tears, she read mingled concern and dissatisfaction on her teacher's face—though that face now was harder to read, thanks to the big scar on her left cheek. It made the Kel Sharha look severe and frightening, no matter what she was actually saying or doing. Or . . . maybe not. Maybe it was scars *inside* that made her look like that. Or maybe Treska was just seeing her that way because she knew she was falling short of what the Kel Sharha expected.

"I'm sorry I've disappointed you again, my Chief. I just . . . I don't know. Maybe the Listeners were wrong; maybe I'm not really meant to be a Healer." She could hardly believe she was saying this to her teacher, to the head of the Order, to the Kel Sharha herself. But since she was, she might as well ask the question she'd been worrying about: "I don't have the . . . capacity, do I?"

"You have it. But you do not yet believe in it; you have not given yourself over to it."

"I don't know how! And even if I did . . . I don't think I'll ever be like you, my Chief."

"I should hope not!" The Kel Sharha laughed, short and sharp.

Treska stared back in mute appeal.

"Be like yourself, Treska, your Healer-self. And know that you are just at the beginning of discovering it; it takes time to grow and find its own way."

"But you need me *now*."

"The *people* need you, and not only now, but for many years to come. I will be gone, and you must carry on. You cannot do that if you allow me to become a shadow over you."

"I don't understand. Why shouldn't I want to be like you? You're my teacher, my Chief—"

"Treska, how do you think I became what I am? I did not spring from my mother's womb a Healer, you know."

"But your gifts—"

"Did not make my apprenticeship any easier than yours, girl. And let me tell you, the Listeners were not even convinced that I *had* the gifts."

That seemed unbelievable.

"They did not place me with the Healers till after I had begun my bleeding cycle. You are already much further along than I was at your age." The Kel Sharha looked off into the distance. "I felt that I was always behind in my learning, and so did the rest of the House. They worked me harder than any of the other apprentices, and the Kel Nira herself undertook to give me extra lessons, even though she was not my covenanted teacher."

"I . . . I'll try harder, my Chief, as you did."

The Kel Sharha sighed, and focused her gaze on Treska again. "Just do your work, and busy your mind with how to serve the people instead of dwelling on your supposed inadequacies." She squeezed Treska's shoulder. "Go down to my garden; pinch back the mints, and have something to eat before you return to the House of Healing. This afternoon I will start teaching you to use touch and your mind to See into a patient's body."

As Treska thanked her teacher, she felt something akin to delight edging out a bit of the sadness and doubt that had filled her throughout the morning. *The Kel Sharha wouldn't teach me the Seeing if she didn't think I could be a Healer.* She went home feeling as near to happy as she had been in a long time.

*****

After Treska had gone, the Kel Sharha lingered on the balcony. Thinking back to her own apprenticeship had given her a peculiar feeling—as though there was an itch in her mind that needed scratching. Really, though, it was Treska's apprenticeship she should be contemplating; what was going to become of the girl after she was gone?

Movement on the green below drew her notice. There was always a group of Forsteners standing watch; now more soldiers were joining them. They came from every direction, having been quartered in houses throughout the Sanctuary (a thought that still rankled), wearing Lord Corvalen's black and red or Torval's blue and white over their mail. Every man had his sword at his side, his shield in his hand, and carried or wore his helm.

This has an ill appearance. She was about to go and send for the Kel Jemya when something else arrested her attention: at the south of the Sanctuary, Lord Corvalen, with Rossen and Torval, emerged from the Champion's house—and Pieran was with them. He looked across the green, saw the Kel Sharha, and waved to her.

She folded her arms and frowned. She did not like the Forstene officers making their quarters in the Champion's house, but she was even less pleased to see her brother among them.

Pieran left Lord Corvalen and made his way up the green toward the Guesthouse, to join the Kel Sharha on the balcony.

"Your Forstener watchdogs met me at the top of the stairs. I thought they might not let me through, but they just asked my name. I suppose they report anyone who speaks with you."

"What are you doing here, Pieran? You were supposed to go back to Redcreek."

He hesitated, and didn't quite look at her when he replied. "They won't let me."

"Won't *let* you? Will they turn the Sanctuary into a place of imprisonment, then?"

Pieran shrugged; his shoulders, settling back into place, sagged a little. "That pup Rossen reminded the Scourge that I know Forstene, and they need translators. So I have to stay."

She began to speak, but he shook his head to forestall her.

"They would have found some reason, Kel Sharha. They know I'm your brother, and that I was the Champion's Second. They're not going to want me out of their sight; if I'd gone away, they just would have sent someone to bring me back."

"I wanted you safe from them," she whispered.

"I know. Anyway"—he put on a smile—"Lillanna's here, and . . ." The smile faded.

"Yes; she would take it hard if you were to leave, especially now." She patted his hand, and thought of her Second's quiet grief for her dead apprentice. At least there had been no new cases of the fever since yesterday; the worst seemed to be over and, with the Mothers' blessing, they would not lose anyone else.

Down on the green, the Forstene soldiers had assembled south of the dais, divided into two ranks facing each other. Lord Corvalen took his place at the head of one group; at the head of the other Rossen waited, evidently standing in for Torval, who still favored his wounded leg and sat now on the dais.

The Kel Sharha ignored Lord Corvalen, whose voice was raised in address to the two groups of soldiers. But her quiet contemplation broke before the onslaught of the bellowed orders that followed.

With answering shouts, the two sides rushed together, swords drawn and shields braced in tight formation. A few men went down from the sheer force of the clashing shield walls. For a short time it seemed that the fight was nothing but shield pushing against shield. Then a group of Rossen's men managed to bullhead their way through Corvalen's front line. A moment later, Corvalen's rear line broke away and ran to circle around Rossen's force, taking his rearguard by surprise. The mass of men fragmented into pairs, fighting hand to hand.

Watching, the Kel Sharha shifted uneasily. The shouting, the metallic ring of sword meeting sword, the duller impact of sword against shield—the walls of the House of Healing would not keep out all this noise of battle. Her patients would surely hear, and what memories would it stir for them?

One sound, at least, was missing: the screams of the wounded and dying.

Lord Corvalen called an abrupt halt to the exercise. He had stepped back from the melee and apparently had seen something not to his liking. He beckoned Rossen to him, and the rest of the men moved to give the two room. Fragments of Lord Corvalen's lecture carried across the green as he and Rossen went through a slow-motion demonstration: ". . . if you hold your shield thus . . . come under . . . your opponent can strike . . ."

The Kel Sharha glanced aside at Pieran. His expression was keen, and his eyes followed Lord Corvalen's every move.

Against her better inclinations, her own attention was drawn back to the two Forstene warriors. Lord Corvalen had finished his explanations. He looked around at the men-at-arms, saying something she could not hear. Then, without warning, he sprang at Rossen. The younger man responded instantly, thrusting his shield upward to block his lord's descending sword.

The two men were matched in reflexes, strength, and skill. Lord Corvalen was a little taller, but not enough to make a difference in their contest. His greater experience was another matter. Unlike Rossen, he fought without his voice, making no sound either when dealing a blow or receiving one. His utter focus was palpable to the Kel Sharha; the achieving of such confidence and discipline, she knew, was the work of many years. She could sense the deep welling of power within him, the flowing of that power into his sword arm, the way that power kindled his mind to act and react.

Her right hand gripped the balcony rail, but she felt as if it were tightening around a sword hilt. Though she was standing still, every muscle in her body was intent on movement. When Lord Corvalen lunged or darted forward, she felt it in her own legs; when he parried a blow with his shield, she felt the impact shiver her own left arm; her right arm shared every muscle contraction of his as he wielded his sword.

She bit her lip; this was a cauldron she would rather not stir, but the odor rising from it was as alluring as it was horrible. What was happening to her?

The Healer in the Kel Sharha snapped awake again when Lord Corvalen brought the flat of his blade down on Rossen's gauntleted sword hand; Rossen cried out and dropped his weapon.

She bit back a swear word. "The fool! He could have broken every bone in Rossen's hand!" At the same time, she knew it was not foolishness that had caused Lord Corvalen to strike such a blow; it was his abandoning of himself to that which she knew as Jemhara, the power wielded by the Guardians. Well, and perhaps such abandonment was foolishness after all.

It had taken Lord Corvalen a moment to regather himself before sheathing his sword. Now he was examining Rossen's hand. He gestured toward the House of Healing. Rossen shook his head, but Yasma was already running from the doorway toward him. The Kel Sharha realized that every doorway around the clearing, in fact, was filled with spectators. She could see some of their faces clearly enough to realize what most of them must be thinking.

"A pretty demonstration," she heard herself say.

"A useful one, at any rate," Pieran replied.

"We know full well how thoroughly we are beaten. He did not have to make such a show for us—and in the very center of the Sanctuary!"

"To be fair, Kel Sharha, I don't think it was done for that purpose—at least not solely. This is how they train, I believe. It's how our warbands should have trained," he added. "If we, too, had drilled every day as though we were in real battle, these Forsteners might not be in our Sanctuary now."

"Their warriors do *nothing* but fight," she answered scornfully. "Ours have farms and vineyards and flocks to tend."

"And that's why they're the conquerors, while we—"

"Oh, let us stop this, Pieran. It does no good now."

"No, perhaps not now. But for the future—"

He was cut off by the winding of a horn, coming from the forest road. The men on the green snapped to attention. A few moments later, two outriders bearing purple and gold standards entered the Sanctuary. They circled around the open area and drew rein near the dais as two dozen armed knights trotted out onto the green. In their midst, tall on his stallion, rode Prince Dursten, with Esban following him like a faithful dog.

Chapter Twenty-One

It was late afternoon when Rossen was dispatched to summon the Kel Sharha. He found her on the ground floor of the House of Healing in a room at the back. It reminded him of an apothecary's shop. Shelves filled with pottery jars and dark glass bottles lined the walls. Bundles of drying herbs hung from the ceiling beams, and on the long oaken worktable were mortars and pestles in a range of sizes, along with two sets of handsome bronze scales.

The Kel Sharha was standing behind the worktable in sleeveless tunic, overdress, and a long russet-colored vest, humming as she ground something in a large stone mortar. Her apprentice stood by; her eyes flickered toward Rossen as he entered, and he thought she might scream, as she had done in the woods the day of the Kel Sharha's escape. But she turned her gaze back to her mistress and her duty.

The Kel Sharha said something, and the girl took a handful of dried leaves out of a jar in front of her and added it to the mortar. Maintaining a steady rhythm with the pestle, the Kel Sharha ground in the new ingredient, though the tune she hummed changed slightly.

Almost seduced by the hypnotic effect of the new melody, Rossen found his eyes focused on the arm that wielded the pestle, watching the play of muscle beneath her lightly tanned skin. She wore no more bandages and seemed utterly unconscious of the scarred-over burns. She had an admirable fortitude; nobility, almost.

If I could love a woman, it might be someone like her. But of course there were no such women in Forstene. And besides—

The humming ceased; the Kel Sharha looked up from her work and caught him staring. She acknowledged his presence with a nod, but spoke instead to the apprentice. She handed the mortar to the girl and watched as she scraped the contents into a bowl, then poured wine over them. A few more instructions, and at last, coming from behind the worktable, she attended to Rossen.

"Let me see your hand, please."

He held it out, and she ran her fingers over the bruised skin.

"The Healer who looked at it on the green told me that nothing is broken," he said.

"Healer Yasma spoke true. But still you have swelling here. . . . Hmm . . ."

She walked over to a shelf and selected a squat clay jar. Returning to him, she uncorked it and, before he could protest, rubbed some kind of ointment into the back of his hand. He wrinkled his nose at the cloying smell of it.

"Does your lord often injure his friends?" she asked lightly.

Rossen tried to match her tone. "Never by intention. He—" No; why should he justify Corvalen's actions to this woman? She would not understand anyway.

His hand tingled, but the sensation faded as she finished with the ointment.

"That will help," she said, disregarding the sentence he had broken off. "But do not use the hand much for the next days; no sword till the moon changes. If you have more pain or swelling—"

"Lady, I did not come to see you about my hand," he interrupted, afraid he was in for a long medical lecture otherwise.

"No; of course. They want to see me."

"Immediately, please. The prince is not in a patient temper."

Her mouth tightened, but she only nodded and led the way out of the House of Healing.

*****

A cold feeling washed over Treska as she watched the Kel Sharha leave with the Forstener. She hadn't understood anything he said, but it couldn't have been good. Still, there was nothing she could do about it. And the Kel Sharha had told her to take the medicine they'd just made to Healer Lillanna. So that was what she ought to be doing. *It is better to work than to worry*—that was something the Kel Sharha was always saying.

As Treska reached the door of the ward, she heard Taras's lute. She recognized the tune: he had been working on it for a long time, ever since the battle of the Lenasha. It was what he'd been able to piece together of the song the dead Celebrant Jedan had sung before the battle, the song that had made the men fight so bravely. Whenever Taras had the chance to talk to warriors who had been there, he asked them if they remembered it. Most of them did—a few well enough to hum a bit of the melody or recite some of the words.

Of course, Taras changed the tune a little when he played it in the House of Healing, to make it more suitable; healing strength was different from battle strength, he said. And in the House of Healing he never sang, but only played the lute. Unless the Kel Sharha happened to be nearby. He knew all her favorite songs, and he made up new ones for her, too. She would listen to a quiet verse or two, then smile at him and go back to work.

Except she hadn't done that since she returned from the Forsteners' camp.

"Treska? You're blocking the door, child."

Treska blinked. Healer Yasma stood in front of her, her cheeks pink, like they always were on hot days, and her eyes all full of pity.

"Sorry; I got lost in thought. I'm, um, supposed to bring this medicine to Healer Lillanna."

"She's gone to lie down for a bit. Perhaps you should, too, dear; you look exhausted."

Treska fought the urge to yawn in response. "I need to wait for the Kel Sharha to come back. One of the Forsteners came and got her, and—"

A voice she didn't know, a man's, interrupted from behind her. "And she'll be busy with them for a good while—so why not take a little nap? She'll never know. Besides, you've got to get used to doing things without her permission sooner or later."

Treska had stepped back from the doorway, and the man strode past her and Yasma into the ward. His appearance surprised her so much that she blurted out, "Who are you?"

He was Sharhay, only he was wearing Forstene clothes. He gave her a lopsided smile, as though he was trying to be charming. He smelled like a wineskin.

"I'm Esban. Perhaps you've heard of me."

Treska shook her head.

Yasma frowned. "You're that boy. . . ."

"Yes, *that* boy. The one your Chief said wasn't good enough for this House. But look: here I am!"

"Well, you're not staying," Yasma said. "You've no reason to be here, so I will thank you to go elsewhere."

"Oh, I have a reason. And maybe I even have some old friends among your patients." He sauntered down the ward, peering at the occupants of the beds. Then he noticed Taras, bent on his music and never so much as glancing at Esban. "And who's this? You, what are you doing here—don't you know there's no place for men among the Ma'Sharha?"

Taras did not stop playing, but Treska could hear a change in the music. "There is always a place for a man who is willing to be of use," he said.

"'Willing to be of use.'" Esban laughed. "I bet you are."

Taras looked directly at Esban for the first time. "I honor our leaders. I help my people. I use the gifts the Mothers gave me." The music grew somehow harsher. "But you are a drunken idler." The lute strings rasped. "You, Esban, are a traitor." The melody finished with a brawling chord. "You are damned."

Esban staggered back as though Taras had knocked the breath out of him. Silence resonated through the ward.

Treska could not keep herself from staring at Taras. He was still sitting, his hands now folded, relaxed, over the belly of his lute. But he was not the gentle singer she had thought. She wondered if the Kel Sharha knew. She must.

Esban, too, stared at Taras. He licked his lips, swallowed, and made a little coughing noise. "Whatever I am, I'm no woman's servant."

"And whose servant are you?" Taras said, but he gave his attention to retuning his lute, making it clear that Esban's answer had no importance to him.

"As a matter of fact, I serve Prince Dursten, and I'm not ashamed to say so. He knows how to value a man's talents: I am helping him build the castle on Summer Bluff. His Highness has been designing it himself, and he has sought my advice at every turn. He was not at all happy, I can tell you, to have to come here to discipline the Kel Sharha when he has a castle to be planning."

Yasma had had enough. "You will leave this House, Esban. You will leave now, or I will summon the Guardians to remove you."

"Keep your Guardians. I've lingered here too long already; His Highness awaits me." He moved toward the door, but turned to look around the ward one more time. "I can't imagine, now, why I ever wanted to be one of you. You Ma'Sharha claim to have power, but the only power you've got is what you take from the rest of us. And I'm not the only one who thinks so."

Not so long ago, Treska would have been shocked to hear anyone voice such a notion. But she had not forgotten the conversation she'd overheard between those refugees. *If I had the power they have*, the one had said.

But even if Esban felt that way, how could he turn against his own people and serve the prince of Forstene?

And what had he meant when he said the prince had come to the Sanctuary to "discipline" the Kel Sharha?

*****

Rossen led the Kel Sharha up the stairs of the Champion's house to the room that Corvalen had chosen for his office. Afternoon sunlight slanted in through the window to reveal Corvalen and the prince seated behind a low Sharhay table. The prince shifted his position every few seconds, obviously not comfortable with having to rest his royal bum on a cushion on the floor; Corvalen was as gracefully at his ease as ever. The only other person in the room, stationed to the prince's right, was Torval, who actually had a stool to sit on—a concession to his bad leg, no doubt.

Rossen saluted the prince and begged pardon for not bringing the Kel Sharha more quickly. Dursten waved him to silence, and Corvalen waved him to a seat beside him.

The prince looked not altogether happy about Rossen's staying, but turned his displeasure on the Kel Sharha instead. "Won't you sit down," he said to her in a parody of courtesy, gesturing to the leaf-patterned rug in the center of the room.

As soon as she had seated herself, legs crossed and hands folded in her lap, Dursten got to his feet, walked around the table, and stood over her. He stared down at her but said nothing. She, too, was looking down, her eyes lowered—yet her unbowed head and straight back told Rossen this was no pose of modesty or submission.

Dursten snapped, "Look at me, woman!"

She raised her eyes and tilted her head back ever so slightly, her face impassive. Dursten waited, evidently hoping to unnerve the Kel Sharha or to win from her some greater show of respect. She was not obliging.

Corvalen shifted on his cushion. Rossen could tell he was out of patience with this battle of wills—although Rossen himself would have been interested to see who came out the winner.

Dursten tossed back his hair, like a horse flicking its tail at a fly, and glared at the Kel Sharha. "I received word late yesterday that two detachments of my soldiers were attacked north of the Lenasha Forest. This morning a messenger brought news that a third detachment has been ambushed some miles northeast of here. It appears that you alone

215

are *not*, after all, a sufficient guarantee for your people keeping the peace. So I wonder: now that they have broken the treaty, what shall we do with you?"

At last the Kel Sharha looked disconcerted. "They cannot even know about the treaty yet. You sent our warriors away on foot, but yours have gone on horse and . . . and ridden far ahead of the news that we have made peace. And none of your men speak Sharhay, do they? They could not explain themselves, or answer questions—"

"Forstene warriors do not explain themselves to the vanquished!"

"Not all of my people know yet that they are"—she had to push the next word out—"vanquished. So if Forstene soldiers come riding onto their lands—"

"Every one of those detachments was bearing the white standard at the fore."

That brought her up short. "White standard? What is that?"

"The white standard, Lady," Corvalen said, "is a plain white flag— a symbol of peaceful intentions."

"Ignorant barbarians," Dursten muttered.

The Kel Sharha sighed. "Blue is our color for peace. White is the color of death."

"But you wear white," Torval pointed out.

She turned to him with an expression almost kindly. "Healers stand before the gates of death, Torval of Caldene. We try to keep them from opening untimely, but still we see many pass through. None must bow to death so often as a Healer does."

Rossen wondered if this was true—a warrior, after all, saw death aplenty—but he could see that Torval was suitably impressed.

Dursten, of course, was not; he had never been one to be engaged by philosophical speculations of any nature. "Whether or not those who attacked my men knew about the treaty, it is broken nonetheless."

In the knife-edge silence that followed this pronouncement, Dursten turned to the table and picked up the copy of the treaty that lay there. He scanned the parchment with deliberation. "Article Two, as you will recall, states that any unrest will result in an extension of curfews and other restrictions. And Article Six promises that force will be used to put down any rebellion."

"'Immediately and indiscriminately,'" she quoted. "So I am here for you to tell me that your soldiers have killed more of my people."

"They got what they deserved. As you said yourself, many of them didn't know yet that they have been vanquished. My men have erased any doubts about the matter. But I wonder"—he paused—"if *you* might not need a reminder that you have been conquered, Kel Sharha."

She stood up with such measured dignity that Rossen knew it was an effort to resist the impulse to jump to her feet. He glanced sidelong at Corvalen, and saw that he was tensed like a cat that might spring at any moment. There was a hardness in his eyes that made even Rossen feel wary; he was glad Dursten could not see it.

"The treaty terms," the Kel Sharha said, "permit you to suppress armed rebellion with as much force as you deem necessary. They permit you to extend the time that Sharhaya is under military rule. They permit you to collect tribute and to parade me in your triumph. They do not permit you to make more 'reminders'—to my people or to myself."

"The treaty does not specify 'armed rebellion,' Kel Sharha." He jabbed a finger at the parchment. "You need to refresh your memory— it says 'rebellion of any nature.' And what is your continued defiance, if not rebellion? I am perfectly within my rights to exercise as much force as *I* deem necessary." He grabbed her arm and thrust his face close to hers. "I am the conqueror of Sharhaya, and I will make you know it—"

"Let go of her!"

To Rossen's surprise, it was Torval who had spoken.

The prince gave the Kel Sharha a little push and stepped away from her with exaggerated deliberation, then turned toward Torval.

Corvalen's heir had risen to his feet, making the most of his impressive height. As Dursten faced him, it flashed through Rossen's mind that it was Torval who carried the real air of command, the true aspect of a prince in that moment. Indeed, he was more the image of the heirs of the Exalted Stennar than Dursten—with the unruly hair and golden eyes of his mother's people—could ever hope to be.

"What did you say, Torval?" the prince asked.

"I pray Your Highness, leave her be."

"And what is your concern in this, my friend?"

"Forgive me for presuming to remind you, Highness, but she is the one who saved my leg, and quite probably my life. I owe her life-debt."

"Life-debt? You cannot owe life-debt to a foreigner—an enemy—a woman!"

"I beg your pardon, my liege, but the Precepts of Vallar do not make such distinctions. This woman gave me my life, and the fact that she is a foreigner—an enemy, even—makes the gift all the greater. I and my kin are bound now to guard her life in return. All of the Exalted

Ones of Forstene have honored the Precepts in this, Your Highness, even if in nothing else; shall we do less?"

Rossen grinned inwardly at the look on the prince's face. Everyone knew Dursten hoped that future generations would rank him among the Exalted Ones, so Torval's question had been well calculated. But the inner smile faded as Rossen saw Dursten's gaze harden on the questioner. It looked as though Torval had gone one step too far—he was like to be out of favor with the prince for some time to come. Torval appeared conscious of this fact, but he held himself with assurance nonetheless.

Rossen stole a glance at Corvalen, who sat at apparent ease now beside him. Rossen knew his lord well enough to sense his pride in Torval's sense of honor. But there was concern there, too; Corvalen had never much liked Torval's friendship with Dursten, but neither did he want enmity between them.

Dursten turned a look on Corvalen that seemed to say, "Damn you for drumming those damn Precepts into his head!" His glare swept on to the Kel Sharha. She stood quietly with her hands folded at her waist in that way of hers. Her face was carefully blank.

So, Rossen noticed, was Corvalen's.

"You," Dursten snarled at her, "may think that now you have powerful friends to protect you. But let me be the first to warn you that even the obligations of life-debt cannot save a rebel or a traitor. I will concede—this time—that you had no hand in the attacks on my soldiers. It is the last such concession I will make."

After another fruitless attempt to stare her into submission, he stalked back to the table and dropped onto his cushion in a state of royal pique. "I am quite done with this person now, Lord Corvalen. Although you have one thing further to say to her, I believe?"

Corvalen turned his full attention on the woman. "Kel Sharha," he said, his voice like velvet wrapped around iron, "I am placing you under house arrest. Henceforward you will not leave your house, nor receive visitors, nor converse with your servants more than is strictly necessary, until or unless I order otherwise." Not giving her a chance to respond but still holding her gaze, he continued, "Rossen, you will inform her guards. Escort her to her house."

"Yes, my lord." Rossen rose, went to the Kel Sharha, and took her by the elbow to steer her out of the room. He could feel the tension that ran through her whole body.

When the door of Corvalen's office had closed behind them and they were on the stairs, Rossen said, "Don't worry, Lady. It's only temporary, I wager. And for your protection, too, while Prince Dursten is in the Sanctuary."

She stopped short, and Rossen wondered how his words could have made her go even more tense—then he looked down and saw Esban below in the vestibule. He clambered up the steps toward them.

"My Lady, what a pleasure to meet you here! I myself have been having a most delightful visit in the House of Healing. And I met the prettiest young man there; he seemed almost one of you. Too bad for me, eh, that I was not a pretty boy with a way with a lute—then maybe I would have been welcome among the Ma'Sharha, too, eh? But perhaps, after all, I should thank you. Because if you'd accepted me, I would now be just one more among the defeated, instead of the aide to a great prince, who will one day be king over you. So thank you, Kel Sharha."

Esban had taken her hand, but before he could bow over it, she snatched it away. And slapped his smirking face, hard enough to make him stumble backward and clutch at the banister to keep from falling down the stairs.

The Kel Sharha gave Esban a scalding glare, said a few words in Sharhay that needed no translation, then walked past him as though he had ceased to exist.

Rossen felt like applauding her, but he followed her on down the steps without saying a word, equally deliberate in paying Esban no further notice.

Chapter Twenty-Two

The Kel Sharha awoke gasping for air, her pulse hammering. She'd had many dreams of fighting, but in none of them had she actually killed anyone. Until now.

In her mind's eye she again saw Dursten dying on her blade, and she shuddered. Yet she was also aware of a feeling of satisfaction, even triumph. In her dream she had smiled, viciously, when she killed Dursten. There was a part of her that wanted to smile now, a part that wanted the dream to be true.

"No!" she whispered fiercely. "I do not take life; I *serve* life!"

Lady, you are a healer; you serve life, Lord Corvalen's voice echoed in her mind.

She scowled, threw aside her coverlet, and began to dress. "Yes, I *am* a healer," she muttered. "And if the Scourge of Cheskara thinks I am going to meekly abandon my work, he can . . . he can . . ."

Tying the last knot in her belt, she gave up thinking of a suitable fate for the Scourge. Instead she slipped her feet into her soft boots, took a breath to compose herself, and went to her chamber door.

She eased it open and peered into the corridor—empty but for a low-burning lamp. She slipped out and padded to the door that led from her residence to the top landing in the House of Healing.

Did Lord Corvalen know about this door? If so, he would certainly have stationed guards outside it. She stood for a moment, listening. But she heard nothing, so she went through, shutting it as quietly as she could.

The door of the upper ward stood open; voices rose and fell just on the other side—Treska's and Lillanna's. The Kel Sharha started across the landing, then hesitated as she heard herself mentioned.

It was Treska speaking. "What if . . . if the king makes her marry him?"

"And why should he do that?" responded Lillanna; her voice sounded weary.

"I don't know. But I heard Healer Yasma say he might."

221

"You should not be listening to gossip, Treska. Pay it no mind." After a pause, Lillanna continued, "It's true that many years ago there was trouble on the border between Forstene and Cheskara and, to make peace, King Delanar—or Prince Delanar, as he was then—was married to the daughter of one of the Cheskari chiefs. But that turned out so badly for him, he is unlikely to want another wife from among his enemies."

"How did it turn out badly?"

"Hm. I suppose the Celebrants don't include it much in their tales anymore—it's, oh, about ten winters now since it was news. Well, I can only tell you the short version: Delanar had become king, the Cheskari woman his queen—and then she took another man to her bed, it seems. When the king found out, he had her executed."

"What? That makes no sense."

"I am afraid it does to Forsteners, Treska," the Kel Sharha said, entering the ward and waving away Lillanna's startled greeting. "My friend Martos, the Ghildaran envoy, explained to me that the queen of Forstene is guilty of treason if she shares the gifts of love with anyone other than the king her husband—her prime duty being to give him sons of undoubted paternity. And so Delanar's poor Cheskari wife was beheaded, and the king has remained wifeless since."

Treska's brow wrinkled as she considered this. "It's odd, isn't it, to think that Prince Dursten's mother was Cheskari? I mean, the Cheskari are much more like us than like the Forsteners, aren't they?"

"I have not met many Cheskari," the Kel Sharha answered thoughtfully, "but I know they honor the Mothers."

"Was the Cheskari War because of the queen's execution?"

"Oh yes," said Lillanna. "The Cheskari were outraged. The northern tribes declared war against Forstene and started raiding across the border on a grand scale."

"But Lord Corvalen and his army defeated them. That's why he's called the Scourge of Cheskara, isn't it?"

"As you say," said the Kel Sharha.

"And then," Treska mused, "the Cheskari started raiding across their border with us. So when Prince Dursten brought his army into Sharhaya, our warbands were busy with the Cheskari raiders. . . . How strangely everything is connected."

"Indeed," the Kel Sharha said. "And there, child, you have a lesson in the web of fate, to which every action adds a new strand—and sometimes begins an entirely new design."

Treska lapsed into silence; Lillanna had turned away to busy herself with a tray of medicines.

The Kel Sharha looked from one to the other. "Have the two of you spent all this night canvassing one grief after another?" She touched her Second on the shoulder and saw, when Lillanna turned, the deep shadows of grief in her eyes.

Reminded of her own lost apprentice, the Kel Sharha felt her throat tighten. "Go and get some rest, Lillanna. I can stay on the ward till dawn."

"My chief—"

"You need sleep. And I need to work."

Lillanna nodded, and left without more words. The Kel Sharha beckoned to Treska; together they began their night's ministrations.

*****

Corvalen was not one of those lords who looked on ball-over-the-line as an occasion for wagering or wild enthusiasm, but he enjoyed the game now and then. And it had its uses, especially when men-at-arms were becoming bored and fractious. Since the arrival of Dursten's troops in the Sanctuary, Torval had already broken up two brawls, one over cheating at dice and another that had started out as a friendly wrestling match between one of his followers and one of Dursten's. A good afternoon of ball-over-the-line seemed just the thing to bring the men together.

Rossen captained one side and Dursten the other, but each team's members were a mix from Torval's, Dursten's, and Corvalen's forces; Corvalen had insisted on this. Now he watched the game from the shade of the Champion's porch. The green wasn't the most convenient playing field, but it was what they had. At least Torval, as referee, had a good vantage from the dais—although Corvalen wondered how closely he was able to follow the game, since Esban stood at his elbow and appeared to pester him with questions whenever he wasn't cheering loudly for the prince. Torval looked none too happy.

There were some Sharhay watching, too—several children, Tigannas the Lawspeaker, a few Guardians, and of course Pieran, who stalked the edge of the green, viewing the game from every angle. Corvalen could sense the keenness of his interest, almost hear his thoughts.

Pieran might be thick-skulled on some matters, but his mind for strategy was finely honed. Corvalen knew it did not escape him that the game was more than a recreation, that it was another form of war practice. When the players of one team pushed their wedge through the other team's defense, it was little different from the wedge formation these same men would take in battle. The men linked together to protect their goal line were locked in a shield wall as much as if they'd actually had their shields on their arms. The teamwork, the attention to the captains' orders, the maintenance of a high state of alertness, the exercise of reflexes, the pushing of the body to its limits of speed and endurance—all this made ball-over-the-line more than a mere game.

Rossen's team scored a goal, and Torval called a break. Pellar and two other squires ran onto the field to give the players towels and cups to dip into the fountains to cool themselves. Dursten simply dunked his whole head into one of the fountains—out of the corner of his eye, Corvalen saw some of the Sharhay onlookers wince—then shook the water out of his eyes and ambled over to Corvalen.

"Excellent game—can't remember the last time I played! You sure you don't want to rotate in, Corvalen?"

"I'm sure, Your Highness, but thank you."

"Gotten too old to play ball-over-the-line, have you? Oh well, I suppose it will happen to all of us."

"Indeed."

"Speaking of getting on in years . . . not much longer now before old Beddar arrives and we can get out of this rusticated backwater. Pretty enough country this, but not a lot of amenities. Give it ten years, though, and our garrisons and settlements will have the place transformed. Maybe I'll bring Heldar to visit then; we'll tour all the inheritance I've won him!" Dursten mopped his face with a towel. "By the Unifier, it will be good to see my boy again."

"I can imagine how much you miss him; I've been away from Mellis for three months, not three years, and yet—"

"Better get used to missing her; she'll be another man's soon enough. That's the trouble with daughters. Got anyone in mind for her husband yet?"

"I've had some ideas."

Dursten cocked his head to one side. "What about Heldar?"

"Your Highness? Are you . . . do you . . . ?"

It was seldom enough that Corvalen found himself wordless, so he did not take offense when Dursten laughed at him. He mustered his faculties, however, and managed to say something coherent and correct. "If I understand you rightly, Highness, you do me a great honor, of which I am not insensible."

"But? Come on, Corvalen; you may be 'honored,' but I can see you're not pleased."

"Prince Heldar is hardly more than a babe, while Mellis is nearly a woman. Forgive me for speaking plainly, but it does not sound like a promising marriage."

"Perhaps not from their point of view, at least not for several years yet—"

"Nine years, at least." Corvalen did not enjoy the thought of his daughter married to a child for nine years—not to mention the thought of Dursten as her guardian until the boy matured.

"Yes, but only think what a thing it would be to unite our families!"

"Mellis would not bring Brintora to the crown. My barony will be Torval's, remember."

"Doesn't matter; whoever holds Brintora holds it in fief. Even if it's not crown lands, in the end it still belongs to the crown."

So Heldar took this land to hold, / His first enrichment of the realm—the lines from *The Battle of Brintora* that Dursten had recited at the signing of the treaty with the Sharhay. The recollection of them gave Corvalen an unexpected twinge, but he said nothing.

"No, it's not about the lands. It's about family, and loyalty. And strength." Dursten's voice dropped. "I hardly need to tell you, Corvalen, that the Blood of Stennar is waning. How many men are left in the direct line? My father, myself, my son. Beddar and his two sons. Uncle Sessal, with his palsy and his barren wife. That's it. If I'm going to bring back the glory of my forefathers, I need strong men and strong families supporting me, bound by blood as well as fealty.

"Just think about it, Corvalen. And think about your daughter. What kind of life do you want for her, after you die and Torval becomes baron of Brintora? If she marries Heldar, she'll be a queen—in due time, of course. Otherwise? You're the most powerful of all the barons. Unless she marries a prince, she'll marry beneath her. Why should she be provided for just out of her dower lands and whatever her husband holds, when she could have the whole kingdom to support her? Think about it."

"I will give it due consideration, Your Highness."

"Good!" Dursten clapped his hands together. "Maybe we'll discuss it further on our ride."

"Our ride?"

"Yes, didn't I tell you? One of my scouts has found a promising site to quarry stone for my castle on the bluff, so after I leave here, I'm off to take a look at it. Then I'm going to ride north and see what we've got up there—choose some watchtower sites, pick some places to settle my lacklands, that sort of thing. Thought you might like to come along."

"I might, but your father ordered me to hold the Sanctuary till the viceroy's arrival."

"So deputize Rossen. Surely he's capable of more than just tagging along with you and running your errands."

"Of course he is."

"Well, then? Come on, Corvalen, you've got to be getting tired of this place—all these trees hemming you in all day long. Wouldn't you like to get out and ride, and see a little more of Sharhaya?"

He would, at that.

"Corvalen, I know we've had our differences—but haven't I already shown you I'm past them? You're not going to make me say *please*, are you?"

"Have you ever said *please* to anyone in your life?"

"No. And I'm not about to start. But the truth is . . . I'm proud of what I've accomplished in Sharhaya, and I wish my father could see it. He's not here—but you are. I want you to see what I've won, Corvalen. Come with me, won't you?"

It was what he wanted to do, after all. "How long a ride do you have in mind?"

"Two weeks, maybe a bit more."

Two weeks of not having to deal with the Kel Sharha or her councillors and their endless problems.

But two weeks with Dursten . . . If Corvalen didn't go along, however, that would be two weeks of Dursten on the loose and unsupervised among the Sharhay.

"I will be honored to accompany you, Your Highness. Shall we leave tomorrow?"

*****

For two more nights after the beginning of her house arrest, the Kel Sharha successfully dared its strictures. When all was quiet in the Sanctuary, she left her private chambers and entered the House of Healing through the second-story door. She stayed on the upper ward to avoid being seen on the stairs and worked quietly, for the most part speaking only to Lillanna, Treska, and her patients, and only when necessary. Working through the night made it easier to accept being shut in her house all day.

Toward the end of the third night, she lingered at a patient's bedside until the oil lamps were extinguished, giving place to the dawn that beamed through the ward's east-facing windows. Hurrying out onto the landing, she pulled up short: Fidden and Gar, evidently just arrived on duty, were taking up places on either side of the door connecting to her private chambers; there appeared to be a whispered argument going on.

Well, she would just have to brazen her way past them. She smoothed the skirt of her overdress, folded her hands, and walked forward, projecting the air of one who is exactly where she is supposed to be.

The guards' argument ended in what seemed typical fashion, with Gar applying a sharp elbow to his companion. Fidden let out a barely muffled oath; Gar uttered a more emphatic one as he caught sight of the Kel Sharha.

Fidden remembered his manners first. "Good morning, M'Lady. Um . . . if you don't mind my saying so, you seem to be on the wrong side of this here door." He tapped the carved wood with his spear for emphasis.

"Good morning to you, Fidden, Gar." She nodded graciously to each in turn. "I promise you, I have not left my House."

There was a moment's silence. Then Gar explained, as if to a rather slow child, "Well, Lady, see, the way house arrest usually works is that you stay in, you know, your *house*. Where you live, like—you know, eating and sleeping and all that."

"Do you tell me that Lord Corvalen wishes to confine me to my *residence* alone?" She widened her eyes in calculated innocence, although she knew that she was fooling no one.

"Residence—just so!" Fidden said.

But Gar shook his head. "Pardon my saying so, but you ought not to play them word games with Lord Corvalen, Lady. He's treated you right well, all things considered, and it's not fitting for you to try to get around him like this."

"I am a Healer," she answered, her voice tight, "and there are people who need me here. I thought"—she paused; it was best to be honest, with herself and with the guards—"I *hoped* it would be overlooked, for me just to cross this hall to work in the House of Healing. I have not even been down the stairs, only to this one ward."

Fidden and Gar were staring at her as if she had done something clearly beneath herself. Perhaps they were right.

"I would have asked permission of Lord Corvalen," she resumed, "but he gave me no chance to speak with him."

"You could have asked one of us to carry a message to him for you," Gar pointed out.

"Will you?"

"Can't now," said Fidden. "He's gone off to ride a circuit of the land with Prince Dursten, he has. Got to see how the watchtowers and barracks and all are coming on."

"He wastes no time, Lord Corvalen," Gar said proudly. "Gets things done quickly and gets them done right. Good King Delanar can always depend on him to sort things out. Why, in the Cheskari War—"

"Perhaps you can take a message to Lord Torval for me instead," she interrupted, in no temper to listen to an encomium on Lord Corvalen.

"We could," Fidden answered good-naturedly. "But he'd just send you back respectful greetings and an apology. Nothing he can do about the terms of your house arrest without our lord's say-so. You're in Lord Corvalen's custody, not anyone else's, remember?"

"And I suppose Rossen is gone with Lord Corvalen?"

"Oh, no; he's stayed behind—as his lordship's deputy, you know."

"We could ask *him* about this Healing House thing for you, if you want us to," Gar offered, as if it were a newly dawning possibility.

"I would be very grateful," she managed.

But when Rossen came to see her that afternoon, he was unbudgeable. His understanding of house arrest did not include her crossing the corridor to the House of Healing, and that was the way it would stay unless he heard differently from his lord. Rossen was as polite about it as he could be, and she could not really fault him for his stance.

In compliment to his courtesy, she invited him to take wine with her in the garden before he left. He demurred; he had responsibilities, he said.

"So have I," she growled at his departing back. She did not think she had ever felt so thwarted in her life.

Chapter Twenty-Three

Rossen left the Kel Sharha's house feeling vaguely uncomfortable. For a moment he had been tempted to accede to her request. He had seen what idleness could do to his lord, and he suspected that the Kel Sharha was of a similar temperament.

He reminded himself who she was. It was not his business to make life easier for a conquered chieftain. It was certainly not his business to enable her to foment rebellion. Allowing her to work in her infirmary would only give her opportunity to plot with her people, under cover of treating their hurts and illnesses. Perhaps she had done so already—had been doing so ever since her return to the Sanctuary.

Corvalen thought not. He believed in her commitment to the peace, and in her sense of honor—though he'd conceded that her understanding of honor might express itself idiosyncratically. He'd decided to keep her confined during his absence partly as a sop to the prince, but mostly so that neither Rossen nor Torval would be awkwardly placed if she were discovered in some transgression on their watch.

Which she had been. *I'll have to order guards on that door at night as well as during the day now.* He hoped he wasn't closing the stable after the horse had already bolted.

As Rossen neared the Champion's House, he encountered Tigannas the Lawspeaker leaving it. The Sharhay man stopped and greeted him almost cordially.

"You have talked with the Kel Sharha?" His Forstene was not entirely fluent, but at least he spoke it without Pieran's execrable accent.

"I have; she is well."

"We have harvest soon. Will you be permitting her to be leading the harvest rites?"

"That is Lord Corvalen's decision to make."

"You will tell him, when he returns? The people will be wanting the rites."

"I'm sure they will." Rossen nodded to the Lawspeaker and continued on his way before the man could speak again. *These Sharhay!* Were they all so determined to ignore the fact that they were under Forstene rule now? *They cling to whatever of theirs they can, I suppose.*

The Cheskari had not. That had been a dirtier war—but in some ways a cleaner one. When it was done, it was done, and no one in the borderlands had been able to pretend otherwise. Of course, there were no Cheskari remaining in the borderlands when Corvalen left—nothing but their bones.

Corvalen had not wanted the same thing to happen in Sharhaya, and Rossen could not but agree. At the same time, he had begun to wonder how much his lord was doing now for the sake of the peace, and how much for the sake of the Kel Sharha. Not consciously, of course—Corvalen would put his actions down to the Precepts of Vallar or to the king's desire for a prosperous and trouble-free province, not to any feelings he might be developing for this woman. He'd never even suspect himself of having such feelings. And maybe Rossen was imagining them, after all, and worrying himself needlessly.

All the same, it's a good thing he's away from her for a time. I wish I were away with him.

Rossen found Torval in the front room of the Champion's house, sharpening a quill pen.

"What did old Tigannas want?" Rossen asked.

"I sent for him. I'm having a record made of the Sharhay laws—do you known they've never before been written down? It takes days to recite them all. Oh, and he's helping me learn Sharhay. Listen to this." He laid down the quill and assumed a declamatory stance. *"Na je'shen boru gan sin gless."*

"What's it mean?"

"'My power tree whispers quiet in the night.'"

"That ought to come in handy."

Torval grinned. "It's from one of their songs, I think."

"Well, you said it like a native—as far as I could tell."

"Sharhay's not terribly difficult, if you know Brintoran."

"Knowing Ghildaran helps too, Corvalen says. But my Ghildaran is pretty rough, and my Brintoran nonexistent, so . . ." He shrugged.

"Ghildaran is a beautiful language. Even as a boy, I didn't mind studying it—but how I hated learning Brintoran! I always thought it was just peasant talk. When was I ever going to use it in Caldene or at court? My uncle insisted, though; he said that since I was going to be baron of Brintora one day, I ought to know at least a little of the people's language."

"True. You won't hear any of Corvalen's knights using the old speech, but a lot of the men-at-arms still speak it among themselves. And it does make a difference to them, having a lord who can give them orders in their own tongue." Rossen picked up the quill and tested its point against his finger. "So why are you learning Sharhay?"

"Oh, it's just something to do. Besides, Pieran's always grumbling under his breath; I'd like to know what he's saying."

"I'll wager it has nothing to do with trees whispering in the night."

"And I'll not take that bet. But if you're really in a wagering mood . . ." Torval rummaged under a stack of parchments and brought out a polished blackwood game board and a velvet pouch. "Fancy a game of starstones?"

He upended the pouch, letting the pieces spill out onto the board.

Rossen caught one and turned it over in his hand. It was the Guidestar marker, a pale-blue star sapphire. The other pieces were also star sapphires, moon white and golden yellow, perfectly matched in size and sheen. "A princely set."

"It is fine, isn't it? It was a gift from King Delanar."

"Ah. Well, he can afford to give the best, after all." *A royal gift indeed. Young Torval must have made quite an impression when he served at court.*

"So are we playing?"

"Oh, we're playing all right." Rossen set the Guidestar marker in its place at the center of the board.

Torval had begun to lay out the other pieces; he paused, considering the blue star sapphire. "It looks like her eyes, doesn't it? The Kel Sharha's, I mean."

I know who you meant.

Torval hesitated as though he might say something else on the subject, but after a moment he resumed setting up the game. "Her brother's got pale eyes too, but not so cold."

"Nothing cold about him—certainly not his temper. He could be trouble, that one."

"He would have been easier to deal with here; I don't like to contemplate the mischief he might cause on this circuit ride. I could wish my uncle hadn't taken him along."

So could I.

"And for what? Corvalen's Sharhay is good enough that he hardly has need of a translator. If he does, the prince has Esban with him."

"But Esban is a traitor to his people; the Sharhay aren't likely to listen to him. I believe your uncle felt that Pieran's presence might help counteract Esban's."

"If anything can. But at least this way, if Corvalen requires information about the countryside or anything, he won't have to ask that little shit."

Rossen gave his companion a sharp look. He'd never heard the courtly Lord Torval speak so bluntly. Or so bitterly.

As Torval turned away to busy himself with filling two wine cups, Rossen sought to lighten the mood. "Well, if I had to choose between Esban and Pieran—and a sorry day when anyone should have to make that choice—I'd certainly opt for the latter. Although a porcupine would be more comfortable company than either, I'd wager. And speaking again of wagering . . ."

Torval wore a fixed smile as he returned to the table and handed Rossen his wine. "Choose your color and name your stake—but I'd advise you to be careful. I don't much feel like losing today."

"Neither do I."

The game was hard-played and ended in a draw. By that time the wine had been poured twice more, and neither player aspired to a rematch.

Torval scooped the pieces into their pouch; one escaped him and rolled away. As he retrieved it, he knocked his stack of parchments to the floor. Rossen bent to help him pick them up.

"No wonder you had to sharpen your quill earlier—look at this load of parchment you've been scratching up. What is all this, anyway?"

"Those you're holding are inventories of the stables. Soon I'll have to start going house to house—well, my men will have to; I'm obviously not doing it all myself—"

"Obviously."

"Orders, you know. Start collecting up tribute and booty from the Sanctuary. His Royal Highness needs more treasure to display in his triumph. Needs to show his father that this has all been worth it."

Rossen moved Torval's cup out of his reach. "Don't ever take to drink, my lord. You're liable to say something indiscreet, with the wrong man listening."

"I concede your point; good thing you're not the wrong man. What was I saying?"

"Tribute?"

"Right. Got to start collecting it." He shook his head. "She's not going to like it, though."

"Not one bit."

"Good thing she's shut up in her house. Maybe she won't notice."

"And if she does? She's not in charge here anymore."

"But she thinks she is." Torval grimaced. "Great Vallar, I sounded like Dursten just then." He reached to grab his wine cup away from Rossen. He drained it, then sat silently for a time, shifting the cup from hand to hand.

Rossen got to his feet. "Perhaps I'd—"

"I've been thinking about the other day—Dursten and the Kel Sharha and . . . Do you remember me saying, back in Dursten's camp, that my uncle has no interest in women?"

"I do."

"I begin to think I was wrong."

"Of course you were." Rossen sat back down. "He's just not interested in the women at Court."

"Beddar's daughter—"

"*You're* interested in the fair Thedis. You know she holds no attraction for Corvalen—except, I warrant, as a potential bride for you."

Torval looked ridiculously pleased at that. After a moment, though, he said, "Yes, but my uncle now. . . . Surely you've noticed."

So much for it being just my imagination.

"He hardly takes his eyes off her," Torval said.

"She's his prisoner; he's responsible for her. He's too conscientious not to be always watching her. It's not as though she's a great beauty or anything."

"She doesn't need to be beautiful. She has something else."

"She's just his prisoner," Rossen repeated, and hoped it was true. The woman would be going back to Forstene in chains, and would probably be killed once she got there. Rossen had seen his lord's heart break once already; he did not relish seeing it again.

*****

Across from Corvalen at the guesthouse table, Dursten's scribe scratched away with his quill, transcribing the rough notes he'd made earlier as they toured this village, reducing every asset to ink markings on parchment. At the end would come the calculations: how much to be carried away now, how much to be left so that there would be lambs and linen and good things to carry away next year. Only one thing did not need to be calculated to percentages: the wine, because every cask was going to Forstene.

Corvalen frowned at his own parchment. He had written *Jewel fruit*, then crossed it out in favor of *Hidden fruit*. This he had changed to *Hidden gems* before finally going on to the second line: *Green glimpses tease.* That didn't seem quite right; none of the words did, though the image was so clear in his mind.

Here, far north of the Lenasha Forest, Corvalen had at last found the Sharhaya celebrated by the minstrels and storytellers. Vineyards cloaked the sloping riverbanks, bearded grain rippled over the fields, and ripening fruit, gleaming among the leaves, bent the boughs of countless orchard trees. Sheep grazed the high hillsides, birds adorned the air; the woods were abundant with game.

No matter where Corvalen and the prince stopped on their circuit, woodlands were always near at hand, as though the Sharhay had carved their country out of a primordial forest and set their villages and fields and orchards and vineyards into it like the jewels inlaid to ornament King Delanar's throne. Corvalen could well understand why they had fought so hard to save all this, and why the Kel Sharha had accepted the treaty rather than let any more be destroyed.

The conventions of the latest fad in court poetry just didn't allow him enough words to portray it all. No doubt a master poet could find a way to distill the vision into twenty-three syllables, but Corvalen had no illusions as to the degree of his own poetic mastery. He passed his borrowed quill back to Dursten's scribe and folded his parchment, tucking it into his belt pouch as he left the guesthouse.

Although the afternoon was mild, the villagers were keeping within doors. Villagers usually did when the Forstene soldiers arrived. Next to the modest guesthouse stood the House of the Ma'Sharha—no separate houses for each Order in these little hamlets—with two unarmed Guardians stationed at the door. One flicked her wary gaze to Corvalen, but the other kept a steady watch on the detachment of soldiers patrolling the green.

He strolled away from the village center, past the retting ponds where the flax crop was soaking—Dursten's scribe had noted that down, too—and past the cluster of new-built huts. Corvalen had seen their like throughout this circuit, all of them sheltering refugees who had fled northward in the hope of safety.

In the last village, North Ferry, he'd had to evict a group of refugees who had unfortunately chosen to start their lives over on the ideal site for a watchtower. Pieran had shown his value there. He'd only needed to talk briefly with the refugees and the village Mothers to keep the situation from turning ugly. Then, not one to wait on circumstance, he'd called together a work group and made an immediate start on building new huts on the other side of the village. He'd labored on them through the moonlit night and ridden his horse in a stupor all the next day.

Corvalen passed through his men-at-arms' encampment, exchanging a word here and there, and continued on up the nearest hill; he expected there would be a fine view from the top.

Dursten was there ahead of him, and greeted him heartily. He directed Corvalen's attention eastward, sweeping his arm to encompass the woodlands beyond the village. "I tell you, Corvalen, have you ever seen such stands of timber?"

"I have not, Your Highness."

"A pity I had to burn so much in the south. But it had to be done."

Corvalen kept his voice neutral. "Why so, Highness?"

Dursten chuckled. "Haven't you seen the way these people act about their trees? A stranger mix of sentiment and superstition I've never encountered."

Indeed.

"Perfect way to demoralize them, destroying their precious forests. Deprived their warbands of places to hide, too."

"Very logical."

"Still plenty of woods left, though—and now they're ours. My father's always wanted a merchant fleet to rival Ghildarna's—and finally we have the timber to build one. In fact . . ." His grin widened; he took Corvalen's arm and turned him to face the other direction.

Below them, in the near distance, flowed the wide Ghil River, Sharhaya's western boundary. On the other side they could make out the red roofs of a Ghildaran town. And just entering their range of vision, as though the prince had planned it that way, a merchant galley worked its way upstream, perhaps carrying sugar and silks from Oversea to trade for gold from the mines of south Ghildarna.

"We could have ships like that," Dursten said. "No—*better* ships. And not just merchantmen. Warships. With our good Sharhay timber, we can build a navy to rival Ghildarna's. To *defeat* it."

"Your Highness . . . do you contemplate the conquest of Ghildarna, then?"

Dursten's avid gaze, fixed on the opposite side of the river, was answer enough.

It was, in any case, all the answer Corvalen would get, for the voice of his squire intruded on them.

"My lord, my lord!" Pellar had run up the slope, but he paused only a moment to catch his breath. "A fight in the camp, my lord. I think you'd best come."

Corvalen heard the shouts, cheers, and jibes even before he reached the outskirts of the camp.

"My money's on the barbarian!" someone yelled.

"Which one?" another man asked, and was answered by a cacophony of laughter.

With Dursten following, Corvalen pushed his way through a knot of men. At its center, Pieran straddled Esban's chest, his knees pinning the younger man's arms, and though Esban's feet were flailing, Pieran seemed no more disturbed than a ship on a smooth sea. His face, however, was set in an expression of cold ferocity. He had one hand on Esban's neck and now drew back his other hand, fisted, ready to pummel his opponent.

Corvalen stepped forward and grabbed the arm. "I wouldn't, if I were you," he said. He pulled the arm back just enough to make his point. His angle gave him the advantage; he could easily dislocate Pieran's shoulder if he chose.

Pieran looked up at him. The fury drained from his face, and he took his hand from Esban's neck.

Corvalen shifted his grip on Pieran's arm and pulled him off of Esban, who scrambled to his feet and darted toward the prince.

Dursten, Corvalen was relieved to see, looked nothing more than entertained, as though the scuffle had been an amusement, like a cockfight.

"My good prince, you are well arrived," Esban said. "Now you see that I warned you true: this man should not be of our company. He is nothing but a . . . a ruffian who takes offense at the smallest word, and the only way he knows to settle a disagreement is with his fists."

Pieran could hold his tongue no longer. "This *ghekkes* insulted the Kel Sharha!"

"Well," Dursten drawled, "I shouldn't be surprised if every man in my army has insulted the Kel Sharha; will you wrestle them all to the ground, one by one?"

"*They* are not Sharhay."

"Nor am I!" Esban said. "I am Forstene now. I serve His Highness, and I am under his protection!"

It was clear from Dursten's expression that he did not in any way consider Esban worthy of the name of Forstener; but on the other hand, the prince could hardly fail to seize on this opportunity to put down the Kel Sharha's troublesome brother.

Dursten opened his mouth to speak; Corvalen was quicker. "And for the moment, at any rate, Pieran is serving me, so I will administer whatever chastisement is necessary." He turned a steely gaze on Pieran. "Come with me." He strode away before anything else could happen.

Pieran followed, staying just behind him but keeping pace. Corvalen finally stopped when they reached a stand of nut trees.

Quick as a springing cat, he turned on Pieran and struck him hard enough to send him to the ground. The Sharhay man scarcely had time to blink before Corvalen's sword was out and at his throat.

"I ought to kill you now and save the hangman a length of rope. If you move, I will." He shifted his blade, laying the tip along Pieran's cheek. Pieran lay stone-still, his eyes wary.

With a deft movement, Corvalen took off a slice of Pieran's beard. "Let that be a reminder to you: we are not at play here."

He sheathed his sword and pulled Pieran to his feet. "Just what did you think you were doing back there?"

Pieran glared at him. "I told you: that traitor insulted the Kel Sharha."

"Deliberately—to your face?"

Pieran nodded.

"That seems a foolish thing to do. You were Second to the Champion; you are a warrior and a hunter, while he—"

"He is a man of no talents, who will not even deign to labor with his hands," Pieran said in Sharhay.

"Just so. You are bigger, stronger, far more skilled in fighting—and, I think, are reputed to have a quick temper. He had to know how you would react to his words. Why risk a beating at your hands? You might easily have killed him, had we not intervened."

Pieran's eyes narrowed. "He insulted her in front of all—to increase our shame, I thought."

"That, too, I'm sure."

"But also . . ."

At last the great simpleton begins to understand.

"He knew I would be stopped before he came to harm."

"As I said, insulting you *seemed* a foolish thing to do. But whatever else Esban may be, he is no fool. He meant to provoke you, to drive you to actions that would bring the Forstene soldiery down on you. Had things gone farther, and had Prince Dursten been in a different mood, you might well have been taken and hanged for insurrection. Although

Dursten probably would have just run you through himself—or I might have."

"But you did not. I suppose I should be grateful." Resentment edged his voice, and his fingers worried at his sword-shorn cheek.

"I require you to be sensible, not grateful. You must know, Pieran, that Esban hates your sister—out of all measure, it seems to me, but the fact is there nonetheless. He will hurt her however he can."

"Is it not enough for him that she is prisoner and will be taken away?"

Corvalen pitied the controlled anguish he heard in the man's voice, but he kept his own voice stern. "Apparently not. At any rate, he is such a man as cannot resist the temptation to cause further harm. What would the Kel Sharha have said if she'd seen you fighting Esban?"

Pieran half smiled. "She would have said, 'Brawling, Pieran; for shame!'"

Corvalen allowed himself a smile, too, but let it fade. Softly, he asked, "And what if that brawling had led to your death, Pieran? What would she have said then?"

Pieran stared at the ground.

"You were the Champion's Second; you are already under suspicion, marked as a troublemaker, a potential rebel. This is the last mercy you will receive from any man of Forstene. I give you fair warning that there is a noose awaiting you—and I would not hesitate to put your neck in it myself, if that is what it takes to keep peace and order here. So stay out of trouble, Pieran. If not for your own sake, then for your sister's."

Corvalen walked away, imagining the Kel Sharha bereft and angry—angry enough, perhaps, to call her people to rise against their new overlords. He hoped that her brother would have the sense to govern himself better henceforward.

*****

The Kel Sharha drew away from the window. It overlooked the green, where the Forstene soldiers, under Torval and Rossen, were gathering now for their daily drill. She did not care to watch their exercises, not since that first time, when she had felt herself wielding the sword with Lord Corvalen.

She still could not understand why that had happened. Was it because of their joint contact with the Watcher of the Beeches? She recoiled from the thought of being linked to him in such a way. Surely

238

that was not what the Watchers had intended. . . . Could the experience have come from her memories of her grandmother's life? But that Finoora had been sworn to the Guardians' Order, and Guardians did not use swords; the Order was adamant about upholding the old customs.

She had dreamed again last night of killing Dursten. Again she had driven a blade through him. A blade, and not even a forester's knife. A sword.

For as long as she could remember, the Kel Sharha had lived with the prohibition against touching weapons. Other Healers were not subject to it, though some had been given prohibitions of their own. She had never questioned hers—Serelha herself had placed it on her— and had never broken it. Not in waking life. Now her dreaming mind broke it almost every night.

Perhaps I need a Mind Healer.

She would settle for just having something to do.

On the stairs she passed Arna carrying a bucket and brush, on her way to scrub the upper hall. The girl looked quickly away, and said not a word.

I am a shadow in my own house. A shadow in my own land.

She knew the servants had been instructed to speak to her no more than necessary; not one of them seemed to have the spirit to disobey. They were trapped within doors, too—not allowed to leave lest they carry messages for her—and soldiers stalked through the house on random patrols every day to make certain nothing untoward was going on. No wonder if Arna and the others were dispirited and nervous—but after a fortnight of house arrest (and no telling when it would end), the Kel Sharha's sympathy for them was all but worn away.

Treska would not acquiesce to the Scourge's orders so easily; we could whisper together when no one else was near. And she would not skulk about, or be ashamed to look at me. But the girl was needed in the House of Healing. At least the Forsteners were letting her work.

Treska was staying with Lillanna now—the Kel Sharha had taken care to arrange that the first night of her house arrest. It made sense, since if the girl returned to the Kel Sharha's house, she would not be permitted to leave again. And perhaps she and Lillanna might be some comfort to each other in the wake of Graysa's death. Treska would fill Graysa's place, too, becoming Lillanna's junior apprentice in all but name. *I shall have to formalize that arrangement, so that Treska will have no difficulty progressing in the Order after I have gone.*

The Kel Sharha entered her workroom and made a slow circuit of the shelves. She had already inventoried her supplies, replenishing them where necessary. She planned to take a store of medicines with her to Forstene, although she doubted it was reasonable to hope she would survive to use many of them. She had made up other tinctures, decoctions, and ointments to boost the stores in the House of Healing, until she had nearly run out of ingredients.

No, there was nothing else to do in the workroom. The Kel Sharha shook her head; it would have been agreeable to grind something to dust in her mortar.

She wandered back to the garden. It was as unsatisfactory as the workroom. As the Kel Sharha paced alongside the beds, she saw not a weed needing to be pulled, not an exhausted flower needing to be pinched off. Everything was perfectly in order; there was nothing to do. *Except meditate. Again.*

Before, she'd always wished for more time to sit in meditation under her arbor or beside her fountain. Now she had the time in abundance. But she was no Listener, to be content spending the entire day in silent contemplation. Certainly not for two uninterrupted sevennights.

Beside her low basket chair, under the arbor, were the things she'd left there yesterday: a small sack of wool roving, a drop spindle, a distaff. She had gotten the wool from the supply in her cellar. The domestic tools had been her mother's; in her boredom and frustration, she had dug them out of an old chest, thinking that they might give her something useful to do.

Now she tucked the distaff under her left arm and took up the spindle. Till yesterday, she'd done no spinning since childhood. Her lack of practice showed in the thick, lumpy thread she'd produced. She would do better today; she would spin thread as fine as any her mother had ever made. She set the spindle twirling, and began to draw out the wool, feeling it twist between her fingers.

The spindle reached the ground, and the Kel Sharha paused to wind the new-spun thread around the spindle shaft. As she did so, the distaff slipped from under her arm, but she managed to catch it before the rovings it held hit the ground. She felt like a juggler—an inept one.

She got distaff and spindle into position again, and spun another length of thread. It was a bit easier this time to get it wound onto the spindle shaft. Still, she had seen any number of women—young girls, too, for that matter—manage spinning not only gracefully but with a speed and efficiency that she could not imagine herself attaining. She'd seen them spinning while they walked, even while they carried out other chores. How did they do it?

At last she got into a rhythm. She was nowhere near to being able to walk and spin at the same time, but her thread was smoother than yesterday's, and she no longer feared dropping the distaff. She remembered her mother spinning as she waited on wine buyers in her shop in the old merchants' quarter of Rezhenet. How had her mother had such presence of mind? The Kel Sharha felt she would be incapable of conversing or conducting business while spinning—there was something almost hypnotic in its rhythm, something too easy to get lost in.

She watched the spindle twirling, the wool twisting and drawing through her fingers, turning into thread, over and over again. She saw herself standing there with the distaff under her arm, saw herself pause to wind the thread, then start again. Again and again.

When had she stepped apart, so that she could now watch herself? She wondered idly at first, and also wondered at it—she had not known she had this ability, except in her dreams.

The dreams where she watched Dursten rape her.

The thought shocked her awareness back into her body. The thread snapped. The spindle clattered onto the flagstones and rolled away. The distaff nearly followed it, but she caught it.

Caught it and grasped it in both hands as though it was a Guardian's ironwood staff, and in the same motion swept it in front of her, as though she meant to knock the breath out of her enemy. She thrust, as though she would drive the distaff's woolly point into his throat. A turn, and the butt of the distaff jabbed his gut. Another turn, and the staff cracked against the backs of his knees.

How long the Kel Sharha went on like this she did not know. When she stopped, she was breathing hard, and her tunic stuck to her sweaty back.

What have I been doing; what was I thinking?

She nearly threw the distaff to the pavement. But it was one of the few things she had of her mother's; she could not bear the thought of breaking it. And . . . her exertions with the distaff, she realized, had brought more calm to her spirit than any morning's meditation had yet done.

That night she did not dream of killing Prince Dursten.

Chapter Twenty-Four

Treska broke into a run—partly for the pleasure of stretching her legs and feeling the air rush past her, and partly because she was eager to get to Lillanna's house and have something to eat. She had worked the night watch in the House of Healing with Lillanna and her apprentice Saffa, and their duties had not let up long enough for them to take any refreshment. Now Lillanna was on her way to breakfast with the Kel Jemya, and Saffa had gone off with a friend from the Listeners' Order. Treska was left on her own with her growly stomach.

When she reached Lillanna's kitchen, Pesha, the cook, was just slicing a loaf of fresh-baked bread. Treska took a thick slice and spread it with butter, then went out into the garden to savor it in the early sunshine. Pesha's children, Mikka and Bannan, were already there, looking sticky—their bread was spread with jam.

Bannan finished his last mouthful and limped over to Treska; he had been born with a clubfoot. "Mam is taking us to the Celebrants' hall in a little while to hear stories. What are you doing today?"

"Sleeping." As if to illustrate how tired she was, her smile turned into a yawn.

"Sleep is boring. After the stories, I'm going to catch butterflies, so I can look at them up close."

"They're very pretty."

Bannan dropped his voice to a conspiratorial whisper. "Did you know they come from *caterpillars*?"

"No, not really!"

Treska's feigned surprise had the desired effect; the little boy puffed up and nodded sagely. "It's true. The caterpillar makes itself a tiny room and takes a long nap inside. And when it wakes up, it's a butterfly!"

"Or a moth," put in Mikka, joining them, with all the authority of her eight winters.

Bannan tilted his head to the side and scratched his chin. "I wonder if the caterpillar knows, when it goes to sleep, what it will be when it wakes up?"

"Well," Treska said, "I'm going to go to bed now, but I don't expect I'll change in my sleep."

"No, you wouldn't," Bannan said. "You have to be a caterpillar to—"

He broke off at the sound of raised voices within the house—some of them men's.

Treska strained to hear what they were saying; Bannan sidled up to Mikka, who drew him close.

Was it Treska's imagination, or were those men speaking Forstene? Should she go find out what was happening? What if it was something terrible?

"Stay here," Treska said to the children, and went back into the house.

There were two Forstene soldiers in the front room, speaking slowly and loudly to Pesha. When she shook her head, not understanding, they just talked louder, and added gestures.

"I'm only a servant," Pesha said, her voice almost trembling. "You need to talk to one of the Ladies. I can't help you. I don't know what you want!"

Treska laid a calming hand on Pesha's arm.

The woman turned to her with a grateful look. "Maybe you can . . . You're Ma'Sharha, anyway—or near enough."

One of the soldiers fixed his gaze on Treska; his eyes were almost black. "Ma'Sharha?"

"No," she said. "Not yet. I'm still just a Daughter of the People, not a Mother."

Now both soldiers were frowning at her.

"No." She pointed at herself, shaking her head. "Not Ma'Sharha. You need Ma'Sharha—not me."

This was going nowhere, and the soldiers were looking more and more unhappy. They were big, battle-worn men—one of them was even missing an ear—and wore metal shirts under their blue-and-white tunics. Treska tried not to look at the long, wicked swords hanging from their belts; she had seen enough injuries in the House of Healing to know what those swords could do.

"Pesha," she said quietly, "go find Healer Lillanna—she's with the Kel Jemya. Tell them both to come."

"But Mikka and Bannan. . ."

"I won't let the soldiers near them. I promise. Go on now, before these two really lose patience with us."

Pesha cast an anxious look at the soldiers in front of her, holding a whispered conversation of their own. She drew in a long breath, then dashed past them.

Black Eyes shouted something, and looked as though he would go after her.

"It's all right!" Treska said. "She's going to get one of the Ma'Sharha. She'll come back with someone who can help." Treska tried to mime her words, but she didn't think she was very successful at communicating her meaning.

Still, Black Eyes gave up on pursuing Pesha. After exchanging a few more words with One Ear, he stepped toward Treska.

"Tri-bute," he said, enunciating carefully. "You show."

Treska shook her head, more in confusion over what she was supposed to show him than anything else. But he took it as refusal to cooperate.

He shrugged and pushed past her. "We take."

For a few heartbeats Treska remained in the front room, weighted in place by her own sense of helplessness. But as she heard the soldiers tramping through the house, she remembered the children, and ran back toward the garden door. Black Eyes was reaching to push it open.

"Not there!" Treska said. "No tribute there. Here!" She gestured to the kitchen, although she couldn't imagine they'd find anything in there that they wanted.

Black Eyes came toward her again. Before she could shrink away, he grabbed her hand; his was rough and scarred, but his grip on her was surprisingly gentle. Then, more surprising still, he bowed over her hand. "Thank you," he said, released her, and went into the kitchen.

One Ear was already there, banging about. She watched from the doorway as they examined pots and cauldrons and helped themselves to hunks of Pesha's fresh bread. Then Black Eyes discovered the cellar door. Down he went; after a brief pause he was handing up sacks of grain and baskets of vegetables.

"Wait—that's our food! Are you taking our food? You can't do that!" As soon as the reckless words were out, Treska wished she could bite them back.

One Ear just glanced at her over his shoulder and laughed.

Treska's throat tightened and her eyes prickled. *No, I won't cry. I won't!*

Instead, she yelped in startlement as a hand landed on her shoulder from behind. But when she turned to see whose it was, she almost melted with relief. "Kel Jemya!"

And behind her was Lillanna, hands on hips, looking as irate as Treska had ever seen her. "Just what is going on here?"

Treska knew the anger wasn't for her, so her voice shook only a little when she answered. "They said 'tribute.' I think they're collecting tribute."

"I think they're committing robbery," the Kel Jemya said, and strode into the kitchen.

Lillanna watched her, her lips pressed together. The Kel Jemya was even taller and stronger than her predecessor, Edda, had been, and she showed no signs of feeling intimidated, even when Black Eyes came out of the cellar. But together the two soldiers far outmatched her in size and strength, and they were armed. She was not, since the Forsteners had forbidden the Guardians the use of their ironwood staves.

Treska could feel Lillanna's anxiety like a physical thing, but she didn't know how to ease it. She voiced the first thought that came into her head. "Why did the soldiers come *here* for tribute?"

"I think the Forsteners are working their way through the whole Sanctuary—on our way here, the Kel Jemya and I saw pairs of soldiers going into several other houses. I sent Pesha on to fetch Tigannas. He's gotten uncommon friendly with the Forsteners, and if he knew this was going to happen . . ."

The Kel Jemya had placed herself between the soldiers and the cellar door. Black Eyes was talking at her, louder and louder, but she merely folded her arms over her chest and settled into her stance. When Black Eyes paused to draw breath, she said, "Treska, start carrying these supplies back down to the cellar."

Treska hesitated, looking to Lillanna for guidance. But Lillanna seemed unsure of herself now; she gave Treska no more than a small shrug.

And that made up Treska's mind. Lillanna was Second in their Order, and these Forsteners dared to come in here and raid her stores? And she was thinking about letting them get away with it?

Treska stomped back into the kitchen and picked up a sack of potatoes. Before she could get to the cellar steps with it, One Ear grabbed it away. She reached to take it back, and he gave her a shove that sent her to the floor. She landed flat on her back, stunned, the wind knocked out of her.

Events were a jumble while she struggled to get her breath. First it seemed everyone was leaning over her, then everyone was yelling, and she could feel anger building all around her. Treska closed her eyes, wishing she could close her ears, too.

Then came a voice louder than all the others—clipped, precise, a voice used to giving orders and having them obeyed. Silence followed, except for a new set of footsteps entering the kitchen.

Treska opened her eyes to see Lord Torval standing over her. "Are you all right?" he asked; he spoke Sharhay with only a light accent.

She took a test breath and nodded. Lord Torval extended a hand and raised her to her feet.

"I am sorry for this," he said.

Treska spoke without thought. "Did you send them to take our food?"

"Hush, child!" Lillanna said, and tried to draw Treska away from the Forsteners.

Treska let her, but she still wanted an answer from Lord Torval. "Did you?"

He met her gaze. "Yes. But not all of it. Tigannas will explain; I must see to my other men. Excuse me." A heartbeat's hesitation, and he made a small bow to her and Lillanna, then left, Black Eyes and One Ear following him.

Tigannas had been waiting in the hallway; Lillanna and the Kel Jemya exchanged looks as he entered the kitchen. The ensuing silence was broken only by the voices of Pesha and her children floating in from the garden.

"So," the Kel Jemya said at length, "explain to us, Tigannas."

"There was a misunderstanding, it appears," he said. "The Forsteners reckon the days differently; I thought the soldiers were not being sent out till tomorrow."

"And were you planning to let any of us know about this?"

"Yes, I was going to visit all of the Council members today, and then each of you could inform your Guilds and Orders, and by day's end everyone would be prepared. And Kel Jemya, I was going to ask you to send a Guardian with each party of soldiers, so that the people would not fear being hurt. I promise you, Lord Torval and I planned very carefully—"

Lillanna had been making sputtery noises beside Treska and could contain herself no longer. "'Lord Torval and I'? I cannot believe this of you, Tigannas—you, the Lawspeaker! Have you stopped to consider what the Kel Sharha will think of this?"

"Of course I have! The Kel Sharha agreed to the treaty; the treaty says that the Forsteners may take tribute from us; the Kel Sharha does not want the treaty broken. She wants peace, and for no more of us to come to harm at Forstene hands. So it would be best if we let these soldiers take what they want, don't you think?"

"And what if what they want is—" Lillanna glanced at Treska and broke off.

"I said, a Guardian can accompany each group of soldiers. Lord Torval is calling them all back; they'll wait until tomorrow now, so that we can prepare better for the tribute collection to start."

The Kel Jemya harrumphed. "I'd better get back to my House, then, and make sure we get everything of value hidden or sent off to safety."

"You can't do that, Kel Jemya," Tigannas said, his voice quiet.

"Are you going to try to tell me it wouldn't be honorable or some such nonsense?"

"The Kel Sharha expects us all to honor the treaty—I need say no more on the matter. And when I say you can't send your valuables away to be hidden, that's what I mean: you can't. No one is allowed to enter or leave the Sanctuary anymore without the Forsteners' permission."

"Who gave that order—Lord Torval? Let me speak to him."

Tigannas grimaced. "The Scourge of Cheskara has command of the Sanctuary. It was his order, given before he left to ride with the prince."

After that there was little more to be said—at least little that was thought fitting to be said in Treska's presence. Lillanna sent her off to the room she was sharing with Saffa, where Treska lay down in Graysa's old bed. She watched the pattern of sunlight and shadow travel across the wall and wondered what she could have done differently that morning, and if there was anything she could do to help the Kel Sharha when she had to go away with the horrible Scourge of Cheskara.

With the Kel Sharha shut up in her house, cut off from the people, it almost felt as though she was gone already. How empty would the Sanctuary feel when she really was gone?

*****

The Kel Sharha tried at first to avoid the distaff, even for spinning. But a couple days were enough to show her that if she did not match her staff against a phantom Dursten by day, she would find her dreamself running at him with a sword by night. She wondered again if she needed a Mind Healer. There was none available to her, however; she went back to the staff.

Three sevennights from the beginning of the house arrest, Fidden and Gar almost surprised her at her exercise. Luckily she'd heard them approaching, and when they entered the garden, she was engaged in the unobjectionable task of binding fresh rovings to the distaff. Never mind the sheen of sweat on her face, nor the fact that the spindle on the ground beside her was nearly empty. The former, in any case, could be attributed to the morning's uncommon warmth.

As Fidden and Gar escorted her across the green, she reflected that it was only a matter of time and chance before someone discovered what she was doing. But if she stopped, the killing dreams would return. She would have to find some other way to fight them.

Perhaps she might try to recreate some of the Guardians' moving-prayer exercise. She had seen it only a few times, as the Guardians usually practiced it in the privacy of their House's garden. It looked, she thought, like a slow, controlled dance, although without music or partners. Yet even if she could recall some of the movements, ought she attempt them? The Guardians' exercise was for Guardians, not Healers. It would not be fitting. But . . . it would be much easier to explain away to her Forstene guards, if they caught her at it, than jabbing invisible foes with a distaff would be.

She put her contemplations aside—they would keep till later—as she entered the Champion's house. Lord Corvalen had returned to the Sanctuary, Fidden said, and awaited her in his office.

He was talking with Rossen by the window when she entered. He did not break his conversation, but indicated she should seat herself.

She settled onto a cushion, frowning inwardly. Something in this room seemed out of place. Certainly, there was the discordance of a Forstene lord occupying the Champion's house. But what she sensed now was something else—subtle . . . not, after all, unharmonious, but unexpected.

A small gilt-edged parchment lying on the table drew her attention. She leaned forward to look at it more closely: it was covered with writing, an elaborate script with the lettering so stylized that she would have had difficulty making it out even if she had been able to read Forstene. But the letters . . . was she mistaken? No—they shimmered ever so slightly in her vision, and her inner ear heard their silent hum.

The discussion by the window—men and horses and provisions, and Sir Somebody to captain some garrison—was concluding. She heard Rossen say, "After this interview—"

"No, no. Go along and get started now; I'd like to put my seal to some of those orders before I dine."

"Shall I send in Fidden and Gar, then?"

"Let them take their ease downstairs; I am well enough on my own here. Really, Rossen. I may have just marked my thirty-sixth year, but I'm hardly in my dotage. I think I'm proof against any harm this woman might offer."

Out of the corner of her eye, the Kel Sharha saw Rossen aim a look at her that surpassed mistrust.

What can I have done to antagonize Rossen? And what does he think I could possibly do to Lord Corvalen? Much as she disliked the man, it was never him she imagined receiving the blows of her distaff. Only now she did find herself picturing it. . . .

"That is beautiful writing," she said as he seated himself across the table from her.

He picked up the scroll and read out what was apparently the first line, his voice taking on a warmth she had not heard in it before. "'A blessing on the man who fares abroad.'" He smiled. "It is from one of our Hero stories: a benediction the Exalted Vallar received from his daughter before he went to war. My own daughter wrote this out as a gift to me; fine writing is an art form much cultivated among the ladies at court."

"You have a family?" This did not fit with her picture of him. Nor did a Forstene lady's working of power fit with the Kel Sharha's idea of court life in Forstene, but she had a feeling it would be unwise to question Lord Corvalen about this. She stored away her new knowledge for future consideration and, for the present, pretended interest in his family life.

"My wife died several years ago; we had but the one child."

"I am sorry."

He shrugged. "Ma'Sharha don't have children, do they?"

"It is a rare thing. When it happens, we give them to be fostered after birth."

"The Mothers of the People do not mother their own children?" He sounded shocked.

"We are mothers to allSharhay; we cannot attach ourselves to any one child more than another." How dare he look at her with such disapprobation? "You do not understand the Ma'Sharha, Lord Corvalen. You do not understand how things are in Sharhaya." She bit down on the rest of the angry words that threatened to pour forth, contenting herself with glowering at him instead.

"I beg your pardon, Lady. I did not mean to insult you or your people. You're right; I do not understand. Frankly, I just . . ." He sighed. "Do you, then, have any children yourself, Kel Sharha?" he asked, with what seemed to her a studied gentleness.

"If I had children, I would not risk their lives or freedom by telling my enemy of them."

"Lady, I am not your enemy."

"But you are not my friend. True, you show me honor . . . and even kindness, generosity, as you can. In another life, perhaps, we might be friends. As things are . . . I must believe that any friendship you show me, or my people, is for your own reasons—and your king's. Would I not be a fool to trust such friendship? An honorable lord of Forstene does not put friendship with the Kel Sharha above the commands of his own king."

"King Delanar follows the Precepts of Vallar as I do—"

"But who has acted for your king in Sharhaya these past years? Are you not honor-bound to the prince as to his father? And we have heard that the father is not well, that he has few winters left to him. When Dursten is king, will that change your loyalty? I cannot think so. If you are not my enemy now, Lord Corvalen, the day comes when you will be."

"I would take no pleasure in the arrival of that day, Lady." He seemed about to say something more, but the moment passed.

The ensuing silence lengthened. The Kel Sharha saw Lord Corvalen's eyes wander to his parchment again and guessed he must be missing his daughter greatly. She felt an unexpected flare of sympathy for him.

"Why did you send for me, Lord Corvalen?"

"Ah. No doubt you heard some of my conversation with Rossen; we are making plans for the disposition of my men—those who will stay and those who will return to Forstene with us."

Us.

"I expect His Grace the viceroy to arrive in little more than a week. It is time to give thought to your departure."

"I see." She heard the tightness in her voice, and made an effort to relax.

"I need to know how many you plan to take in your retinue."

"My—? I do not understand you."

"Servants, attendants. Your apprentice, perhaps?"

"Lord Corvalen, I have agreed to be shown off in your prince's triumph, but I would not allow even my *horse* to share in that . . .

251

humiliation!" She took a moment to compose herself again. "And what awaits me after the triumph? Your hostages from the Cheskari War, we have heard, are confined in strongholds throughout your country, and so they will spend the rest of their days. I can accept such a fate for myself, as the price of peace—but the price is mine to pay, no one else's."

"We had assumed that you would be accompanied by at least some of your following—that is how it would be for a noble of Forstene in the same situation."

"I am not a noble of Forstene," she said, leaning forward and fixing him with her gaze. "I am the First of Mothers—the mother of all Sharhaya. Can you really think I would allow any of my children to suffer humiliation and exile, even at my side?"

"No, Lady; when you put it in such terms, I cannot think that." His brow furrowed. "Prince Dursten will not be pleased."

All the better. "I am sure he would like a grander show in his triumph, but the treaty requires no one's . . . participation but mine. I go alone to Forstene."

*****

The sun was near its zenith by the time the Kel Sharha left the Champion's house. She took a deep breath, for the moment feeling something like happiness: she had been released from house arrest. This had come after further wrangling over the details of the triumph—which was going to be a thoroughly disgusting affair, no doubt about it. But that was more than a moon away, and for a brief while longer she had a measure of freedom. Tomorrow she would have to begin her preparations for the journey to Forstene. Today . . .

Her train of thought was interrupted by grumblings from her stomach. She had seen enough of her own house recently and decided not to go back for luncheon. Turning toward the Kel Mona's house, she thought of the old pleasures of a chatty meal with her friend. And after that, she would return to work in the House of Healing. Perhaps she would send for Taras to come and play his lute in the wards—music could be a powerful ally in healing—and while he was there, he might sing a song or two for her. Yes. All things considered, it would be a good day.

Then she heard Fidden and Gar scuffing along behind her, trading jibes. The sounds tore the thin fabric of her optimism like shears shredding fine linen.

She turned to glare the guards into silence, and found her gaze drawn by the sword at Fidden's side. For a searing moment her hand itched to grasp that leather-bound hilt.

"All right, M'Lady?" Fidden asked.

The genuine concern in his voice brought her back to herself. She nodded to him, swallowed, and turned her steps toward the Kel Sula's house. She would chat with the Kel Mona some other time.

The Kel Sula seemed almost to be expecting her; she met her on the porch, and one of the servants deftly ushered Fidden and Gar toward the kitchen with an offer of refreshment. Gar looked back over his shoulder at the Kel Sharha, clearly reluctant to leave her unsupervised, then shrugged and went along as the Kel Sula led her upstairs.

"I hope you don't mind not going to the garden," the Kel Sula said. "I thought your guards would be less likely to follow if we went to my private chambers. I'm sure you could do with a break from them."

"Yes." The Kel Sharha paused outside the bedroom door. She had not been in this house since the day Serelha asked for her crossing.

"Here, my chief," the Kel Sula said from across the hall; she was holding open the door to the sitting room.

"I should go; the House of Healing—"

"Can wait a little. Or you would not have come to me."

The Kel Sharha allowed herself to be led to a low basket chair; it had been Serelha's favorite seat during her last years.

The Kel Sula sat on a cushion close by, expectation and encouragement mingled in her expression.

Serelha must have taught her that look. Somehow the thought rankled. *Well, I am here; I may as well ask.* But she would have to feel her way gently toward what she wanted to know.

"Before she died, Serelha said there were things I should know about the life I lived before this one."

"Did she indeed?" The Kel Sula shook her head. "That is generally not thought wise."

The Kel Sharha could not help noticing that the other woman seemed reluctant to meet her gaze. "'Generally'? Or in my case in particular?"

After some hesitation: "Both."

"I see. Do you . . . do you know what Serelha knew, then, about who I was?"

"It's not so simple, you know, as to say that such a person *was* such another person—"

"Kel Sula, I did not come here to be lectured on the subtleties of your Order's philosophy." She paused to steady herself, then resumed more quietly. "When I returned from Prince Dursten's camp, you told me you would be at my service at any time I wished to talk with you. I am holding you to your word now and asking you for your service."

"The trouble is, Lady, that I'm not sure it *would* be of service for you to know. There are good reasons why the Mothers veil our other lives from us. To carry old memories into a new lifetime—it leads to confusion at best . . . madness at worst."

"It is madness that I fear, Kel Sula. I would not court it, yet . . . there are uncertainties . . . they sap my strength of mind and spirit. . . . I need to *know*."

"You already know, Kel Sharha." She sighed. "But I will say it aloud and plain for you if you like: when last your spirit walked in this world, it walked in the guise of Finoora of Redcreek—your grandmother."

"And she was a Guardian, I know. But why does no one speak of her? Why have I never been told more about her?"

"Because no one knows much to tell. She left Sharhaya not long after your mother was born; she returned but once, and then only briefly."

"Where did she go?"

"To Ghildarna, perhaps, or Cheskara. Or across the sea—who can tell? She is no longer spoken of by her Order, nor by anyone else."

"The Order . . . disowned her?"

"So it would seem."

We will speak well of you were the words said at funerals—unless the deceased had died dishonored. *No one speaks well of my grandmother; what can she have done?* Then came a more disturbing thought: *What part of her dishonor do I still carry within me?*

The Kel Sharha realized she had been sliding her fingers back and forth over the wicker chair arms. She took a slow breath and folded her hands in her lap. "How do you know all this, Kel Sula?"

"Serelha told me. When she was a girl, she was acquainted with Finoora; they were friends, of a sort. Serelha recognized you early in your training, she said, but she kept that knowledge to herself till she was dying. Only then did she tell me, and swore me to equal secrecy, except if you should ask—and if I should think you ready to hear."

"But *why* make such a secret of it?"

"To protect you, of course."

"Yes, yes—confusion, madness; I know."

"Not only that. I assure you, if it had been known that you carried the spirit of a renegade Guardian, you would not now be chief of your Order, let alone Kel Sharha."

Better for me had I been neither. It took her some moments to dislodge the unworthy reflections that followed—and she saw that the Kel Sula was not displeased that she'd been distracted. Then something occurred to her. "But Serelha, who knew, accepted me as Kel Nira, and made no difficulty about it."

"Before her illness, Serelha always saw farther and clearer than anyone else—patterns that no other could discern. She was a great woman."

"Yes, she was."

"So are you, Kel Sharha. And though you carry the spirit of Finoora of Redcreek, you are not her, but yourself."

"Then why have her memories awakened in me?" she whispered.

"To help you, to teach you; that is the usual reason."

"They do not help me, and they teach— She was a fighter, a warrior, a killer; she lived by violence! But I am a *Healer.* I do not want her memories of war."

"Perhaps," the Kel Sula said, "they are meant to balance *your* memories of war."

"Hmph."

"Kel Sharha . . . I don't know exactly what Serelha saw in your heart, or in your grandmother's. But what I see now is that there is something Finoora of Redcreek began that you must complete—and something that you have begun and cannot complete without her."

Chapter Twenty-Five

The Kel Sharha had no time to digest what the Kel Sula had told her. There were footsteps in the hallway, a knock on the door, and one of the Kel Sula's servants entered. She carried a tray bearing a small wheel of cheese, a plate of oatcakes, two plain earthenware jugs, and three cups. She was followed by the Kel Mona, who bowed to her fellow Chiefs in turn.

"I hope you don't mind my telling the girl to bring up a tray for you; knowing you both, I was pretty certain neither of you had eaten yet."

"We haven't," the Kel Sula said. She held the plate out to the Kel Sharha. "Eat, my Chief; it will do you good."

She nibbled at an oatcake without tasting it, watching the others. The Kel Mona busied herself with slicing the cheese, pointedly not looking at her. The Kel Sula poured water, then wine, into each of the cups; the Kel Sharha noticed that she measured out a good deal less wine than was usual.

"Your habits have become ascetic, Kel Sula," she said.

"Not by my own choice, Lady; and I certainly would not offer you such poor hospitality if I could do otherwise."

The Kel Sharha frowned in puzzlement.

"It's those covetous Forsteners," the Kel Mona said. "While you were shut up in your house, they went all through the Sanctuary, requisitioning provisions and making inventories of our furniture, our clothes—everything."

"How did I hear nothing of this?"

"You were shut up in your house," the Kel Mona repeated, "and no one was allowed in or out."

"But surely there was an outcry, there were protests . . . ?" Had it happened while she was playing at sparring with her distaff? Had she been so oblivious to all else?

The Kel Sula said, "We wished to keep the peace for you. So we stayed quiet and out of the way while the soldiers took what they wanted."

The Kel Sharha ducked her head. "Was anyone injured?"

"Some of the soldiers were either clumsy or inconsiderate, and there was some blustering and shouting. But no one was hurt."

"Except by the loss of wine casks and food stores and good linens and woolens," the Kel Mona said.

"That is harm enough. What else did they take?"

The Kel Mona shrugged. "Rugs, wall hangings, jewelry, that sort of thing. They about emptied the Artisans' Hall. There's scarcely anything left except the artisans' tools."

"At least they have those." The Kel Sharha thought of the detachments Prince Dursten had sent out. "This must be happening all over Sharhaya."

"Well, they've got to have their tribute, don't they?" the Kel Mona said.

The Kel Sharha gave her a sharp look. But her friend did not seem to be blaming her for the treaty and its terms. *She does not need to; I can lay the blame well enough myself.*

Her thought was answered by the Kel Sula. "It is not your fault, my Chief."

"Whose then?"

"The Forsteners have done this, not you."

"But I chose—"

"Peace."

"And what sort of peace is this?"

"One that lets us live, my Chief," the Kel Sula said. "And hope. Remember?"

Freedom with despair, or survival with hope. That was how the Kel Sula had summed up the alternatives, at that long-ago Council meeting.

But how long could hope endure if the Forsteners took everything her people needed to live?

And she would not be here to help them—not for a long time. Probably not ever again. It would be an extraordinary thing indeed if the king of Forstene let her return after she made her homage. There was no guarantee he would even let her live.

It was time to face that possibility.

The Kel Sharha looked from the Kel Sula to the Kel Mona. "The people will live, but I may not—or I may well live the rest of my life in Forstene. Kel Sula, have the trees told you what lies ahead for me?"

"Only possibilities and likelihoods, Kel Sharha. And . . . but perhaps I shouldn't mention it now."

"Lord Corvalen has told me that we will be leaving in a sevennight, or soon after. If you do not mention whatever it is now, you may not have another chance."

"Well . . . it's about Lord Corvalen, actually. It seems he is known to the Watchers."

"Yes."

The Kel Mona raised an eyebrow. "That's all you're going to say about it?"

"They asked me to make him known to them. I did not understand why—nor do I now—but one does not question the Watchers."

"Not if one is at all wise." The Kel Mona directed her next words to the Kel Sula. "What do you think it means—have the Watchers given him blessing or doom?"

"Perhaps both."

"Well, what might it mean for the Kel Sharha?" The Kel Mona turned to her. "Could they have marked him for your protector, do you think?"

"Not if they've doomed him, surely. At least I hope not." The Kel Sharha laughed, but sobered quickly. "In any case, Lord Corvalen has already made it quite clear that there is a limit to his goodwill. He will protect me so far as it suits his own purposes and his own notions of honor, but no more. His will is his king's to command. If his king says I die, then I die."

The Kel Mona looked away. "I don't care to think about that."

"You must, my friend. You are next for the keeping of the Motherland, and we must make certain the Mayahara can pass to you even if I die far away."

"The Mayahara always finds its channel," the Kel Sula said.

"Yes, but it flows strongest when it can be passed direct, through touch." Especially when passed at the moment of death, when all the force of a soul breaking from its physical form was added to the transfer—but this discussion was distressing enough for the Kel Mona, so the Kel Sharha decided to say no more about dying. "What I want to find out is if there is a way we can be linked together so that we can simulate that direct connection if . . . if we ever need to."

The Kel Mona twisted the end of her braid. "You worry too much, Kel Nira."

"I agree," the Kel Sula said.

"Then the two of you should be glad to find a way to help me worry less."

After a few heartbeats' silence, the Kel Sula said slowly, "Perhaps it's not that you worry too much, Kel Sharha, but that you may be worrying about the wrong thing. The channel for receiving the Mayahara was set in each of us when we became Chiefs of the Ma'Sharha. But this situation . . ." She shook her head. "There is no precedent—no Kel Sharha has ever left the Land before; even the trees have no memories of such a thing. It's very difficult to foresee what the effects will be, especially on you, on your Power."

The Kel Sharha sat very still. "On the Mayahara itself?"

"I don't know."

Silence descended around the three women again. The Kel Sharha stared down at her hands, her mind seeing a new truth unveiling itself. *What have I done? What if I have taken the first steps in destroying all that I sought to save?*

The Kel Mona knelt in front of her and stroked her hands until they unclenched. "Please don't worry so, and please stop blaming yourself."

"I carry the Mayahara, and I have agreed to take it out of Sharhaya!"

The Kel Sula said, "The Power of the Mothers is not so small. You may be its human vessel, but do you really think it resides only in you? What about the trees and the rivers and the rocks; the birds, the creatures of the forest, the—"

"Yes." The Kel Sharha drew a long breath. "Yes, of course you are right. Thank you; I will need to remember that. I beg your pardon for my hubris. It is just, now that I am leaving so soon, the prospect of being separated from Sharhaya . . ." She stopped before her voice gave way.

The Kel Mona, still kneeling before her, took her hands again and pressed them over her own heart. "You shall not lose your strength, Kel Sharha; I will not let you. I am going to find a way to safeguard your bond to the Land. I swear it."

*****

The Kel Sharha walked slowly back toward the House of Healing after leaving the Kel Sula's house. Still deep in thought, she nearly bumped into Lord Corvalen and Torval crossing the green.

"Are you all right, Lady?" the younger man asked.

"I am not." She turned her glare on Lord Corvalen. "I have just learned that your soldiers have all but sacked this Sanctuary!" No wonder he had wanted her shut away in her house.

Torval did not give his uncle a chance to reply. "Those were my soldiers, Lady. I was commanded to collect tribute, but I gave orders that no household should be entirely stripped of its goods or provisions and that all should be done without violence. If I find that any of my men have disobeyed, I assure you I will take disciplinary action."

The Kel Sharha regarded him narrowly as another thought occurred to her. "The House of Healing—"

"Is untouched; we have no wish to endanger the ill and injured."

"So there is little harm done," Lord Corvalen said mildly.

"Little harm? When the Chief of the Sula must eat stale oatcakes and drink water scarce purpled with wine, what can your collectors of tribute have left for others?"

"But Lady, doesn't your harvest begin soon?" Torval asked. "I hope I did not judge wrongly—I thought it would be best to take the tribute now, and then your people would be able to keep most of their harvest."

She folded her arms and looked from Torval to Lord Corvalen. "And how much harvest do you think we shall reap?" she asked. "You came through the south, Lord Corvalen. Did you see the grain in the fields? Did you see the flocks on the hills? Did you see vines and trees heavy with fruit? Did you see strong farmers tending the land? No? None of this?"

"Not in the south, Lady," Lord Corvalen conceded. "But over these recent weeks I have seen great abundance north of the Lenasha."

"And you think that the farms of the north can alone produce enough for us, now that war has left so many fewer people to feed. So many fewer it will surely be no burden to us to provide for your garrisons through the winter." She stopped herself, realizing that she was on the verge of an unbecoming display of anger.

"Your northern lands are beautiful and abundant, as I said. But even there I saw many farms and vineyards untended. It is one of the costs of war, especially when farmers must take up arms to defend their land instead of cultivating it. The garrisons, however, will be provisioned out of Forstene at least until the next planting comes ripe, when they will have sown their own fields."

So Forstene soldiers would be appropriating Sharhay cropland.

The bitterness overflowed into her next words. "I am relieved to know that your soldiers will eat well even if my people are starving."

"What do you expect me to do, Lady?" For the first time there was a hint of impatience in Lord Corvalen's voice.

Composing herself, the Kel Sharha considered the question seriously. "I am in no position to expectyou to do anything, Lord Corvalen," she said. "Neither you nor I will even be here this winter to see what becomes of my people. The Listeners foresee a hard season, and I must hope the viceroy and soldiers show the people compassion."

"What about . . ." Torval hesitated. "What about magic?"

"Magic?"

"Supernatural powers."

The Kel Sharha was not certain what *supernatural* meant, but she smiled wistfully. "Did you ever hear of a power that could make crops grow where none had been planted, or burnt trees bear fruit? There is no such 'magic' in Sharhaya, no more than anywhere else."

"But there is magic here," Torval insisted. "I've seen it: the strange mists, the solid ground turning boggy, that Kel Sula reading men's minds. And the way you healed my leg."

"That is not 'magic.' It comes from—" But perhaps it would be better not to say more.

"From the trees. Your power comes from the trees." Lord Corvalen said it with quiet certainty, his gaze fixed on her.

She would have to give him some explanation; she did not want the Forsteners thinking they could cripple the Ma'Sharha by cutting down the forests. "The power comes from the Mothers. It is in the land, and in everything that grows from the land. It is a part of all."

"Yet not all can wield it."

The Kel Sharha sighed inwardly. "Always some are born who are like . . . who have a hollow place inside, where the power comes up, like water from a spring. With teaching and practice, this spring can become a river. This is why, in the long-ago, Ma'Sharha were called River Women."

"River Wives," said Torval, nodding. "We have stories about them—and their magic."

"Stories, Torval. That's all—and that's the only place you will find magic." Lord Corvalen's tone made it clear that he disdained to discuss this subject further. And yet, after a moment, his face relaxed into an expression almost contemplative.

Was he remembering his encounter with the Watchers? But he had been angry about that afterward, had accused her of trickery; did he now wonder if there might have been "magic" in it? Yet he claimed there was no such thing. . . .

"I think you are right, Lord Corvalen," the Kel Sharha said, treading carefully, "but we do have many rites that some might call magic. For us, they are for prayer and for keeping the"—she searched for words he would understand—"the rightness of things. The balance. There are ceremonies such as we perform in this season to welcome Harvest, to offer to the Mothers and Watchers, and to prepare for Vintage. You may imagine how important this is to us."

"Harvest is a time of thanksgiving and celebration in Forstene, too, especially in the countryside. I suppose you would like permission to hold these ceremonies?"

"The people will feel more secure knowing the proper rites are done." *And so will I.*

"I must give this some thought, Kel Sharha. You'll have my decision tomorrow." He bowed to her, and she thought it wise to honor him with a bow in return.

*****

Elder Rimenna clasped Corvalen's hand, thanking him again. "It has been a great oppression—a source of unhappiness to many—to know that we might nevermore gather for the celebrations that have been ours since the long-ago," she said.

"One cannot celebrate with only six," agreed Falessan, the Elder of the Vintners' Guild.

"You understand," Corvalen said in his halting Sharhay, "this is for tomorrow only. I am lifting the assembly limit for only the one day, remember."

But that was enough to make a difference, and as the two Elders left his office, Corvalen congratulated himself on the decision he'd made a few mornings earlier.

While the Sanctuary people had behaved peaceably enough since the war's end, they'd nevertheless made no secret of their hostility toward the Forstene occupiers. This, Corvalen thought, did not bode well for his hopes that the viceroy would be able to work with and through the Sharhay leadership after the Kel Sharha's departure. Now, with the prospect of the upcoming festival, the Sanctuary's residents seemed more inclined to treat the Forsteners with something at least approaching courtesy.

And we have won over that Tigannas almost completely. Torval had already been cultivating the Lawspeaker's goodwill, and when Corvalen sent to consult with him after his last conversation with the

Kel Sharha, the man made no effort to hide his sense of gratification. Yet there was none of Esban's fawning obsequiousness about him. He was an earnest man, but a serious one. His desire for peace seemed at least as strong as the Kel Sharha's. For the sake of maintaining that state, he was more than happy to explain anything Corvalen wanted to know about Sharhaya's laws and customs. And he was much more forthcoming than the Kel Sharha. Much less prickly, too.

Once Corvalen intimated that he was inclined to allow the Sanctuary folk a modified version of their traditional Harvest observances, Tigannas did not hesitate to recommend adjustments, or to agree to those Corvalen suggested. One day of rites instead of three, no visits to or from the surrounding countryside, and so on. What was left of the celebration was apparently enough to satisfy, the more so since none of the Sharhay had expected to be allowed their rites at all.

Certainly Prince Dursten would rather not have permitted them. But Dursten was back at Summer Bluff, busy planning castles and deploying men-at-arms to garrisons and veterans' settlements. The king had given Corvalen charge over the Sanctuary, and Corvalen was sure he would be vindicated for his belief that the Sharhay would respond best to a beneficent administration, one that had the flexibility to interpret the treaty in such a way as to mitigate some of its stricter terms. He would write as much in the report he was composing for Duke Beddar.

Sounds from the green drifted through the open window of his office and nibbled at the edges of his concentration. He laid aside his pen and went to look out over the preparations taking place below. Although the harvest celebration would not be held until the morrow, a tentatively festive air was already making itself felt, even among the Forstene soldiers. Corvalen and Torval had both cautioned their troops to show restraint, however—the delicate peace could easily be overbalanced by even one or two unduly rambunctious Forstene revelers.

Tigannas had advised that the soldiers be clear on one point in particular: Sharhay women were quick to take offense.

Remembering this, Corvalen found himself involuntarily looking up the green to the Kel Sharha's house. He was surprised to see a number of people, in carefully spaced clusters of no more than six individuals each, lingering in the area. The loiterers were orderly, but there was also a subdued boisterousness about them, and he could see a number of soldiers nearby keeping them under surveillance.

After lifting the house arrest, he had felt it safe to allow the residents of the Sanctuary access to the Kel Sharha again. For one thing, Fidden and Gar were faithful and intelligent fellows—and Brintoran speakers, rapidly advancing in their comprehension of Sharhay. They were staying closer to their charge now and would quickly scent out any plotting that might be going on between the Kel Sharha and her visitors.

Besides, as anxious as the Kel Sharha was to avoid further violence in Sharhaya, he doubted she would condone, let alone foment, any kind of rebellious conspiracy. And she spent most of her time in the House of Healing, where visitors were generally in no condition to bother themselves with seditious plots.

For these reasons Corvalen felt more curious than worried about the small crowd outside the Kel Sharha's house. He decided that satisfying his curiosity had more appeal than working on his report.

The clusters of people drifted apart as Corvalen approached. Before he could knock at the door, it opened, and Corvalen stood aside to let a woman and two children pass. One of the little ones was limping, but smiling widely, with eyes only for the carved wooden rabbit he cradled in his hands. The family left the door standing open, so Corvalen went on through.

He had never yet been inside the Kel Sharha's house, although of course Fidden and Gar had briefed him on its layout. He knew that the ground floor had a kitchen (with cellar beneath), a parlor, a workroom, and a storeroom; that the Kel Sharha's private chambers and bedrooms for her apprentice and a few servants were upstairs; and that behind the house was a small garden.

But Fidden and Gar had no eyes for art or craftsmanship. They had not mentioned the fine carved and painted wall panels of the little entrance hall or its intricate parquet floor or the plush, deep-hued carpet at the foot of the narrow stairway. As Corvalen's eyes adjusted from the bright sunlight outside, he took in still more details, such as the banister of rich wood, worked to look like a wild growth of shrubs and vines in which half-seen creatures lurked; the eyes of the creatures gleamed with inlaid stones.

A servant came down the stairs and audibly caught her breath at sight of him, nearly dropping the bundles she carried. She hastily deposited them near the door. Only then did Corvalen register the presence in the front hall of a number of cloth bundles, pottery vessels, and baskets containing jars and packets of he knew not what.

The servant was eyeing him apprehensively. He smiled at her and used his gentlest tones to inform her that he wished to see the Kel Sharha.

The girl led him through to the back of the house. She seemed in a hurry; following her, he caught only glimpses of the house's comforts and ornaments. Although the Kel Sharha's residence was hardly palatial, everything he saw appeared to be of the highest quality. Passing out through a door with colored glass panels, Corvalen entered the garden.

The Kel Sharha, seated in a low wickerwork chair in the shade of a vine-covered pergola, did not seem at all surprised to see him—she must have expected that the people gathered outside would attract his attention sooner or later. Beside her stood a small table bearing a pitcher and two glasses, and next to that was another wickerwork chair. She nodded toward it, and Corvalen sat down, looking about for the guards. They stood discreetly at attention near some tall shrubbery at the back of the garden, and he gestured them to take their ease.

The Kel Sharha was evidently feeling in the mood to play gracious hostess. Lifting the pitcher, she said, "Because of the rites tomorrow, I drink only water today, but if you prefer something other . . ."

"Water is sufficient," he answered, and accepted the glass she offered. "Since you are here and not in the House of Healing, may I take it that your patients are well on the road to health?"

"Most are, indeed. But today I would be here, or out on the green, in any case. It is our custom that on the day before a great ceremony the Kel Sharha receives any of the people who desire a blessing from her."

"Ah." A detail Tigannas had not remembered—or chosen?—to tell him. "That is the reason for the people gathered outside. And the bundles and baskets in your hallway?" He hoped that was not the way she was packing for the journey to Forstene.

"Gifts."

Understanding came over him. "Are you giving away your possessions, Kel Sharha?"

"All but the things my Second will need; she is to live here after I am gone."

"Ah."

"There is a problem, Lord Corvalen?"

He should have learned by now not to make assumptions about these people. "It was thought that most of your possessions would go with you to Forstene."

"Will I need them?" she asked.

He answered the underlying question. "I do not know what will become of you after you make your homage to the king." The rebellious jut of her chin made him lean toward her and add, "You do realize that you will be killed if you refuse to render homage."

"I know well that my life is of small value once I cross the mountains into Forstene." After a moment she smiled a little, making an open-handed gesture as though giving the matter over to fate. "However, I will pack for the journey as though I expect to live. I assure you I will be well provided with heavy tunics and cloaks against the winter." She stopped, and the smile became one of cynical amusement. "But of course that is not your concern. You were thinking to display my possessions in the triumph. And then . . . I suppose they would make part of the spoil, or the tribute."

He eyed her steadily to let her know he did not flinch from the truth. "That is what was intended, yes."

The Kel Sharha returned his look in silence. Her eyes were shadowed, as though she had not slept well for several nights running.

"Tell me plain, Lord Corvalen: Have your people gathered enough for the tribute?"

He nodded slowly, knowing she would be furious to discover how much timber had been taken from the Lenasha Forest, how many fleeces had been claimed from farmers and woolworkers, how few wine casks were left in the cellars of Sharhaya. "Most of it has already been loaded and is even now being carted to Forstene—the wagons go slowly, and His Highness has soldiers glad to undertake the guarding of them so that they might already be on their way home. Yes," he assured her, "there is enough."

"Then there can be no need to take my possessions as well. Besides, my belongings from the Winter Sanctuary are already among the spoils. Here in this Sanctuary, my house was the only one Lord Torval left untouched during his tribute collection—and now I see why—so I believe it is fitting to share with my people. This is the . . . noble thing to do, would you not agree?"

Her slight emphasis on the word *noble* was not lost on Corvalen, but he admired her shrewdness. When they conversed, he often felt they were engaged in some sort of contest to discover who was cleverest, or strongest willed. He realized he rather enjoyed the sparring, and decided he would let her win this time.

"You are right, of course. By all means, distribute your gifts, Lady."

She inclined her head, and he stood to take his leave. But plainly she knew that this was a small victory, and likely one of the last she would achieve. "Lord Corvalen." Her voice was very soft, very grave as she rose from her chair.

She was standing quite close to him; a scent of sweet herbs hung about her. Corvalen waited.

"Lord Corvalen," she began again in the same quiet voice, "you must know that taking away spoils and tribute together, you leave my people more to fear than the coming winter. With our resources so low now, it will not be easy to make the tribute for next year—perhaps for many years."

He did not think the appeal in her eyes was the effect of artifice or calculation, and he hardly liked the answer he had to give. He tried to speak gently. "I know this, Kel Sharha, but there is little I can do. You must, I suppose, put your hope in tomorrow's ceremonies."

Chapter Twenty-Six

"The gathering, the gathering,
Come all you now to gather in!"

The chant woke Corvalen at dawn on the festival day. He pulled on a tunic and went to the window.

Below him, the Celebrants circled the green, some drumming, some dancing, all singing-shouting the chant. The summons was answered by doors opening, by people leaving the houses in twos and threes to trickle out onto the paths that led to the green like streams feeding into a lake. They joined their voices to the Celebrants', and their clapping hands echoed the drumbeats.

Since Corvalen's coming, the Sanctuary had never been filled with such movement and color. The earthy tones that garbed the humbler folk were punctuated by the rich dyes of the guild members' robes— blues for the Celebrants, yellows and oranges for the Artisans, and red-purples, of course, for the Vintners. When all the people had arranged themselves around the center dais, the pattern was a delight to behold. And from this distance there were no patches or frayed hems to be seen, even though Corvalen knew that the best garments had all been taken by Torval's soldiers for the Sanctuary's tribute.

A double patrol of those soldiers stood around the green, in the shadows of the houses, aloof and on watch.

As the colors still swirled, the guild Elders had mounted the dais. Now Elder Rimenna of the Celebrants stepped to the center, holding up a large bronze bell. She paused dramatically, then struck it with a mallet three times. The bell's reverberation stilled the crowd.

"We welcome Harvest with thanks for our voices," Rimenna proclaimed, and bowed to the people.

"The Mothers' blessing!" they responded.

Rimenna passed the bell and mallet to Ingas of the Artisans' Guild. He, too, struck three times. "We welcome Harvest with thanks for our skills!" He bowed.

"The Mothers' blessing!"

Falessan of the Vintners stepped up and took his turn with the bell. "We welcome Harvest with thanks for our sustenance!"

"The Mothers' blessing!" rang out as a cheer as the Elder Vintner executed his bow.

Rimenna took back the bell and struck it three more times. Some of the Celebrants, gathered now in front of the dais, had exchanged their drums for pipehorns and struck up a slow march. The Listeners, Summoners, and Guardians emerged from their Houses in a stately procession. They looked more grave than festive, Corvalen thought, and the march sounded harsh and bleak in his ears.

When the three Chiefs had mounted the dais and the others had ranged themselves at the front of the crowd, Rimenna struck her bell thrice again. Like the people gathered below, Corvalen looked toward the House of Healing.

Lillanna led the Healers out, their overdresses gleaming like fresh snow. The Celebrants added high shrill flutes to their pipehorns, rattles and tambourines to their drums. The Healers took their places to a crescendo of jangling sounds, and Rimenna struck the bell a final time.

The Kel Sharha stepped out onto the green.

She was dressed like a queen—which, Corvalen reflected, she was, whether or not her people would use the title. But more than the rich embroidery down the front of her overdress and around the trailing sleeves of her tunic, more than the golden diadem woven with vines and flowers, more even than the serene dignity of her face and carriage, his attention was arrested by her hair. Unbraided, it reached to her waist, flowing down her back like a river fired by the sunrise.

As he watched her progress to the center of the Sanctuary, the song of a single flute all the music that accompanied her, Corvalen could not help seeing how her people also watched. He realized more forcefully than ever the extent to which the Sharhay's hopes and aspirations— even their very sense of themselves—were focused on their First of Mothers. *She is their heart. And I am going to cut her out.*

His thoughts tumbling over one another, it took Corvalen some moments to translate what she said after she mounted the dais: "My people, behold: I am your servant." She bent her knees in a deep curtsy and simultaneously bowed low, a form of obeisance he had never seen before. Her hair spilled over her shoulders, obscuring her face. She rose slowly and opened her arms as the people, in unison, bowed from the waist, hands over heart and belly, in the formal Sharhay gesture of respect and homage.

There was an awkward pause; it occurred to Corvalen that perhaps tradition called for the Champion to play some role at this point, and the Sharhay were at a loss as to how to proceed without him.

The Kel Sharha was equal to banishing the uncertainty. She gathered herself and smiled radiantly. Raising her arms high, she called, "Bring forth the cart!"

The crowd took up the cry, with the encouragement of the Celebrants turning it into a staccato chant: "Bring forth the cart! Bring forth the cart!"

Not far from the Champion's house, the people were jostling one another aside. Corvalen soon saw what they were making way for—and he knew why many of the Sharhay fell silent when they saw it. It was an ordinary wicker-sided farm cart, bedecked in garlands and pulled by two small horses with braided manes and tails. This was not what the Sanctuary dwellers were accustomed to. Corvalen had seen some of the goods collected for the tribute, and one thing that had caught his eye was an exquisitely crafted cart, its wooden sides carved all over with images of fruit, grain, trees, and other growing things, alongside symbols that he thought might indicate sun and rain and the like. He had wondered what such a cart could have been made for, and now he knew: it was a ritual vehicle, used in this ceremony and perhaps others.

The Kel Sharha gave no sign of dismay. Corvalen remembered that she had fasted the previous day and wondered what other preparations she had made, for there was something great and remote about her on this morning. He remembered her pressing his hand into the beech tree and telling him that the Watchers stood between living people and "the Mothers Beyond." That was how she seemed herself now—a link between ordinary humans and the greater powers.

Then his native skepticism reasserted itself. He shook his head and smiled at his momentary gullibility. He already knew how well the Kel Sharha could play any role she felt called to act; clearly, he had let the sight of her unbound hair befuddle him. Exhorting himself to better self-governance, he shut the gate on any further thoughts along those lines and returned his attention to the ceremony below.

The cart had stopped in front of the dais, the horses' withers even with the platform. The Kel Sharha was holding a bundle of herbs in one hand and a wooden bowl in the other. Ingas poured water from an earthenware pitcher into the bowl; Falessan came forward to add wine. As the Elders stepped back to their places, the Kel Sharha began a singsong chant, but the words were obviously not meant to carry beyond the dais. Dipping the bundle of herbs into the mingled wine and water, she proceeded to asperge the cart and horses.

She handed the bowl off to the Kel Mona and stepped to the edge of the dais. "Make ready!" she called out. The people cheered as she jumped lightly down into the cart, raised the bundle of herbs high, and threw it into the crowd.

Another shout went up, and a young man danced forward, waving the bouquet triumphantly. He climbed into the cart and bowed to the Kel Sharha, who placed her hand briefly on top of his head. Then it was his turn to throw the herb bundle out, winning the catcher a place in the cart. Corvalen smiled at the similarity between this part of the ceremony and the harvest games he had sometimes seen among the peasants on his lands. With that reflection, he finally felt able to turn away from the window.

But as he finished dressing, he found himself thinking again of the Kel Sharha's hair, and drifted back to look at it again. The last woman he had seen with her hair long and loose was Neldis the courtesan—for his money (he grimaced at the unfortunate aptness of the expression) the most beautiful woman in Forstene. Yet even as he recalled the luster of her thick chestnut tresses, the knowing wit that sparked in her eyes, the generous curve of her lips, he felt no more emotion than if he were remembering a portrait once seen in a fellow baron's collection. An exquisite portrait, to be sure, but still . . .

He summoned up memories of the warmth of Neldis's coppery skin, the feel of his hands tracing the curves of her body—and remained unmoved. Indeed, his mind could not even retain the remembered images and sensations. His inner and outer eyes alike seemed to be only for the Kel Sharha. How had he never noticed that she was beautiful?

He wished he had not noticed it now. *But I will soon be able to forget*, he told himself. *After this festival she will braid her hair again, and be severe and proud. Another conquered chief clinging to dignity. I have seen the like before.*

But a deeper part of him whispered, *You have never seen her like before, nor shall you again.*

*****

Although the Kel Sharha seemed content so far with the modified harvest festival, clearly Pieran was not. Rossen felt as though he and Torval were standing next to a thundercloud as they watched from the portico of the Champion's house. Torval's curiosity was nevertheless undaunted, and he asked Pieran dozens of questions about various aspects of the ceremony, ignoring the grudging tone of the answers.

With a bit of envy, Rossen noted how easily his companions switched back and forth between Forstene and Sharhay. He really had no gift for languages; it had taken him years to become competent in Ghildaran. Sharhay was almost beyond attempting; he certainly entertained no hope of ever approaching Torval's fluency. But even without understanding everything, he found the ceremony enjoyable—a sort of refined peasant pageant, he thought, and utterly charming. Of course, no Forstene village could ever boast a Harvest Queen to compare with the Kel Sharha.

He caught himself in the thought with surprise, then wondered if Corvalen shared it.

The wagon was full of laughing men, women, and children. The Kel Sharha had moved to sit beside the driver, and a procession of Ma'Sharha and Guild members was forming up behind the cart. The driver gave the reins a shake, and the vehicle creaked into motion, with the Celebrants blowing a jolly-sounding air on their pipehorns. Fidden and Gar scurried to mingle with the Guild members, one of whom thrust a tambourine at Fidden. He began to bang away at it gleefully, to Gar's quite obvious disgust.

"Where are they going?" Torval asked.

Pieran frowned. "They would go to meet carts coming from the farmland near the Parasha. The Kel Sharha would bless the carts, and they would come back with grain for the Sanctuary. But"—the scowl deepened—"many of those farms were not worked this year. And no one enters or leaves the Sanctuary today"—this with a quelling look for Torval.

"So what will they do?" Torval prompted.

Pieran shrugged. "Gather from the gardens here."

"Will that be enough?" Rossen asked.

"Not likely. We will make our bread from acorn meal before winter ends."

Even Torval could think of no answer to that, and soon afterward Pieran begged leave to spend the rest of the day with his countrymen.

For a time Rossen and Torval quietly observed the activity on the green. Those Sharhay who had not followed the cart were gathering in small groups to breakfast together out of doors. They spread out rugs or blankets over dusty patches and much-trampled grass and shared around pottery jars of drink and baskets of oatcakes.

The talk and laughter became more subdued as the Sharhay seemed increasingly aware of the Forsteners on watch around the green. Every so often, a few children would break away from their families and dash about in a game of chase, only to be hastily summoned back to their rugs. The adults would scold and glance around at the soldiers.

Rossen was trying to picture what this festival had been like before the war when Torval interrupted his thoughts, speaking as though he had just reached a decision. "I'm going to stay."

"Here? Whatever for?"

"To assist His Grace." Rossen must have looked skeptical, because Torval added, a little defensively, "The duke and I got on very well when I was his squire, and I can be useful to him here. I've learned a lot about this country, and I know the language, too. I think he will be glad of my help."

And you will be glad to attach yourself to another member of the royal family now that you're out of favor with the prince. "What does Lord Corvalen think of this notion?"

"My uncle respects Duke Beddar; I'm sure he'll recommend me to His Grace's service."

"Perhaps your uncle would prefer to have you with *him.* And doubtless your lady mother would like to see you back at court."

Torval shook his head. "I have no wish to live at court."

"And what of your barony?" came Corvalen's voice behind them. Rossen turned to see him leaning in the doorway.

"Good morning, Uncle," Torval said. "May I ask how long you've been listening?"

"Long enough to surmise that you are not intending to return to Forstene with us. But you have been away three years; your lands could do with your attention."

"You were in Cheskara for five years, sir, and have been mostly at court since then. Your lands are far more extensive than mine, and if you can entrust them to your stewards, then why cannot I do the same?"

Rossen felt he ought to take himself off at this point, but Corvalen was blocking the way into the house, and Torval was blocking the steps leading down from the portico to the green. Since he couldn't leave discreetly, Rossen tried to fade into the background and minimize his appearance of listening in on this family controversy.

"You are painting in broad strokes, Torval," Corvalen said quietly. "You know full well that I returned home for at least part of every winter during the Cheskari campaign."

Rossen winced for his lord, knowing what had come of two of those all-too-brief visits home. After each there was joy when the letters arrived in camp to inform Corvalen that his wife was with child. Then came the news, both times, that there would be no child after all: the first pregnancy ended in miscarriage, the second in stillbirth. Corvalen had killed a Cheskari warrior-woman that season, only to discover afterward that she had been pregnant. He was still atoning for his breaking of the Precepts of Vallar when he received word of his stillborn son.

Absorbed by his recollections, Rossen had lost the thread of Corvalen and Torval's argument. It seemed, however, that Torval was close to winning his point. "It might be well at that," Corvalen was saying thoughtfully.

Torval pressed his advantage. "Duke Beddar will make his residence in the keep on the bluff, if I know him. But he will surely want a deputy and troops here in the Sanctuary. We can even barrack the men in the Guesthouse once the Sharhay are done using it as an infirmary."

"There is justice in all you say, Torval. But could you really be content living here?"

"I will be doing my duty, sir. That should be enough to content me, should it not?"

Just the sort of argument Corvalen was most susceptible to; Rossen feared for the day when someone might turn it against him.

Corvalen gave Torval a measuring look. "I will speak to His Grace on your behalf. But *you* will have to write and explain yourself to your mother—that task is more than I am equal to, even for your sake." Allowing himself a smile, he treated Torval to a rough embrace and drew him toward the door.

Rossen, forgotten, followed them in silence.

*****

As the day progressed, Corvalen found the festival spirit taking hold of him. He, Torval, and Rossen passed the afternoon among the crowd watching and cheering the games and competitions on the green. It was the kind of thing he and his men enjoyed every bit as much as the Sharhay did. He and Torval were forced, however, to dissuade several of their followers from competing in the foot races and wrestling matches—further resentment would surely be the result if Forstene warriors bested the Sharhay in these contests.

From overheard remarks, Corvalen gathered that in the past the Champion had presided over this portion of the festivities. Now Tigannas the Lawspeaker took his place, seated on a cushioned stool on the dais, calling start and stop to the contests and proclaiming the victors, his voice carrying across the green as resonant as Elder Rimenna's bronze bell. When the games ended with evening's arrival, he summoned all of the winners to the dais, crowning each with a garland of leaves. A number of Celebrants had returned to the green and beat their drums in a rhythmic fanfare while the crowd cheered.

As the winners left the dais, they were enveloped by well wishers and admirers. Seeing people gathered around one man in particular, Corvalen remarked to Torval, "Our friend Pieran appears to be the hero of the day."

"He wrestled well. But in previous years, I'm told, he always took the prizes for things like archery and ax throwing."

Rossen chuckled. "It's as well we prohibited weapons contests, then. I don't like the thought of sharp objects in the hands of that man."

"He was formidable in battle," Torval recalled. "I never faced him directly, but I saw what happened to those who did."

"He was the Champion's Second," Corvalen said thoughtfully. "I expect he had designs to become Champion himself one day. You'll need to keep him under your eye, Torval."

"I agree he bears watching, sir—though he wouldn't become Champion now, even if the office were restored. The Champion is the consort of the Kel Sharha, after all."

"I thought the Holy Women didn't marry," said Rossen.

"It's not considered a marriage," Torval explained, "since the Champion only visits the Kel Sharha, so to speak, and only on ceremonial occasions—they don't live together. But he has to swear himself to her, and he's not allowed to marry anyone else."

The conversation was interrupted by another loud tattoo from the Celebrants' drums. This appeared to be the signal for a procession to form up, led by the Lawspeaker and the day's victors. The Celebrants took their places next and began to beat out a heartbeat-like rhythm. The other Sanctuary people, with much excited whispering, began to jostle themselves into a queue.

On an impulse, Corvalen decided he would take part as well. Stepping into line, he found himself behind the same woman and children he had met coming out of the Kel Sharha's residence the previous day. He smiled to see that the boy was still clutching his wooden rabbit.

Rossen and Torval joined him. "Are you certain this is a good idea, sir?" Torval asked in a low voice.

"We'll soon find out."

"If you're going to stay among these people," Rossen said to Torval, "you ought to know what kind of things they get up to, don't you think?"

The woman in front of them turned her head, regarding them with suspicion, and Corvalen gestured his companions to silence. Feeling the weight of stares bearing down on the three of them, he assumed an attitude of reverence, hoping to make it clear that he had no wish to disrupt the ceremony. Gradually the people around him seemed to relax—or simply decided to ignore the three Forsteners.

Darkness was descending as the procession surged into motion. Corvalen, near the end of the queue, became aware that the Sharhays' sociable whispers had given way to murmured prayers. These people had much to pray for, he reflected soberly as he shuffled forward with the crowd. He thought he might pray, too, but he did not feel it would be proper for him to call on Vallar or any of the other Exalted Ones during this foreign rite; neither could he see himself petitioning the Mothers and Watchers of Sharhaya.

Looking up, he saw the Guide Star glimmer into visibility against the deepening indigo of the heavens. He was not a great devotee of the Celestials—they were too far distant—but he reflected that this same sky arched over Forstene and Sharhaya alike. Yet even as he made up his mind that it would be permissible to send an appeal to the Guide Star, he was struck with confusion, not knowing what he ought to pray for.

He returned his attention to his nearer surroundings. The procession was winding its way around behind the House of the Listeners. He made out two ranks of torchlight ahead, as though outlining a path, and soon found that this was so.

The torches were spaced far enough apart that the night pooled between them. In the islands of light, the path's white paving stones took on a lunar sheen. White, the color of death. There was only one white pathway in the Sanctuary; the rest were paved with river-stone cobbles or flags of slate or granite, all in as wide a range of colors as the bones of the earth would yield. The white path was the processional way to what the Sharhay called their chapel. That, Corvalen thought, must be where the Kel Sharha was.

Must be, must be, echoed the drums, muffled by the darkness, seeming to come from every direction.

The path was wide, and the procession kept to the left of it. Another procession seemed to be moving in the opposite direction, along the right-hand side of the path. The leader moved into a circle of torchlight—it was Tigannas, and Corvalen understood that the Lawspeaker and those behind him were now returning from the chapel. Immediately behind the Lawspeaker followed Pieran. He met Corvalen's gaze with obvious surprise. Corvalen gave him a small, swift bow, then the movement of the procession carried them both away from the torches and back into darkness.

The drums pulsed, the sound approaching and receding like a tide.

The woman in front of Corvalen heaved a weary sigh. She had been carrying her boy—Corvalen had made out that he had a clubfoot—since entering the white path. As they approached the next pool of light, Corvalen leaned forward and whispered in his most careful Sharhay, "Madam, I should be very happy if you would permit me to help you. I can carry the child easily, and you may have some rest."

The woman turned toward him and stared, her pupils reflecting the torch. Corvalen smiled and held out his arms. After a moment's indecision, her exhaustion apparently won out; cautiously, she passed the child to Corvalen. The boy was asleep. Stirring a bit, he snuggled against Corvalen's shoulder. Corvalen flushed with pleasure—it had been so long since he had cradled a child in his arms. His rush of paternal feeling must have shown in his face, for the woman gave him a smile, wan though it was. The procession moved on.

At last they neared the chapel. The Celebrants were there somewhere beyond the torchlight, the heartbeat of their drums echoing out of the night as loud and soft as ever. In spite of himself, Corvalen felt the back of his neck prickle. The repeated passage from darkness to torchlight must have bemused his eyes, for the chapel emerged from the shadows like a living thing, crouched and waiting. The next moment it seemed as still and dead as a burial mound; it was the same shape. The forest loomed just beyond it—and reached to embrace it, too, for the outer walls of the chapel appeared to be made from living trees and vines bent and trained to this form.

Corvalen had been to some of Vallar's woodland shrines, but none had been so wild as this.

He was nearly to the open doorway; it glowed palely from within. In a pause between drumbeats, he heard an owl's drawn-out *hu-hoo* from among the trees. The sound seemed to call up a breeze, which brought the loamy scent of the forest to him.

Corvalen ducked his head under the low lintel and entered the chapel. The woman in front of him halted. Looking past her, Corvalen took in his surroundings. In spite of the lamps in their bronze stands, the interior was murky—with incense smoke, he realized. The scent was not a familiar one, though; it had a tang of burning herbs rather than the resinous sweetness that clung about the shrines and temples of Forstene. There was also a small, smoky fire burning in the low hearth at the chapel's center. The atmosphere was close and hot.

A tomb, a tomb, the drums outside seemed to say. Inside, they were counterpointed by the ebb-and-flow susurration of women's voices.

The procession wended sunwise around the building, each participant pausing at the cardinal directions. Directly opposite the door, near the back of the chapel, sat the Kel Sharha, a winnowing basket in her lap. A man approached and knelt in front of her. Something passed between them, then she reached forward and kissed him on the forehead.

As the man rose and moved on, the Kel Sharha raised her eyes to the doorway.

Her gaze touched Corvalen's for a moment, and her eyebrows lifted. The expression vanished as another of her people came to her, and she returned her attention to the ritual.

Corvalen no longer knew whether he was hearing the drums or the beat of his own blood.

In front of him, the boy's mother took a step forward, to be stopped by the Kel Jemya, who intoned something as she held out a bowl from which blue-hearted flames licked. Corvalen watched as the woman bowed to the Guardians' Chief—or to the fire?—and plucked a strand of hair from her own head. This she dropped into the flames. The Kel Jemya motioned her to proceed, but she hesitated. She turned to Corvalen and wordlessly gathered up her son from his arms, ducking her head in thanks before hastening to the next ceremonial station.

This left Corvalen face-to-face with the Kel Jemya. He wondered if she would demand that he leave the chapel; she looked as though she wanted to. And perhaps he ought to go, at that. But she thrust the bowl of fire toward him and said, "You may not receive until you have given." As he had observed the woman ahead of him do, Corvalen bowed, pulled out a strand of hair, and consigned it to the flames.

Apparently he had shown sufficient reverence, for he was allowed to continue on. He came next before the Kel Mona, who asperged him with water, so entranced by her own chanting, it seemed, that she did not register who he was.

He slowed his steps as he approached the Kel Sharha, waiting for the woman and her children to get to their feet and proceed; the boy had awakened but was moving sluggishly.

As Corvalen waited, he realized what it was he was about to do, and his heart rebelled. Never in his life had he bent his knee to anyone save his king. But to turn back from the rite now would give offense in the extreme. He must go through with this.

His turn came. He hesitated. *This means nothing; nothing.*

As he had seen the others do, he knelt before the Kel Sharha.

She held out her hand to him, showing a single kernel of wheat resting on her palm. "Here is the promise of abundance. May it nourish your spirit through the coming seasons."

He searched her face for a cue as to what he was supposed to do; her skin was golden in the lamplight.

She leaned forward, dropping her voice. "You are supposed to take this grain and eat it now, Lord Corvalen."

Of course. The wheat kernel, small as it was, felt weighty as he lifted it to his lips. The Kel Sharha took his head between her hands. He almost drew back; he had not expected she would do this to him. The kiss she left on his forehead was feather light, but as incendiary as a stray spark from an unguarded fire. He got to his feet as soon as she released him, and avoided looking at her again.

It was almost over. Ahead of him at the side of the building was another open doorway, leading back out into the night. He had only to get past the Kel Sula, who bore a pottery bowl, the source of the incense smoke. It stung his eyes as he passed through it. He was aware of the Kel Sula staring at him and exhorting him to "walk forth under the protection of the Watchers," but his only thought was escape.

Chapter Twenty-Seven

Corvalen did not wait for Rossen and Torval to emerge from the chapel. Let them follow as they might, but he would not linger in this place.

He had been almost at the end of the procession, and those who had been behind him were all in the chapel now. The white path was empty. He could stride on up it as fast as he pleased and not worry that anyone might see him making unseemly haste. He could run if he wanted to.

Anything to forget that he had knelt. And that she had kissed him.

It was just a ceremony. None of it meant anything.

No, the kneeling meant nothing to him, and the kiss nothing to the Kel Sharha. But what did the kneeling mean to her? And, Vallar help him, what had that kiss opened up in him?

He gripped the hilt of his sword. He probably should not have worn a weapon into the chapel, but he was glad he had it at his side. He felt an urge to draw it. *I shall go back to the Champion's house and do sword practice. I shall perform my devotions to the Exalted One. I shall finish writing my report to Duke Beddar.*

Anything to forget that he had knelt. And that she had kissed him.

As he rounded a bend, the clubfooted boy and his mother and sister appeared on the path ahead. Corvalen slowed his steps so that he would stay well behind them. He could no longer hear the drums back at the chapel, but there was music coming from the green now. Lively, passionate music.

Her hair, her kiss—what wonder if they had awakened his lust? He'd not been with a woman since his last visit to Neldis, and that had been some time before his departure on this mission. But lust posed him no great challenge; he had conquered it before, and he would conquer it now.

And he would forget how her hand had pressed against his under that beech tree.

He could see the end of the path, and beyond it the green, lit by torches and lanterns, vibrant with music and movement: the feasting and merrymaking were under way.

"Now that's more like it!" Rossen exclaimed, coming up behind him. His voice was a bit too loud, and Torval told him so.

Corvalen frowned them both to silence. It was somehow wrenching, disorienting, to leave the quiet shadows of the white path for the festive activity on the green. And as he, Rossen, and Torval made their way forward among the Sharhay, at close-up he could not help seeing that the revelers' smiles seldom lit their eyes. Their laughter sounded as though it came not from a deep place of joy but as though it echoed from the depths of a dry well. A group of young people whirled about in a ring dance nearby; none were lithe, but all were thin. The piper accompanying them played as though he were running for his life. It was all uncomfortably surreal.

When they passed the Guesthouse, Corvalen decided to tell his companions that he intended to forego the rest of the festivities. Before he could speak, Tigannas the Lawspeaker accosted him.

"Lord Corvalen," the man said, executing a small bow, "you have done us honor to take part in our rite."

Corvalen matched the bow, and forced a smile as he saw Pieran standing, arms folded across his chest, behind the Lawspeaker. "I fear, sir, that some of your people may feel our attendance did you insult, not honor—but it was honor that we intended."

"Of course it was, and we would like to show you honor in return. Would you and these knights care to join the Elders and myself at feast on the porch of the Artisans' Hall? You will have a very good place there to see the Celebrants perform."

Corvalen's suspicions were awakened, but he said, "This is unlooked-for hospitality, Master Tigannas; there is little my friends and I would enjoy more this night."

They made their way along the periphery of the green, past the House of Healing, the Kel Sharha's residence, and the Vintners' Hall. As they went, Corvalen noted with approval that the Forstene patrols were staying at the fringes of the celebration—on hand in case of trouble, but not like to cause any themselves. If only he could be sure that his scamp of a squire was keeping to the Champion's house as ordered. Corvalen had caught Pellar making eyes at some Ma'Sharha apprentices a day or two ago, and this was certainly not the time or place for him to explore his newfound interest in girls.

Upon reaching the Artisans' Hall, Pieran took his leave with more than his usual brusqueness. The Lawspeaker turned an apologetic smile to Corvalen. "I hope you will excuse Pieran. This day has brought him sore reminders. We have never had a festival without a Champion to play his role beside the Kel Sharha. And the winners of the festival games have always feasted with the Champion in the porch of his house."

"I see." Corvalen saw, too, at least one reason for Tigannas's hospitality: better to have the porch of the Champion's house empty this night than to have it occupied by Forsteners. "Have the winners somewhere else to feast?"

"The Kel Sharha has thought of everything and has made a new place of honor. See, she has arranged a table there for them, before the House of the Guardians."

"The Kel Sharha is all graciousness," murmured Corvalen.

"Ah—and here she comes." Tigannas, who was shorter than Corvalen, craned his neck for a better view over the crowd.

The four Chiefs rode to the dais in the harvest cart. The Sharhay danced out of the way but by no means stilled themselves; evidently the time for solemn ceremony was over. If anything, the pipers played more loudly. The Kel Sharha and her companions mounted the dais and took up positions at the cardinal directions. Each woman held a sheaf of wheat cradled low over her belly.

The sounds of merrymaking dwindled into expectancy as the Chiefs stood motionless. When the silence broke, with a trilling of bells and the beginning of a new music, the Chiefs raised their wheat sheaves to heart level. Four young Celebrants vaulted onto the dais, each more acrobatic than the last. There were two women and two men, all dressed alike in clinging trousers and tunics of pearl gray, with green and red ribbons trailing from their arms and hair.

As the drums pounded and the hornpipes skirled, the Celebrants danced in pantomimes of asking, begging, enticing, and beguiling, trying to coax the four Chiefs into giving up their sheaves. Laughing the whole time, the Kel Sharha played along, offering her sheaf and then snatching it back, making a dancer follow her around on his knees. At last she yielded up the sheaf in exchange for a comically exaggerated kiss. The crowd laughed and applauded as the Chiefs took their seats on cushions at the back of the dais.

The music changed, and so did the dance, at turns robust and lyrical. The dancers were superb, but Corvalen hardly noticed. He had seen the Kel Sharha laugh. He had not heard her, though, not over the music and the noise of the crowd. He wondered what her laugh sounded like—high or low, throaty or sweet?

The performance ended with the dancers leaping off the dais and distributing stalks of grain among the audience. That seemed to be the signal for feasting to begin in earnest.

Corvalen ate and drank somewhat sparingly, for it was plain the tables were not laid in as much abundance as they would have been in years past. He tried to converse politely with the Elders, but he soon realized they all wanted something of him. Oh, they expressed their desires indirectly, but their guileless looks did not deceive him. Ingas wondered aloud where his Artisans would get some of their raw materials if trade with Ghildarna was cut off; he hoped it would not be. Falessan talked of the upcoming Vintage: the wine they pressed this autumn would take time to mature, and would folk have the patience to wait for it, or would they spoil it by shipping it off before its time? Rimenna discoursed on the importance of allowing Celebrants to travel widely. Luckily she directed her remarks to Torval as well, so Corvalen felt no compunction in not answering her.

Let Torval carry the conversation; he's the one staying, the one who needs to know them and work with them, the one who can intercede for them with the viceroy. I will be away from here soon. Away with the Kel Sharha.

Rimenna continued to extol her Celebrants until they reappeared to resume their entertainment. First a children's chorus sang a stanza or two. They were followed by a pair of dancers, then a juggler. Corvalen had begun to mentally recite the sayings of Vallar, but as the performances continued, their excellence came to command his full attention. He found himself laughing and applauding along with all the rest. Even Rossen, who understood so little of the Sharhay language, appeared to be beguiled by the entertainment; his gaze never left the dais except when he reached to refill his wine cup—though that was often enough.

Rimenna leaned toward Torval and Corvalen. "I am so glad you have allowed my Celebrants to perform tonight; you can see how they lift everyone's spirits. Ah, and here is one of the finest of all: my former apprentice, Taras. He attained mastery just last winter, but already he is thought to be one of the best singers in Sharhaya."

Corvalen recognized the young man as the singer whom he had seen in the House of Healing on his first day in the Sanctuary. He'd observed him around the Sanctuary on a few other occasions, but hadn't paid him much attention—in Corvalen's experience, most minstrels were worthy of notice only when they were performing. Now, however, it occurred to Corvalen that this one might be different.

Lute in hand, Taras took his place at the center of the dais. He bowed to the audience, then to the Chiefs as he plucked the introductory notes of his song. The Kel Sharha smiled at him, and he began to sing. His voice was a clear tenor, its inflection exquisite.

"Good neighbor, will you drink with me
for what has been and what will be,
for sorrow and for gaiety
that mix like wine and water?

"Good neighbor, will you raise your glass?
For whatever comes to pass
is ours to share, though griefs amass
and flow like wine and water.

"Good neighbor, will you take in hand
goblet, cup, or bowl, and stand
to drink your pledge to this kind land?
Raise up your wine and water."

Taras held the population of the Sanctuary entranced. Corvalen felt his own soul stirred—and by such a simple song. But the way it was sung, and the way Taras made his lute strings sigh and soar . . .

As the last notes faded on the night air, the Kel Sharha stood and came forward. She raised her wine cup; behind her, the other Chiefs did the same. In a moment all the gathered Sharhay were on their feet as well, and Corvalen, Rossen, and Torval with them.

The Kel Sharha's voice resonated through the Sanctuary. "To the kindness of the Land!"

"The kindness of the Land!" echoed all the people, and drank.

The Kel Sharha passed her cup to Taras. When they had both drunk, she gestured to him, and he played a final stanza:

"Good neighbor, when my song is done,
remember still the lesson sung:
though all things change, Beyond they're one,
and life is wine and water."

When Taras finished, it took everyone some moments to gather themselves together before breaking into applause. Corvalen noticed that the eyes of most of those around him glistened with tears, even as voices were raised to cheer for the singer.

Taras bowed graciously, his smile modest.

A rare fellow.

That was the end of the formal entertainment. Food remains (there were not many) were cleared away, rings of dancers once more formed up on the green, and here and there couples stole away into the darkness arm in arm.

On the dais, Taras had seated himself before the Kel Sharha. Corvalen could see his fingers moving on the lute's neck; he could tell, from the attentive look on her face, that Taras was singing to her.

Beside Corvalen, Rossen murmured, "She might almost be beautiful, were it not for that scar on her cheek."

Corvalen had ceased to notice the scar. He pretended not to notice that Rossen had spoken; he did not think his friend had meant to speak aloud. Then he realized that Rossen was staring at him, watching him watch the Kel Sharha.

He made himself be jovial as he turned to Rossen. "Well, whatever else may be said about the Sharhay, they have talent. That young Taras sang as fine as any of our Brintoran minstrels."

"Indeed, my lord. And his talents seem to be amply appreciated by"—Rossen glanced at the dais—"his own people."

"As well they might be."

"My lord . . ." Rossen hesitated, then shifted a bit closer. Corvalen could smell the wine on his breath; Rossen had drunk much more than his wont. "The woman is not to be trusted, my lord. Nor is her pretty singer."

"Nor are any of them, so far as we are concerned. But it is not politic, Rossen, to speak of it here."

Rossen dropped his voice. "She has been manipulating you, my lord."

"She has been trying to, no doubt," Corvalen said mildly. "Do you think I am not proof against a woman's wiles?"

Beside them Torval, in conversation with Tigannas, was also speaking of the Kel Sharha. "She's offered herself as hostage for the peace of Sharhaya, and I wish I could guarantee that the king will accept her as such, but I can't. Though I can tell you that much depends on *how* she renders homage."

"*If* she renders it," Rossen remarked, perhaps not meaning for the others to hear.

"She has said she would; she will," Tigannas asserted.

286

"I have no doubt of her intention," Torval said. "But she doesn't know all that lies ahead of her—nor do I, so don't bother asking me."

"Then I will ask something else." Tigannas turned to Corvalen. "You can see that she lives, my lord, can you not?"

"Only till she reaches Forstene City. After that . . . I am the king's man. I must abide by whatever fate he decides for her." And if she was to die, what then of the life-debt he and Torval owed her? Some would say he'd already repaid it, but did not the Precepts of Vallar demand more?

The Lawspeaker sat straighter; there was a shadow of steel in his voice when he spoke again. "If King Delanar kills the First of Mothers, he will not find Sharhaya an easy province."

"I will tell him so, Master Tigannas."

"Your king would do better to accept her homage and send her back to us."

"His Majesty will decide himself what is best for him to do. And you, Master, would do better to remember that he is not only my king but yours as well."

Corvalen had spoken more coldly than he'd intended; Tigannas gaped at him, as did the others. *Best to take my leave now; Torval can stay to make certain they don't start plotting together as soon as they see my back.*

As he stood, he saw Pellar dodging his way through the crowd in front of the Artisans' Hall. The squire clambered up the steps to the porch and saluted Corvalen.

"Here's a message come for you, my lord. From Sir Rindal." He proffered a folded quarter of parchment sealed with a dribble of plain wax.

Corvalen broke the seal and angled the parchment to catch the light of the nearest lantern. *My lord,* read the missive, *His Grace Duke Beddar is arrived at His Royal Highness Prince Dursten's camp this afternoon.* The viceroy had made good time; this was days ahead of Corvalen's expectation. *His Grace begs you to attend him there tomorrow at your convenience.* That, of course, meant as early in the morning as possible—Beddar was notoriously impatient and had no tolerance for slugabeds.

Corvalen looked up to see the Kel Sharha's seat on the dais empty. Good; this gathering would be breaking up soon. As briefly and politely as possible, he thanked the Elders for their hospitality and bid them good night.

287

"My lord." Rossen caught up with him as he descended the steps, and nodded in the direction of a pool of torchlight across the green.

The Kel Sharha stood there, Taras with her. As Corvalen watched, she offered her hand to the young Celebrant. Together, they made their languid way in the direction of the white path. One last rite to perform in the chapel, Corvalen supposed, the thought souring within him.

"Where are her night guards? Go and find them, Rossen; send them after her."

"Shall I order them to bring her back?"

Corvalen hesitated. "Not unless she goes farther than the chapel. Tell them to keep their distance but to keep watch."

It was too late to stop the Kel Sharha and Taras without making a scene, and he would not have her humiliated, not if he could help it.

But, Harvest rites or no, she should have known better than to behave like a wanton where everyone could see. He had thought her wiser than that. He had thought her a woman of discretion and honor. He had thought he could trust her.

Chapter Twenty-Eight

Taras's hands hesitated on her back, and the Kel Sharha wondered what her scars must feel like under his sensitive fingers. He pulled away a bit to look at her. Was that pity in his eyes? Before he could say anything, she pressed herself against him and kissed him, hard. They were well entwined by the time they tumbled down onto the cushions beside the hearth.

"O Mothers and Watchers, accept our offering," she remembered to whisper.

He took this as his signal, and she did not blame him for that. Too late, she realized she was not ready—no, not ready for this at all.

He was so eager, so happy. And, it occurred to her, inexperienced. The fact that she was not moving in response to him, not keeping up her part of their joint rhythm, seemed not to register with him.

Memories insinuated themselves around the edges of her consciousness. Dursten. She mustered her will and pushed him out of her mind. Instead she made herself see Taras, only Taras, his beautiful intent face, his fair hair spilling over his shoulders, the muscles of his arms taut with bearing his weight over her.

But even as she waged her battle against visual memory, the fear and rage and desperate helplessness she had felt under Dursten's assault resurged.

O Watchers, O Mothers Beyond, help me!

In the heartbeat after she released her prayer, Taras had his own release. It was over.

She could not stop herself from breathing a sigh of relief when he rolled off of her.

He took her hand. "Thank you," he slurred.

She took refuge in the ritual benediction. "The gift is given; may the Land thrive in love and plenty."

Taras was already drifting into sleep.

The Kel Sharha let him doze awhile. As soon as he stirred, she sent him away to his own bed.

It was plain he had hoped to share the gifts of love again, and there was puzzlement in his eyes. Had he not pleased? She assured him he had. "But there is one rite more I must perform here tonight, and it must be done alone." The clouds passed away from his face so swiftly that she could not regret the lie. He kissed her again, and left.

She had regrets enough. Taras was young and beautiful and devoted and ardent. Yet she had been unable to lose herself to the rite with him, unable to give herself to the great current of the living world. Though Taras had entered her with reverent abandon, she had still needed to throw up walls against the recollection of the prince's brutal invasion. The walls had separated her from Taras and from the life current as well.

Another wave of anger hit her—and more: bereavement. Another joy stolen, perhaps never recoverable.

Curse Dursten!

The thought came unbidden, and uncoiled like a snake. It was justice, after all. He who misused his manhood would suffer the loss of it. That was the law.

Being a Healer, she had never been taught the cursing ritual. But it was easy to summon the prince's image in her mindsight, easier still to gather up her hatred, her shame, her rage—all of it. She made of it a fire, fashioned an arrow in her mind, and lit it at the heart of the flames. It was the act of a single thought to aim and loose that arrow. It pierced Dursten's thigh, and she watched the fire consume him. . . .

She came to herself standing over the chapel hearth, her hands outstretched with clenched fists, her face burning as the fire flared high. She opened her hands, turned her palms as though emptying the contents of her fists onto the flames. The prince's image crumpled into ash, and the blaze calmed.

What have I done?

She did not want to think about it. She banked the hearthfire, then circled the chapel, wearily extinguishing the lamps. She lay down again among the cushions, and breathed in Taras's scent as the darkness settled around her.

*****

She was awakened shortly after dawn by an apprentice from the Listeners' Order, whose turn it was to tend the hearthfire for the day. The Kel Sharha stretched and went to the east door of the chapel to say the morning prayer. Then she walked into the forest, to a brook where the Ma'Sharha often washed before and after chapel rites.

The water was cold enough to make her gasp as she splashed it over her breasts. The air, however, already promised a sultry day, so she held her breath and plunged her head into the water, and then savored the feel of cool rivulets running down her back. But as she sat on a rock beside the stream, finger-combing her hair, she began to brood once more on her failures of the previous night.

She had gone through the form of the rite with Taras, but she had not really given herself to it. Coupling on a festival night was supposed to be like the sacred dance of sun and rain upon the land, a union that would send the blessings of the holy balance rippling out over Sharhaya. But she had not danced, and what further suffering might now befall her people because of this new failure?

Remonstrate with yourself all you like, but what good will it do you or anyone else? She made herself listen to the morning greetings of the birds until she felt calmer, then returned to the chapel and shrugged into her clothes. She bid the apprentice good morning, and left her to her solitary task.

She had not gone very far up the white path when she saw Fidden and Gar ahead, waiting for her. They nodded to her cordially as she approached, but seemed to have no more desire for conversation than she did. They let her pass them, then fell in behind her in an almost companionable silence.

Finches bickered in the gardens alongside the path, and bees buzzed, but the trees were silent; no air moved in the branches this morning. The leaves were looking dry, too; soon they would begin to change and fall. Already some garden plants were dying back, and some were all gone to seed.

She passed between the Guesthouse and the House of the Listeners, and then she was out on the green, alone there except for Forstene soldiers.

Looking down toward her residence, she saw Lord Corvalen dismounting his horse in front of her porch. He was wearing his mail; his helm rested on the pommel of his saddle. Beyond him, Rossen and half a dozen other men, fully armed, sat their horses as though they were waiting for something. For her? Were they going to take her away *now*?

Lord Corvalen held himself stiffly, offering no greeting as she drew near. He did not seem the same man who had come to the chapel last night. Whatever all this meant, she was certain it did not bode well.

"Good morning, Lord Corvalen," she said, as pleasantly as she could manage.

"A good day to you, Kel Sharha," he answered, but he did not sound as though he meant it.

Formal politeness seemed the best way to lift the moody silence that hung about him. "I see you have early business. I hope the revels last night did not keep you from your rest."

"I am well enough. But you, I am sure, must be fatigued indeed if you are only now returning to your house." There was an odd quality in his voice, and she did not quite like the way he was regarding her.

She strove to maintain her composure. "Our Harvest Welcome has been always three days; to fit all the rites into the one day was . . . wearying."

His voice grew colder still. "Surely you did not need to perform every one of those rites."

"Surely we did. Sharhaya has never had more need of the Mothers' blessings. You must see that, Lord Corvalen."

"I see only that Prince Dursten was correct when he said *you* must to be made to realize the truth: you and your nation have been conquered."

The words hit her like a blow. She tried to step away from him; he grabbed her by the arms and held tightly.

His voice dropped, cutting like an icy wind. "Do you *want* to die, Kel Sharha? Do you want more of your people to die, to suffer?"

She shook her head, stupefied by his behavior.

"Then why do you flout us? You do what you have always done, without regard for how it appears. You will not survive a week in Forstene if you continue to behave in this manner!"

She took a deep breath, and kept her voice firm but quiet. "Let go of me, Corvalen."

He seemed to suddenly become conscious of what he was doing, to notice for the first time his hands gripping, almost crushing, her arms; she would have bruises. A confusion of emotions played over his countenance, and he released her. She backed up a step.

"Where is the Celebrant?" he asked.

"Taras?" Her heart tightened. "Why?"

"What do you think will happen to him if Prince Dursten or the viceroy find out about him; what if they believe that you have set him up as your consort?"

"But—no!" Understanding dawned, and hatred for the Forsteners and all their ways washed over her anew.

"The viceroy arrived in the prince's camp yesterday; I am on my way to meet with him. I will say nothing about what has happened— this time. But I do not believe now that I can trust you to conduct yourself appropriately." He turned to Fidden and Gar. "See that the Kel Sharha goes inside and speaks to no one; she is not to leave her residence or receive any visitors until I return."

He mounted his horse. The reins were in his hands as he stared down at her from the saddle, but the fierce sternness was gone from his look. "I'm sorry, Kel Sharha. You were right: I am your enemy." He rode away, and the other horsemen fell in behind him.

She watched them out of sight before entering her house, Fidden and Gar close behind. Feeling all at once weary to the core of her soul, she dragged herself up the stairs to her private chambers, stripped down to her trousers, and climbed into bed. She lay for a long time staring at the fretted ceiling, tracing its patterns, unwilling to consider any of the thoughts that were nearest the surface of her mind.

Treska tiptoed into the room, left without a word, and returned a short time later with a sleeping draught. The Kel Sharha drank it gratefully, conjuring the drink to drive away nightmares as well as bring on swift and merciful sleep.

*****

O Exalted One, I, Corvalen of Brintora, mindful of your deeds, pledge that my own will follow the same path of honor, that I may be worthy to be counted among your following.

Corvalen had mentally recited the names of the Exalted Vallar's warriors, from greatest to least, and still Duke Beddar was not done reading. Just so had Beddar used silence and concentrated inattention to put Corvalen in his place during the long-ago days of his squiring. Corvalen did not enjoy the recollection.

Outside the pavilion he could hear the hammers and saws of the carpenters who were building Beddar's winter lodgings. The first of the castle's stone towers was under construction as well, but even the expert masons whom Dursten had included among his troops could work only so fast—it would be nearly a year before the tower was ready for any kind of occupancy. Not a situation that would sweeten Beddar's temper.

Corvalen studied the man who had taught him to be a knight. The years had not been altogether kind to him—wrinkles seamed his face, and his jowls sagged. From the way he moved when he walked,

Corvalen could tell he was troubled by aching joints. Yet he had all his hair still—gone iron gray—and his sword arm bulged with no less muscle than it had in the days of Corvalen's youth.

At last Beddar looked up from the report in his hands. "You allowed them to gather for their harvest ceremonies? By Heldar, man, what has happened to your common sense?"

A very good question, but not one Corvalen intended to answer. He was glad Dursten wasn't present—taken ill in the small hours of the morning, Beddar had said—for he would almost certainly have seized the opportunity to make some barbed remark. A sleepless night had left Corvalen feeling less than his usual diplomatic self and definitely not in the mood for awkward situations.

"Your Grace will note that the celebration was much curtailed from what it had been under native rule, and in particular we permitted no Sharhay to enter or leave the Sanctuary during the occasion." He cleared his throat. "Your Grace will find also, as you continue to read, that I have taken full responsibility for this experiment in leniency—and for its failure."

"The barbarians got out of hand, did they?"

"I can assure you there was no uprising or anything of the kind."

"Then what? What made your 'experiment in leniency' a failure?"

Corvalen had expected some such question. "These people are difficult to understand, Your Grace, and more difficult still to master. Their leaders adjure them to give way to us but at the same time act as though they still hold sovereignty."

"Their leaders? Or do you mean the Kel Sharha?"

"As you say."

"Ah well, you'll be taking her away in a few days' time—and we will make clear who holds the sovereignty. With no Kel Sharha to rally around, do you think the Sharhay will be manageable?"

"It's hard to know. She says 'peace,' and there is peace. If she is not here to keep saying it . . ."

"Hotter heads might prevail?"

"They might. But probably most Sharhay will heed the Kel Sharha's stated wishes and ignore any rabble-rousers."

"I doubt there will be many of those—make an example of the first few troublemakers who come along, and you're not likely to have many willing to follow in their footsteps."

"So I found in Cheskara, Your Grace. But here, I am not sure it will be productive to make such examples."

"We must have order, Corvalen."

"Indeed we must. And I think we will, so long as the land is under good governance. For the most part, these are a peaceable people; unprovoked, they do not look for trouble. But they do not think like us, so we must make our expectations of them clear." Something that Beddar would no doubt manage better than he had.

Beddar gave him a skeptical look. "Your report concludes with specific recommendations, I assume?" He turned to the last page and skimmed down it. "Hm . . . they certainly have a high opinion of their women."

"The Ma'Sharha—their Holy Women—in particular."

With a snort of disgust, Beddar dropped the report onto the table in front of him. "A most unvirile lot these Sharhay men must be!"

"They do not seem so, Your Grace."

"No? To let themselves be ruled by a gaggle of loose-moraled women with supposedly supernatural powers?"

Corvalen shrugged with affected indifference. "If we would be exact, it is the entire Council of Chiefs and Elders that rules, and some of the Elders are men. Still," he conceded, "the Chiefs of the Ma'Sharha do have pride of place—though I believe the Sharhay consider themselves to be not so much ruled as guided by them."

"By a council of women!"

"Strange as it might seem to us, Your Grace, it appears to me that the Ma'Sharha have earned their people's devotion. They spend many years in training and take great vows dedicating themselves solely to the welfare of their country. It is also my observation that people seem to do the Kel Sharha's will not so much because she commands them to but because she wishes them to. Their respect for her office, even apart from the individual woman holding it, is such that few of them would contemplate displeasing her."

"Indeed? And do you, Corvalen, believe that any woman can be as wise and worthy of devotion as that?"

"It hardly matters what you or I believe, Your Grace. Our concern here must be with what the Sharhay believe."

Beddar stood up, stretched, and cracked his knuckles with impressive deliberation before turning a calculating eye on Corvalen. "Dursten has suggested that we abolish the office of Kel Sharha. I believe the king will incline to agree. What do you think of that plan?"

"I thought," Corvalen said carefully, "that His Majesty desired the Kel Sharha to do homage to him, that he planned for Sharhaya to become a vassal state once we are certain the people will not rebel."

"And that has not changed. But it is likely this Kel Sharha will be the last of her line. Once she is gone, I think we will be safer from rebellion if we do not allow that office to pass to another."

To Corvalen's immense relief, Beddar did not seek his opinion on the matter again. Corvalen could not have said at that moment what he thought of Sharhaya's future; he could only wonder how much of a future the current Kel Sharha had.

*****

While Corvalen met with Duke Beddar, Rossen went in search of the portion of Torval's following that had remained on the bluff when Torval went to the Sanctuary. The Forstene soldiery here was less numerous than it had been, since Dursten had dispatched many of his soldiers to posts elsewhere in the country. Most of the remaining men were quartered in tents ringing the perimeter, the camp having been rearranged to accommodate the construction at its center.

Rossen paused to look over the castle layout, indicated by surveyors' marks. In one grid a band of Sharhay laborers were digging a foundation. Elsewhere Rossen saw more Sharhay men working under Forstene supervision, but none of them were doing anything that required much skill—they were being used almost as draft animals, and, from the look of them, treated that way, too. Rossen wondered how they had been recruited. Perhaps the promise of occasional food and some kind of shelter from the elements had been enough.

It was not his concern. And all the construction noise was serving to remind him again that he had drunk too much last night. He just wanted to get Corvalen's errand done and then find someplace out of the sun to rest while he waited for his lord to finish with the duke. Then they could go down to the riverside camp where most of Corvalen's following had remained under Rindal's command. There would be plenty to do there, but in the evening they'd have gaming and ballad singing and—

"Sir Rossen, what a fine delight to meet you here!"

Rossen turned his coldest glare on Esban, who had sidled up next to him and whose voice was not what Rossen's hangover needed.

Esban continued, oblivious. "I see you admire our castle—well, what will be our castle. This is only the beginning, of course; His Highness says that one day it will cover the entire bluff, and below it will grow a town. A real town, and a real castle, in Sharhaya—do you not think it fine?"

"And what about those fellows?" Rossen nodded toward a group of Sharhay laborers, wheeling barrows filled with stone. "Do they think it fine?"

"They have nowhere else to go; for now, they are glad enough to have a living. But when this great castle is complete, they will be proud to have been part of its making—almost as proud as me."

Rossen knew Esban was waiting to be asked why he took so much pride in the castle's construction, so he made a point of saying nothing, but scanned the surrounding area for Torval's banners.

Esban was not to be discouraged that easily. "I am so proud, you see, because His Highness has made me assistant to the master of works. At first I was unhappy that I would not go back to your wonderful Forstene with His Highness, but he has more need of me here, for I can make liaison"—he spoke the word with savor; it was no doubt a recent addition to his Forstene vocabulary—"with the Sharhay workers, to recruit, to translate, to oversee. It is a position of great worth and much honor."

"I can see how important that is to you," Rossen said, hoping to pave his way toward ending this conversation.

Esban nodded ponderously. "Yes, of course you understand. You must know how it is, you who are always in a great man's shadow. Well, in Sharhaya, we all of us are in the shadow of the Ma'Sharha. Even the so-great Champion was. Even a man who rises to Lawspeaker or Guild Elder. None have any chance at greatness save the Ma'Sharha. Or that is how it was, before your people came. It is a fine gift you have brought to this country: the chance for a man to rise to greatness!"

Esban had been so far from noticing Rossen's growing coldness that he actually slapped him on the back now, a flawed imitation of Forstene camaraderie.

Rossen took a step away before he could be overwhelmed by the temptation to return the slap with a blow. "You still have much to learn about greatness, Esban. Excuse me; I have business elsewhere." He strode away, praying that Esban would not tag after him—because then he really would hit the little bastard, and Corvalen did not need him stirring up that kind of trouble.

Corvalen had been moodily silent all the way from the Sanctuary, and he'd seemed almost nervous as they entered the camp. Rossen knew many a man who retained a lifelong awe of the knight who had trained him, although he'd never thought Corvalen was one of them. But if there was anyone who could intimidate Corvalen, it would be Beddar, simply because of that old relationship—even though Corvalen had become a far greater man than Beddar, blood of Stennar though he was, could ever hope to be.

Unbidden, Esban's words played through Rossen's mind again: *you who are always in a great man's shadow.*

No, not in his shadow. In his service. There was a big difference—but Esban was simply not the kind of man to see that, let alone understand it.

It was with a sense of relief that Rossen finally spotted Torval's banners. Now he just had to hope that Jennis was still within the encampment. So long as he could find her, he was certain she would gladly give up the life of a camp follower for that of a lady's maid, at least for the journey back to Forstene. Because Corvalen was not about to let the Kel Sharha travel without an attendant, no matter how proudly she disclaimed the need for one.

One should always observe the proprieties.

*****

"Finoora, what have you done?"

The Kel Sharha bolted upright. "Who is there?" She had slept through the entire day—the room was in darkness except for the weak flickering of a single lamp flame. A steady rain pattered on the roof overhead, but there was no other sound. She was alone in the room.

Whose voice had she heard? The Kel Sharha hugged her knees to her chest, frowning. She must have been dreaming, yet the voice had been so clear and had seemed to come from outside of herself.

There was a soft tapping at the door—Treska's knock. The door opened just wide enough for the girl to slip through. When she saw the Kel Sharha sitting up in bed, she muffled an exclamation. "Forgive me for disturbing you," she whispered, and turned to go.

"No, Treska, stay a bit."

"Yes, my Chief. Only we must be very quiet. The guard on you has been increased; there are two soldiers at the bottom of the stair. They'll come up if we make any sound—no one is to speak with you out of the guards' hearing."

Lord Corvalen's maddening efficiency at work. But at least Treska seemed to be permitted to come and go as she pleased—so long as she wasn't caught in private conversation with her Chief.

"Come sit beside me, then," the Kel Sharha whispered. "How much of the night is gone?"

"It's past midnight, Lady."

The Kel Sharha frowned. "What draught did you give me that would keep me asleep so long?"

"It was the four-ingredient draught you taught me to make during the winter. Only . . ."

"Yes? Did you put an extra charm on it?" But she could not remember having taught Treska any charm that would double a medicine's efficacy in this way.

"Just the one you taught me. Only . . ."

"Treska, I am not angry with you. Just tell me what you did."

"When I thought the draught would be wearing off, I came in to check on you, and it seemed to me that you were having a terrible nightmare. So I . . . I . . . Forgive me, my Chief; I shouldn't have dared, but I could feel you suffering so much, so I went over to you and placed my hands the way you do—"

"You tried to give me Nihara?" It took considerable effort to keep her voice from rising. The girl was nowhere near ready to attempt Nihara, and the Kel Sharha had told her in no uncertain terms not even to think of learning it until she was nearing the end of her apprenticeship. There was always an element of danger in the procedure, which could easily sap a Healer of her own life strength. For one as young and inexperienced as Treska . . . "You tried to give me Nihara?" the Kel Sharha asked again.

"I—well, I meant to, but I think something else happened instead."

Abruptly, the Kel Sharha remembered the nightmare that had taken hold of her as she began to emerge from her drugged sleep. Again the beating, the flogging, the burning, the unrelenting questions, the leers of the guards. Then the prince had turned his back and somehow begun to change. Her dreamself knew that when he turned around he would be wearing Lord Corvalen's face—and that meant that even the slightest hope of mercy and deliverance were gone. But before he could turn, a radiance suddenly flooded her dream vision, as though she were in the midst of a clear midwinter dawn. The light had wrapped around her like a cloak, becoming a shield that emanated outward to push back every ugliness and cruelty until they were nothing but dust motes caught in the light. Then even the motes dissipated into nothingness, leaving the radiant purity shimmering around her. The light faded until she relaxed into the velvet blackness of peaceful sleep, hearing a far-off crooning that might have been a lullaby sung by the Mothers themselves.

The Kel Sharha stared at her apprentice in something approaching awe, as new understanding came to her. No wonder the girl had been so

clumsy with surgical procedures and the like—her gifts lay elsewhere.
"Treska," she said, "what did you see in my mind?"

"It was like looking into storm clouds, or the river at full flood. It's
hard to describe. I didn't see what you were dreaming, though; should I
have?"

"No. Although, if you were a full Listener, you might have caught
glimpses." And thank the Mothers that she hadn't.

"Listener? I'm not . . ."

"But you have some of the Listener gift—much more than the
average Healer does. You can reach into a person's mind."

"Don't all Healers do that, to calm patients' fears or help them cope
with pain? You taught me those things, my Chief."

"But I did not teach you how to enter and stop a nightmare. Nor
can I; I cannot do it."

"You . . . you can do anything, heal anyone, my Chief!"

The Kel Sharha smiled ruefully into the darkness. "No Healer can
defeat every injury or disease; you know I could not heal Serelha. And
even if I might cure every imbalance of the body, to rebalance a
disarray of the mind would still be beyond me in almost every case.
The Kel Nira who came before me, though—she could do this. She was
a Mind Healer. And so are you."

She let Treska sit with the new knowledge in silence. Her own
thoughts turned to the past. During her early years with the Order, she
had spent many and long hours with the Chief for special training. But
not training in the skills of mind healing. No, she had not been a
student, she realized now—she had been a patient. She was apprenticed
to another Healer, learning from her to heal the body. At the same time,
the Kel Nira was healing her, restoring balance to her mind. But . . .
why?

"My chief, I wish you would let me go with you to Forstene,"
Treska said.

The remark seemed such an odd response to the news the girl had
just received that the Kel Sharha's growing unease dissolved as she
considered her reply. "Even if I would have allowed it before, I could
not do so now. I cannot train you in mind healing, Treska. You must
stay in Sharhaya and apprentice to someone who can."

"But . . . I want to help you. With the nightmares, I mean." Her
voice dropped so low that it was difficult to hear her. "I'm afraid they'll
be even worse for you, when you are all alone among the Forsteners."

The girl was thinking like a Healer indeed—and she was probably right. For the space of a heartbeat, the Kel Sharha was tempted. But it was not to be thought of.

"Treska, I am not the only one in Sharhaya to have suffered at the Forsteners' hands—and many have suffered far worse. You owe it to the People to stay here and master your gift, for many are sore afflicted and will never regain their strength of mind without healing from those like you."

"But there are no Mind Healers in the Sanctuary since Halla died of the winter fever. Who will teach me?"

The Kel Sharha frowned. So many of her Order's Houses had been destroyed by the Forstene invaders. Some of the Healers had been able to flee to safety, but many had been killed. It was difficult, now, to know who was left and where they were. One Mind Healer, she knew, had crossed the river to Ghildarna. She was fairly certain that another had gone into hiding, along with other refugees, in the mountains on the Cheskari border.

"When the treaty was signed," she said slowly, "all of our Houses north of the Lenasha still stood. But the Forsteners went to subdue that part of our country, too, and I do not know how much damage they have done. There were Mind Healers at the Houses in Redcreek, Roundhill, and North Ferry. You must ask the Kel Sula to divine which you should go to; I pray they are all still there."

"What if the Forsteners won't let me leave the Sanctuary?"

"Then Lillanna will continue to teach you Healing, you will go to the Listeners for some of their training, and you will pray to the Mothers and Watchers to help your gift develop as it should."

"Yes, my Chief." Treska paused. "Nothing will ever be the way it was, will it? In Sharhaya, I mean; we won't be . . . us. Will we?"

The Kel Sharha drew breath. "That is a question for the Listeners, Treska. But for my part, I will never give up hope. Nor should you."

Chapter Twenty-Nine

It had been decided that the formal transfer of governance to the viceroy would take place in the Sanctuary. But the grand display that had been planned was marred by an unrelenting downpour. Privately, Rossen suspected the Ma'Sharha of prolonging the rain for the express purpose of inconveniencing his people.

The storm had begun the night after the Harvest rites, and continued on for two more days while Corvalen made the necessary arrangements for the bulk of his army to break camp and return to Forstene. On the morning when Duke Beddar, Prince Dursten, Corvalen, and their respective retinues set out for the Sanctuary, it seemed the weather was clearing. But as they entered the Sacred Forest, the skies opened again. Instead of galloping triumphantly into the Sanctuary with banners flying and trumpets blaring, the troop plodded through mud, the fanfares bleated damply, and the banners clung to their poles.

Few Sharhay were about, though Rossen distinguished some faces at windows. He glanced toward the Kel Sharha's house. Of course she was too proud to allow herself to be seen looking out. But he could imagine her standing just back from the window, her arms folded across her chest and her eyebrows raised as she watched them all ride onto the green. Perhaps she was even smiling, enjoying the sight of them being discomfited by the weather.

A messenger had ridden ahead, so in front of the dais waited Torval and a cadre of his men, seemingly oblivious to the rain pouring down their backs. Torval came forward now to hold the bridle of the viceroy's horse as he dismounted. Duke Beddar rewarded his former squire with a squeeze to his shoulder and a "Good to see you, my boy!"

As the horses were led away, Beddar looked around him. He was plainly unimpressed by what he saw. Rossen found the gabled wooden houses of the Sharhay charming, but clearly the viceroy felt they did not compare favorably to the sprawling, stone-built palaces of the Forstene aristocracy.

"This is where their leaders live?" the duke said, not bothering to keep the incredulous scorn from his voice.

"It is, Your Grace," Dursten answered.

Corvalen added, "It is also a kind of ceremonial center, like the precincts of our temples."

"I see no temple."

"They conduct many of their ceremonies here"—Corvalen indicated the dais—"under the open sky. There is also a small ritual building, a chapel, at the edge of the forest." He gestured in the direction of the white path.

"And where is the Kel Sharha's palace?"

"Because she is also Chief of the Healers' Order, she lives adjacent to the House of Healing, there."

Duke Beddar regarded the Kel Sharha's house with open amazement. Even with its balconies, its elaborately carved door and porch pillars, and its painted window frames, it hardly looked palatial—not at all, Rossen had to admit, like the residence of a queen.

"Barbaric!" the viceroy muttered. He turned to Prince Dursten. "Congratulations, boy. You've conquered a nation of peasants. Now let's get in out of this damned rain."

The weather finally began to clear as they sat down to a dinner featuring roast woodhen stuffed with the last of the nuts and dried berries that had been stored in the pantries of the Champion's house. Beddar occupied the head place, with Dursten to his right and Corvalen to his left. Rossen sat next to Corvalen, and Pellar waited on them both; Dursten's squire served him and the lieutenant he had brought along, a man named Uthal.

Not so long ago, Torval would have had that place at the prince's right. But now Torval had his own place at the other end of the table, his own lieutenant at his side—Corvalen's heir had gotten his wish and was to be Beddar's official representative in the Sanctuary. It was a request the viceroy had granted without hesitation—clearly, the less he had to do with, in his words, "this monument of rusticity," the better. The keep on the bluff might be only in the beginning stages of construction, but it would be a proper fortress, a fit dwelling and symbol of might for a scion of the House of Stennar.

There was one other guest at the table: Esban. He sat between Torval and Uthal, and none of the squires knew which of them was to wait on him. When Torval's squire moved to refill Esban's glass, Torval gave the boy a quelling look that sent him away and kept him from that side of the table for the rest of the meal. And that was as close as Torval came to acknowledging Esban's presence. The others ignored him almost as successfully.

It was not a relaxing meal. Corvalen was quiet, his composure coming to him less easily than usual, Rossen thought, while the duke seemed in a mood to be pleased by nothing.

The prince was unabashedly in an ill temper, perhaps not yet wholly recovered from the sudden fever that had struck him a few nights previously. Uthal's assiduous flattery of his lord was ignored by its object and served only to irritate the other diners, particularly Beddar. Uthal, undaunted, continued to laud Dursten's "genius" in overcoming the Sharhay—until he happened to utter the unfortunate phrase, "covered in glory."

"Covered in something, all right," Beddar muttered into his wine glass, "but I wouldn't have called it glory." The remark was just loud enough for everyone to hear, but quiet enough that courtesy demanded they pretend not to have heard.

Dursten drained his goblet and slammed it onto the table with such force that he shattered the glass—Ghildaran, beautifully worked, and formerly quite valuable. "Do you disdain my achievements here, sir?" he asked Beddar. "I have enlarged our realm and brought glory to our house!"

The older man eyed him with calculation. "Ah! And here I was thinking that three years, thousands of lives, and half the war treasury seemed like much to expend in the conquest of a countryful of woman-ruled, superstitious rustics. But perhaps I was too harsh." His smile was completely unapologetic. "It is a good deal of rich land, after all, and we should get some profit from it—if the natives don't give us too much trouble."

"That is Your Grace's job to ensure—as my father and I are counting on you to do."

Rossen would have expected some reaction to this pointed reminder that Dursten, as heir to the throne, outranked his father's cousin, for all Beddar's experience and reputation. But the viceroy answered smoothly, "Then let us establish my authority in this place without further delay. Have your men call the Sharhay to assemble immediately. I want every man, woman, and child in this 'Sanctuary' out on that common by the time I have finished my fruit and cheese."

"What about those who are too sick or injured to leave their beds?" Torval asked.

Beddar glared. "Let them stay in their damn beds, then. Otherwise, no exceptions. And I want that Kel Sharha front and center."

*****

"Time to take your place, M'Lady," Fidden said at the Kel Sharha's elbow.

She took a moment to smooth the fringes of her woolen belt before stepping out of her porch's shade into the steaming afternoon heat. The people assembled on the green fell silent and bowed as she passed. Tension thrummed in the air; she felt the same kind of foreboding that had plagued her on the morning the Council rode to the ford to hear the Forsteners' treaty terms.

Fidden and Gar directed her to the front of the crowd and settled her into place between the Kel Jemya and the Kel Mona; the Kel Sula stood at the Kel Mona's other side. The two guards joined a line of soldiers formed up just below the dais, their backs to it so that they faced the assembled Sharhay. The Forsteners all stood at attention, their stares raking the crowd. They had the air of men prepared for trouble.

The Kel Sharha felt a hand on her shoulder—a thing only one person would dare to do. She reached back to grasp Pieran's sturdy fingers. But with the soldiers watching them, he dropped his hand, and they waited in silence like everyone else.

At last the Forstene leaders emerged from the Champion's house, each preceded by a contingent of his own men. More of Beddar's soldiers brought up the rear. They distributed themselves on either side of the pathway cleared by the Sharhay crowd as Lord Corvalen and the others took up positions on the dais.

A herald stepped forward, Esban following him like a shadow. The Kel Sharha sensed the people around her tightening in anger at the sight of the traitor, there smiling in pride that he had a place on the dais. The breast of his jerkin sported a badge with the same sword-and-stars design that decorated Prince Dursten's surcoat.

The herald cleared his throat. "People of Sharhaya, greet your most royal lord, His Highness Prince Dursten, heir to the throne of Forstene, carrier of the Light of Stennar, beloved of the Celestials, inheritor of his ancestors' might, like in greatness to Heldar the Unifier of heroic memory!"

The words struck dully against the humid silence on the green. Their impact was not increased by the time it took for Esban to translate them.

Beddar frowned. He stepped forward and muttered something to the herald.

The herald tried again. "People of Sharhaya, bow to your liege!" Esban was quicker in his translation this time.

The Kel Sharha felt eyes on her; the people would do what she did. Fidden and Gar were mouthing, "Bow! Bow!" at her. She glanced up at the dais. Lord Corvalen's expression was impossible to read; Torval looked worried; Duke Beddar had folded his arms in stern expectation. The prince's eyes were alight with malice, but she met them with ice in her own.

She did not look away as she slowly executed the smallest bow possible, one in which the angle of her back scarcely changed, with her arms rigid at her sides—the kind of bow any Sharhay would regard as a studied insult. She held the pose for half a dozen heartbeats to make certain the rest would see and imitate her. When she straightened, Dursten was smirking, and the viceroy looked satisfied. Torval seemed relieved. But Lord Corvalen's brows were drawn together; he had recognized her gesture for what it was.

The herald stepped back, and Dursten commanded the gathering's attention. "My people"—he shot a glance at the Kel Sharha—"this is a great day for the province of Sharhaya. Today you welcome Duke Beddar of Stenhal, of the Blood of Stennar, beloved of the Celestials, who comes to lead you out of your barbarity and teach you the ways of civilized men. He stands here before you with all the authority of the king himself, His Most Solemn Majesty Delanar, Sovereign of Forstene, Heir to the Exalted Stennar, Merciful and Just—"

Dursten stumbled over the next words and broke off, flustered by a disturbance at the back of the dais. Two soldiers in Beddar's colors had mounted the stairs on that side. They were dragging something between them but, with the cluster of Forsteners on the dais blocking much of her view, the Kel Sharha could not make it out at first.

One of the soldiers released his grip on whatever it was and came forward to salute Beddar. As the man spoke to him, the viceroy's look of annoyance at the interruption changed to one that bespoke a kind of hardened gratification. He turned again to the waiting crowd, addressing the Sharhay and his man simultaneously: "Make your report, soldier, so that all may hear."

"Yes sir! While patrolling the streets as ordered, we happened upon a malingerer in a hut back at the edge of the woods. We informed this person that all Sharhay were required to assemble here and, giving her the benefit of the doubt, we urged her to hurry along. When she refused to leave, we undertook to bring her by force, but she resisted. We managed to subdue her. . . ."

The man was speaking rapid Forstene, and Esban was having difficulty keeping up, so few in the crowd knew what he was saying. The Kel Sharha, though she understood most of the words, found it difficult to make sense of them. A "malingerer" in a hut? What hut was there at the edge of the woods? Could the man mean the chapel? But if that was so—

Behind her Pieran sucked in his breath. He had just pieced it together, too. The "malingerer" could only be a Ma'Sharha apprentice, doing her turn at tending the chapel hearthfire, determined not to leave her sacred duty for any cause—and not understanding a word the Forstene soldiers said.

Dear Mothers! Today it had been Treska's turn to tend the fire.

The Forsteners had rearranged themselves on the dais, and now everyone could clearly see as the second soldier pushed the girl forward and dropped her, like an armful of wet laundry, at the viceroy's feet. It was indeed Treska, disheveled, bleeding, quietly weeping.

Uneasy murmurs welled around and behind the Kel Sharha as the people started to understand the sacrilege that had been committed. Through her own shock, it took her a moment to realize Duke Beddar was speaking again, Esban echoing his words in Sharhay.

". . . the rule of law. When a command is given, it will be obeyed. If it is not, punishment will be swift and sure. We will have order, and so an example must be made of the lawless and disobedient."

The Kel Sharha felt as though a fist were closing around her heart.

As Esban finished translating, the viceroy drew his sword—but Dursten's was already out.

No, this cannot be. . . .

The blade came down before anyone could react; Dursten drove the point into Treska's chest.

A collective scream erupted from the Sharhay, but the Kel Sharha herself was struck dumb as she watched the blood well up from her apprentice's death wound.

The fist around her heart gave a final squeeze.

She heard herself cry out, a wordless sound that was grief, prayer, protest, anger, and imprecation all at once. And with the sound something uncoiled within her.

It was the occurrence of an instant, but she felt a power released. Her lungs were full of fire and her blood pulsed like the drums of war. There was violence in her, and it was strong and purposeful—and familiar. And welcome.

The people were surging and shouting behind her. Someone in the crowd to her right let fly a rock, and it struck one of the soldiers lined up in front of the dais. But she had no need of rocks. She could feel the power building in her, nearly ready to be released. She raised her arm, fiery energy surging to the palm of her hand, her fingertips—

Strong hands grabbed at her, pinning her arms to her sides. She struggled briefly, till a voice cut through the rush of blood that all but filled her hearing.

It was the Kel Mona, pleading. "If you take part in this, they'll kill you, and then what will become of us?"

"But now is our chance!" She struggled again to free herself from the joint grip of Pieran and the Kel Jemya. "The prince, the viceroy, Esban, Lord Corvalen—they are all together. We can kill them all at once!"

"With what?" Pieran said. "Our bare hands against their steel?"

The Kel Jemya added, "Even Jemhara is not enough to defeat them without weapons." Her own command of the power was wavering in the face of the Kel Sharha's force, and she grunted as the Kel Sharha pushed against her.

"The power *is* the weapon!" The Kel Sharha twisted and broke free. Her purpose was clear. Forstene soldiers advanced toward her; she forged ahead. When Fidden and Gar reached for her, she wrapped the power around herself in a tight shield, then made it into a wedge at the front. It was the work of only a few moments more to push her way to the dais steps.

The sounds of the crowd and the soldiers came to her distantly, as if floating on mist across a lake. As she reached the top of the dais, she realized she was indeed surrounded by mist, and one of the sounds that drifted to her was the Kel Mona's chanting. The fog would conceal her movements from the Forsteners for only a brief time, she knew—then they would simply charge into it. And she did not know how long she could sustain the Jemhara at this intensity; she must act quickly. She turned, orienting herself, seeking out Duke Beddar or Prince Dursten. Esban blundered past her, unseeing. The risen Jemhara kept her own vision clear even while her enemies' sight was clouded.

The viceroy was standing at the front edge of the platform, bellowing commands. She made a quick loop, to stalk up behind him. But when she turned her eyes forward, she saw beyond Beddar to the rioting crowd of Sharhay, screaming, throwing stones and clods of mud, pushing and panicking. And she saw that the Forstene soldiers had remembered their discipline and fallen into ranks. They were marching, inexorably, their swords and spears leveled at her people—and most of those people did not have Jemhara with which to fight back.

Yet her own power inflamed her and screamed for release, overwhelming the brief flicker of Healer's compassion.

A soldier tottered as a rock struck him in the temple; he dropped and lay still. A shout went up from the nearby Sharhay, and they surged forward. Among them was a young woman with a babe in arms—she was trying to work her way out of the crowd, but the mindless current of the mob caught her and pushed her to the front.

There was a spray of blood as a Forstene spear ran through mother and child in a single thrust.

"Hold!" roared the Kel Sharha. The power had reached release, but it was the Healer in her who wielded it now, called forth by this second spilling of innocent blood.

She seized and gathered the power again, thrust away the mists, and magnified her voice. "People of Sharhaya, I bid you hold! This is what they want: a reason to kill us all. Do not give it to them! *Hold!*"

Her words rolled out over the crowd, and all became still, Sharhay and Forsteners alike. Breath alone stirred among them.

In the pause, Dursten shouldered his way out from behind the shield wall his men had made to protect him. "This outrage will not go unpunished!" he bellowed.

"You dare speak of outrage?" the Kel Sharha said, barely able to keep her fury from rising again.

Duke Beddar shouted over them both, addressing himself to the Sharhay. "This assembly is ended! Return to your homes immediately and in an orderly fashion; you will stay within doors until we give you liberty to do otherwise. Be advised that in the meantime we will find out the instigators of this riot, who shall be punished accordingly!"

Most of the people stood still in confusion, waiting for a translation that did not come; Esban had fled.

The Kel Sharha took it on herself to interpret the viceroy's command. "My people, I beg you to keep yourselves safe! You must go to your homes and stay there, and call on the protection of the Watchers. If anyone near you is wounded, take them first to the House of Healing, but then look to your own safety."

The viceroy turned on her. "You do not rule here now, woman! What did you just say?"

Lord Corvalen stepped between them. "Most Sharhay do not understand Forstene, Your Grace. The Kel Sharha has simply translated your command."

"Unaltered?"

"Let us say . . . mitigated. And I think wisely so—I think we would not wish to create further resentment among the people here this day."

Dursten was practically sputtering in indignation. "These people have offered violence to the Blood of Stennar, and you're just going to let them go quietly home? We should—"

Lord Corvalen interrupted in a placating tone, but the Kel Sharha did not hear the rest of what they said. The power was ebbing, leaving behind it a clawing emptiness. She turned her back on her departing people so that none would see her weakness—and there was Treska, lying bloodied on the dais, almost at her feet.

The Kel Sharha fell on her knees and gathered the girl's body into her arms. It was deceptively warm still, but there was no trace of life remaining. Treska's spirit was gone, completely, already winging back to the Mothers. Tears came to the Kel Sharha's eyes before she could think to stop them, and she abandoned herself to weeping.

Pieran pulled her away from the body. Step by bitter step, he and the Kel Mona led her back to her house and up the stairs to her bedchamber.

Even under the ancient beech tree she had not sobbed like this. All that was good in the world was broken. Treska was the true daughter of her heart, and she had not realized it in time to tell her or to love her as she deserved. And the girl was a Mind Healer—such promise; a gift so rare. . . .

The Kel Mona took her by the shoulders and gave her a shake. "Kel Sharha! Remember yourself!"

"Finoora!" pleaded Pieran. It was the sound of her birth name that cut through. She drew a steadying breath and rubbed the tears from her eyes.

"The Forsteners will not let us stay long," the Kel Mona whispered. "This may be the last chance we have to speak with you."

"Tell us what you want us to do," Pieran said.

She closed her eyes and took another long breath. She exhaled, opening her eyes slowly. "Prepare for war."

"Kel Sharha?"

"We cannot live under the rule of men such as Prince Dursten and that viceroy. We must drive them out. Not now—we are too weak. But when I return, the People must be ready, strong in body and spirit."

"And if . . . if you don't return? If you can't?"

"I will. I swear before the Watchers that if I die in Forstene, I will take no rest with the Mothers Beyond; if I return not in this life, believe that I will in the next. Let the People bide their time till then. Let them keep the truce but never concede victory in their hearts. Strengthen them, and strengthen the Ma'Sharha. Our powers can do more, far more, against our enemies than we have allowed even yet."

From below came the sound of the door to her house opening and shutting, then a rumble of Forstene voices in the entryway.

"Understand me, both of you?"

"Yes, First of Mothers," they murmured.

"Pieran," she said in a rush, "if Torval keeps you here, saying he wants your assistance, then you must assist him. Turn it to our good. Turn as many Forsteners as you can to our cause. But be careful, and keep yourself alive; I need you here when I return."

The Kel Mona knelt beside her. "You must be careful, too, Kel Sharha. Only those of us standing near felt the change in you out there, and I cloaked you in the mists before any could see. But you must watch yourself. Do not reveal yourself too soon."

They were out of time—heavy footsteps could be heard progressing up the stairs.

The Kel Sharha sagged against Pieran, allowing herself to be racked by sobs once more. Pieran took the cue and clumsily patted her back, making comforting noises.

The door opened. Lord Corvalen stepped into the room. Lifting her head from Pieran's shoulder, the Kel Sharha looked up at the Scourge through a haze of unfeigned tears. The Kel Mona, still kneeling next to her, reached out to rest a sympathetic hand on her arm.

"Your friends must leave now," Lord Corvalen said.

"For pity's sake—," Pieran began.

"Don't make things more difficult for yourselves. Stay any longer, and the viceroy will be certain you are planning an uprising."

The Kel Mona answered him with brittle dignity. "We were planning the funeral."

"The girl's body has been taken to the House of Healing; Healer Lillanna is . . . dealing with it. There's nothing else for you to do now. Go back to your homes."

Under his watchful eye, there could be no more than silent embraces as first the Kel Mona and then Pieran took their leave. The room seemed to grow darker as the Kel Sharha listened to their retreating footsteps.

Lord Corvalen stepped full into her field of vision. "I'm afraid there will be more than one funeral. I took a swift count, and at least six others were killed." He paused. "I'm sorry about your apprentice, Kel Sharha."

His sympathy, sincere or not, meant nothing to her. She packed her anger into her next words, making each syllable a blow: "Get out of my house."

He took a step backward, as if she had indeed struck him. Then he appeared to collect himself. "The bodies will be burnt tonight. We can allow only one of the Ma'Sharha to be in attendance. Not you."

Not her? He would not allow her to make her final farewell to Treska, to stand beside the pyre and speak aloud her love for the daughter of her heart? "Please . . . she was my child—or as close as I have ever had."

"I'm sorry," he repeated. "No."

"Then the Kel Mona will oversee the rite," she managed.

"Very good."

As he hesitated, she turned her back on him, willing him to leave.

"One thing more, Kel Sharha. Esban was one of those killed."

"He will not be mourned." She refused to face the Scourge again; she wanted him gone.

"Your people will not be blamed for his death. It happened in the confusion. He was struck down by one of our guardsmen."

"Good; he will feed the vultures."

She thought she heard Lord Corvalen sigh, but when he spoke again, his voice was cold as iron. "I'll impose on you no longer, except to say that we depart for Forstene at first light the day after tomorrow. I have sent for Jennis to attend you on the journey. Make yourself ready."

She waited until she heard his boots on the stairs. Then she crossed to the door, which he had left standing open. Though she longed to slam it shut with all the force of her anger and pain, she would not display her emotions to any listening Forstener. She pushed the door closed slowly, letting the latch fall into place with quiet inevitability.

*****

Corvalen returned to the Champion's house and sought Torval's room. The young man was at the washbasin, scrubbing.

Corvalen pulled a knife from his belt and tossed it into the basin; the blood on the blade turned the water a sickly pink.

313

Torval stared at the knife for several heartbeats, then fished it out. He turned to Corvalen.

"I gave you that knife when you were a boy," Corvalen said.

"So you did, sir, and so I grieved when I . . . misplaced it."

"Ah. It's good I can return it, and bestow it on you again. Do you want to know where I found it?"

"If you wish to tell me, sir."

"I found it between Esban's ribs. Perhaps there was some accident?"

Torval bowed his head. "No accident, sir. I . . . he . . . When the Sharhay rioted, he panicked. He turned and ran, and I saw him coming toward me. I stepped in front of him; the knife was already in my hand. It was no accident. I saw my moment and I seized it. But he was no fighting man." Torval swallowed, and whispered, "He was unarmed. It was not honorably done."

Corvalen laid a hand on his nephew's shoulder. "Why?"

"He betrayed her." Torval looked up and met Corvalen's gaze; his voice strengthened. "She saved my life, but Esban took the good she did me and turned it to an evil. He used her own compassion and honor to trap her and deliver her to be tortured and violated."

Corvalen let Torval's emotion pass before he spoke. "It was a betrayal of the worst sort," he agreed quietly. "Honor was wronged; but now wronged honor has been avenged. You have returned the scales to balance, as Vallar would will." Solemnly, he saluted Torval, then left him alone to his devotions.

Chapter Thirty

The Kel Sharha sat by her window late into the night, staring down into her garden but seeing little besides the recurring vision of Treska's corpse.

The odor of smoke from the pyre—Treska's pyre, Treska's smoke—hung in the air until a light rain began to fall, and eventually the scent of damp earth reached the Kel Sharha. This had once been a fragrance full of promise and reassurance—but not tonight, and perhaps never again.

First Deela, now Treska. My children. My poor children.

She did not wish to sleep, but she wished to think even less, and not only about today's fresh deaths. She had channeled Jemhara, and done so as though it were the most natural thing in the world. She had opened to it, welcomed it; nothing within her had resisted. And she had meant to wield it, a wildfire that would kill all in its path. *I am a healer, not a destroyer!*

She hugged her knees, rocked, hummed, pushed away the images that assailed her inner eye. The fourth time she caught herself falling into a doze, she gave up and climbed into bed. How much worse could the nightmares be than what she had lived through this day?

It was the old nightmare that came: the bloody face, screaming. But for the first time, her dream vision widened, and she saw the whole scene.

The face belonged to a girl, twelve or thirteen winters old, clad as an apprentice of the Guardians' Order. Another girl, about the same age and in the same garb, dropped to her knees and bent over her.

"Finoora, what have you done?" shrieked a woman from somewhere near.

The second girl glanced round at the voice, and the Kel Sharha saw that it was herself.

Finoora turned back to her fallen companion and without any hesitation placed her hands in the Healers' manner. The Nihara—absolutely pure, absolutely powerful—began to flow.

The injured girl had stopped screaming, had nearly stopped breathing. But now she shuddered and gasped; her lungs filled with air, and her eyes, which moments before had been fixed at nothing, blinked and filled with tears.

She sat up, smiling uncertainly. It was Edda.

"Finoora? What did you do?"

"I thought I had killed you! But then . . . I don't know!" Finoora, weak and swaying, turned to one of the women who had run up to them. "Please, Guardian, what did I do?"

The dream faded then, and the Kel Sharha drifted awake. "You became a Healer, child," she answered her younger self.

She lay listening to the rain on the roof. A sense of the brokenness of her life, of her country's life, still resided within her like a constant ache. But another part of her being felt as though a missing limb had been miraculously restored. It was still confusing; there was still much she didn't understand, might never understand. Even so . . . she remembered.

She remembered her tenth winter, and the Ma'Sharha taking her not for the Healers but for the Guardians.

She remembered the Guardians' House in Redcreek, and the early training with the ironwood staff, and her first experience of the dancelike exercises to focus mind and strength. She remembered her teachers exclaiming over her precociousness, the rate of her progress, and showing her the first steps in channeling the Jemhara.

She had been in the Order for a bit more than two years when the House from Redcreek met for training matches with the House from a neighboring village. Her match was against Edda, a three-year apprentice of apparently the same skill level. But Edda was the bigger of the two girls, and something of a bully besides. Finoora spoke Sharhay with a Ghildaran accent, and Edda made fun of her as they fought. Although Finoora had learned much from her teachers, their lessons in detachment and self-control had made almost no lasting impression. She was already frustrated by the advantages Edda had from her size, and then Edda made one teasing remark too many.

Finoora opened to the Jemhara, channeling it sure and swift, knocking Edda to the ground and unconscious. Then, the moment she realized what she had done, and just as surely and swiftly, she used her need to shift the Jemhara, to reshape the channel, and to pour out Nihara instead. In less than forty heartbeats, she had all but killed Edda and then healed her completely.

What happened next was a confusion of exclamations, recriminations, questions, and silences. The case was finally referred to the Chiefs of the Orders themselves, and she and Edda were taken to the Summer Sanctuary. Neither had ever been there before, but they were too afraid, too awestruck, to take in much of anything but the long winding of the white path back to the chapel.

Their teachers told the Chiefs what had happened; the Chiefs asked some questions. The Kel Nira, pointing to Finoora, asked, "If this one has so strong a gift for healing, why did her village's Listener place her in the Guardians' Order?"

Serelha—Kel Sula Kel Sharha then—beckoned to Finoora and took her by the chin, stared into her eyes. She pulled back at last, looking wan but with an air of pleased certainty. "There was nothing wrong with the Listener's seeing. This girl carries a spirit that belonged to the Guardians before resting with the Mothers; that imprint is still strong, and there would have been no reason to look beyond it. But now that I do look deeper, I see such a channel for the Nihara. . . ."

"You would remove her from my Order, then?" said the Kel Jemya.

"If the Healers will accept her, yes."

The Kel Nira tilted her head to the side, considering. "Send the children out, and we will discuss it."

When Edda and Finoora were summoned back, the Chiefs gave their judgments.

"This one"—the Kel Jemya pointed to Edda—"shall remain with the Jemya. She shows great promise, but she shall finish her training in the south so that she will not be every day reminded of this incident. The Kel Mona will put a bond on her not to speak of it, and she will be encouraged to forget it."

Edda and their teachers were dismissed; Finoora faced the Chiefs alone.

The Kel Sharha eyed her silently a long while before speaking. "You, girl, are going to be a problem if we are not very careful of you."

She found courage to answer, "First of Mothers, I do not wish to be trouble to anyone, least of all the Ma'Sharha."

"The only place for you is among the Ma'Sharha. We have decided to take you from the Guardians, however, and train you as a Healer. You have been accepted into the Healers' Order on the condition that you be taught to forget all you have learned among the Guardians. Moreover, you are henceforward forbidden to touch any weapon, and your lessons in self-control will be even more stringent than those normally taught to apprentices. I should add that you have no choice in these matters. Without the measures I have just outlined, you pose a danger to yourself and others; but with them, you may grow into such a woman as may live to serve the People in their greatest need."

Finoora remained in the Sanctuary after that. On the morning she was to begin her training with the Healers' Order, the Kel Sharha summoned her and spoke to her confidentially. "This day will be remembered as your first among the Ma'Sharha, Finoora. You and everyone else will forget the two years you spent with the Guardians, and it will never be spoken of again. But I want you to know that *I* will remember there are two rivers whose waters conjoin in you. I will watch the weaving of your fate, and if the day ever comes when you have need of your memories, I will help you wake them. May the Mothers and Watchers grant that I do the right thing now, and that I will do it then."

*****

The rooftops of the Sanctuary were just brightening under the rising sun when the Kel Sharha stepped out onto her porch for the last time. The air was chill, and there was a breeze that breathed of autumn. *Our summer is ending.*

No one was on the green save for Forstene soldiers, and Jennis. Torval's men all appeared to be staying. Some were engaged in their usual morning patrol, while others exchanged farewells with Lord Corvalen's followers.

The Kel Sharha had already said good-bye to her servants, under the watchful eyes of Fidden and Gar. Her cook and two maids stood silently now behind her. Apparently no one else would be allowed to see her off. Well, what else could she have expected? And the tears of the servants were difficult enough. . . .

She watched two Forsteners load her travel chest into a covered baggage wagon. She had packed some changes of clothing, her warm riding coat, and a small selection of personal items, but mostly the trunk contained medicines and other healing supplies. She wore her medicine bag slung over her shoulder, too, and now found herself patting its reassuring bulk.

Lord Corvalen approached on horseback, leading a smallish bay gelding. She did not advance to meet him, but waited for him to reach the bottom of her porch steps.

318

He wasted no time with morning pleasantries. "I believe you did not wish to subject your own horse to the journey to Forstene. I hope this mount will suit."

"It will." She beckoned to her maid Arna, and the young woman hurried to secure a rain cloak and a few other supplies behind the gelding's saddle.

"Well then . . ." Lord Corvalen nodded to Fidden and Gar. "Get to your horses. You'll ride with the Lady in the middle of the column." As they moved off, he turned his attention back to the Kel Sharha. "It's time. Make your farewells, but make them quickly."

She frowned, then her brow cleared as she realized his gaze had shifted. Following its direction, she saw Torval and two of his men escorting a small group toward her. Her throat contracted at the sight of those well-loved faces: all of the Council members, as well as Lillanna and Pieran. She wanted to rush to them, but knew she must be mindful of her dignity in front of the Forsteners. She knew, too, that Torval might turn his back discreetly while she made her farewells, but that he would nonetheless be listening to every syllable exchanged.

She had had weeks to ponder the final words she would leave with her people, but now, as she walked toward the gathered friends and Councillors, nothing she could say seemed appropriate or sufficient.

Tigannas the Lawspeaker stepped forward to meet her. He bowed, then fervently clasped her hands, but he was as tongue-tied as she. She finally got out, "Keep our laws and our ways, Tigannas; do not let them be forgotten." He nodded, and wiped at his eyes.

Falessan and Ingas were next. They pressed into her hands a red-glazed pottery flask, finely incised with a design of beech leaves. The Vintner explained tremulously, "This contains the last of the four-year vintage"—the last of the wine made before the Forstene invasion.

The Kel Sharha nodded. "May we have many years of peace and bountiful vintages before us," she managed, and passed the strap of the flask over her shoulder as she moved to the next of the Councillors.

Elder Rimenna bowed low. "We will sing of you, First of Mothers," she whispered.

"Thank you, Rimenna, but I would rather you sing *for* me—and for us all."

"Yes, of course; as you wish."

"I know you and your guild will help the people keep their spirit, as you have always done."

She turned now to her fellow Chiefs. The Kel Jemya's bow was stiff and formal, her expression set and impenetrable. "What would you have my Order do in your absence, First of Mothers?"

It was impossible to truly respond to the question, with all its undercurrents, within the hearing of the Forsteners. "The Guardians may be denied use of arms," the Kel Sharha said, "but Lord Torval, by his good grace, may well give you hearing on matters of justice, so that you may fulfill your calling to defend our women, our children, and our holy places. And when your spirits flag"—she leaned forward—"remember to *dance*."

The Kel Jemya's jaw relaxed as she grasped the Kel Sharha's meaning. She nodded slowly. "Perhaps my Order might encourage others to follow your advice, First of Mothers, that all who are able may have a means of strengthening their spirits?"

"Indeed, Kel Jemya. Indeed."

Behind her, Lord Corvalen cleared his throat, and a horse stamped. She was taking longer than the Forsteners would like, she knew, but she refused to be hurried. She moved on to the Kel Sula, who looked at her with wide pupils.

"I see you are awake now, Kel Sharha. Two rivers, flowing together."

"Yes. My eyes are open, and I hear the trees, more than before. You and your Order, Kel Sula, will also need to see and hear more than you did before, till I return."

"We look to the future, Kel Sharha. And if you—" She broke off; Torval had taken a step closer to them. The Kel Sula composed herself. "Live, First of Mothers. Just live."

"This may help," the Kel Mona offered, coming forward to tuck a cork-stoppered clay pot into the Kel Sharha's medicine bag. "Charcoal and ash from the seven-woods Harvest fire," she explained quietly. "The strength of the trees and the earth that nourished them remains in the coals. There is power there for you, to help you keep your bond to the land. As I swore." She grasped the Kel Sharha gently by the arms and traced symbols down their length, then kissed her tenderly on each cheek.

"My dear friend—"

"No more, no more." Her voice caught, and she gently pushed the Kel Sharha toward Lillanna.

"My Chief." Lillanna bowed.

For the first time that day—in many days, it seemed—the Kel Sharha smiled. She had seen Lillanna grow from an awkward young apprentice into an extremely capable Healer, and a fine woman. "I am happy the Order will be in your hands, Lillanna. You must take the Healers' seat in Council while I am gone. I know you will care for our people as I would."

"You have my word on that, my Chief." She smiled a wobbly smile.

At last the Kel Sharha came to her brother. They embraced in silence.

"Stay out of trouble, Pieran," she whispered as they separated.

"You, too."

The Kel Sharha gazed at him a few heartbeats more, inscribing every line of his face in her memory. Then she backed a few steps away, until she could see the whole group.

She took a deep breath. "Elders, Chiefs, Friends, I thank you all." She sank into the ritual obeisance. As she straightened to face them again, she drew a breath that filled her through every pore. Feeling the power of the deep earth coursing up into her, she extended her hands in blessing. "May we all walk under the protection of the Watchers, with spirits true to the Mothers."

"So may it be," came the response, and all bowed.

While their eyes were still downcast, she turned away. Torval made to speak to her, but she brushed past him and mounted her horse.

Feeling the weight of Lord Corvalen's gaze, she busied herself with pulling on her riding gloves. Out of the corner of her eye she saw him hesitate, then move off to take his place at the head of the column of soldiers.

As they set out, she cast one look backward at Pieran and the Councillors. But Fidden, Gar, Jennis, and other riders were moving into position around her, and her friends were soon lost to sight.

Amid the calls of the men, the jangle of harness, the hoofsteps and other equine noises, a clear-pitched sound somehow carried over all the rest to catch her attention. She found its source quickly enough: Taras stood on the balcony of his guildhall, plucking his lute. Their gazes touched for a moment, and he began to sing.

"If I should leave behind the sacred wood,
I swear it shall not be for good.
If from the orchards I should roam,
I swear I'll not forget my home.
Though the fields and vineyard hills,
The meadows, downs, and singing rills

Be present only to my mind,
While I am far from all my kind,
I swear I will not long depart.
I swear it as the bond of my heart:
And all to which I turn my hand
Shall bring me again to the Mothers' land."

Borne away by the column of riders like a leaf caught in a river current, still she heard the song following after her as she left the Sanctuary. Passing under the chiming boughs of the Sacred Forest, she turned the last words into a prayer, and repeated it over and over to herself:

May all to which I turn my hand
Bring me back to free my Motherland.

A NOTE ON PRONUNCIATIONS

All Sharhay names and terms have the accent on the second-to-last syllable. The same is true for Ghildaran and Cheskari.

All Forstene names and terms have the accent on the first syllable, with the exception of Brintora, which is accented on the second-to-last syllable.

THE HIGH COUNCIL OF SHARHAYA

Sharhaya is governed by a council made up of the four Chiefs of the Ma'Sharha Orders, the three Elders of the Greater Guilds, the Champion, and the Lawspeaker. The head of the Council is the Kel Sharha, who is simultaneously Chief of one of the Orders. The rank of Kel Sharha, held for life, passes from the Chief of one Order to another in the sequence given below.

The Orders
The Mona (Summoners)—ritual leaders, weather workers, game callers
The Sula (Listeners)—diviners, counselors
The Jemya (Guardians)—keepers of the peace, executors of justice
The Nira (Healers)—healers

The Greater Guilds
The Vintners—makers of wines and spirits
The Artisans—woodworkers, metalworkers, jewelers, potters
The Celebrants—singers, dancers, musicians, poets, storytellers

The Champion
A man nominated by the leaders of Sharhaya's regional Hunt Councils, subsequently accepted by the Kel Sharha (who may, however, reject the nomination and ask for another). He is expected to have an intimate relationship with the Kel Sharha and to have ties with no other woman, since she shares her Power with him. He is responsible for the defense of Sharhaya.

The Lawspeaker
An authority on the laws and customs of Sharhaya, which he or she has committed to memory; elected for a lifetime term by the regional lawspeakers, but can be recalled either by them or at the request of the Kel Sharha. Lawspeakers are literate and act as scribes, ambassadors, and the like as necessary.

Every High Councillor has a Second who may attend all Council meetings but may only speak if sitting in for an absent Councillor.

SHARHAY GLOSSARY

borend = to whisper
dan-ajlas = a mintlike herb that grows in damp places
gan = quiet, quietly
ghekkes = a useless man, a man without honor
gless = night
hara = literally "flood," used of Ma'Sharha powers at their fullest strength
je'shen = tree of power, guardian tree
Jemaya = a member of the Jemya Order
Jemhara = Power wielded by Jemya
Jemya = defenders, peacekeepers, executors of justice
jess = power, especially spiritual power
kel = chief, first
len = west
may = mother
Mayahara = Power of the Mothers
Mona = literally, "Summoners"
Monaya = a member of the Mona Order
na = my
Nihara = healing Power
Nira = Healers
Nirayna = a healer in Orders
par = east
shar = people, country
shen = tree
sin = in

Sula = diviners, counselors (literally, "Listeners")
Sulayna = a member of the Sula Order

CHARACTER LIST

Sharhay (in order of appearance)
the Kel Nira (Finoora), Chief of the Healers' Order
Fama, a member of the Guardians' Order
Treska, the Kel Nira's junior apprentice
Deela, the Kel Nira's senior apprentice
Pieran, the Champion's second, the Kel Nira's brother
Reshtas, the Champion
Luma, the Kel Nira's horse
Lillanna, the Kel Nira's second
Wennas, a vinedresser
Yasma, a member of the Healers' Order
Arna, one of the Kel Nira's servants
Taras, a member of the Celebrants' Guild
Rimenna, Elder of the Celebrants' Guild
Jedan, a member of the Celebrants' Guild
the Kel Mona, Chief of the Summoners' Order
the Kel Sula Kel Sharha (Serelha), Chief of the Listeners' Order and
    leader of the High Council
the Kel Jemya (Edda), Chief of the Guardians' Order
Taja, the Kel Sula's second
Esban, a collaborator with the Forsteners
Kirtana, a member of the Guardians' Order
Graysa, Lillanna's junior apprentice
Saffa, Lillanna's senior apprentice
Falessan, Elder of the Vintners' Guild
Tigannas, the Lawspeaker
Ingas, Elder of the Artisans' Guild
Hoba, aunt to the Kel Nira and Pieran
Silna, Pieran's ex-wife
Pesha, Lillanna's cook
Mikka, Pesha's daughter
Bannan, Pesha's son

Forsteners (in order of appearance)
Lord Torval of Caldene, friend of Dursten, nephew of Corvalen
Lord Corvalen of Brintora, Lord Marshal of Forstene
Rossen of Barasel, Corvalen's aide
Pellar, Corvalen's squire
Prince Dursten, heir to the throne of Forstene
King Delanar, Dursten's father, king of Forstene
Mellis, Corvalen's daughter
Fengal of Telthene, commander of Southwood Fort
Prince Heldar, Dursten's son
Princess Hannalis, Dursten's wife
Thannen, a star reader
Rindal, one of Corvalen's lieutenants
Lady Ardalis of Brintora and Caldene, Corvalen's sister, Torval's mother
Caunar, a star reader, formerly Dursten's and Torval's tutor
Ildanis, one of Torval's sisters
Fidden, one of Corvalen's bodyguard
Gar, one of Corvalen's bodyguard
Jennis, a camp follower
Duke Beddar, King Delanar's cousin
Thedis, Beddar's daughter
Odasen Swordplayer, a show-swordsman
Neldis, a courtesan
Sessal, Dursten's uncle, Delanar's younger brother
Uthal, one of Dursten's lieutenants

Ghildarans
Martos, Viscount of the Fifth District, a diplomat
King Zhorzos, ruler of Ghildarna

ABOUT THE AUTHOR

Kathryn Hinds grew up near Rochester, NY, then moved to New York City to attend Barnard College and the Graduate Center of the City University of New York, where she did work in Comparative Literature and Medieval Studies. She now lives in the mountains of north Georgia, but migrates back to the southern shore of Lake Ontario nearly every summer. Although Kathryn has held a variety of jobs—waitress, administrative assistant, early childhood educator, library information specialist, and freelance editor—writing has been her enduring passion since elementary school. Her published works include poetry, short stories, a coauthored book on Celtic mythology, and more than fifty nonfiction books for children and young adults. Kathryn also teaches English composition and early British literature at the University of North Georgia, and she occasionally moonlights as a belly dancer. Her primary job, however—according to certain members of her household—is to ensure that cat food is always available on demand.